I0610816

# Wolf Within

MOONLIGHT TERRITORY

By
M.A. Kastle

This is a dream come true.


To Mr. K and the Minions- Love you always.

Books by M.A. Kastle

**Cascade Saga**
Bone Chimes
Dark Awakening

**Cascade Wolves – Crimson Series**
Crimson Moon

**Horror**
Tales of Woe (Collection)
A Curse Revisited – The Legend of Noah Blyth (Novella)

# CHAPTER ONE

*No service.*

He gauged his surroundings at the same time he tossed the worthless cell to the center console, the rubber case making a thud as it hit. What had he gotten himself into? The tip he received sounded legit—a warehouse in an abandoned industrial area surrounded by desert, light traffic, and no witnesses was the perfect place for Hunter Wolves. He desperately wanted to believe it was real. Needed to believe. The vampire hadn't called Agent Sinclair with the Department of Justice ... no, he called Kayne Sinclair, alpha of the Garrick pack. It had been personal. It made it believable.

"I swallowed it hook, line, and sinker," he mumbled to the inside of the cab.

Kayne eased the truck off the highway, his tires crunching broken asphalt like it was consuming it while gusts of wind sent sand drifts snaking across what was left of the two-lane road. As if escaping the desert, tumbleweeds rolled out in front of him like they were tempting him to hit them to end their misery while the temps increased to one hundred despite it being early morning. He didn't know why anyone in their right mind would live in a barren land that felt like the face of the sun. There were no trees, grass, or water ... just heat, sand, wind, and broken buildings the weather had destroyed. Pulling off the road, his tires sank in soft sand, and stopping he checked his cell, the two words no service mocking him.

Like a giant black box, the warehouse loomed in front of him, its shape and color standing out against the beige rolling landscape peppered with specks of darker beige and rogue greens. This was where a deranged madman was creating his monstrosities, planning his war on mortals, and hiding? Kayne hated himself for letting his single-minded revenge drive him to another dead end. Over the years, his pride had been turned to shreds, then torched and made ash with every failure. He sat back in the seat with defeat, and was relieved no one was there to witness it, like Commander Wilson and Daeland. Especially Daeland. With a grunt, he accepted the tip was a bust and put the truck in reverse. Kayne had a job to do, and it wasn't sitting and staring at a forgotten warehouse in the middle of nowhere, without cell service. What if Commander Wilson was trying to get a hold of him? He couldn't afford another reprimand added to his stellar career with the DOJ.

When he backed up his tires spun, creating a cloud of dust. If he wasn't careful, he was going to be stuck. Hissing a string of curses, he put the truck in four-wheel drive, and as he was easing on the pedal the weak feel of Otherkin crawled over his senses. Kayne stopped and searched the area, his hopes soaring then crashing when he didn't see anything or anyone, and mumbled more curses. There were miles of open desert, it didn't mean it came from the warehouse. Anyway, he was looking for shapeshifters, Hunter Wolves, not Otherkin. He didn't need a witch, an empath, or a Fae. Slowly backing up, he could picture getting stuck, then having the DOJ or a detective from the Bureau of Paranormal Investigations find him. The questions would never end, and it would ruin his investigation. Out of the corner of his eye,

Kayne saw the massive shadow a second before the Hunter Wolf landed on the hood of his truck, crushing the passenger side. Its weight rocked the full-size vehicle and threw him into the driver's side door. He gripped the steering wheel, grappled with the gear, and shifted the truck into park.

The Hunter Wolf bellowed an angry roar as it jumped up then landed in the bed of the truck, the force causing windows to burst that sent glass flying, and he heard the frame groan. Scrambling for the handle, Kayne wrenched on the metal, prayed it held, shoved the door open to hear metal grind on metal, and fell out to land on the scorching ground. He rolled to his side, his T-shirt catching thorns and leaves as he tried to get to his feet when the Hunter Wolf landed next to him, making a plume of dust. Shoving him down, it forced his hands to slip in the heated sand while Kayne's rapid pulse thundered in his ears. When it released him, he fought to get to his feet, but lost traction when the ground beneath him gave way. As he fell, it laughed a rough, grating rumble that had his frustration turning to fury, and consuming him it focused on his mistake. This was going to be bad. Like he disobeyed a direct order and hadn't checked in with local law enforcement bad.

Kayne's boots dug into the sand as he scrambled, got to his feet and stood to face the eight-foot tall, twisted version of werewolf and mortal, known as their Hunter Wolf form. Its yellow glare held his for a breath before it loped in the direction of the warehouse. Its swinging arms weren't those of a mortal or a wolf but a dangerous merging of corded muscle and strength, while its long fingers and sharp nails made up its clawed hands. Taking chase, he could hear Commander Wilson's condescending voice warning him about working on his own and his failure to follow protocol. *The hell with it,* he wanted to yell. His boots sank as he staggered past his truck, the thorns from tumbleweeds and creosote brush catching his jeans. Finally escaping the soft sand and reaching asphalt, the sudden difference jarred his knees, making vibrations sink into his muscles.

The Hunter Wolf didn't pause, didn't check to see if he was following, it continued creating distance as it headed for safety. Like the distance between them, its howl mocked Kayne, his attempt to catch up, and forced him to run faster. He wasn't going to let it make it inside only for it to lock him out. He had reasons for chasing the Hunter Wolf, reasons for entering the warehouse, and maybe it was enough to appease Commander Wilson and he wouldn't bust him for not following his order. The tip he received, the Hunter Wolf, its attack, and how it was all coming together meant this was his chance to get the evidence he needed to prove he was right. And not losing his mind with his need to avenge the death of his alpha and the alpha's family. Maybe it would be enough for Daeland, a demanding vampire lord, to believe him. He would have laughed if he wasn't running all out to catch up with his evidence. If there was a chance he was right and was in the clear with both Commander Wilson and Daeland, he wouldn't know how to live.

Kayne's instincts roared a warning as a rusted metal roll-up door clanged, shuddered, then began too slowly open. Like the giant maw of a monster, its insides sat dark and waited for its victim because that's what he was going to find. He knew this. The buzzing in his head told him there was more than the Hunter Wolf in the warehouse, and it wasn't human, or at least its powers weren't. With his proximity the feeling of jagged metal grated over his senses in a desperate warning of Otherkin and death, but it wasn't going to stop him when he was so close. Having to squint his eyes against the late morning sun, Kayne gained on the Hunter Wolf as it ate up the distance to the opening, and once inside the shadows swallowed its massive body.

He was only seconds behind the beast, and entering the warehouse, its smells assaulted him. The roll-up door slammed closed behind him to create a dingy cloud of sand, debris, and a howl echoed on metal. Kayne stopped before he ran headlong into a shipping container, and covered his nose and mouth in the bend of his elbow as the tang of rot, blood, mortal and shifter waste shrouded him. Death rested its cold hand on his shoulders as he gagged, his stomach rolled, and he forced himself to breathe through his mouth which wasn't better. The tainted air coated his exposed flesh, and sitting on his tongue it felt like thick grease while it slid down his throat.

He fought against the instinct to get the hell out of there and get away from the death, magic, and torture holding the warehouse captive. Kayne nearly failed when an eerie silence settled in the massive expanse, giving him the sounds of the wind rattling tin, sand hitting the roll-up door, and nails scrapping metal. With the need to distract himself from the smell, he searched his immediate area to get his bearings. He stilled as he looked at the rows and rows of shipping containers, towering three high, and seemingly going on for miles as they cut the warehouse into sections. The containers in front of him wore scars, were riddled down their sides like mini explosions had gone off, and metal flared where shapeshifters had punctured the sides with their claws.

"Fighting to escape," he growled. He no longer worried about Commander Wilson ... no, he had reasonable doubt and evidence to justify his presence. All he had to was convince Daeland.

Unable to take his eyes off the mangled, curved edges or the crimson lines following the raised contours, he couldn't stop thinking what it meant to the DOJ's case, and his own selfish revenge. He sucked in a breath of rancid air only decomposing bodies in the desert heat could create, and it made his wolf howl over the denigrate for the dead and their brutal deaths. As the situation landed on him like a ton of bricks, urgency drove through him as he fought to focus on the warehouse, containers, the deaths, and the Hunter Wolf. Wherever it had gone. He needed to get to his truck, grab his cell, find reception, and call for backup. He didn't care if the BPI responded. If he found what he was looking for, he would walk away from the DOJ. Simple. His pack might even appreciate it.

The hit came out of nowhere, making him stumble into the ravaged metal side, its sharp edges ripping his T-shirt as he jerked backward. He hadn't sensed the Hunter Wolf's approach, hadn't heard it. Damn. Kayne twisted from the next blow, its giant fisted hand connected with the back of Kayne's head, its force propelling him into the side of another container. His mind had been elsewhere, a deadly mistake that made his reaction time slow and sloppy. Hitting headfirst, Kayne felt his skin split and warm blood run down the side of his face at the same time the world went black for agonizing seconds. Before he was able to regain his balance and stand, its heavy steps sounded over his pulse rushing in his ears, then its clawed hands grabbed him, its nails puncturing his skin, and tossed him to the other side. If he didn't get his shit together, it was going to kill him.

Kayne landed hard on the concrete, his shoulder screaming with pain, his head throbbing, and his vision blurring. Using precious moments to heal the superficial wounds, he gripped the container, climbed up its side, and stood.

The Hunter Wolf was gone.

With his back to the container, he tested his shoulder, wiped the blood from his face with the hem of his T-shirt, then released a low growl that vibrated his chest. He'd been sloppy; if the Hunter Wolf wanted to kill him, he would be dead. Eyeing the warehouse, he listened to the sounds, then opened his senses to search. The slightest hum of werewolf teased him, its presence drifting like sand in the wind, making it impossible to pinpoint where it had gone.

*What the hell?* In answer to his question, a strike of power, feeling like a hammer, slammed into his skull, burrowed down to his spine, and latched on. Kayne clasped the sides of his head with his hands, and squeezing, collapsed to his knees from the pain and heard cracking as he landed. Images of his life tumbled in front of him, giving him the years of humiliation, his territory, Alpha Garrick's rough voice, and silver eyes stained with crimson.

"No."

He couldn't stop the deluge of his fears, regrets, and sorrows from grabbing him and pulling him into their black hole where she was waiting for him.

"It isn't real," he whispered. "She's dead."


**The Bureau** of Paranormal Investigations team wearing black on black BDUs, face masks, and holding their weapons, backed up to slip behind Detective Macy Gray, leaving her in front and with a clear shot. She took her stance, tucked the butt of the H&K rifle loaded with synthetic silver into the curve of her shoulder, and tracked her target. Mrs. Barrett. With an ungainly bearing, the naked woman ran over pieces of shattered glass and wood from fallen picture frames, and debris from the crumbling walls. Trailing behind her were crimson footprints that stained the plush, off-white carpet while tranquilizer darts tore from her skin, leaving bleeding holes as they fell to the floor.

Macy slid her finger to the trigger, feathering the metal, in preparation of firing. With her mark in sight, a calm swept over her, taking the team's voices, the target's heavy breathing, the heat in the hallway, and left her waiting for the shot. Then she hesitated. Going against her training and instincts, she listened to the target's weakened heartbeat as it blasted through the barrier of her carefully crafted defense and into her ears. Its drumming slowed, one, two, and Macy heard Mrs. Barrett's blood pulsing through collapsing veins to the muscle struggling to keep her alive. *Target*, Macy yelled at herself. The target's heart was failing.

"I have no idea why you're here. You don't have it anymore, the edge. You risk lives, proving you don't have what it takes to do this job. Competently." Sergeant Mayco's voice disrupted the memory and jerked her back to the present. He inhaled, exhaled, the knuckles of his fingers blazed white as he gripped the steering wheel of the BPI's SUV, like he was transferring his anger to the thing. "You don't give a damn about your team," he accused. His jaw clenched, his chest rose with another full inhale, pulling the black BDU top tight around his torso. As if he could get away from her, he pushed the speed to eighty, and equipment bounced, making dull thuds as the SUV bounded over potholes in the asphalt.

*Not true,* Macy wanted to argue. Ignoring his increasing speed, she struggled to shake the memory of her failure.

Was she going to wait for the avalanche of accusations coming at her to bury her, then defend herself? Staring at the side of his face nothing came to her, and when he didn't acknowledge her, she shook her head, sat back as far as her utility belt would allow, and wondered if Sergeant Mayco was finished with his rant. The same rant he said every time they worked together. And every damn time she ended up feeling the same way ... defeated and without a shred of confidence. In truth, she was never going to win the argument, any defense would be ripped to shreds, so like the dozen times before Macy gave up trying.

She stared forward, concentrating on the desert, and did the job that stuck them together. They were looking for a truck. A black truck. The missing Department of Justice agent didn't deter her attention from having an internal argument with Sergeant Mayco. Damn him, she did care about her team. The tension in the SUV gained weight and made the whining air conditioner grate on her fragile nerves. If it wasn't closing in on one hundred and five degrees, she would have turned it off and stopped the irritating noise. Then it started whistling, like there was a leaf suck in the ventilation, and Macy cringed. *Hold it together.* She rubbed the back of her neck with her right hand, trying to ease the tension in her tight muscles while cool air blew loose strands of her hair.

"I have no idea why you're here," Sergeant Mayco grunted. He craned his neck to the left, as if he saw something, then back to the road. "No fucking idea."

*Can't let it go.* No, so how many times? Ten, maybe twelve repetitions of 'I have no idea why you're here'. He kept proving to her he had no problem stating his dislikes despite her being able to file a grievance against him for creating a hostile work environment. She wouldn't dare do it, it would make her look guilty, and might change the minds of the few detectives who still trusted her. Between a rock and hard place. She kept quiet, knowing better than to add fuel to the fire. His personal inferno.

*Damn, Harmony Grove,* Macy cursed.

A semi-truck blew past them, its force pushing on the SUV as it headed north while they drove south. She watched small dust devils twist on the shoulder, their hazy fingers catching leaves and tumbleweeds, carrying them and releasing them when its strength died. Her attention was focused on Sergeant Mayco, but her mind latched onto the reason her once immaculate career with the Bureau of Paranormal Investigations had been ruined and her reputation as a trusted detective destroyed. Yes, Detective Macy Gray had been formally put on the shit list. Because of shapeshifters. The hurt had her glaring forward as unquenched rage simmered.

Behind the elaborate wrought iron gates of Harmony Grove sat decadent estates built on two acre lots for the elite lycans, therians, the Otherkin, and humans. The combination gave the development a reputation of hedonism, fantasy with an edge of danger, and had created one of the wealthiest developments in the High Desert ... hell, Southern California. Despite the decadence and wealth involved, Harmony Grove had its secrets. Like domestic violence. That's what started the whole mess, a freaking domestic disturbance call.

"Do you think you can keep an eye out for the agent's truck? Or would it be to taxing?" Sergeant Mayco mocked.

*I am.* "Affirmative, sir."

Macy scanned the desert, her eyes skating over the seemingly bleak terrain, blends of taupe, fawn, various states of green, and deceptive visibility. She knew hidden in the beige landscape dotted with skeletal creosote bushes were ravines perfect for hiding anything from a person to a vehicle, but doubted the agent was taking in the sights of the desert. During the brief, Captain Dixon told them he had been investigating a warehouse, hadn't checked in when scheduled to, and wasn't answering their calls. The DOJ followed protocol and alerted his commander, who authorized personnel to track the agent's cell phone by GPS. She understood finding him, especially if the agent was investigating the possibility lycans were using a warehouse to imprison humans. With an increase in shapeshifter crime, it didn't take much for Macy to imagine shapeshifters kidnapping innocents, holding them prisoner, and torturing them. Or, dear god, infecting them against their will. And when the public found out shapeshifters were kidnapping and infecting humans, the sale of White Cell was going to skyrocket.

No matter what happened, death was going to be part of the equation. The horror of it sat like a weight in her soul. What was the chance the agent had been found trespassing and the shapeshifters locked him up? Too damn good. She didn't believe they would risk holding a DOJ agent when his disappearance would bring every Southern California law enforcement agency down on them. Macy inwardly shrugged her shoulders. She was having the conversation with herself, and hated the mounting questions and lack of answers. The one bugging her most was if the agent found a warehouse, how had the BPI missed it? And why was the DOJ using an outside agency? The answer didn't matter when they went straight to the one person, Captain Dixon, who wouldn't refuse helping what he viewed as a superior agency. *Leave it alone, he isn't your target.*

While they continued down the highway, the questions, lack of answers, and the agent faded into the background as she fought the trails her mind wanted to chase. Harmony

Grove. After dispatch received the call and confirmed the residents identified as humanoids, a team from the Desert Rock Police Department responded. From there it turned into a nightmare. The officers quickly found out the residents weren't completely human and faced two therians in different states of transforming. There was nothing but trouble when dealing with shapeshifters, let alone therians. Beside her, Sergeant Mayco's low mumble continued, and he grunted his dislike for the DOJ and her work ethic.

When they confronted the couple the situation escalated and Mr. Barrette pushed his animal and tried to complete shapeshifting into a lion, which made both officers draw their weapons and order him to standdown. The officers created a hostile environment by taking the alpha role in the male's lair and then threatening the female. God forbid they hand the scene over to the BPI. While the officers were focused on Mr. Barrette, Mrs. Barrette began crying and begging them not to hurt her husband, which provoked the male's protective instincts. Both officers then lowered their weapons, explained they weren't there to hurt anyone, and tried to clarify a report had been made stating someone needed assistance.

Mrs. Barrette used the opportunity to run through the house, and while in a hysterical state, headed upstairs and out of sight. With Mr. Barrette in a vulnerable condition, and Mrs. Barrette hiding from them, they had become the agitators and chose to leave the scene. The officers failed to apprehend the suspect, Mr. Barrette, or to help the alleged victim, Mrs. Barrette. Per standard procedure when facing a shapeshifter or Otherkin, they contacted the BPI. By the time DRPD released the scene to the BPI, Mr. Barrette had fled the premises, and no one knew if Mrs. Barrette had gone with him. The situation forced the BPI to stop all traffic and close the entrances into Harmony Grove, while DRPD units searched the development. With the community closed to traffic, the BPI team geared up and entered the house in search of Mrs. Barrette. It had been dark, dirty, musky, and smelled like animals had been living in the sprawling mansion instead of the reported human couple. It was obvious Mr. and Mrs. Barrette were slowly turning their home into a lair. Macy held her breath as the memory of the stringent scent magnified by the heat invaded her, and she slowly exhaled. In the beginning, evidence and the atmosphere proved they had purposely been infected, then the BPI detectives found dozens of empty vials of White Cell. Which proved they were trying to stop the contagion.

Macy slowly inhaled, rubbed her neck, then moved strands of chestnut hair from her cheek, careful to not aggravate the healing scratches and tender bruises. To explain the White Cell, the BPI wanted to know if the couple been infected through force or fear, or had they planned a controlled crossover and changed their minds? With no one to give them answers and the evidence pointing in every direction, it caused the investigation to stall. Maybe the couple feared public scrutiny, though Macy didn't know why. Mr. Barrette owned Golden State Shipping, the largest shipping company for nationwide rail and trucking. With their money and influence, and living in Harmony Grove, making the decision to become therians would have made them celebrities in the upper cusp of the paranormal community.

Even with their status, the presence of White Cell bothered everyone. The illegal and less effective version of CD4-T, the antiserum for therianthropy and lycanthropy contagions was regulated by the medical industry and could only be administered by a doctor. The law helped keep track of the spread of the contagion. It was the hospital's responsibility to record if the human had been a victim of a rogue shapeshifter attack or if it was through force or fear, then the hospital's adjuster generated documentation of the case and passed the file onto law enforcement for investigation. In the event a human requested infection, the applicant was required to choose an animal form, clan, pass a psychological test, an emotional endurance test, and a physical stress test. Once the applicant had been cleared, they were injected with the contagion.

*Damn fools.*

Sanative Medical Center—a paranormal specific hospital—then secured the applicant in its guidance center. Observing the crossover was the alpha of the chosen clan, Dr. Locke, the hospital's chief physician and alpha of the local lycan clan, and a team of medical personnel. With every crossover the risk of a Death Bloom, the sign the contagion destroyed the human body's ability to accept the transformation, kept the attending physicians on edge. When the transformation was complete and the applicant was stable, the information was entered in the National Chronicle of Anthropomorphism, NCA, and could be accessed by law enforcement agencies and hospital personnel throughout the nation.

Macy drifted from her thoughts to Sergeant Mayco, who had stopped his tirade long enough to explain their location and progress to dispatch. Remaining silent, she continued to search the terrain while eavesdropping. It was the only way she was going to find out *the plan* because he wasn't speaking to her unless it was to complain. They were continuing south, would search the off-road areas to cover their bases, then he advised dispatch to keep track of their movement via GPS from the Mobil Digital Terminal, MDT, because cell service wasn't reliable. When he turned his attention back to the road, Macy fought to let go of the rest of the scene.

The BPI team found Mrs. Barrette upstairs alone and struggling to shapeshift. Her sweat-damp skin appeared translucent, her veins sticking out from her pale flesh, and she stood on misshaped legs with her warped arms hanging at her sides and her twisted, human cat eyes glaring. Detective Gaines, a trained high-risk negotiator, approached the woman and tried to convince her the BPI was there to help, and she needed medical attention. To prove their intentions were for her safety and she would receive medical help, Detective Gaines explained there was an ambulance from Sanative waiting for her. Mrs. Barrette's eyes clouded, turned empty, and her face became a blank mask, then her body began trembling. Detective Gaines was in the middle of repeating her statement when Mrs. Barrette cried, a high-pitched mix of feline and woman, and ignoring Detective Gaines, ran naked and half shifted in their direction. Her advance forced Sergeant Mayco to order tranquillizers, and immediately soft shots sounded. When darts riddled her body and she continued her attack, he gave the order to kill.

End of report.

Mrs. Barrette no longer existed. She had become a target. As the sharpshooter for the team, it was Macy's job to take her down. Damn, if only she could go back and change it. Using both hands on her shoulders, she kneaded the tension, trying to untie the stress knots and stop from reliving her failure. Her defense had been the Death Bloom. Named for resembling a rose bud and the first indication the victim wasn't going to live through the shift, it curved up and around Mrs. Barrette's bare shoulder. She was dying. Seeing the tightly wound scarlet-and-violet-colored blossom giving away Mrs. Barrette's failing body and pending death, Macy hadn't added a bullet.

She should have. It would have been like dotting an I on a report.

"I can't work like this," Sergeant Mayco blurted out, his tone jolting her from her thoughts. "One shot."

Was he reading her mind? Macy turned to watch his body tense with his frustration.

"Watching you stand by as a therian ran at your team is enough to have you relieved of your duties and kicked out of the BPI. You would never be hired by another law enforcement agency." He did the breathing thing again—in, out, in, out. "My concern during a conflict shouldn't be if you can do your job. I don't doubt, right now, you would freeze, and your hesitation would cost someone their life. I shouldn't have to work with you. Your weakness is an embarrassment to the bureau."

*That's a new one,* she thought, *and I didn't freeze.* Macy wanted to remind him that Mrs. Barrette never attacked, she collapsed, facedown, and died. *Right in front of me.* The remaining darts plunged deeper into her body, and her cat-shaped, emerald eyes stared at her own damn carpet.

"I can't pretend to understand what Commander Arden is doing or his methods, but I know you shouldn't be here." Sergeant Mayco didn't bother looking at her. Instead, he kept his ice blue gaze on the road.

No, he didn't know what Commander Arden was doing.

Macy checked her work cell for messages from her commander, and seeing he hadn't checked in with her, replaced it in the center console. Sergeant Mayco's rant wasn't about Mrs. Barrette and the failed shot, not entirely, it didn't change the fact it was the final nail in her coffin. He was reminding her of Officer David Murphy, DRPD, human, and her partner when the Desert Rock Police Department and the BPI worked together.

*That also turned to shit,* Macy thought.

Realizing she wasn't going to take the bait and defend Commander Arden or herself, Sergeant Mayco huffed, and silently brooding, drove on. To distract herself, and hoping for information, she checked the MDT to see if dispatch had an update on their current call, and at the same time she made sure the GPS was tracking their position. When dispatch recognized their location and clarified they didn't have an update, Macy couldn't stop herself from mumbling, "We were ambushed."

Sergeant Mayco ignored her.

She couldn't remember a time when she had gripped her gun as tightly as when she fired on the first shifted lycan. The eight-foot tall, twisted version of lycan and human merged into one, creating what became recognized as their *Hunter Wolf form.* In their animal forms, lycans and therians carried the contagion in their nails and were able to release the toxin at will. One scratch and you're fighting an aggressive contagion intent on changing your DNA and damning you to a future as a shifter. The Hunter Wolf form was different. While their claws held the contagion, it was their bite causing the most damage. Inside of their mouths were multiple glands containing a concentrated version they were able to inject with their bites. The contagion didn't infect its victim, it killed them. She always thought it was better than being turned.

The Hunter Wolf form had jumped from a shipping container to stand on elongated hind legs and towered over them. They were separated from the team and it left them standing side by side with their guns drawn as it backed them into a corner. She ordered it to stop, to go to the ground, and shift into its humanoid form, then warned it, she was going to open fire. Blatantly disregarding her threat, it began stalking forward, its dull yellow eyes displaying its weakness and status among its own, and tracked their movements. With its approach, Officer Murphy spotted an opening, and taking the left side where he could get a better shot, left her in the path of the Hunter Wolf form. It had opened its mouth, baring its teeth, its body growing tense with its imminent attack, then it loped straight toward her.

Macy risked a quick look at Officer Murphy, who hadn't engaged, hadn't attempted to stop it, and realized she was on her own. With its advance, her reaction time felt uncoordinated and her movements sluggish as she raised her H&K .45 loaded with syn silver and fired, twice. It stumbled, its body hitting the floor with force, and she tried to escape the corner. Macy believed she was going to make it to safety and to the team when a second jumped from a container. The consuming feel of being trapped blasted through her, nearly crippling her, and she retreated to the corner where she burned through her magazine. Eleven rounds into one Hunter Wolf form. Eleven. It hadn't stumbled or showed signs of slowing. Sudden doubt made her hesitate when Officer Murphy's order, hard with anxiety, told her to reload while he covered her. Without thinking and working on instinct, she hurriedly jerked a magazine from her vest.

No, she hadn't watched it attack him.

The wounded Hunter Wolf form punched her, the force sending her backward, and passing her, it attacked Officer Murphy. Macy's face erupted in pain at the same time she hit a container, causing her back to scream in agony while her tactical helmet did little to protect her from the threads of unconsciousness. Officer Murphy's rough yells kept the fog at a distance as she struggled to get her footing. It wasn't her fault. She assessed the situation and proceeded accordingly. Macy radioed for backup, watched for an opening, and ignored the feeling of helplessness when the Hunter Wolf form took Officer Murphy to the ground. The haunting resonance of his missed shots and the echo of his gun clicking empty played in her ears. Moments filled with the combinations of growls and screams ticked by when he gave up the fight and his body went limp. The lycan's slashes tore through his protective gear, allowing blood to pool at his sides, and sated with his death, it turned its attention to her.

Black blood had clung to its straw-colored fur, marking the bullet wounds while its bright eyes paled from syn silver poisoning, and its fading pupils struggled to narrow on her. Macy backed up, determined to keep her eyes on the Hunter Wolf form and not on the rips and slices in Officer Murphy's vest and compression shirt. The last layer of protection against the contagion. With an officer down, she fought for composure and felt it splinter when the lycan backed her into another corner, ending her retreat. Alone and trapped, Macy raised her gun. *Thought I was going to die.* She inhaled, focused, and the world went silent. The only sound was her pulse in her ears and the feel of her heart pounding in her chest. *Hold tight,* she repeated as it stalked forward, closing the distance between them. Macy waited. One step. Two steps. Three steps. And with a controlled exhale, she fired.

*I killed it.*

Macy looked at the side of Sergeant Mayco's face. *I killed it.* Internal Affairs read her report, questioned the officers and detectives involved, and conducted their investigation into Officer Murphy's death. IA concluded there was no negligence on her part and confirmed they had been ambushed.

She was cleared of any wrongdoing in the death of Officer Murphy. The report hadn't helped her case, when Sergeant Mayco was quick to point out, 'It was a weak defense,' and reminded her Dr. Locke, a lycan, had transported her to Sanative for precautionary medical care. First on scene, she didn't have control over what the head doctor of Sanative did or did not do.

She wanted to ask Sergeant Mayco why she was there if he didn't trust her, as team leader he had a choice. He wasn't her only problem ... no, it was only the beginning. Macy was lucky to be alive. She was lucky she hadn't been infected. Too bad he didn't care. Part of her saw it from his point of view. He wanted someone to blame. Desperately needed someone to blame. Macy understood, she yearned for the same damn thing. Except she blamed the Hunter Wolf forms and not one of her team.

Static from the radio broke through the thickening tension inside the SUV, and she hoped dispatch was going to give them information. *Please. Please. Please.* With the break in silence, Macy turned to see Sergeant Mayco giving her a sideways glance, his sunglasses hiding his crystal blue eyes. Seconds moved between them, then he dismissed her, and looked back to the road. They both waited to hear the familiar voice and anticipated an update. The silence remained, Sergeant Mayco ignored her, and they continued down the highway with the open desert on both sides and no sign of the damn truck.

---

# CHAPTER TWO

**Kayne** clutched his side, his head pounded and seeping blood, his wolf weaved inside of him to tease him with the power he could have if he allowed himself to shapeshift. All he needed to do was shift and end some of his misery. Closing his eyes—gods how he wanted his wolf—he gained control, snuffed the pressure, and reminded himself he was an agent with the DOJ and there were strict rules. Remaining in human form was one of them, if not the most important.

*Being in mortal form is no different than being bound in chains.*

With his mental walls back in place to stop the onslaught of the empaths, he searched the tops the of the containers, then the aisle. *Where the hell did it go?*

"I expected more!" Kayne yelled. *Why the hell am I yelling at it? Am I losing it?* "I didn't expect a coward." *Losing it.*

In response, a sharp bark of laughter tangled with an ear-piercing whine of grinding metal, had Kayne craning his neck to look up. The Hunter Wolf used its massive body, its shoulders bunching as it pushed a shipping container. A squeal echoed a second before the forty-eight-foot stack started to shift. Kayne deserted his hiding place in the shadows, and with curses leaving his lips, raced to the end of the aisle. Behind him, the stack tumbled, creating a clang of breaking cement, metal, and wood as it sent fist-sized pieces of debris ricocheting off containers and pelting his back. The intensity sent him to the ground, where he landed on his side, his ribs cracked, and his ears rang. Ignoring the searing pain wrapping around his chest, he scurried to his feet, covered his face in the bend of his elbow, and worked to get out of the fray. After a few dozen yards, he skidded to a stop at the end of the aisle, his boots grating on the concrete, and he struggled to search through the dense cloud of sand and dust. What was left of the containers released a fetid smell, infusing the air with decay.

Torture. Pain. Blood. They resonated around him as if warning him he was next.

Kayne took several steps backward as the sickly yellow eyes of the Hunter Wolf glared through the thinning cloud while heat exhaustion turned his mood dark, and dehydration and pain from his wounds ate his muscles. As the Hunter Wolf easily corralled him into another aisle, he felt like he was retreating, and his opportunity to get his cell taken from him. A whispered voice invaded his mind, bringing the feeling of loss and fear, and it grew into panic, forcing him to face the truth.

*I'm not going to make it out. I'm going to lose the fight,* he thought with defeat. *I'm going to die like the others.*

With no other options, he raised his gun, and threatened, "I'll kill you."

"No." Its muzzle pointed to the ceiling, and it roared.

Kayne refused to holster his pistol to cover his ears and save himself from the thunderous howl. When it ended and silence took the warehouse, he listened to its nails click on the concrete. Each thick thump matched the hard beats of Kayne's heart. It wasn't fear. The instinct to shapeshift into his Hunter Wolf gripped him in its primal need to survive. As an alpha, he possessed the strength to defeat the werewolf threatening his life, but shifting wouldn't give him Elijah. It would create more problems. His wolf pushed harder, rising to the surface and filling his ears with its wailing. *Ignore the voice.* He could beat the Hunter Wolf and stay alive. He didn't have to shift. Gripping his gun, he knew he needed one shot. The one shot guaranteed to destroy his evidence.

Damn syn silver.

It's technical name, synthetic silver, had been created from breaking down the natural chemical elements of silver when the mortals needed a less expensive alternative. Finding the precise combination for optimal destruction, they tested it on imprisoned shapeshifters, Otherkin, and paranormals. Once the tests proved its effectiveness, they synthesized what became known as synthetic silver. Syn silver was now everywhere from jail cells, handcuffs, cages, ammunition, and anything else used to control all paranormals. Kayne growled, his frustration feeding the indecision plaguing him. He was about to use an ammunition perfected by torturing paranormals on a werewolf, like a mortal, for the mortals.

"I'm going to tear you apart." With its struggle to speak, drool slid from his thick jowls, then the corners of its gapping mouth. The green/yellow goo hit the sand-dusted floor between them in soft pats.

One shot.

"He'll give me a reward." It shook, like a tremor shot through the length of its massive body, its fur ruffled, and it steadied itself.

*A reward, from Elijah?*

It was almost enough for him to holster his weapon. Kayne couldn't control the conflict ragging inside of him. Dead wouldn't get him anywhere. Despite needing answers, he had to get out the warehouse. As if sensing his inner struggle, the Hunter Wolf lunged, and Kayne stumbled backward, his muscles burning with pain and fatigue, making his retreat shoddy. His back hit the container in a crunch of bones, and sliding sideways a claw missed his chest, sliced across his shoulder, then grated against steel. He went to his knees as fire spread out from the cuts and electric shots of pain burst down his spine. Thrusting his hand out to stop himself from face planting on the concrete, he felt fiery nails cut across his back, bringing a growl, and he stood and ran. The Hunter Wolf tailed him, its long strides swallowing his attempt and easily catching up, its sharp nails shredded the remainder of his T-shirt. Each deep bite of flesh brought fire to his skin, its flames emanating throughout his body, forcing him to push harder even as warm blood cooled on heated skin.

Near the end of the aisle Kayne picked up speed, skidded around the corner, and his eyes widened in shock when he saw the Hunter Wolf. *How?* It swung its massive arm, its clenched fist colliding into his chest and sending him flying. Pain exploded inside him as if his chest burst open, and felt like his bones and breath were being pushed into the warehouse. Watching the distance between them grow, his body tensed with anticipation for the crash. In a cloud of dust, metal met skin, bones broke, and his damaged body folded in on itself.

Thankful he hadn't broken his arms, hands, or legs, he ignored the pain, and with listless movements struggled to get up from underneath his own weight. He made it to his knees when claws sank into his upper arm, grabbed him, and lifting him off the floor tossed him into another container. With the cuts in his shoulder creating a puddle of blood, muscle turned to mush for a second as bones gave under the pressure and Kayne slumped to the floor. The damn thing was playing with him like he was a toy. He was bleeding, his broken ribs acted like knives inside of his body, making him thankful they hadn't punctured a lung, and making it worse his wolf pushed against the hurt. On his side and through half closed eyes, Kayne saw the grip of his Colt 1911 peeking out from a clump of straw. He didn't know when he lost it, but if he was going to survive, he needed it back. Desperate to save himself, every fiber of his wolf rose in protest with his next thought.

Inhaling through the pain, Kayne sat up, kept his head low, his rage-filled, amber eyes staring at the floor, and raised his right hand in defeat. "Enough," he pleaded, as his hot breath stung his lips. "Enough."

"I will kill you." It inhaled, its wide chest expanding to show its dominance, then collapsed with its exhale.

"Yes," Kayne agreed through clenched teeth.

*If it kills me? In a warehouse surrounded by the forgotten.*

Dried blood pulled the skin across his back taut, opening deeper cuts while crimson seeped from slashes to stain his shoulder. If his wounds were minor Kayne would heal them, but broken bones, blood loss, bruised muscles, and a variety of cuts and slices from nails containing the contagion went beyond being able to heal them without shifting.

*You're supposed to be immortal.*

Kayne wanted to laugh. Immortal if you were able to repair the damage. As a werewolf, he healed faster than a mortal and shifting amplified the wolf spirit's power, enabling him to heal even quicker. If he shifted. If he hadn't been in a warehouse with an empath bent on driving him insane while an ersatz tried killing him.

"What will you get?" Kayne asked, each word burning his throat while his breath felt like sandpaper. On his knees, he forced himself to keep his eyes on the floor.

"A reward."

"A reward for my life?" he growled and looked up. If he didn't get his gun, he was a dead man.

"Your life? No, your head. I'll deliver it to him," it laughed as its narrowed yellow eyes landed on Kayne.

A wave of chills gripped him, making him shudder and causing broken bones to grind against one another. As if fighting the attack, his corded muscles tightened around the shattered ends as blood seeped from a dozen wounds. He needed his gun. He needed help. Damn, he was going to have to kill it. Showing submission, Kayne held his breath, struggled to his knees, and with his eyes downcast gauged the distance to his weapon. He slowly exhaled. Doubt wove into his plan, and he wondered if he would have enough strength to cross the distance.

"Fighting in human form," it mocked. "He should see your weakness."

"Elijah?" Kayne asked as he brought one knee up. Nausea churned in his stomach, its sour taste threatening his throat, while thunder roared in his skull.

*Get the damn gun.*

It let a guttural howl rumble from its chest as its response, and taking its eyes off Kayne, he risked throwing himself in the direction of the grip. Landing hard on his side, he sucked in a breath as fire erupted, its threads sinking into his legs, and hurriedly rolled to his knees. Inches. Growling in frustration and pain, he pushed off the toes of his boots and crawled. When his fingers curled around the grip and the gun was cradled in his palm, adrenalin fueled a false sense of strength and he stood. The Hunter Wolf roared in fury, marched closer, and closed in. Kayne raised the gun and leveled the barrel at its muzzle, stopping its advance.

"You won't shoot. Your need for retribution is your lifeforce." There was no fear, its yellow eyes tinged in red as it spoke, only anger and insanity. Dark insanity. Keeping its narrowed stare on Kayne, it took another step, its chest heaving, its arms hanging at its sides as if mocking his threat.

*My lifeforce.*

It's the reason you've chased Elijah for twenty-three years, left your pack, and traveled ten hours south of your home.

"If this is his revenge, why isn't he here?" Kayne forced himself to stand straight and not give into the need to sink to the concrete.

Gauging him, its head cocked to the left with consideration and clarity. "You are nothing. A toy for my enjoyment. He found what he was looking for."

*Found what?*

The question couldn't compete with his racing mind, pain fighting for attention, and the need to stay alive. The Hunter Wolf stared at the barrel of the gun and tilted its head again, its glare meeting Kayne's. There was something happening to it, its clarity slipping, and it wasn't the same, like its body was deteriorating. Red lines reached out from the corner of its eyes and bled into yellow, turning its entire eye a dirty rust color.

*Blood rage.*

A shapeshifter's eye color became a twist between the mortal and the animal, the animal being dominate, and symbolized their power and strength. If the mortal's eyes were blue and mixed with brown, its combination might be hazel. A pale hazel signified weakness, where a strong hazel with bold golds, greens, and browns signified strength. When those colors were overtaken by red, it meant the shifter had lost control of the animal and had given into its primal roots and Blood Rage. It became deranged, cannibalistic, and evil, and if it wasn't stopped, mortals, shapeshifters, and the Otherkin were at its mercy. No one was safe from its brutality or the claws of its maliciousness.

Kayne's gun was going to be useless if it sank into Blood Rage. Damn, he was close to finding Elijah. He needed one shot.

The answers to his questions would die with the Hunter Wolf.

One shot.

How much more damage was he willing to take for the vengeance fueling his life? His lifeforce. He wanted to laugh. Telling himself he hadn't been living and he didn't want retribution was a lie. Kayne was feeding off revenge's poison and simply existing. Elijah knew it and easily manipulated him. The warehouse was a trap he walked into like a lamb to slaughter.

As if its time has come to an end and Blood Rage had taken its mind, the Hunter Wolf roared, the sound bouncing off containers and the heated air between them. Kayne waited, indecision weighing heavy on him. When it flexed its claws and rushed forward, instinct took over. Three shots swallowed the warehouse in a blaze of blasts, leaving blue-gray smoke curling around the barrel of the gun. The sharp lightning strikes of pain fired into his wrists as its roars went unheard. He watched three dark crimson blooms soak through russet fur, and holding his breath, waited for it to die.

Its scarlet eyes dimmed, it roared an angry, crazed sound, and struggled to take another step when its muscles bunched. The wounded werewolf lurched, tittered, then stumbled backward. The next shot sent it reeling. Unbalanced, the Hunter Wolf hit the ground in a loud, bone-crushing smack. Relief swept over Kayne and the breath he held exploded from his chest. Around him, the scent of syn silver clung to the air a second before drifting on its own smoky sweetness. He backed up, hit a container, and slid down its side to slump on the concrete. Resting the gun on his thigh, he inhaled a slow, controlled breath, while a mixture of blood and sweat covered his skin and soaked into what was left of his T-shirt. The wet cotton clung to him like a second skin, but he didn't give damn ... he was focused on the syn silver destroying his evidence. He needed evidence. With one last hard pull of air, he controlled his breathing and listened to its dying heart.

One. Two. Three. He waited. Ten. Eleven. His heart pounded. Twenty. If a shapeshifter, in one of its animal forms, was injured or dying it converted to the easiest form to hold, its natural form. Humanoid. Thirty. The Hunter Wolf remained. An anxious energy teased Kayne.

"They're real," he mumbled to himself, disbelief in his voice. "It's an ersatz."

It was Blood Rain's responsibility to investigate paranormal cases exhibiting irregularities. With reports of werewolves and therianthropes having superior strength, speed, and the ability to withstand syn silver, the DOJ started their investigation and named the altered shapeshifters *ersatz*. The distinction separating them from the uncontaminated shapeshifters and explained they weren't natural or of nature. The evidence needed to prove someone, or something, had altered the Hunter Wolf was destroyed by syn silver. There was no denying the ersatz was different, and maybe forensics would be able to test its DNA despite it having been shot. If it carried the abnormality like the others, it would prove Kayne was on the right track. Time would tell, but he was sure he knew what was happening in Desert Rock. Elijah was infecting his victims with a corrupted contagion, making disposable shapeshifters, and using them to build an army. He would use them to destroy the vulnerable relationship between mortals, shapeshifters, and the Otherkin.

Mortals on one side and paranormals on the other.

If the relationship crumbled, the divide would provoke another war. The Requiem, the deaths, sacrifices, hunts, and then peace on both sides would have been for nothing. Kayne wanted to know why. After twenty-three years, why did he expose himself? Why a city in the middle of nowhere? What did Desert Rock have?

*He found what he was looking for.*

It didn't make sense.

As syn silver ate through flesh, turning the ersatz's body to mush, dark crimson seeped from matted fur to coat the concrete, and a new stench joined the rot inside the warehouse. Normally, it would take a couple of hours for syn silver to render a shapeshifter into a puddle of thick liquid with bones and hair in its mix, but with the heat, time worked against him. Kayne holstered his pistol, kept his eyes on the ersatz, and cradling his left arm, scooted up the side of the container. Skirting the expanding pool of silver-polluted blood, he cautiously approached the body, stopping at its muzzle. It landed stretched out on its stomach, its lower jaw propping its head up, almost as if it was going to laugh at Kayne one last time. Kneeling, he watched its red eyes and graying pupils roll up and out of sight.

*Damn thing is dying and taking my answers.* Chills sank into his core with the realization that had he continued to fight, he might have ended up like the beast in front of him. He would have lost everything.

Once he confirmed the ersatz was dead, he was going straight to his truck and calling for backup. He would risk the Bureau of Paranormal Investigations, but ideally wanted the DOJ or local police. The warehouse was holding back its dirty secrets, the bodies of the dead, and Elijah's victims. *Not for long.* Kayne moved closer, and with a dirt-stained hand covered in blood and scratches, reached out and pushed on the ersatz's shoulder. Its weak growl faded as it rolled to its side, its mouth snapping closed with clashing teeth. Thinking about who he was going to call, and lost in thought and half dazed by the loss of evidence, he watched it continue to liquefy in front of him.

In a blur, the ersatz's arm shot up, grabbed him, drove its nails into his shoulder, and growled, "Traitor."

Kayne choked on his roar as he reared backward, trying to free himself from the ersatz's nails. His back erupted in pain, and tight and sore, his legs weakened, and his muscles didn't respond to his demands. The ersatz forced its ashen nails deeper into the flesh of his shoulder, tightening its grip so its poisoned tips sank in, only stopping when they reached Kayne's shoulder blade. Nails grated against bone, causing flames to spread out and snaking into his arms, up his neck, and down his sides.

He yelled when ersatz jerked on his shoulder, his knees hit the concrete, his body leaning into its face. A sliver separated them when their gazes locked, one set amber wild with fear, and the other scarlet from Blood Rage and dying from syn silver. It sucked in a breath, working its collapsing throat, clumsily shifted its bulk, and held Kayne with its weight. His fight turned desperate when the first stings of poison penetrated his flesh, entered his bloodstream, and began its assault. The lycanthrope contagion wasn't going to kill him, it would weaken him like it had after the ersatz clawed him, except it wasn't natural, it was carrying a tainted version, and syn silver. As more contagion seeped from its nails, it pushed syn silver into Kayne's body. He felt it burn, cursed, and let a frustrated growl loose from his chest. He needed to calm down before his rapid heart rate carried the poisoned combination through his veins.

A heated mixture of blood and silver drifted on its breath, misting Kayne's face as its garbled words tumbled from its gaping maw. Panicking he jerked his gun from the holster, and with a shaking hand, placed the barrel against its head and pulled the trigger. The ersatz's body seized, turning to stone for a heartbeat, its nails like daggers in his flesh, then sagged with the weight of the dead. Kayne shoved backward, tearing the claw free, and the limp appendage fell to its body. A mist of scarlet and onyx blood covered him, the floor, and the container, while brain matter and skull fragments peppered the background.

The toxic concoction of contagion and syn silver quickly coursing through his veins weakened Kayne's hands, and unable to keep his grip, he dropped the gun and watched it land with a metal clang. He scrambled away from the ruined body, wanting to howl, curse, and kill the ersatz all over again. Inhaling and exhaling his panic, he couldn't stop his fingers from curling into the palms of his sweat-damp hands. Kayne hissed curses, his words slow and distorted as his throat tightened with each garbled phrase.

After chasing the ersatz into the warehouse, an empath attacked Kayne's emotions and memories, forcing him to abandon his senses and struggle to fortify the walls around his thoughts. With confidence, he knew he could keep it out of his head and protect himself from falling into the depths of his emotions. That was before he had been beaten, given a corrupted contagion, and syn silver. With the poison moving through him, his defenses began crumbling and the pressure intensified, letting the empath's hooks screw into his head. *Empath.* He should have known Elijah would have a guard dog.

Whispers from his past breezed in his ears, then growing louder thundered and sounded like they were coming from all directions. Kayne frantically searched the containers and aisles, then checked and rechecked. Nothing. He was losing his mind to the poison as it continued to corrode his body and control. With his defenses rotted like the dead surrounding him, he didn't possess the strength to protect himself and the gates to his thoughts opened and ushered in his nightmares. The madness from failure, loss, and sorrow came crashing down, twisting his revenge and playing in his memories. He wasn't as strong as Alpha Garrick and would never be the man he had been. He would never get validation as an alpha. His mind gave him his ruin, a pack without an alpha, a territory without a master, and the haunting images of ghostly eyes that would never turn silver.

*It's not real.*

The heavy feel of emotion rushed forward, pulsed, and the delicate face haunting his dreams came alive. Years of regret brought the smell of burning fuel, tires, hair and flesh to his nose as the bitter tang of her blood sat in his mouth. He was kneeling in dirt, glass, and metal on the side of the road, praying she would live long enough he could save her.

"A child," he mumbled.

Her singed hair sat close to her skull while her skin scarred by burns, peeled, and blistered, as soft cries escaped from between crimson-stained lips. He felt her pain and grief roll from her at the same time Kayne begged her to stay awake.

*I'm losing you.*

Silver gleamed as if the last of her strength erupted, she closed her eyes, her heart beat for the last time, and he felt her body go limp in his arms. Staring at the lost girl, his wolf enveloped him, and he roared.

Kayne exhaled and closed his eyes, praying the emotions of the memory cut him loose and would leave him the hell alone. As the sickening fumes slowly vanished and the girl's face blurred and faded, his memories sank back into the shadows, and he relaxed. It was a false sense of ease. The girl may have retracted her claws from him, but the decades of regret coursed through him like the syn silver. He failed then and he failed now. He didn't make it out of the warehouse, guaranteeing Elijah would continue mutating shapeshifters and threatening the future.

A seizure gripped his body, turning the knuckles of his fingers white, then as if someone had yanked on his spine, his knees bent and were drawn to his chest. Kayne's body curled in a ball and the fire spread, engulfing him while his wolf howled in his ears and clawed at the darkness swallowing him.

*If I give up ... if I stay where I am, I'm going to die.* A low growl froze in his chest when he rolled to his side, struggled to his knees, and with his palms flat on the concrete, he stopped. From between the frayed edges of his shirt tainted blood dripped and hit the sand-dusted floor. He watched a slow line of scarlet crawl into a crack, while chasing the red line were black fingers of syn silver reaching out into healthy blood.

*Time for you to let go.* Death waited patiently for its prey, and he had become its next victim.

*Damn, silver is a painful way to die,* Kayne thought and lowered his head.

Darkness slid into his mind, promising him death and turning his thoughts toward evanescence dragged him into the enervate. The *enervate,* the werewolf drift, a place between worlds where the wolf spirit and the human merged into one. Bound in ties of weakness, they would slip from the world and meet death together, as one.

A round of shudders racked him, sending weakness over him, and taking his balance stole the strength in his legs and he fell to his side landing with a thump. His mind flooded with voices, memories, and the faces from his life. Part of him thought he deserved death. He knew he hadn't been the best alpha, failed as a lord with the Council, failed as a sentinel for Alpha Garrick, and was an inept friend. To everyone. How he remained alpha of his pack he had no idea. And what would the pack do without him? He laughed—it sounded insane—coughed, and a mist of blood coated his lips and chin. He was an unvalidated, absentee alpha. The pack didn't depend on him, didn't expect anything from him, and survived without him. Despite abandoning them to chase his ghosts, they would address his death with tradition and respect. The pack would wait through the appropriate grieving period, then follow the guidelines set by the Council and appoint a new alpha. Maybe Michael. Whomever it was, the pack wouldn't end, it would go on and on. His thoughts drifted from his pack to the humiliation of dying on the floor in a warehouse in the middle of the desert, in a town he couldn't remember the name of.

*It's the silver,* he reminded himself, *it's ripping my mind apart.*

Files. Reports. Background information on every BPI detective in the Southern California office sat in his truck. The first thing they would find if they found the warehouse. A spasm gripped Kayne's muscles, and he groaned from pain. When the worst of the agony ebbed, he wondered if the information mattered. He was going to die permanently ending his part of the investigation.

The BPI would care. They'll find his truck, the files, his body, and the ersatz. Only they won't recognize it as an ersatz. No, they'll follow protocol, and after finding him and the evidence, they'll call Commander Wilson. After that, it would be a matter time before they learn why he was sent to *help* them.

What will they do when they learn the commissioner of the BPI ordered the DOJ and its Blood Rain team of shapeshifters to investigate them? The BPI. Mortals. Investigated. By paranormals.

His chest tightened with a building cough, and merging with a tremor the force caused his back to arch off the concrete and his breath burned his lungs. Fresh blood sat on his lips, its bitterness telling him he didn't have long, and promised his suffering had only begun. The nightmares haunting him broke through his ramparts, and breaking him down gave him the girl. The zenith of his ruin. In front of him, her eyes melted to molten silver faded and bled to cinnamon as if silently accepting his failure to keep her safe. She crept toward him, her mouth opened, and her lips curved around her accusation.

"Gods, no," Kayne mumbled in feeble protest.

*"They're dead,"* she breathed as a mixture of blood and tears slid from the corners of her eyes. *"My mom and dad. Burned."*

"I couldn't save her. Them," Kayne mumbled. Thick spit bubbled from between his dry lips and slid from his mouth as he begged for her forgiveness. Sinking further in the silver's poison, it damaged every part of him, its pain reaching into his muscles turned ropes that curled and tightened around bone. He moaned as the agony washed over him, twisted inside of him, and he prayed death would take him and end his suffering.

*"Death is coming for you,"* a whisper promised.

No. He was going to find Elijah and take the murdering bastard to Daeland. He needed to save himself, and to do that the voices in his head and the nightmares had to stop. Kayne inhaled through a seizure and ordered himself to shapeshift.

*"Death has chosen."*

*Yes. What's done is done.* Kayne let go of the fight, and giving up, released the breath in his burning lungs and sank into the concrete.

Silence.

His mind stopped, his body stilled, and silence wrapped around him.

"Wake up. Hey, wake up."

The voice sounded metallic and sharp as it reverberated in his skull, disrupted the fog, and lifted him from the concrete. Seconds of clarity brought questions. How long before someone found him? How long before Elijah found him? It was his warehouse. His ersatz.

"Wake. Up. Now." The demand sounded angry, female, and weak.

*Not real.* Kayne jerked and sucked in a breath with the splinter of consciousness, then struggled to defend himself when hot fingers touched his forehead. He grabbed the thin wrist, squeezed, and heard a surprised yelp. Through half opened eyes, he saw his worst nightmare come true. Detective Gray stood over him, her chestnut hair hanging by the sides of her face, her dark eyes gazing down. They found him. He released her for fear his blood would infect her, and his arm dropped to his chest.

"Detective Gray?" he whispered. Did she see his truck and the files?

# CHAPTER THREE

---

"Well? Is it the agent's or not?" Sergeant Mayco demanded.

Macy met his glare with her own. "Negative. The truck is registered to someone in Desert Rock," she replied. "And his tags are expired."

Sergeant Mayco cursed under his breath, put the SUV in gear, and pulled back on to the highway. As with every stop, tension quickly dominated, and like the silence, its electric edges found her nerves and created pressure points of frustration. Macy fidgeted, took her cell from the center console, and checked her messages. Nothing. All day without a word from the man. A feeling of abandonment crept in, and she wondered if Commander Arden had taken Captain Dixon and Sergeant Mayco's advice and cut his losses. Ordered to do an investigation, she was positive he would tell her before ending it since she was working directly for him. Right.

She shoved the feeling down, replaced her cell, checked the MDT for an update, and saw there was nothing new. With Sergeant Mayco engrossed in his mumblings she took the time to go over the information they had learned from the DOJ. When the agent went dark and before they lost his signal, they tracked his cell to a section along Highway 395. Most of the area was open desert as far as the eye could see, then it ran into Desert's Gateway, a once busy industrial hub with warehouses, coffee shops, and had been home to a half dozen food trucks. Desert's Gateway shutdown shortly after a territory fight between two therian-cougar prides destroyed a warehouse, killed six humans, wounded four DRPD officers, and infected three other officers. All of which died from Death Blooms. The therians responsible had been killed on sight, while the others were arrested and taken into custody.

With human deaths and the those of the officers, California declared a state of emergency and implemented the Requiem Preternatural Act to seize all industrial property owned by paranormals. Then it instated regulations prohibiting paranormals from purchasing large parcels of land to prevent them from gathering in groups. Statewide outcry spurred a standoff between pro-human groups and pro-paranormal groups, with both sides confronting the corporations. Rather than fight either side, and spend millions in court battles, the human-owned businesses closed their doors, packed up, and abandoned the area. The warehouses were left to squatters, stripped by scavengers, and what they didn't take time and the desert's extreme weather destroyed.

Where the hell was dispatch with an update and why wasn't the Department of Justice searching for their agent? After another dirt road and no agent, Macy sat in the passenger seat listening to Sergeant Mayco's breathing. Chatter from the radio broke up the silence while the tires created their own noise. If the BPI knew what was going on, they would have searched every warehouse, investigated the owners, and arrested the shapeshifters before the kidnapping started.

*Maybe,* she thought, *eventually.* It was the reason she was taking orders from Commander Arden. Her directive was to find out why cases weren't being investigated and if she could prove the alleged spy had anything to do with the mishandling of evidence. Despite the BPI being under-manned—it was always undermanned—the caseloads were possible. Her involvement went deeper than investigating unworked cases. Unknown to Sergeant Mayco and the other BPI detectives, the result of disobeying Sergeant Mayco's direct order to fire on the target, Mrs. Barrette, had gotten Macy separation papers. In a desperate bid to save her career, she pleaded her case to Commander Arden. He listened, and when Macy finished begging, he offered her a deal. *A deal.* He was blackmailing her. Macy either spied on the detectives of the BPI and Officer Murphy, or she walked out of the BPI office for good. Sergeant Mayco's statement was spot on, she would never work with another law enforcement agency. Ever. Macy took the deal, turned traitor, and was given her badge and gun back.

Out of nervous habit, she checked her phone. *Nothing. Damn it.*

"Why do keep checking your phone? Expecting a call?" Sergeant Mayco asked. "Maybe a message?"

It wasn't delivered as a simple question. He targeted her with an accusation. "Nervous habit," Macy replied. She ignored his grunt of disapproval when he expressed his lack of confidence in her answer. *What else is new?* Inwardly sighing, a warning went off in her head and told her why she was with him. "Is this your way of keeping your friends close and your enemies closer?" she asked. "You want to watch me?"

Sergeant Mayco turned his head enough to glare at her. "Don't flatter yourself." His attention went back to the road.

*Right. Thanks for clearing things up.*

If the agent was chasing a bad lead, the DOJ was making a bold accusation. And if they were right and they found lycans were involved? They would be arrested, tried in court, and no doubt found guilty, and would spend the rest of their lives in silver-lined cages waiting for the death penalty. Or given a lifelong sentence and used as test subjects which was nothing more than a death sentence itself. If extended torture, over years, could be a sentence.

She asked herself how an agent with the DOJ, not from the area, could find one warehouse out of dozens in the desert. The BPI had no knowledge of the warehouse, the lycans involved, or had been contacted about missing persons. How did the agent get his information? And why hadn't he called for backup? There were to many variables, and Macy imagined every scenario, and if the past month was any indication of how things were going to turn out, it wasn't going to be good. She couldn't control the nervous energy coursing through her, and shifting in the seat, her thigh holster caught the edge, and her utility belt dug into her waist.

*Come on, dispatch.* She prayed they told them something. Anything to end the search. Along the shoulder of the road, paper and trash drifted in the breeze as trash bags clung to creosote limbs waiting for the wind to set them free. While they searched, the afternoon temperature climbed to over a hundred and ten, its heat emanating from the black-top in waves and turning oncoming headlights into blurred waves floating in a haze. The desert in July was unforgiving, brutal, and hot. As the sun traveled across the sky, the temperatures were going to get worse, and if the DOJ agent was imprisoned in a warehouse, the building was going to become a hot box. What would kill him first; the lycans, heat exhaustion, or the desert? Macy didn't have an answer. Maybe he was lost, got his truck stuck, and they were going to find him along the road.

Sure they were. There's no way she was going to be that lucky.

Macy looked at Sergeant Mayco, his clenched jaw, the tension in his shoulders, and his unsaid accusations. Lycans attacked both the BPI and DRPD, killed an officer, and law enforcement didn't have any leads. They were ambushed, meaning someone knew they were going to be there. What had she leaned from Harper's warehouse? The Hunter Wolf forms were hard to fucking kill and didn't shift back into their humanoid forms after they died. It made identifying the body impossible, and with syn silver corrupting them, it made DNA tests more difficult. An added problem, they weren't able to run the DNA through the NCA, the database of every registered shapeshifter to get their identities, backgrounds, including next of kin, current address, and criminal history.

Her thoughts of a future where there were super shapeshifters with no respect for the law blocked out the rough terrain of the desert and the afternoon sun. If the lycans pushed the BPI, they would be forced to tighten their hold on the paranormal community. The public would see it as an assault on a specific faction and the pro-paranormal groups would do everything in their power to stop the BPI, then the pro-human groups would enter the fray. No one would admit a battle between species would threaten everyone's safety or put the advances they had made since the Requiem at risk. For her, Officer Murphy's death had done more than rock law enforcement, it added another reason to hate lycans to her growing list. Lycans? Macy was an equal opportunist; she hated all shapeshifters.

With her thoughts feeding frustration's fire, she touched the screen on the MDT, bringing the call log up, and skipping to the menu screen, it blinked, changed, and gave her a dozen options. Choosing active calls, Macy saw Detective Gaines had a therian in custody and was running his name through the NCA. That's what she should be doing, working, investigating, not looking for a lost agent. When she touched an arrow, the screen switched to a map, and brought up their position. They were at least thirty minutes outside of the city limits. *Stuck with each other in the middle of nowhere and on nothing more than an errand for the DOJ,* she thought with annoyance.

**Kayne** imagined Detective Gray sifting through the files in his truck and finding the information he had on her. Like her photograph. He had stared at it, admittedly losing himself in her frozen gaze, but it hadn't prepared him for her intense stare as her cinnamon eyes searched him. Their feel traveled over the wound in his shoulder, his torn T-shirt, and back to his eyes. When she held his stare, a feather of familiarity touched him, drifted through his memoires like a ghost, and at the same time he knew his eyes reflected his wolf.

*Cautionary. Has expressed prejudice toward all shapeshifters. Abrasive towards paranormals.* Detective Gray understood what he was. Would she help him knowing he was a werewolf, or because she hated shapeshifters, would she leave him to die?

Detective Gray leaned down, eyes narrowed, hair falling forward, and asked, "Did that thing do this to you?"

When he tried to answer, mumbled moans and grunts escaped from his numb lips. He couldn't form words. Syn silver held him in its grasp, crippling his senses and ability to speak.

"Did you kill it?" she demanded, her voice high with desperation.

He was going to report her for not following protocol. Barely able to keep his eyes open, he held his breath when Detective Gray's face blurred, and her dark hair melted into hanging clumps of greasy blonde strands sticking to the sides of her bruised and broken face. *No, it's a delusion.* The BPI wasn't there. He wasn't saved. His blood turned cold realizing a victim had found him. The woman knelt beside him on scraped knees, her bloodshot eyes ringed with dried, cracked blood, and her skin held yellow bruises.

"Did you kill it?" she repeated, every word ending in a whistle.

*Yes. Can't you see?* Kayne stared at the dirt covering her thighs, arms, bare stomach, and the shredded shirt hanging off her scratched left shoulder. What he saw explained everything and nothing. A jagged bite made from human teeth disfigured the exposed shoulder while the bitterness of blood, both werewolf and mortal, shrouded her in its stench. Kayne wanted to answer her. He wanted to say yes, that thing did do this, and yes, he killed it, but the sound forced from his mouth was a groan, not a word. *Can't you see it?*

"Answer me," she screamed.

*Yes.*

The woman's presence and her yelling breached his self-induced shame. Pulled back from death, Kayne focused on shapeshifting, healing his superficial wounds, and saving himself. Like a battle of wills, the same haunting whisper refused to let him go.

*"You can't be saved."*

He was meant to die. Like his lost girl.

"Shut up," Kayne mumbled to the whisper.

When the woman scooted toward him, her hate rolled from her in waves. He didn't need her getting any closer and corrupting his already warped thoughts and pushing his instincts. Ignoring her, he focused on surviving as he fought against the stronger surges of nausea roiling in his stomach. Sour bile burned his throat while tremors gripped his core and tumbled through him making him curl into the fetal position. His laugh sounded in his head, rough and unstable, then as the tremor eased, he straightened his legs.

*Time is wasting*, he told himself.

"Is it silver?" the woman demanded.

*Yes.* "Clothes. Off," he whispered through swollen lips, and hoped she understood. Silence followed, and he feared she left him to die. *I was meant to die.* Kayne opened his eyes to make sure it wasn't another delusion and saw the truth in the dirty crimson caked to the side of her face. "Clothes." *There isn't enough time.* "Off."

With the first tug, his back grated against the sand-covered concrete, opening cuts and spreading flames over his skin. Sucking in a breath, he grunted when a second, harder yank freed his foot from his boot, and she started on his left. She dragged him with each jerk, his entire body clenching in defense, his stomach roiling with the pain. When her fingers grazed the skin at his waist, he tried to defend himself. Her touch was too hot, and he bet the contagion was making quick work of her. Kayne moaned, his thoughts slugging along, trying to tell him what was going on when she inhaled in an exaggerated breath laced with a whistle.

"Your veins. You're ... There's black blood," she mumbled, with a tremble in her words.

*I'm dying.* Kayne tried raising his arms off the ground to work his jeans and quit when he was too weak to move. "Hurry," he slurred.

No answer. No sound. He was finished.

"Don't touch me. I hate this. I hate you. I hate your kind," she hissed.

*Noted,* he thought. *Now hurry.*

With a grunt, the woman shoved his hands from his body and away from her, and hesitantly her fingers fumbled with his belt. Seconds ticked by and her work turned to angry jerks, and her fingers inched under the waist of his jeans to wrestle with the button. Her whispered curses continued as she moved him with rough pulls and shoves, then she rummaged through his pockets.

*Good luck.* He had nothing. Everything was in his damn truck where he left it. Like a fool. He held his breath when her trembling fingers grazed his thighs as she yanked each pant leg down his legs.

"Okay, I got your clothes off," she hissed, pushing against his broken ribs. "Get up, I need your help."

He tried rolling to his side. The broken bones grated, and pain screamed at the same time his head drummed and he swam in nausea.

"Get up. Shift. Do something, you worthless lycan." She inhaled, a whistle following. "You're supposed to be immortal. Get the fuck up."

*"Immortal. Rest easy, everyone dies in the end."*

*Not my thought.* Kayne lifted his right arm, releasing flames in his veins and into his shoulder. His arm hit the concrete with a smack as another spasm gripped his legs and torso.

"Get. Up," she ordered. The constant whistle was fading in her anger, as if she was clenching her teeth. "Get. Up," she repeated. She exhaled as she hit his chest, shoulder, and his face. "Damn you, get up."

Kayne rolled to the left, trying to escape the woman's attack, but he was too slow, and she blasted another round to his back and side. "Stop," he begged.

"No. Not until you get up." She landed several more punches, breathing in quick gasps.

Out of desperation, he cleared his mind, called the wolf within, and clutched the threads of power. In the depths of evanescence his wolf clawed its way to the surface, its howls in his ears to steal the noise of the warehouse. The air thickened around him, acted as a protective barrier separating him from the world to usher his wolf forward. He wasn't in the solid, living, breathing plain of mortals, the shift put him in the enervate and the drift where he receded deeper inside of himself. His wolf gained strength from both places as they evolved from one and into another. Usually the shift passed quickly, the morphing of bones, skin, hair, and tendons moving over him in a painless blur, and was quickly forgotten. Nothing about the day had been normal. As his essence sank into the static of the enervate and then held in the werewolf drift, he saw silver eyes as if she was there watching him.

*Not possible.* With his next breath, the energy wrapped around him, and touching his skin with its magic it warmed his body. Throwing his head back despite the pain, he howled, his grief at seeing the child's eyes and his crumbling boundaries gave the wolf's spirit full access to his body. He wanted out of the drift. Power poured over him like a white-hot liquid, plunging into his changing limbs and forcing the silver from his veins. When his wolf broke the surface, Kayne couldn't stop the roar as new energy swept him up in its coil of his wolf.

Syn silver oozed from wounds, making shiny puddles lined with black next to the nails of his clawed feet. Skin stretched over bone while muscles and tendons reformed and softened, and his arms and legs reshaped. Soon the warehouse faded and refocused as his eyes shifted with his body. He imagined how he must look, his eyes gleaming amber, his human body melting and continuing to morph into his Hunter Wolf form. With a final rush of strength and energy, his lesser wounds closed, his bones mended, his body finished shifting, and his instincts exploded with information. Kayne stood, his massive chest rising and falling as he stretched to the eight-foot height of his Hunter Wolf. With most of the silver out of his veins and the deepest wounds healed, he looked for the woman who saved his life.

In search of her, he made a half circle when he saw her huddled beside a container, her knees drawn up to her chest and the bones of her spine pushing against her ashen skin. He took a step toward her, felt her unrestrained loathing, and from dark sockets, her bloodshot eyes stared up at him, betraying her fear.

"I won't hurt you," Kayne assured. He spoke slowly, carefully, making it easier for her to understand him. "I am not one of them." His deep voice thundered through the silence of the warehouse.

She didn't move. The bruises marking the left side of her face ranged in colors from green to purple to yellow, gleaming from sweat while scrapes crisscrossed her sunken nose and forehead. In his Hunter Wolf his senses were stronger, clearer, and told him what he suspected. The lycanthrope contagion had taken over her body and was actively changing her DNA.

Kayne took a hesitant step and watched the woman push herself against the container, attempting to dig into the metal. He stopped, raised his large, clawed hands, showing he understood her fear, and slowly backed up to give her space. As much as he wanted to stay in his current form, for the strength, senses, and relief from the empath's mental torture he wasn't going to get any answers from her. Stepping back, he put greater distance between them, and stopped beside his crumpled pile of clothing he could smell, and did not want to put them back on. Left without a choice, he checked on her one last time, gave her his back, and trying for manners on his part, privacy for her, shifted into his humanoid form.

The shift progressed slowly, and he felt every second of his muscles, bones, and skin transforming into another form. Keeping his back to the woman, since he wasn't wearing clothing, he tested his right shoulder, then his left, twisted to check his ribs, and felt the pain ease. Tomorrow was going to be hell, but it would be all right, he was alive. Dressing quickly, before he went to his truck in search of clean clothes, he pulled on the shredded shirt, sweat-soaked boxers, stained jeans, socks, and boots. The damage done to his leather shoulder holster bothered him the most. He was going to have get a new one. When he was dressed and wearing his holster and gun, he faced the woman.

"I'm not one of them," Kayne assured as he gauged her reaction. He waited for her to say something, anything to acknowledge him, and letting seconds burn in the heat she stared at him with her fearful gaze. "I'm Agent Kayne Sinclair with the Department of Justice."

The woman remained hunched down next to the container, her knees by her face, her grimy feet as close to her body as she could get them. Silence sat thick, and Kayne started to think she wasn't going to move or talk.

"I'm Grace," she finally mumbled. "What is the Department of Justice doing with a lycan?"

"Do you want some help up?" Kayne asked, ignoring her question.

"Don't touch me," Grace snapped. Her eyes remained on him for a second before she started to stand and slowly inched up the side of the container.

*Fine.* "Grace, I'm part of a task force investigating the presence of shapeshifters in this warehouse. Who did this to you?"

She cringed like she hated him saying her name, and ignoring him clung to metal. Watching her deliberate progress, Kayne saw the problem. She had broken her ankle. If the lycanthrope contagion was altering her mortal DNA, like he thought, and if she was close to shifting, like he thought, it should have healed a portion of her wounds. Whatever was happening was wrong.

"You're infected and it's a matter of time before the contagion completely intertwines with your DNA and changes its function to adapt to the wolf. You're hours away from shifting." Kayne regretted his brash approach. Grace had been infected against her will, but it was too late, she was already staring at him with wide, hurt eyes. With guilt simmering inside of him, he watched tears slip down her cheeks, leaving wet lines through dirt and old blood.

"I could have done without that," Grace mumbled and looked away. "I know."

"I'm sorry. Time is something neither of us have." Someone would eventually check on the warehouse and the prisoners. "If you're going to shift, you're going to need help." He searched her with his senses, felt the contagion, but not her crux, the wolf's essence, and not her wolf's spirit. She didn't have one. The contagion was erasing the wolf's spirit and leaving a void behind. The cavity reminded him of victims of a Death Bloom, when their bodies rejected the wolf spirit. How was she alive?

Without a word, Grace used the side of the container as a crutch and started down an aisle. After a few hobbling steps, her foot caught on the open edge of metal, causing her to stumble and cry out from the pain. Kayne quickly stepped in to help but stopped before touching her when she cowered from him.

"I can help you," Kayne offered. *Please let me help you.* Watching the bones move under her bruised skin, and the strength it took to drag her foot, sent chills down his spine.

Grace gave him a sideways glance, disregarded him, and continued forward. "They came for Henry and kidnapped us from our house," she started to explain, through broken teeth. "They wore black, grabbed us, drugged us, and we woke up here. I think it's been a week. I'm not sure."

Her body wore an array of colors, starting with the deep bruises on her arms, legs, and most of her exposed flesh. Fear, mortal waste, and the sour smell of infection floated around her. If she was infected a week ago, the transformation shouldn't take place for another week, the night of the full moon. That wasn't the case. How did the lycanthropy contagion work so damn fast?

"Do you know who they were?" Kayne asked as he kept pace with her.

"Yes." The word came out slowly, dripping with caution.

"Can you tell me?" he pressed. Kayne might have healed his wounds but the remnants of silver in his body made him weak and the empath in the warehouse made him wary of his senses. Judging her reaction was difficult and he couldn't tell if she was lying or not.

"I know how it works. Cops protect each other. Brothers in arms and all that. You said you were DOJ." She scooted along the side of the container, her fingertips leaving a trail of grime in her wake.

Kayne stopped, her broken ankle and greasy smudges forgotten. "A cop did this? Kidnapped you and Henry from your house?"

"Cops," Grace mumbled through a painful laugh laced with fury. "It was the fucking BPI."

"Why? Why would they take the both of you?" Kayne demanded. "You said they came for Henry, why did they take you?" Two steps and he caught up to her. "Were they the people who did this to you? Beat you, infected you?"

Grace stopped, lowered her head, stared at the floor, and her body shook. "No, they didn't *do this*. Henry used to sell White Cell. He doesn't anymore and hasn't for a long time," she replied, quickly turning her eyes to Kayne. "He knew a manufacturer, and they said he wasn't keeping up his end, and they took us. They told us we were expendable." Grace stopped talking, and favoring her broken ankle, limped along the side.

Kayne understood who hurt her and hated him. "Were they male or female?" He didn't need any more evidence Elijah was using the warehouse to imprison mortals, and it had been a trap. The ersatz knew who he was, knew he was searching for Elijah, and would have gotten a reward for killing him. Kayne wanted Grace to tell him the names of the BPI agents and those giving Elijah information.

Grace stopped, caught her breath, and rested for second. "Male. I think. Only one of them talked, but they were all big, their faces hidden behind those black masks. I couldn't tell because their entire bodies were covered."

He had heard how the BPI cloaked their physical appearances by using masks, all black uniforms, and were trained to mirror shadows when dealing with paranormals. Their ghost-like appearances, rumors of their tactical training, and armed with syn silver, they executed their mission with precision. With a reputation of violence and death, even mortals feared them.

"Do you know the name Elijah?" Kayne asked as he followed her. He cringed with each pained step but could do nothing except watch her hobble down another container as she led them deeper into the warehouse.

"No." Grace kept ambling.

Kayne wished he could tell if she was lying and wanted to ask her a dozen questions about the BPI detectives, but he wasn't going to push her. He was lucky she told him anything at all. His investigation into the detectives was ongoing and his questions were going to be answered. Passing Grace, he left the aisle and entered an open, U-shaped area made from more containers. They sat lengthwise, end to end, their sides had been cut out and bars and doors replaced metal. Each one of them were fitted with new locks.

Grace made her way to a stack, stopped, took a deep breath, sagged against it, and without looking at him, pointed and said, "He's up there."

He wasn't paying attention to the direction she was pointing and wasn't staring at the open container. He was staring at her hand and arm. Sets of teeth marks punctured through cuts and defense wounds as they carved a path while giving away her attempt to protect herself.

Glancing at him, Grace found him staring, looked at her arm, and a swath of crimson crept up her throat to her cheeks. She studied her wounds as if for the first time, as if seeing them through a different set of eyes, and her shoulders sank. After clearing her throat and gathering herself, she straightened as much as she was able.

"Up there."

"If you were able to get out, why wasn't he?" Kayne checked the distance from the top container to the ground and was surprised she had broken an ankle and not a leg or her neck. "What is he doing?"

With a weak cry turned rough cough, she met his gaze, her eyes bloodshot and tears welling. "He's stuck."

Newly turned werewolves don't possess the strength to control the wolf spirit. The wolf has no reasoning, doesn't give in, its primal need forces it to fight and survive, regardless of its broken, bleeding mortal body. Kayne knew the werewolf was in that state, hurt, its mind struggling to understand what was happening, while the mortal's body was dying. As death created desperation, the wolf spirit pushed forward to gain dominance. It made Henry dangerous. For Kayne to help him, he would have to force the shift, gain control over the wolf, and hope his mortal body endured the transition.

"Stuck?" Kayne dreaded her explanation.

Mortals believed shapeshifters purposely set out to infect others. It explained the black-market White Cell, but what they didn't understand or believe, few mortals survived the initial infection of the contagion, and less made it through the first transformation. The lesson for infecting a weak mortal had been learned through pain and death. Because mortal deaths brought attention to the paranormals and the Veiled—those living in secret, from the Council, an organization of the oldest and most powerful factions of the paranormal world—crossovers were strictly regulated. Unless the shapeshifter turned rogue and attacked an innocent, an act punishable by death.

It didn't make sense for Elijah to blatantly kidnap and infect mortals when it would get the attention of the Council and human law enforcement. Kayne believed the Council members were too old, too powerful, and too bored, and the inertness of their existence made them dangerous. Their years were substantial and creativity among them vast, allowing them to think of new ways to torture their prisoners. Why risk their retribution? So, the Council hadn't listened to his ramblings whenever he approached them about Elijah, but Kayne convinced himself, they couldn't deny hardcore evidence. Henry and Grace were his evidence. All he had to do was get them out of the warehouse. Alive.

"Between human and animal." Tears slipped down her cheeks, her shoulders gave up their strength, and she shook her head like she didn't believe what she was saying. "Animal and human. Wolf and Henry."

The haunted look in her eyes, and the grief etched on her face, told him she didn't understand what was happening. Her mind was having a hard time accepting what she was seeing, but knew she feared for her husband and he disgusted her. The sadness radiating from her gave away her self-loathing for feeling both. Kayne nodded. It wasn't a response, more of a weak acknowledgement he'd heard her. She stared at him with tears falling, her chest heaving with her breathes, and her heart pounding. He stared back, not having a choice and regretting every minute of it. For fear the empath would attack his thoughts, Kayne tested the strength of his senses and wondered what monstrosity he was going to face.

---

# CHAPTER FOUR

"Here's another one." Sergeant Mayco's gruff voice made her jump, and she gave him a sideways glance. "I think this leads to the Pennsky warehouse."

Thinking he saw her jump, she expected to hear how she wasn't good enough for the job, followed by a fifteen-minute rant. To her surprise, if he did notice, he ignored her. His attention was on what lay ahead as he pointed toward another entrance to yet another warehouse. They were making their way through Desert Gateway and the shells of what was left.

She thought she knew the name. "Are you sure it's Pennsky?" Not that it mattered, she would do anything to get out of the SUV and the suffocating silence. Sergeant Mayco didn't answer, and Macy inwardly shook her head. Leaning forward, she searched for evidence the agent had been there or was there.

The entrance was missing a company sign, and nothing told them what its purpose had been. The area resembled a ghost town inhabited by husks of warehouses that had been blasted by sand and the elements. Rusted siding, broken windows, crumbling asphalt driveways, and overgrown weeds pushing through the broken pavement of the parking lot made doubt surge. There were no lines defining the sides of the road as sand crept up the edges and then over the crumbling parking spaces, and any definition defining the front and back of the warehouse had been erased.

"It matches the others, run down and deserted. I wouldn't be surprised if scrappers have stripped it clean," Macy said as she searched the road and surrounding desert.

"We'll see," Sergeant Mayco replied as he turned left off the highway and onto Rattler Lane. A sharp right turn and several rough splits in the road later, they were on Pennsky Way.

*Damn, he was right.*

Macy took a pen from her pocket, looked at her cell, wished Commander Arden would freaking message her, then took a notepad from her left side cargo pocket. She flipped through several pages, marked with rushed handwriting, and stopped when she saw the notes about the Barrettes. She should have taken the shot. Dead, almost dead, at least it would have been one less problem. The thought made her feel guilty and frustrated. Flipping to the next page, she wrote down 'Rattler Lane' and 'Pennsky Way'. Rattler Lane might seem out of place anywhere else, but in the barren desert surrounded by sweeping hills and skeleton brush trying to make it through another summer, it fit.

She stared at the page, information about the case surfacing through her thoughts, and nearly blurted out Officer Murphy's name. Macy was positive there had been a report about White Cell and Desert Gateway, just like she was positive Officer Murphy's task force had overseen the investigation into the claim. Continuing to stare at the notebook page, she struggled to remember why the BPI hadn't been notified. She gave Sergeant Mayco a sideways glance as she weighed her options and wondered if asking him was worth the cost.

Negative. There was no way in hell she was going to say anything about Officer Murphy failing to check the warehouse, and the BPI hadn't done a follow up. The fear she would be walking into another 'I don't know why you're here' rant made her pause. Plus, she would be making an accusation against a dead officer, the sole reason Sergeant Mayco didn't want to work with her. For the moment, Macy would keep her thoughts to herself, and when she was back at the office, she would check the BPI logs.

The law stated if a shapeshifter, Otherkin, or anyone identifying as a paranormal wanted to purchase large parcels of property, like a warehouse, they would have to request permits for the building and there would be a background investigation on the individual. The purchaser's information would be entered into the NCA along with their animal, DNA, fingerprints, and other properties in connection to the purchased parcel. If Officer Murphy's task force investigated and a crime had been committed, he would have to file a report with the DRPD, the Building Division, and if it had been a paranormal crime, the BPI. Plus, he would have entered the information into the NCA. She could check the database, but Officer Murphy's report would be at the DRPD office, and they weren't going to share information anytime soon. They barely tolerated her as it was. The cold reception she received at the Barrettes' house was proof. But she didn't need them if he filed with the Building Division. She circled the word *investigation*, it being her main concern, and when she finished, she stuffed the notebook in her pocket.

"If lycans are using the warehouse, why don't we know about it? And how the hell does the DOJ?" Macy asked. The SUV bounced, jarring her in her seat and tightening the seatbelt. She grabbed the door handle with her right hand and the console with her left as the SUV's front tires dipped in another rut. In the rear of the vehicle, gear rattled, metal on metal, letting loose a screeching sound only comparable to fingernails on a chalkboard.

"I don't know. We can ask him when we find him," Sergeant Mayco answered. His curt response didn't go unnoticed. "Look."

Macy let his distant tone dissolve and looked up the crumbling asphalt road. The driver parked the black truck, at least one hundred yards from the warehouse, where the parking lot used to be, and in soft sand. After an entire afternoon of checking trucks, vans, and cars parked in the desert, and talking to people who were playing with their off-road toys, she knew only someone from out of town would park in soft sand. One spin of the tires and you were going to dig yourself a hole.

"The truck matches the description. Let this be the agent," Macy prayed.

Sergeant Mayco remained silent as he slowly drove toward the vehicle. Ignoring him, she let her hopes get the better of her, unbuckled her seatbelt, and sat forward, trying to get a better look.

"You'll check the vehicle. If it checks out, I'll call Captain Dixon," Sergeant Mayco explained. He eased the SUV over ruts and broken pavement, drove another twenty feet to leave plenty of space between them, and parked on the opposite side of the road.

Frustration brewed. He wasn't getting out to check, a real shocker. When she had a view of the truck her heart pounded, blood rushed through her veins, and a little shot of adrenaline hit her. "Damn, the passenger side window is broken." Shards of glass glittered in the sun, reflecting a throng of primary colors against the window of the SUV. For a second, she ignored Sergeant Mayco's sideways glance and slipped back into her old self. "Backup?"

"Negative."

Macy wore a neutral expression on her face to cover the shock of his reply. Negative. A missing DOJ agent, a wrecked truck, possible shapeshifter presence, and he responded with negative. What the hell? A little backup would be nice. Sure, part of her wanted to be out from under his glare, but if the truck belonged to the agent and there were lycans in the vicinity, she needed Mayco. Macy stared, tried reading his face, then understating hit her like he had punched her. This was what she gets. Should have taken the shot. His sunglasses sat on his forehead, leaving his ice blue eyes unveiled, his defiance wrapped in a challenge, and his rage creasing his face.

Giving him her back, she opened the door and escaped the SUV.

A dry wave of heat wrapped around her, chased the chill from the air conditioner, and blowing strands of hair around her face, it couldn't unleash the tension gripping her shoulders. She tried shrugging off Sergeant Mayco's glance, his one-word answer, and his intent. She failed. She failed the detectives of the BPI. More than once. She was investigating them. Carrying the weight of her lies, Macy approached the truck, her right hand on the butt of her gun while she listened to the surrounding area. Traffic from the 395 increased and hummed, the wind blew through drying brush, and the engine of the idling SUV purred. There were no noises. Voices. People struggling. Macy's questions about the agent, the warehouse, and why he was investigating by himself multiplied with his truck. Aftermarket additions lifted the vehicle while the off-road tires made it sit even higher. It had to be his POV, because she was sure the DOJ didn't issue four-wheel drive trucks to its agents. What was the DOJ agent doing at a warehouse with his personal vehicle if he was there on official business? She walked closer, noticing the passenger side wore dents where something had landed on the hood ... hard and heavy enough to bend the frame and break the windows.

"A damn lycan," she mumbled. It was always damn lycans. Resentment quickly worked her attitude, and like water through rocks, it flooded her with memories of Officer Murphy, Mrs. Barrette, and Sergeant Mayco and his tirades.

As a precaution, because Sergeant Mayco refused her backup, Macy pulled her gun from its holster. Her instincts sang with a warning as awareness snaked across her shoulders and tightened its grip. Hunter Wolf forms.

*Calm down.* Sergeant Mayco was watching and judging. Leaving several feet between her and the truck, she knelt in the gravel, checked underneath, and saw the engine was purging fluids. A couple more steps, she stood on the toes of her boots and with her gun raised, checked the truck's bed. One suitcase, a duffle bag, nothing else. The evidence of Hunter Wolf forms and their violence fueled the resentment building inside of her at the same time feeding the confidence they weren't going to find him. They were going to find his body. Macy walked down the side of the truck, taking in the dents, chipping paint, and the flat tire while glass crunched under her boots with each step. She rounded the front, approached the half open door, raised her gun, and peered inside. She released the breath she didn't know she was holding when there was no one inside.

With the cab clear, Macy stepped backward, stared at the crunched door like it would tell her what had happened, then went to the front of the truck. The driver's side headlight hung like it had been squeezed from its socket while a cluster of wires kept it from hitting the ground. Standing in front of the license plate, Macy pressed the button on the mic clipped to her shoulder, read the numbers to dispatch, and waited for a response. Around her, a strong breeze pushed the headlight against the truck's grille, glass gleamed, and the world moved forward as if she wasn't standing in front of a wrecked vehicle.

"Charlie-Eight, the vehicle is registered to Kayne Sinclair out of Feather River, California," the female voice reported into her earpiece.

"Affirmative," Macy replied absently.

When Sergeant Mayco told her the agent was from out of town, he hadn't mentioned he was from Feather River. Would have been nice to know she was looking for someone from her hometown. *I don't know anyone there*, she reminded herself. Mixed with tension, a sad laugh sat in her throat, wanting its freedom. The name of the town drifted through her memory, and reaching out fell into nothing. Those days felt like a thousand years in the past, and since she spent a lifetime trying to forget them, she wasn't going to hold onto them. She marched to the driver's door and with her left hand—no way in hell was she holstering her gun—she tugged, hard. Metal squealed, chunks of glass fell to the ground, and the door grudgingly opened, and she took in what the agent had left behind.

"Dispatch confirmed it's the agent's truck. There's an extra magazine and a DOJ badge sitting inside," Macy confirmed. "By the look of it, he was attacked."

"Shapeshifter?" Sergeant Mayco asked.

*No shit.* "Hunter Wolf form," she answered.

"You're positive?" His tone questioned why she specified it was a Hunter Wolf form and not a shapeshifter.

"Affirmative." Macy wasn't going to argue. The tension racing across her shoulders was all the confirmation she needed.

"I'm calling Captain Dixon and getting a team out here," Sergeant Mayco replied from the SUV. "The DOJ have their team on stand-by. The warehouse is the only place he can be, if he didn't run out into the desert."

*He didn't run.* Macy nodded as if he could see her, then searched for blood, a struggle, any evidence showing the agent was hurt, dead, or had been dragged from his truck. A human against a lycan, DOJ or not, would have been a tough fight. If the lycan was one of the hard to kill kind, the agent didn't have a chance. An ammo magazine sat in the center console beside a cell phone, pack of gum, and receipts. Rookie move leaving your cell behind. Macy moved on. The black interior made finding blood difficult, but there were no bullet holes and nothing showing a struggle took place inside of the cab. In fact, his dark blue suit jacket draped over the seat hadn't been touched, its dangling sleeve grazed a worn leather briefcase. With a gust of wind her attention went to a charm hanging from the rearview mirror. Carved into the reddish-brown wood, a wolf's head pointed up, howling as if at the moon, and swayed in the breeze. She watched it turn, took another step closer, and leaned farther into the truck to get a better look. The charm danced with a stronger gust, the wind blowing into the cab carrying different scents, and rustled papers.

*Papers?* Macy turned her attention to the floorboard and the scattered stack of pages, files, and manilla envelopes. Her breath caught, her heart pounded, and an empty feeling sank inside of her as she leaned closer and read her name.

She vaguely listened to Sergeant Mayco as he relayed information to Captain Dixon about the truck, its condition, and they could download their location from the MDT. Even with a team on standby, it would take several minutes before the BPI and the DOJ were en route. What would happen when the DOJ arrived? Would one of the agents retrieve the files? She didn't know, and at the moment, didn't care. Macy climbed into the truck, stretched over the console, and using the barrel of her gun, pushed her file to the side and saw her picture.

It wasn't the one from her state-issued ID card. No, it was a copy of the one the disciplinary committee looked at while they read through Internal Affairs report on her conduct regarding Officer Murphy's death. He had IA's report? Using the barrel, she slid the picture to the side, and saw she wasn't alone. Every detective from the Southern California BPI unit sat staring up at her from the floor. A face holding a permanent scowl and narrowed blue eyes framed by lines fanning out from their corners stared at her. Sergeant Emmitt Mayco. Equal parts of fear and anger came to life. She imagined Sergeant Mayco telling Captain Dixon she shouldn't be there, she was responsible for Officer Murphy's death, and he didn't want to work with her because 'she didn't have it anymore'. IA cleared her of any wrongdoing with the case and Sergeant Mayco couldn't change the outcome.

"I'm paranoid," Macy whispered. Nope. Paranoid and scared. The evidence someone was investigating her and the BPI sat in front of her. She did what Commander Arden asked, because if she didn't, he had her separation papers, and she wouldn't have a job.

The sad truth was the DRPD didn't trust her, and her fellow BPI detectives were divided. The DOJ didn't have a reason to have interest in her. Now an agent had her file, her picture, and there was a team of agents with Captain Dixon headed her way. She needed to talk to Commander Arden and find out if he knew anything about the investigation, and if he did, why hadn't he warned her? Macy saw Mrs. Barrette running at her and wondered if it had anything to do with failing to take the shot and failing to protect her team. Negative. Maybe the DOJ was there because of the hard to kill lycans.

Static buzzed in her ear when the radio teased communication, at the same time her heart pounded and she took several deep breaths, trying to calm her nerves. The hot summer breeze blew through the open door to escape out the broken passenger window. The heated air stirred the scents drifting inside the cab, bringing a man's rich cologne fused with the smell of the woods to her nose. The familiar scent brought back memories of Feather River, and while her mind strayed, she watched the charm. In every turn the wolf howled at the sky.

"Charlie-Eight, standby," the female voice ordered.

Her call sign mixed in static jerked Macy to the present and she told herself to get out of the truck. *Get out of the truck.* She didn't. The charm turned, heat surrounded her, and sweat beaded on her forehead.

"Charlie-Eight, code red. I repeat, code red," the dispatcher ordered, and her voice cut off.

*A hostile detective.* Code red meant a BPI detective or other law enforcement personnel had gone rogue and was threatening the lives of law enforcement or civilians. She was supposed to be ready to fire on a BPI detective.

"Affirmative," Macy replied. Who the hell was the code about? She looked at Sergeant Mayco through the passenger window. Negative. If it was him, dispatch would have told her. If it was her, dispatch would have told him. And he would waste no time implementing code red. It didn't make sense.

"Charlie-Eight, be advised a team from the BPI and DOJ are en route."

"Affirmative. ETA?" Macy asked. *Let it be quick.*

"Thirty minutes."

*Shit.* "Code red, clarify," Macy demanded.

Silence. She should get out of the truck, go to the SUV, and wait for backup. One second, two, and time ticked.

"Charlie-Eight, stand by," a male voice ordered.

It wasn't the same dispatcher. Why did that small detail shake her confidence? And why did she think the situation just got worse? Macy looked at the files. Over the months, her confidence had taken hits one after another, then keeping the appearance she was in control had exhausted her. She was heading full speed into a wall.

"Charlie-Eight, Kayne Sinclair is a lycanthrope and team leader of the Department of Justice's Blood Rain force. Code red is directed at Agent Sinclair. I repeat, he is a lycanthrope and part of the Blood Rain force. You've been ordered to stay with your vehicle, do not engage. Do not search for the agent, the Blood Rain force is en route. I repeat, do not engage," the male voice ordered.

*Team leader?* "Affirmative," Macy answered, an edge of frustration threading in her words.

"If confronted, use restrained force. Repeat, if confronted, use restrained force. No hard ammo."

She would use any force she deemed necessary. Blood Rain, a paranormal team made up of shapeshifters and the Otherkin, had a reputation for doing the jobs humans weren't capable of surviving. If they were called to a scene, things had truly turned to shit. She had only heard rumors of their tactics and the messes they responded to and the outcomes. With enhanced senses, strength, the ability to heal, and no fear of the contagion twisting their bodies, the mobile unit was the perfect team. The perfect weapon. Her fear and worry over Agent Sinclair felt betrayed. Not only should Agent Sinclair be able to take care of himself as a trained agent, but he's a damned lycan. A shapeshifter and the real enemy. What would demand the presence of both the DOJ and the Blood Rain task force?

Blind, stupid, and otherwise concerned about her future the truth had escaped her. They were there for the same reason Commander Arden told Captain Dixon to keep her on duty despite objections. Hard to kill shapeshifters. The spy. She looked at the files. Spy. They were there to investigate the BPI. She needed to talk to Commander Arden.

Whoever set the trap at Harper's warehouse had lycans waiting for the BPI and DRPD to arrive. Officer Murphy's death created fear and brought to life the rumor there was a spy among the officers and the detectives of the BPI. Who better to investigate humans than a shapeshifter, like Agent Sinclair and the Blood Rain team? They sensed lies, and no doubt there would be an Otherkin or two, like empaths, thrown into the mix to help them. A chill raced down her spine and over her skin despite the one-hundred-and-ten-degree heat. She wanted to hit something, like Agent Sinclair, his truck, and maybe Sergeant Mayco.

*Mayco.* Her glare targeted him.

Trust was hard to come by and made harder with the threat of a detective turned traitor. The unanswered question was whether the DOJ contacted the BPI or Captain Dixon contacted the DOJ? Macy would never understand the need for an outside agency; you didn't take your problems out of house. You protected your own and kept them in house. Showing a weakness wasn't an option. But Captain Dixon wasn't the commanding officer you wanted if you thought you were in trouble. He craved attention and loved authority, and didn't stand behind his team and wouldn't risk his career. With an outside agency, he could pass the blame to them if anything went wrong. *If* that was the case and she wasn't losing her mind. So why was the agent alone?

*Because he's a lycan and doesn't fear confronting another lycan.* Macy got out of the truck, leaving the files where they were, and standing in front of the broken headlight, like a dangling eye, looked at Sergeant Mayco. He hadn't given her information and hadn't been honest with her all day, and she feared what else he didn't tell her. With every vehicle she searched, she had put her life on the line, and he sat in the SUV and watched. The report from dispatch aired to both their radios and he heard the issue of code red, Agent Sinclair, and the arrival of the Blood Rain team. Sergeant Mayco stared back at her, his reactions and emotions covered by his sunglasses.

"You knew," Macy accused, as she approached him. "You knew we were looking for a lycan and he's the damn team leader of Blood Rain."

"And?" Sergeant Mayco replied absently as if gaffing her off.

Macy looked in the direction of the highway and tried to control her anger, then met his glare. "The DOJ believe the agent is injured or worse, or they wouldn't have ordered a damn code red." She kept her voice as neutral as possible, desperately wanting to keep her worry restrained and her frustration further away. This was not the time to lose control. Not after failing. If she could talk to Commander Arden and find out what the hell was going on, she would feel better. While her thoughts chased one another, she started a mental countdown of time. Twenty-five minutes.

"We'll keep surveillance on the warehouse while we wait for his team. Once they arrive, both agencies will search the warehouse for him. Now you know why I don't want you here, Detective. I have to go into the warehouse with *you*, the person who refused to take the shot after a direct order, and I have to depend on you. We'll be surrounded by shapeshifters, but that doesn't bother you, does it? You'll feel right at home with them." Through his body armor his shoulders tensed as sweat beaded on his forehead and he gripped the butt of his gun.

While she was investigating the truck, he had put on his tactical gear.

For a split second, Macy envisioned him using the code red to gun her down for being the traitor, for not taking the shot, and telling her as she bled out that he was judge, jury, and executioner. She deserved her punishment. No one would question him if he accused her of being the spy. His rants about not wanting to work with her made sense. So obvious now.

"What the hell are you talking about?" Macy asked with her back straight and her hand resting on her gun. She would take his verbal insults about the Barrettes and Harper's warehouse, she deserved them, but that's where it ended.

Laughing, he shook his head at her question. "Shapeshifters. One of those monsters destroyed Officer Murphy's armor and tore into his body. He was a human and fellow brother, who was lying in a pool of his cooling blood, when a lycan took you to Sanative for medical. You could have said no. You could have refused medical and requested transport from Rapid Response." He squared his shoulders as if his body was trying to contain his anger.

"Take a good, hard look. I'm still sporting the bruises from the attack. Per protocol, Doctor Locke followed procedure when the life of a law enforcement officer is at risk, and it was," Macy said in defense. *My life.*

"I saw Doctor Locke at the Barrettes' house and I watched him watch you. If that wasn't bad enough, he talked to you and not one of the others. He found you. Why would he do that?" Sergeant Mayco stepped back, looked around, and back at her. "You're supposed to keep your distance, but you don't, you talk *to them* as if they're equals."

*Looking for your backup.* The idea of an ambush hit to close to home and almost had her checking her surroundings. "Let me remind you, he's in charge of Sanative, and when there's a paranormal body, he's the coroner. He asked when he would be granted entrance to the scene, and I told him he would have to wait for the county coroner to release the scene and the body. He had to wait because Mrs. Barrette didn't have a chance to shapeshift and was registered as a humanoid. Doctor Locke assumed shots were fired, not tranqs, and assumed I did it because I'm the sharpshooter. I didn't do anything."

*She had a Death Bloom,* Macy thought, laughing at the absurdity, and the sound hurt her ears. "He blames me for killing Mrs. Barrette, and you're pissed off I didn't. Sergeant Mayco, our work, my job, means I have to see him. It means you have to see him." She couldn't believe, she was defending herself. Her truth didn't matter when Dr. Locke would always be there. Shapeshifters would always be there to invade her life. "Next time I'll let you explain the scene."

Macy told herself she felt Officer Murphy, David's loss, and understood it wasn't as much as she should. Between Harper's warehouse and the Barrette fiasco, Macy's focus had been on Internal Affairs, saving her career, and freaking Commander Arden and his damn orders. Maybe one day the truth would come out, but today was not that day. Macy's mind didn't race over everything she had said over the past week and her actions at the house, it analyzed every single move and word. She hadn't let anything slip, not once. She acted as natural as she could under the circumstances. Like dealing with Sergeant Bailey of the Desert Rock Police Department when they were at the Barrettes' house. He had questioned her about David, and when she looked to Sergeant Mayco for backup, he deserted her. *Your weakness is an embarrassment to the bureau.* He kept it all business knowing people would judge him.

"Do you think, after everything, I could see them as anything but the monsters they are? I fight them, too. I kill them. It's my job." Macy wanted the conversation to end.

"I don't know what you think. Right now, I don't give a shit. The only thing we're going to do is get through the day." He turned away from her, one step, and rounded on her, his fury controlling him. "Can you do your job? If we face Hunter Wolf forms, I don't want it to tear me to pieces."

"We were ambushed. Fuck, I get it, I should have taken the shot. I didn't. She was the walking dead." Macy's heart rose to her throat, and she knew her voice was getting higher. She was wading into waters with Sergeant Mayco she didn't want to be in ... ever. The sight of the files, the DOJ, Blood Rain, and his anger came full circle. "You think I'm siding with shifters. You think I'm the spy," Macy started. "Is Agent Sinclair here looking for altered Hunter Wolf forms or the spy?" She hated the conversation they were having. She hated baiting him. But if he knew about the DOJ, he knew about the files, and to save her ass, because no one else was going to, she would do whatever it took. And she was going to report everything he said, and his lack of backup, to Commander Arden.

"Altered Hunter Wolf forms. Quite a revelation, and it's funny how you thought of that. These cases have everyone questioning themselves, and to be clear, no one said you were the spy, you are part of the team. Detective Gray, the way you work gets attention." Sergeant Mayco rechecked the area, his eyes skating as his thoughts consumed him.

Macy noted how he avoided mentioning the files, referred to her as Detective Gray, but accused her of naming the hard to kill lycans. *Nice.* "You practically said I was when you didn't give me critical intel. I walked up to an unknown vehicle, associated with a lycan, who happens to be a DOJ Blood Rain agent, without knowing what the hell was going on. He could have been hiding, wounded, or insane. They ordered a *code red.*" Macy repeated the code, like he didn't understand the severity of the situation. He understood because he didn't leave the SUV. Damn, she needed to get her tactical gear.

"Maybe it was a test," Sergeant Mayco countered through clenched teeth. His professional façade crashed and burned when his voice lowered enough it carried the sharp edge of his anger for her to feel.

"Test?" He wavered between thinking she was the enemy and thinking she was part of his team. Macy wondered which side would win.

"I always thought you were different. You're too young to be as jaded as you are. Then there's the fact, out of all the veteran detectives in the BPI, you're a junior team leader and sharpshooter for a response team. You handle situations as if you're a seasoned killer and not a thirty-something woman who's been on the bureau for what, a couple of years? And that's after serving with the Emergency Retraction Team. I tried to ignore it, but Harper's warehouse was proof you're different. Officer Murphy was dying, yet you kept your mark. You didn't lose control, and you didn't let his death stop you from killing the damn thing. That doesn't cover what I saw at Harmony Grove."

"What are you scared of? I can do my job, or I can't do my job?" Macy challenged. "You want me to kill them or not?"

"Harmony Grove," Sergeant Mayco seethed through clenched teeth.

"Everyone knew she was going to die, she had a Death Bloom," Macy repeated her defense. It was in the report.

The weak beat of Mrs. Barrette's heart sounding in her ears had nothing to do with it, and suddenly her anger fell flat and tasted wasted. By making her search the truck alone, he had taken a chance with her life. The only emotions she felt were betrayal and hurt. Macy looked at him and wanted to make excuses for her detachment. Jaded. Team leader. Sharpshooter. Dead parents. Raised by her grandparents who had passed away after she graduated high school. They weren't bad people and had done their best to raise her, but they weren't caring people. There was no love between them, and it taught her to rely on herself and gave her the detachment she needed to leave Feather River and start a new life. Which she did, and achieved her goals, only to see them going up in flames.

Why was she thinking about her family when she left them in the past? It was being one wrong move from fired. She was dealing with it alone. And damn Feather River. Macy cut the thoughts loose and focused on the present. She was good at her job, because the BPI had become her family, and she needed to protect them. If he didn't get it, she would be damned if she was going to explain it to him.

"I didn't see it until she was upon us. I don't think you saw it." He did his breathing thing, inhaling and exhaling in exaggerated huffs. "Every time Commander Arden demands your presence at a scene, it makes the rest of us wonder why. We have listened to the talk. This morning, I told Captain Dixon I didn't want you with me. I said you weren't ready, trying to be kind. I should have told him you were a liability." He kicked at a rock, and she heard it skipping along the broken blacktop. "Do you know what he said? Do you?"

*I saw it,* she tried convincing herself. Did she see it? Macy wanted to hang her head with her doubt, and tell him she didn't care and didn't want to talk about this anymore. She knew why she was there. She could tell Sergeant Mayco the truth, that she wasn't against him, that she was working for Commander Arden. No way confessing was an option, not with a lycan's truck sitting behind her.

"He said Commander Arden needed you on this case. You know shifters. Like insisting a Hunter Wolf form attacked the agent."

"What else could have done the damage? The truck is a wreck."

His stare shifted to the wreak and back to her. "A lycan in humanoid form, a therian in humanoid form can do the same damage. That shit tells me you know shifters, like you have a connection with them. It makes you too damn good for my liking. It makes you look like a shifter. Screw it, though, you know it's not about what I think. It's about results, and I can't deny you get results." Sergeant Mayco let out a sarcastic laugh tangled with his exasperated breath.

*I'm not a shifter.* "I passed all the requirements for reinstatement." It was a halfhearted defense.

The Hunter Wolf form never scratched her, and while David's infected blood covered her uniform, it didn't touch her. At Sanative they gave her the antiserum; the yellow bruises on the back of her knees, along her spine, and in the bend of her elbows from needles served as proof of the treatments. Sergeant Mayco knew better than anyone. It didn't change his need to argue with her, blame her, and let his anger have its way with her. She was the connection to David. Had been there when he was killed. It left her with little defense and even less fight to fuel her argument. There was nothing she could do when she felt like she deserved the punishment.

"So I'm told," he mumbled with indifference. His hand rested on the butt of his gun, and he squared his shoulders, his tactical gear moving with him.

"I know you want someone to blame, and I know I'm an easy target. I made a mistake." Macy studied his face, his stance, and pushed forward. "Let me ask you, do you think you'll be around after today, *Sergeant Mayco*? Inside the agent's truck are all of our files, even yours. I'm not the first one on the spy list. It's a spot we share. And while you're blaming me, and everyone wants to know why I kill things and am good at my job, there is a team of shapeshifters here to test us. By the way, I don't have a connection with them. I have studied them."

*Knowledge is power, dumb ass.*

"Here's why Blood Rain is here ... they sense your lies by the sound of your heartbeat. Your human heartbeat. It gives you away. And it's admissible in court when testified by a government agent, which as of right now, the lycan is." She took three steps toward Sergeant Mayco. "If he catches you in a lie, where do you think you will be? Will your friends talk about you next? I have a job, and it's learning how to deal with them. Shapeshifters. The Requiem was the wakeup call. You can hate it, but you still have to deal with it, and you're behind." Macy took a deep breath, her hands on her hips, and her shoulders straight. Damn him, she wasn't giving in. "Denial will be your death sentence."

They stood across from each other in silence while the heated July breeze carried gnarled branches and dried leaves across the crumbling parking lot to an open field. The gusts weren't enough to dry the sweat on her neck and face, they added to her discomfort. Minutes and silence sat between them, and they were still glaring each other to death when two dark blue four door SUVs bearing the BPI's emblem approached. Following close behind were two white SUVs with the DOJ's emblem on its doors. Macy took an easy, controlled breath and watched as all four vehicles drove by them, their SUV, and parked. It had been about fifteen minutes. As she watched, she questioned if they had been following them using the GPS locations. *Doesn't matter.* Quicker was better, and after they found the agent, the day would be over.

Macy gave Sergeant Mayco her back; his verbal assault was over when witnesses arrived. *Let's see who showed.* The first person out of the DOJ's vehicle was a tall, thin man with short, black hair, sunglasses, and wearing a white T-shirt, blue BDU trousers, boots, and a badge clipped to his belt. Behind him was a woman. Her short, fire-red hair shimmered in the sunlight, and she was dressed the same way as the man, her badge clipped at her waist. *The people in charge.*

They cast shielded looks through sunglasses, and ignoring them, walked to Agent Sinclair's truck.

"This isn't over, Gray," Sergeant Mayco threatened.

"Never thought it was," Macy mumbled to herself.

Deep down she knew she should have fought a harder fight. She wasn't the person he described. Scarred. Jaded. Human criminals left destruction and tragedy in their wake and abused the court system. Paranormal criminals took it to a new level, leaving human law enforcement trying to fig- ure out how to handle them. She had a job to protect the innocent, and she took it seriously, and wasn't going to stop because of him. Macy watched Sergeant Mayco walk toward the BPI's SUV, every worry about being Commander Arden's spy consuming her. She didn't want anyone knowing she was spying on her own damn team and several officers, in- cluding David. There was a spy, the shapeshifters were changing, and she put herself in the middle of it all. *Good job.*

The price for living with shapeshifters was taking its toll. It was taking lives.

---

# CHAPTER FIVE

"Better off dead," Kayne whispered. His wolf howled in his ears as every detail of the monstrosity lying before him burned into his memory. What he saw, he didn't want to believe. Grace's description of her husband's condition was subtle. *Stuck* didn't begin to describe what was happening. How he was alive, Kayne didn't know.

Being the strongest in the pack, the alpha shouldered the responsibility to provide strength, control, and balance to a potentially violent situation. A mortal's spirit naturally fought against becoming one with the wolf spirit. Once they were intertwined, and the balance between the two matured, it gave the body its ability to shift and made controlling the wolf and shifting between the two easier, almost natural. The first time they came together, the mortal's morals and ideals battled for dominance against the wolf's strength and primal instinct. The victims who lost their mortal half and gave into the wolf's domination eventually lost the wolf spirit and were scarred with a Death Bloom as they died.

Kayne considered shapeshifting a spiritual transition and called the pair—his mortal spirit and wolf spirit—his *Soma*. His mortal body separate from his wolf spirit, rather than his body separate from his mind. For him it explained the nature of the beast. Henry was not in his humanoid form or wolf form. His body was suspended in the enervate and his spirits battling to meet in the drift. His body was a mangled distortion as if the worst and most painful had come from both and erupted from within him. Kayne sucked in a breath as pale eyes, a sign of weakness, opened to slits and gazed from sunken sockets. Henry lay on his left side, his human arm extended, his sinuous muscles cradling his misshapen head while in front of a wolf's rib cage his right arm and right front leg twitched. Translucent skin stretched tight over his arching spine, defining his vertebrae, and like netting, black veins covered straining, jerking muscles. From his head, chest, arms, and legs, tufts of brown hair were damp from sweat. He looked at Henry's feet and found they were paws while his thighs remained in humanoid form. Grace escaped the container and had broken her ankle to chance help.

Negative. She left the container wishing a Hunter Wolf found her and ended her misery.

In the moments he stared at Henry, he could imagine the creamy liquid in the vials as a sweet, tangy, metallic smell hovered in the air. The sourness of it coated his mouth like a thick syrup from a poisoned well. Kayne stepped back from Henry, the half-human, half-wolf atrocity, and wanted to know who gave him White Cell? And why hadn't it killed the contagion?

"Grace," Henry groaned, his thick lips snagging on his sharp, canine teeth.

"She's all right," Kayne assured. "She's waiting for you."

"Liar," Henry growled. Clumps of glutinous drool dropped to his chest and clung to a thatch of short wolf hair. When the shift rolled through him, he choked on his saliva, his humanoid mouth began elongating, his lips stretching, and his neck thickened, then it stopped.

"What's happening?" Grace's small voice asked. Her fear soaked each word, her splintered teeth making them sound sad and broken.

The warehouse won. Created to destroy its victims, it chewed them up and spit their broken bodies out. Henry whimpered while fresh blood seeped from his knees and knuckles, and he twisted his head toward Kayne. Struggling to get off the floor, his skin grew tighter around his joints, turning them violet, and the muscles of his arms quivered. He might have fought his captors, his wolf, and after they left, himself, but the moment they left him to fight his wife, things in his mind began breaking down. No one came back from that. Letting go of your sanity and giving your pain to someone else broke a thread inside, and you didn't come back, not entirely. Kayne's skin chilled from the thought. If this had been a different situation, he would have killed Henry. A mercy killing. No one deserved the agony and torture he was going through. But Kayne was selfish and needed evidence.

"Grace is safe. I'm not the one who put you in here. I can help you, but you're going to have to trust me." Kayne's voice echoed in the container as he pulled his force from the wolf within. As it increased his strength, it surrounded them, and the power of his wolf began feeding him the information he needed to help Henry.

The wolf inside the man felt distant, buried, the same way it felt when he tried to sense Grace's wolf. They were missing their spirit. Neither were complete, and Kayne feared they wouldn't make a full recovery, emotionally or physically even if they safely shapeshifted. It was bad enough the couple had been infected by an ersatz, left alone in a warehouse, then were subject to an empath's wrath. It wasn't right. It was torture. At least Henry hadn't killed his wife. He beat her up, yes, but he didn't kill her. It meant he restrained himself, and Kayne hoped it was enough to keep the man alive. All Henry needed to do was hang onto the strength and control for a little longer.

"Help." Henry strained to push the word from his mutating muzzle and gagged when he tried repeating himself.

Kayne's ears ached with the choking sound coming from Henry's throat and he wanted to tell him to stop talking. Henry's eyes left Kayne's, his head teetering on uneven shoulders as he turned to look toward the open door. Drifting up to him were his wife's soft sobs, and soon tears slipped down his pale cheeks. The varied whimpers of their weeping traveled in the silence surrounding them, and Kayne let the moment linger. They were both infected, both beaten, and now they needed to hear the pain they shared and the pain they survived for what may be the last time. If they survived, they needed each other. Werewolves were pack animals. However, if they hated being werewolves all Kayne was doing was guaranteeing them a life of self-loathing and riddled with regret. Over the two hundred plus years he had been alive, he had witnessed the destruction those feelings caused.

"Henry," he began, "I am Kayne Sinclair, Alpha of the Garrick pack. As they run through the Moonlight Territory, their power flows through me." Just saying the traditional words of the alpha ignited the strongest power, the heat of it sweeping through the dark spaces deep within him while the forest came alive inside of the sweltering container, bringing his territory to him. The rush of water, the rich scent of soil, and the calming taste of pine ate at the air, replacing the dead with life. He opened his eyes, felt the change in them, and pictured them blazing amber with his wolf while held in a humanoid face. Henry whimpered as Kayne turned his attention to him, and when he met the pale yellow gaze of the half-man, half-wolf he saw new terror.

Henry's nails scratched the steel floor, his thigh muscles struggling to control his jerky movements in his attempt to get away from Kayne. "You kill," he breathed. "Your own. Us."

Henry's words cut straight through Kayne. "What?"

"You kill," Henry growled, arching up on his humanoid hand. "Assassin."

"Who said this?" Kayne demanded with a growl in his words. "Who?"

Henry's sagging lips lifted, exposing short, undeveloped canine teeth while slack skin wrinkled. "Elijah."

Grace lied to him. Why?

*Because I'm the enemy.* "You're bait," Kayne mumbled, his lips barely moving around the words. Why would Elijah use a stranger? Unless the bait wasn't for him.

The ersatz.

He left toys for his creations. Why wasn't Elijah monitoring the warehouse? Because he found what he was looking for. Who? Kayne didn't know. With his frustration driving him, he focused his hate, anger, and impatience on Henry.

"Are you going to kill us?" Henry asked, his words barely audible.

"I should," Kayne answered coldly. He didn't need to save products of Elijah's madness. "It would be a mercy kill."

Henry mumbled, his sloppy words sounding wet as they made spit spray from between his misshaped muzzle, and yellow liquid mixed with blood stained his chest and arms. "Do it."

"You can believe the madman who left you here or I can help you," Kayne offered with indifference.

Henry cried Grace's name, lowered himself to the floor in defeat, and begged, "Help."

If he stayed true to the canons of the Council, he would kill the abominations Henry and Grace were, walk away from the fucking warehouse, and go to his truck to call for help. He wanted Elijah, and to get him, Kayne needed Henry.

The man whimpered as tremors gripped his body and nails shaped like a wolf's broke through the skin of his right hand. Henry knew Elijah, and if he lived, would be a witness for the DOJ and the Council. Without a word, Kayne slowly reached out and flattened his hand on Henry's ribcage. Bones, sharp and close to the surface, nudged his palm with each harsh inhale.

Henry tried scooting backward, the stretching and crawling tore his skin and fresh blood seeped from open wounds. Kayne needed to be quick, he didn't want a Death Bloom, and didn't want Henry damaging his body any more than he had. Closing his eyes, he brought his wolf to the surface, and letting it wash over him, his strength increased, and the familiar hum of power traveled over his skin. With his force saturating the container, Henry sank lower into the wet straw, giving life to a wave of rotting fumes. Ignoring it, Kayne reached out to the man. It should have been easy to feel the wolf spirit struggling to make the shift. The ersatz didn't change back to their humanoid form and he assumed the wolf spirit and the mortal hadn't fully merged in the drift. They were lost. The ersatz were soulless beasts controlled by hate and rage and fed off fear. The information was going to help them stop them, Elijah, and Kayne would finally have his revenge.

With that thought, he looked down on Henry and knew the threat of turning into an ersatz loomed over him. "I feel your wolf," Kayne whispered.

Henry looked up into his wolf eyes, like he needed an anchor, opened his mouth, and his lips curved around a silent plea. Power rushed between them, and the next time Henry opened his mouth, he screamed. The cry grew louder and became a howl of pain that died when his mouth extended into a muzzle. Throughout his body, bones reformed under stretching skin and thickening fur as his wolf emerged. With the shift in motion, Henry was lost to the outside world, his spirits combining for the first time in the enervate and the drift of the werewolf world.

Kayne backed up, giving Henry room, at the same time maintaining his power and control over the wolf spirit. When time continued and the shift stalled, Kayne feared it was too late to save him from a Death Bloom, and Henry was lost. A rumble of a guttural moan was stifled by the final surge in the transformation, and Henry lay in the muck in wolf form, breathing and alive. Kayne cut his power, the sharpness causing him to waver, and with his energy burned from him, his wounds erupted with pain.

"One down, one to go," Kayne mumbled. He knelt, making sure his knee didn't sink into the wet straw, and waited for the worst of the queasiness to end.

While he waited, he watched Henry to see if he would wake up, but the wolf remained motionless, its rib cage rising and falling with its easy breaths. To ensure Kayne knew what was happening to Henry, he used his wolf's essence to establish a mental link. With it embedded inside of Henry's mind, Kayne listened to his heartbeat and felt his calm as he slept. There was more to do, and before he collapsed from exhaustion, he needed to tell Grace Henry had shifted. He stood, stretched his throbbing muscles, walked to the edge of the container, jumped, and landed softly on the concrete.

His weak legs lasted a second before giving out and he was on his hands and knees, the weakness quickly reminding him of his wounds and the silver poisoning. *Later.* He would deal with it later. Fighting through the pain, he looked up, expecting to see Grace waiting for him, not the empty room. She disappeared.

*Damn it all to bloody hell.* Kayne stood, fear snaking through him, and repeated his feeble search of the room. Area. He yelled for her, listened, and yelled again to receive no answer. Risking using his senses to find her, he searched the warehouse and found nothing. He couldn't get past the empath, if he was right about that, and didn't have the energy to waste. He needed to go look for her. How far could she have gone on a broken ankle? He had no clue. She survived her husband. Anything was possible.

Kayne retraced his steps, heading back to where Grace had found him, hoping she had started toward the front of the warehouse without him. He did tell her his cell was in his truck. She lied to him about knowing Elijah and now she knew there was an escape. His cell. If she thought she was leaving in his truck, she was mistaken. It wasn't going anywhere. Down an aisle he saw her dirty fingerprints smeared on metal as she used the container as a crutch. Seeing her progress sent an electric current through him. Why? Because he would find her, get to his truck, and get help before whoever was in charge of the warehouse came back. Keeping his mind open to Henry and his senses focused to feel others, like the ersatz and Grace, he maneuvered through the aisles. He believed he was making progress and hope's bright star grabbed him when the soft hum of intruders inched over his skin. Hope crashed. He had run out of time.

**It came** as no surprise when Captain Dixon jumped at the chance to work with the DOJ, gave them every resource available, including detectives, to help them find their agent. Maybe he was working with them. Sergeant Mayco should question him.

With no intel on the warehouse and unsure of the conditions inside, Blood Rain decided it was their job to protect the human BPI detectives. Macy had winced when she heard a shifter/human partnership gave them a better chance of winning a fight than a human/human combination. No amount of warning could have prepared her for the reality of the BPI and DOJ's Blood Rain team working together. Sergeant Mayco's accusation that she sided with shifters made her furious, and knowing she was going to have to work with him, depend on him for backup, created a new kind of rage. Like the BPI detectives, whose sole job was to investigate, arrest, and dispatch paranormals were expected to put their lives in the hands of shifters. *Rage.* With Captain Dixon's glare on everyone, the threat of a spy among them, no one objected to the decision, and without objections, Commander Wilson ended the briefing.

When the captain and commander stood beside one another, Macy watched the two interact and knew Commander Wilson was human. His talk about working together was a little less impressive when the DOJ didn't trust shapeshifters enough to put one in charge. She nearly laughed, then the humor died when he announced who would partner up, and Macy was introduced to Agent Logue, Blood Rain team member. His bulk stood beside her, taking short inhales, holding them for a second, and letting them out. She did her best to ignore him by concentrating on the door, what they might find inside, and Agent Sinclair's physical condition.

Finding his wrecked truck and his cell sitting in the console told her he wasn't able to get out, was either injured, locked up, or dead. Not great options.

Inhale. Exhale. Agent Logue continued his breathing exercise, and she continued to ignore him.

Side by side, they waited in front of the door while the lineup included Detective Ramirez and Agent Kriss, Detective Cutler, Agent Flynn, and bringing up the rear was Sergeant Mayco and Agent Pixley. Inhale. Exhale. It was grating on her nerves. Macy wanted to yell at him to stop but knew shapeshifters didn't depend entirely on their sense of smell. They combined smelling the air with tasting the scents it held. The two together surpassed a human's ability, making them incredible trackers, and if a shapeshifter smelled you, it had your scent in their head. If they wanted to find you, they could. There were drawbacks, nothing was perfect, like wind, animals, or a smell overpowering their olfactory organs. It appeared as Agent Logue inhaled and exhaled, he was having a hard time discerning what he was smelling/tasting. It made everything worse. She didn't want to know what he tasted, what he didn't taste, what he smelled, what he didn't smell. And she didn't want him as a partner. She didn't trust the shapeshifters and knew she wasn't alone. Tension reached, wove, and touched everyone, proving no one trusted the other.

"There are people inside," Agent Pixley started from behind them. "Lycans. I'm not sure of the number. There's interference coming from somewhere."

"What kind?" Commander Wilson asked as he looked at the agent.

"Empaths," Agent Pixley responded coldly. She hated fighting other empaths. Without her talent giving her information she couldn't sense Agent Sinclair, his condition, and was letting her team, and the BPI walk into the warehouse blind. "They're blocking me. I don't know what they're doing to those inside."

The BPI didn't depend on empaths, going in without proper intel was standard business. Macy shifted, easing the weight from her right side, the small step causing Agent Logue's sleeve to brush hers, and she barely stopped herself from cringing. She might be standing beside a shapeshifter, but Sergeant Mayco was standing beside an empath. *Serves him right,* she thought bitterly. Empaths, their name taken from the word empathy, were part of the group known as Otherkin. Their talents allowed them to absorb emotions like sorrow, anger, and happiness as if they were a physical energy, then use the force as they chose. Macy knew Dr. Locke used empaths to monitor fluctuating emotions at Sanative and at scenes involving paranormals. If a shifter turned violent, the empath simply absorbed the anger and projected a calmer environment. Sometimes it worked. Sometimes syn silver worked better.

As they waited for the order to enter the warehouse, Macy could swear she heard the seconds ticking and turning into minutes they fed her anxiety. The faded and weather-beaten paint telling her it was Pennsky blended into the sand beaten, white faux wood siding as it rippled along its seam while the breeze tossed the peeling strips of paint like ribbons. The Building Division should have closed and boarded the warehouse's doors until it passed inspection from the surveyors. There were no 'keep out' signs, no evidence of an alarm system, nothing to hinder teenagers, the homeless, or scrappers from trespassing. The warehouse sat a quarter mile off the highway and down a crumbling road. If someone broke in there weren't going to be any witnesses. Which explained why a lycan in Hunter Wolf form attacked a truck and an agent and no one saw them.

Despite trying to make mental notes about the warehouse and the chance there might be a connection to David, she felt Agent Logue's energy wrap around him. He was swimming in adrenaline, and she was jealous. The feel of adrenaline pulsing through her veins usually brought a surge of excited energy. She didn't feel it now and hadn't felt it since David's death, resentment and fear taking its place. Macy gave Agent Logue a sideways glance, struggled to study him, the breaths he was taking, and tried to catch a glimpse of his face. She guessed his height was a little over six feet, which meant he was nearly a foot taller than she was, so spying on him was difficult. Trying for natural, she adjusted her tactical helmet, accidently grazed the bruises on the side of her face, cursed, then secretly studied him.

Her eyes moved over his bronzed skin, a result of both his Native American heritage and the sun. She took in the shape of his mouth, jaw, neck, and muscles from time in a gym, each tightening and flexing as he scanned the door in front of them. The ends of his black hair sat at the collar of his dark blue T-shirt, his body armor and vest declaring him DOJ. Despite the layers, his chest rose and fell with easy breaths and didn't give away the animal lurking inside.

Macy couldn't see the front patch identifying him as a Blood Rain member, or his animal. If she kept staring, he was going to notice, and it would make matters worse. Figuring she would find out eventually, she slipped into her routine, and ran a hand over her extra magazines, across the Velcro BPI patch identifying her as a detective, her rank, and sharpshooter for her team, then checked her knife. Agent Logue turned toward the line of agents and detectives and her eyes automatically narrowed on his patch. Against its black material, white stitching carved out the head of a wolf, under it in gold stitching it spelled out DOJ, Blood Rain, Lycan-thrope.

*Lycanthrope. This is too damn soon to be close to a lycan. Too soon to deal with a lycan. Sergeant Mayco was right, I'm going to be a liability.* Macy fought for her next breath as her chest tightened and squeezed the air from her lungs. She didn't want to go into the warehouse knowing she was sur-rounded by them and he was her backup.

"Ready," Agent Logue called. He manipulated his deep voice, so it didn't thunder over them; it flowed over them, getting everyone's attention.

Macy took her gun from its holster. Agent Logue did not. Not good when she was going to have him as backup. *Can't be worse than Sergeant Mayco.* Maybe the lycan agent was planning to beat whoever was behind the door with his bare hands. Perhaps he would strip out of his uniform, shift into his Hunter Wolf form, and rip them apart. Maybe he would shift and turn his uniform into shreds like an overdramatic Hollywood movie. He could do any of those things because that's what he was. Staring at the lycan, she tightened her fingers around the grip of her gun, and as if he sensed her his body tensed through his shoulders. He took another small breath of air, at the same time he looked down on her, his body language proving her mistake.

She's an idiot. She let her emotions get the better of her and she broke the first rule.

Macy let her fear and anger move through her, allowing the lycan to sense her feelings. Struggling to ignore him, she began counting to calm down. With an inhale, she shoved the chaos down, hoping its flames died and she could sal-vage her dignity, then reminded herself Captain Dixon was there, and she was being watched by everyone. If she wanted to prove she could her job and wasn't the liability Sergeant Mayco thought she was, she needed to stay calm and focused. The truth washed over her like cold water and doused the worst of her emotions. Agent Logue didn't move, the weight of his stare making her want to run. Macy forced herself to keep her eyes forward while acting as natural as possible, as if she was waiting like the rest of the team. He finally shifted his gaze and attention from her to the line. She slowly released the breath she had been holding, the tension in her shoulders eased enough it wasn't painful, and she took her normal stance.

"We're going in," Agent Logue ordered.

He reached for the rusted handle, and securing his grip, the team waited and watched in silence despite the tension teasing their patience. Macy mentally readied for whatever was waiting for her on the other side as Agent Logue took a deep breath, his entire body acting as one muscle. His forearm bulged as he pulled the door while his back flexed, causing his body armor and tactical vest to stretch with his body. A sharp squeal sounded, as if metal had been torn free, and Macy watched in surprise as the sandblasted door flew open on silent hinges. *Oh damn.* Her attention focused on the door as it flew from Agent Logue's hands, and automatically took a step backward out of its way. She watched the agent's momentum throw him off balance, and his eyes widened as he stumbled in her direction.

*No. No.* In two semi-controlled steps, he pushed her to the side, making sure they didn't stumble into the waiting agents and detectives, causing everyone to fall like dominoes. When he slammed her into the side of the warehouse, his left boot was beside her left boot, his right hand wrapped around her wrist at the same time he gripped her left wrist and pinned her arms and body against the wall. With a sliver of space separating them, she sucked in a breath and tried to quench the recoil from touching him. Keeping her eyes locked on his chest, his patch, anywhere but his face, she felt his glare on her for the second time. Macy stopped breathing and holding her breath, she realized even as he lost his balance, his muscles flowed like the predator he was. With his body weight, and the strength he used to pull the steel door from its hinges, he could have sent her into the wall, the ground, anywhere he liked. Instead, he shifted them, and while her back was against the wall and he was gripping her wrists, he hadn't hurt her.

"Agent Kriss, Detective Ramirez, take the lead," Commander Wilson ordered. "Move."

No one said anything to them as they followed orders and two at a time entered the warehouse. Macy silently begged the commander to order the agent to let her go and get the hell away from her. As the others continued to pass them, Agent Logue didn't move; he kept her pinned, using enough strength to remind her she couldn't free herself and he was holding her gun hand.

"Are you hurt?" Agent Logue asked through clenched teeth.

Macy released her breath, craned her head, causing her helmet to graze the siding, and met his downcast gaze. This was going to cost her. Agent Logue's body covered hers, completely, and she imagined what was being said about her. As if to confirm her worries, Sergeant Mayco stalked by them, and she heard him cursing. No doubt he was planning on reporting to Captain Dixon it was her fault the door's appearance was deceiving, Agent Logue pinned her to the wall, and then held her there. She took a deep breath—in through her nose, out through her mouth—attempting to swallow her anger. The only thing it did was bring the smell of his clothing into her head where it joined her frustration.

"Negative," Macy answered sternly.

His fingers tightened around her wrists, sending electric currents into her skin, and she feared he was going to make her drop her gun. Not making a sound, Macy didn't move and wasn't going to give into her fear. *Damn lycan.*

Agent Logue took a slow, purposeful breath, pushed his body against hers, and as if reading the hate from her thoughts, squeezed harder. Seconds spread out between them, and in a quick motion, he stepped backward, leaving her where she stood, and entered the warehouse. At once the blood flow returned to her hands, making them tingle at the same time heat swept up her neck and into her cheeks. Macy refused to holster her gun to touch her wrists or look at the red marks he left behind. Lycans and their damn games. One breath, then another. *Don't fail.* She swallowed her anger, and wearing a mask of indifference, entered the warehouse.

The entrance led to a narrow room, resembling a reception area, where chairs, desks, and filing cabinets cluttered the space and looked as if they had been thrown haphazardly. Around them, shredded pieces of paper and plastic drifted from their footsteps while above them the roof rattled from gusts of wind, bringing down sparkling veils of dust and sand. Against the walls, and piled at the bottom of each container, miniature dunes of sand reached up toward the ceiling. It set a desolate mood. And that said nothing of the gagging smell. Macy fought to keep herself from covering her mouth with her hand.

"Everyone, stop," Agent Pixley ordered. Like an attacking army, death rolled throughout the warehouse and sent her instincts reeling.

"What the hell?" Agent Kriss mumbled.

Agent Logue stopped, and searching the room, looked up at the tops of the stacks. "I do not like this."

With guns drawn, the teams stood before a wall of blue, green, and red shipping containers, each sitting end to end, and stacked nearly to the ceiling. Narrow aisles cut through the far ends where shadows darkened the entrances. Macy expected to see something in the warehouse, maybe a twin to Harper's, a couple containers, semi-truck trailers, giving the ersatz places to hide. But she never expected it to be crammed with shipping containers. There was another world hidden behind the wall and it was going to take them hours to search and longer to reach the back of the warehouse. Where the hell was Agent Sinclair?

"Something is dead in here. Like an animal or two," Detective Ramirez said around a cough.

"Not something, someone," Agent Logue countered. He turned to Macy, his eyes narrowing, and moved to Agent Pixley. "Several, if I had to guess. And it has been going on for a long time."

"I agree," Agent Kriss replied. "This is ripe with death."

"Agent Sinclair is here. Somewhere," Agent Pixley reminded them, and tried keeping them on track. She turned in a circle and looked at the surroundings, and like everyone else, was in total disbelief.

"Confirming there are enough people patrolling the outside?" Detective Ramirez asked.

"Affirmative," Agent Pixley answered. "The rest of the team has arrived along with another unit from the BPI. Local law enforcement has been alerted to the situation and will be engaged if the suspect or suspects break the containment area."

Of course they thought there was enough manpower. One shapeshifter was comparable to six humans. Macy watched Agent Pixley, her green eyes narrowing as if she was trying to sense something. Ahead of her, Agent Logue faced the front, where Agent Pixley stood, and lifted his face. He kept his mouth open, and Macy closed her eyes and changed her view. It didn't block him out, but it helped.

"The sooner we find Agent Sinclair, the quicker we can get out of here." Sergeant Mayco's drawn brows gave away his doubt.

He didn't believe what he said and neither did Macy, not when it made the BPI look incompetent. There was going to be a full investigation into the warehouse, those associated with it, and the detectives and officers who were supposed to have run background checks. More than ever, she was convinced David had been involved. What would she find when she checked the records? Wasn't going to be good. *Investigate a dead officer you're suspected of failing to protect ... smooth, Macy.*

Agent Logue faced her, nodded, and with his strength rolling over him strode to the left side of the room. Macy's mind wanted to focus on Sergeant Mayco, David, but she resisted, and slipped into Detective Gray mode and surveyed the group. Detective Ramirez and Agent Kriss went to the right side with Detective Cutler and Agent Flynn following. Captain Dixon and Commander Wilson remained outside to keep contact with the perimeter and watch for incoming threats while Detective Elston and Detective Lebere, along with Agents Brecht and Lyrick, patrolled the perimeter. With the other's locations memorized, her nerves calmed and kept her from thinking about her partner. Which was why she was hanging several feet back before following him into the aisle.

*Too soon*, Macy repeated. Reminding herself she wasn't ready to quit her job, or get fired, she stepped toward the aisle. She wasn't seeing the darkened corridor as much as she was watching the way the agent's body flowed, like the animal he was, all fluid motion and predator. Taking a deep breath, she decided the warehouse was an opportunity to find the Hunter Wolf forms and the people responsible for David's death. The need pushed her. It forced her to believe in the hope they would finally be brought to justice. But first she needed evidence the Hunter Wolf forms were different. Altered. That they were more dangerous than the average shapeshifter. She also wanted to prove there was a spy. All while trying to keep herself from being a suspect. No problem.

Kayne rounded a corner, abruptly twisted back as faint sounds of people drifted on the air and their essences proved the uselessness of his senses. He cursed as he automatically pulled his gun from its holster and waited for someone to show themselves. Time seemed to slow down as silence sat thick, and he checked his remaining rounds. One. If it was another ersatz, he was going to shift and kill the thing. It was all he had. One round wasn't going to slow it down, let alone kill it, and he wasn't going to be death's next victim. Gods knows he didn't want to see or feel the nightmares from his past again.

*A child.* Her molten silver eyes held him, making him stop to shake his head, and closing his senses, he concentrated on the voices. Lost in his past and the chaos of the warehouse, he turned in a circle while frustration took bites from him as the feeling he was nothing more than rat in a maze mocked him. Coming to a stop, he listened, shoved his impatience down, and checked the tops of the surrounding containers. He didn't need to find Grace. Kayne needed to get to his truck, get his cell, and call for help. He was beyond doing it by himself. A team of officers would be better than them all dying by the hands of an ersatz. Looking back and forth, he jumped to the top of the nearest container where he was able to look out over the warehouse.

It occurred to him, with the view, he should have been searching from the top the entire time, not running blind in the maze, and the familiar feeling of frustration burned, bringing a growl to his lips. Black squares and rectangles interrupted the sea of green, red, and blue tops. He wasn't as close to the front as he thought and found himself in the middle of the massive warehouse. Somewhere along the way, he took a wrong turn or two. Being able to see it in its entirety, he finally understood the layout of the place. Intentionally planned from front to back each half was opposite of the other. Beyond the walls of containers, small rooms, aisles, and narrow spaces interconnected each side while in the middle, a wall separated the front from the back. You had to know where you were going or risked missing one of the three aisles to the other side. Like he had.

People were in the warehouse, time was running out for all of them, and soon they would find Grace or Henry. Guilt and exhaustion rode his regrets of should have, could have, and would have. He stopped, his boots scraping the metal, and tried to shut down the racing chaos brewing in his head when voices echoed. Facing the direction of the noises, he looked at the back of the warehouse, feared Grace was trying to find him, and he was failing her. No. He needed to get to his truck. While he wrestled with the decision to go to his truck or find Grace, anger burned inside of him. A growl started in his chest and a low rumble crossed his lips as he turned in a circle, went to one knee, and stared at the front of the warehouse. Grace was hiding and she knew they were there.

# CHAPTER SIX

Kayne pushed doubt to the side and headed to the back in search for a way out. Then he wouldn't have to confront the invaders while armed with one round. Reminding him time was running out, beads of sweat slipped down the sides of his forehead to his cheek and he felt slick skin sticking to his leather holster. He wiped most of the sweat from his face with the bend of his left arm, but refused to touch his face with his shirt; it left a salty, drying film behind. With the increasing heat, it took seconds for it to get sticky with sweat. Another gap and he slowed to a jog, a walk, and stopped altogether. He inhaled, smelling more than the rotten stink he had smelled for hours. There was blood, Henry and Grace's dying humanity, and another. With one breath, he caught more than one scent.

"Mortals. Shapeshifters," Kayne mumbled. Their crux, the essence of what they were, slid over his senses and a hum itched at the base of his neck.

He leapt from the container, landed on the concrete with the weight of the warehouse bearing down on him and wanted to give up. The warehouse was beating him down the same way it had Grace. Henry. The ersatz. As if admitting he was losing, Kayne gave into the despair, stumbled, and walking aimlessly, made a right, left, backed up, and tripped over his boots. He fell against a wall, sank to the floor, his head resting on the wall behind him, his arms hanging at his sides, and let out a weak howl. He took a deep breath and laughed, the insane rumble echoing. His hands felt the wall and he laughed again. The wall wasn't corrugated, it wasn't metal, and it wasn't a container. Its cool paint sank into his hot skin, feeling like an anchor in the sea of heat. He leaned forward, took his shredded T-shirt off, and wiped sweat and grime from his face. Then, rubbing his eyes, he checked again making sure he wasn't delusional. Glass, stainless steel, and plastic gleamed in the sunlight. It was real. Kayne couldn't believe what he found.

"Out in three, two, one," Agent Logue reported. "There's a body in here," he said over his shoulder.

Macy assumed it wasn't Agent Sinclair when the agent didn't charge in to get him. She cautiously continued while her fear started getting the best of her, then she saw the Hunter Wolf form on its back, one arm stretched out, part of its head missing, and beside it, thick clumps of flesh and bone littered the floor. The syn silver was continuing to eat its way through the body, letting Macy see the expanding wound and the sludge its organs had turned into. Around the glittering mess was more blood, torn material, and debris. She stopped a safe distance from the body and the pool of gleaming black blood.

"Agent Sinclair did this?" Detective Cutler asked as he looked at the crashed containers. "He killed a Hunter Wolf form?"

"It didn't return to its humanoid form," Detective Ramirez pointed out as he met Macy's gaze, and quickly turned his stare to the agents.

"Negative." Agent Kriss bent down and picked up a piece of cotton. "This is Agent Sinclair's. It smells like syn silver." His slow words gave his fear weight, his eyes focusing on the material and the oozing holes in the Hunter Wolf form. He dropped the scrap, stood up, and wiped his hands on his pants.

"Agent Sinclair would not kill if he did not have to. He is here as an agent and would not risk the punishment," Agent Logue assured. "The Hunter Wolf must have caused the stack to fall."

"Affirmative. It would explain Agent Sinclair's need to protect himself," Agent Kriss added.

Macy heard the agents trying to convince the humans their team leader, Agent Sinclair, wasn't in a warehouse shooting up Hunter Wolf forms without a reason. No one needed to make excuses when it didn't take a lycan with senses to know there was a fight and the agent defended himself. As it lay dead and turning to goo, the Hunter Wolf form was larger than those at Harper's warehouse, and after it died, it didn't shift. The chilling idea they were witnessing the beginning of a nightmare sat in her thoughts. Taking a step backwards, she told herself to get away from it while her heart pounded and its empty, dead eye bled into David's familiar brown.

"Detective Gray, you alright?" Sergeant Mayco's face wore a professional mask, but his eyes glittered with his accusations.

"Affirmative," Macy responded slowly. *Get it together. "Your weakness is an embarrassment to the bureau."* Meeting his gaze, she took another uneasy step back. They weren't going to find survivors. No one, human or paranormal, could survive the warehouse.

"This proves the warehouse is being used by shapeshifters. We find Agent Sinclair, make sure the place is clear, and have forensics in here to collect evidence," Agent Pixley explained to the group. "The DOJ is taking command of the investigation and I'm having another team, White Rain, respond."

Another paranormal team. Macy wanted to leave it to them.

"Copy. This is a possible hostage situation and an official investigation. I'll call and advise the appropriate teams to back up your agency." Sergeant Mayco added, "I'm alerting medical and Sanative of the situation."

Macy's gaze narrowed on Agent Logue, her thoughts going straight to the fact any minute, any second, he possessed the same power as the thing lying dead in front of them. Worse, she was surrounded by shifters. She took another step backward as Agent Logue turned and watched her with calculating eyes. She met his stare and saw the animal, the beast living in all lycans sitting in the shadows, waiting to be let loose, and as if it knew she saw it, its eyes gleamed bronze. She cringed as she saw the monster responsible for killing David.

*It's my imagination, brought on by fear,* she told herself, *seeing the wolf inside the man.* If she had the time and was able to put her anxiety aside to think about it sanely, she would tell herself it wasn't real. But she wasn't thinking straight. She didn't like seeing it ... no, she hated it, and she hated them.

"We need to continue the search," Agent Pixley ordered loud enough so everyone heard her. "There are four aisles, pick one and keep us informed."

"Agent Flynn and I are going to the right and will follow the aisle to the end," Detective Cutler replied.

Agent Logue joined Macy and stood beside her. "Detective Gray and I will take the left."

"Detective Ramirez and I will take the next," Agent Kriss reported.

"That leaves one aisle. Agent Pixley and I will follow it. We won't go too far, in case there's a problem at the entrance," Sergeant Mayco explained.

Macy absently nodded her head, and pushing herself trailed after Agent Logue. When they reached the aisle's mouth, the agent took his gun from its holster, turned, looked at her for far too long with the same calculating gaze, and went around the corner.

*He sees a liability and a threat to his life.* Macy shook her head as she counted to five and entered the aisle with her gun at the ready. Agent Logue stood in an empty walkway made from damaged containers and piled junk while darkness hung despite the sunlight coming in from skylights and windows set high along the ceiling. His dark bulk stopped three feet in front of her, his body going still, not rigid, as if his muscles flowed under his skin as he waited for his prey. Macy remained behind him, silent, watching and waiting. They stood in silence, alone, waiting for him to do what, she had no idea. What the hell he was doing? Did she ask? And if she did, with no commanding officers, and no one forcing them to play nice, would he answer her?

He knew she didn't like shifters, her attitude betraying her calm demeanor. If she questioned him, would he act like Sergeant Mayco and turn on her? And then when they were in front of people would he pretend everything was normal? As normal as it could be. Probably. He had no reason to treat her as an equal. Her line of thinking stopped cold when a whisper of a warning burned through her and filled her head. Death was matching her footsteps, and with her next breath, she felt it place its icy hand on her shoulder. Macy knew without a doubt the warehouse was the final resting place for dozens of people. They were going to find bodies there, and it wasn't going to be only humans. There would be a mix of human, shifter, and Otherkin. The feeling sank into her bones with such power it made her want to turn and run.

"What?" Agent Logue rounded to face her and stared into her goggles. "What did you say?"

A step backwards. "Nothing. I didn't say anything," she answered.

"Nothing?"

"Nothing." Macy cringed.

Agent Logue studied her, eyes skating over her face, then abruptly turned. "The aisle ends in four feet." His voice drifted back to her. "Detective Gray? Three feet."

"Three feet," Macy repeated absently. Deep in her head, the whisper created a montage of images from David, the nightmare of Harper's warehouse, and the Barrettes to fuel her imagination. *Cut it lose.*

"Three, two, one. We are in the open." Agent Logue searched the room, gazing at the stacks of containers, and more aisles.

"Copy," Macy replied. She stopped, letting the agent leave the aisle, and walk into the open alone while she hung back and kept a safe distance between them. She also would have his back if a Hunter Wolf form came from one of the other aisles.

Detective Ramirez emerged, and closing the distance approached Agent Logue. When he was several feet from the agent, he raised his hands, his gun held in his left, and each step slower than the first. Detective Ramirez hadn't checked the aisle; instead, he fixed his attention on Agent Logue. Macy shook her head. Did she look like that? Paranoid? Sloppy? Her hate for shapeshifters causing her to make mistakes? *Affirmative.* To her left, Agent Kriss walked out of the aisle, saw Agent Logue with Detective Ramirez, and stood beside her.

"Where's Detective Gray?" Detective Ramirez asked.

Agent Logue didn't have time to respond before Agent Kriss, understanding the underlying accusation, and with his anger rolling off him, stormed over to take his place beside the other agent. Knowing what was about to happen, she moved toward the group.

"You're a detective, figure it out," Agent Kriss mocked with disdain riddling his voice and a growl running through his words.

Detective Ramirez clearly heard the growl, took a step back at the same time he made a scoffing noise like it didn't bother him. Macy knew it did. He lowered his hands, didn't holster his gun, and took another step.

"Detective, she is behind you. Considering we are here searching for a missing person and have found a body, you should be aware of your surroundings," Agent Logue advised calmly. He turned slightly to meet the other agent's gaze. "Stand down."

Detective Ramirez hesitantly gave them his back to look at her. Why? Was he checking to see if she jumped the human ship and joined up with the shifters or maybe ran out of the warehouse? *Because I'm a liability.* In silence, he closed the distance, keeping his eyes narrowed on her. Despite his obvious doubt about her, she was better than the shifters, making her the lesser of two evils. Together they automatically created two teams. Two against two. It wasn't the DOJ and the BPI. It was human against lycan.

"The death, heat, and possibility of facing Hunter Wolves is pushing our anxiety and tempters." Agent Logue met their gazes. His words were steady, convincing, and he focused his attention on Agent Kriss. "Remember why we are here."

*Why are you here? Why is your team leader here?* Macy wanted to ask. "There are four more aisles. We could continue searching in pairs, taking up twice the time or we can search them separately," Macy said, trying to keep the focus on the mission.

"Separate," Agent Logue quickly replied. They shared a look before turning their attention to Agent Kriss and Detective Ramirez.

"Separate," they answered in unison.

*Surprise.* "Separate it is," Macy confirmed. She might be drowning in her own misery, but the current shit show needed to get underway. "I'll take the farthest aisle to the right. Agent Logue will take the next, then Detective Ramirez, and last Agent Kriss."

"Affirmative, ma'am," Agent Logue replied.

Macy gave the agent a sideways glance and saw her reflection in his goggles. Sand dusted her black uniform and helmet, and her face gleamed with sweat, highlighting the bruises and the scabbed over scraps. *Nice.* "Detective Ramirez, update Sergeant Mayco."

Detective Ramirez glanced at her and took his radio. "Captain Dixon, there are four more aisles leading out from the first room, advise, we are moving forward separately," he reported.

Purposely defying an order. All right, if that's the game he wants to play, Macy would have to watch her back.

As they waited for Captain Dixon to confirm their position, Macy wiped sweat from her cheeks with her sleeve, then the area around her eyes where her goggles sat against her skin. The bulky, protective eyewear cut her field of vision in half, added to her frustration, and wasn't going to save her from a Hunter Wolf form. Needing to get rid of at least one frustration—she was maxed out—she chose the goggles. Macy holstered her gun, reached up and lifted the eyewear off her face, and placed them on her helmet. At once, the not so fresh air cooled the skin trapped under the polycarbonate.

"I advise you to wear your goggles, Detective Gray," Detective Ramirez warned. "We don't know what's in here."

"Noted, Detective Ramirez. We've been in here for nearly an hour ... if anything airborne was going to kill us it would have," she replied, giving him her best Detective Gray smile. "They're constricting my field of vision, especially in the aisles." Her smile didn't fill her eyes ... hell, it barely tugged at the corners of her mouth. It did convey she was in control of her actions, and he should leave her alone.

"I'm not worried about airborne contagions. My concern is the lycanthrope contagion," Detective Ramirez explained as he held Agent Kriss' glare.

"Eye protection isn't going to save you from the contagion," Macy pointed out. Not much in the world was.

"I have to agree with Detective Gray," Agent Logue began as he removed his goggles.

"I can't stand the damn things. And it's not like *we* need them," Agent Kriss responded to Detective Ramirez. "The two of you might want to keep them on. Big, bad contagion will hurt a mortal."

Agent Kriss smiled as he met Macy's gaze. She didn't smile back at him. Instead, she drew her gun from its holster.

Not getting the rise out of her as he wanted, he turned his attention to Detective Ramirez.

"Affirmative, I don't want the dog contagion." Detective Ramirez glared back.

"Did you call me a dog?" Agent Kriss asked through a low growl.

*Perfect, that's what I need*, Macy thought.

"You are the one growling," Detective Ramirez shot back as he took an easy stand with a smirk curving his lips. "Is your bite as bad as your bark?"

*Shit.* They were supposed to be searching for a missing agent, in a warehouse where they were surrounded by the dead, had already found a dead Hunter Wolf form—they weren't supposed to be fighting. Sergeant Mayco would note she was there when the fight between agencies broke out. Between species. Agent Logue meet her unshielded gaze, his challenge sitting in the caramel depths, his authority radiating from him while he silently explained to her it was Macy's responsibility to stop her fellow human. He was doing his intimidation thing with her, the same way he had at the door. The freedom with which he worked had her wondering what position he held in his clan. Close to the alpha if she was pushed to guess, although it didn't matter. Agent Logue's bullying was nothing compared to whether or not Detective Ramirez was going to listen to her. Yes, Macy was senior, possessed the rank and authority to order him around all day, maybe, before her world started to crumble, and no one trusted her. He already challenged her when he didn't radio Sergeant Mayco.

Keeps getting better. Macy stared back at Agent Logue, contemplating her options. There weren't any. Either she ordered Detective Ramirez to stand down, proving her authority, or she looked like a fool in front of the DOJ, who were lycans, and whose power base was authority. *Here goes.* "Detective Ramirez, stand down," Macy ordered sternly, and met his gaze. Was that a spark of humor? *Not backing down.* "There is a missing DOJ agent, its importance has Captain Dixon here. We don't need a fight with an allied agency."

Detective Ramirez stared at her patch and slowly met her narrowed gaze. "Right. Allied agency." His face contorted with his smugness, telling her she was right, he didn't respect her.

When Detective Ramirez stared at her patch, Macy wondered why. Was it a reminder of her authority and position? A senior detective, sharpshooter for her team, and second in command of said team. Or did he want to take it from her? No doubt he was thinking Macy needed to practice what she preached. Her job was at stake, not his. He could get into a verbal battle with Kriss or Logue because, in the end, he was human, they weren't, and he obeyed orders.

And ... well, she didn't.

"Russell, back down," Agent Logue warned. "You do not need the attention from Commander Wilson, not to mention Kayne." If only for a moment, his order eased the tension rising around them.

Agent Kriss shot Detective Ramirez a death stare, minus wolf eyes, and grudgingly met Agent Logue's gaze. The two men stared at each other, each battling for his place, and when Macy had had enough and considered leaving them to their scowl battle, Agent Kriss cast his eyes to the floor. She watched his show of submission and was curious to know how much more was going on than a subordinate submitting to a senior. She could feel the energy coming from them, its fingers wanting to crawl over her heated skin. It was an abrupt reminder of what they were. This had to end before she lost her mind and Ramirez searched for Sergeant Mayco to tell him he shouldn't have to work with her because she didn't have it anymore.

Macy cleared her throat to get their attention and tried to get them back on track by saying, "While we wait for an answer, Agent Logue, how are your senses?"

"Not good," he answered, and faced her.

"And yours, Agent Kriss?" Macy asked.

"The same," he admitted, grudgingly.

"Taking that into consideration, is splitting up the best decision?" Macy asked the group. Her attention stayed on Detective Ramirez, his reaction to the agents, and their conversation.

"Even without our senses, we are stronger than you and able to defend ourselves against another werewolf without fear of infection," Agent Logue explained. "If we remain in pairs, we are capable of getting between you and a Hunter Wolf. It is your call."

His use of the term werewolf was typical of a lycan. Of course, her use of lycan was typical of a human. Werewolves became lycanthropes, beast walkers became therianthropes, any shapeshifter other than a lycan, aptly named after their diseases. Both names were quickly shortened to lycan and therian, attempting to make their genera, and their beast, less intimidating, less unknown, and more human. Macy wasn't fooled, knew the truth about them, and saw it every time she responded to a call. No matter what they called themselves, she didn't trust them. Their display of proving who was in charge only added fuel to her fire. They were monsters dressed in human skins.

"Detective Gray," Captain Dixon's voice tangled in static over the radio. His tone sounded stressed, and she figured he was having as much fun as she was. His allied agency was more than he could handle. *Good.* "Confirm." The radio cut out.

It was all she needed. "You heard him. Let's move," Macy ordered, and turning, headed to the first aisle. Their movements started on the left and went to the right, each giving the aisle a number. As she approached the mouth, she relayed her position over the radio. "Gray, heading into aisle one."

"Ramirez, aisle three."

Macy turned to meet Detective Ramirez's stare, her eyes darting from the entrance, the serious expression on his face, and his conflict. He wasn't happy about the goggles, wasn't happy about the lycans, and she knew he was following Captain Dixon's orders, not hers. They were staring at each other when Agent Logue stepped into her line of vision. The agent's eyes blazed for a split second before he disappeared.

A warning? Chills skated down her spine, the feel of death creeping in, and fighting the dread threading around her, Macy entered the aisle and headed toward its end.

"Room." The static grew worse as Agent Logue's voice came over the radio. "Gray. One for backup."

Macy listened to the agent's broken order demanding her presence and rolled her eyes with the request. Damn, she covered one aisle and Agent Logue was calling for backup. How was a human going to help a lycan? The warehouse was a network of aisles and chambers, some small and some large, so she assumed the aisles divided another section making it impossible for Agent Kriss to respond. Because, she was positive, Agent Logue didn't purposely request her over his own kind. She stared at the end of the aisle, her nerves on edge, her thoughts racing as she waited for Agent Logue to repeat the order. She wanted confirmation he did in fact request *her*. Bowing her head, she cursed knowing Sergeant Mayco was listening to radio chatter and he heard Agent Logue specifically request her for backup.

Add it to the list, sir. First, Agent Logue pinned her to the warehouse. Second, he called her for backup. That was going to be hard to explain. The agent didn't know what was going on in the world of the BPI, or he did—every DOJ agent probably had copies of the files sitting in Agent Sinclair's truck and were briefed on the disfunction inside the BPI. Not to mention Internal Affairs investigation into her conduct.

"Gray. Backup," Agent Logue ordered.

*Fuck.* "Copy. On my way," Macy answered. *Taking notes, Mayco?* Leaving her aisle, she started backtracking while keeping mental notes of the layout. The scene was becoming too familiar. Way too familiar.

Seconds later, she slowly approached the agent from behind, his body visibly tense with his concentration. Hearing her approach, Agent Logue slowly lowered himself to one knee and staring forward drew a breath. Why was she there? With tension tracing across her shoulders, she raised her gun and closed the distance between them. Agent Logue didn't acknowledge her, his attention remaining on whatever was in front of him, his unwavering focus creating apprehension with each step.

"Behind you," Macy warned. She stood directly behind him, his head even with her shoulders. "What is it?" She made sure her voice was soft, firm, relaying she was covering him and awaiting orders.

"Someone is hurt." Agent Logue looked at the ground, and with a fingertip touched the concrete.

"You're sure?"

"Affirmative. I am unsure if it is a shapeshifter or a human." Agent Logue stood, hesitated, then raised his head and smelled the air. "There is blood."

While Agent Logue smelled the air, Macy was trying not to. She didn't want the rancid mix of the dead in her nose and head, and didn't need it adding a flare to the nightmares she harbored. Against her better judgement, she inhaled, and there under the sour scent was blood from fresh wounds. It brought the taste of warm rain on rusted metal to her tongue. As it circled her, the sweet scents mingled with a sharper, tangy smell stabbed at her memory. It wrapped itself in the heated air, touched her throat, and slid to her stomach. Macy covered her mouth with the back of her left hand, trying to stifle a gag.

"Without full use of my senses, I do not trust this. The rogue werewolf remains a threat," Agent Logue advised, frustration plain in his voice.

"Is it a single person?" she asked. Macy didn't ask about Agent Sinclair. He obviously wasn't in there.

"Affirmative. Fear rides the air." Agent Logue stilled, like before, the pause causing her to hesitate.

*What else is going on*? "Do you want me to call Agent Kriss and Detective Ramirez for backup?" Macy hated the doubt riddling her. She hated working with a lycan. Frustrated, she thought if Detective Ramirez took the next aisle over, which he did, he should have been the backup, not her. Why didn't he respond? Easy, he didn't want her fate.

"Negative." Agent Logue turned and looked at her over his shoulder, his dark eyes narrowing. "I think the room is small. If you cover the entrance and the aisle it should be enough. I want to be able to defend if we are attacked," he explained.

Macy nodded her response, his gaze taking her in, then giving her his back he stalked into the room. The wide aisle allowed four people to walk side by side, for several feet, and slowly bottlenecked leaving room for one person. Escape wasn't likely. The aisle and entry would trap them, giving the guards time to capture and kill. She stood at the widest point, making sure Agent Logue had enough room to back out and fight if attacked while leaving herself enough room to fire on whatever came out of the chamber. There she waited. And waited. She hated waiting. Waiting gave her time to chase the fears tormenting her and what might sit in the deepest part of the warehouse.

The question remained, where was their Agent Sinclair? He had to have heard them, must have sensed them. Unless, like Agent Logue, his senses were skewed, and he was seriously injured, the Hunter Wolf form clearly wounded him, there was syn silver on his clothing. Or he thought they were the enemy and was stalking them, the code red hadn't been cancelled, its risk level in effect and reminding them the person they were trying to find might turn on them. Agent Sinclair and the rogue lycan were both threats. Macy scanned the aisle, her eyes searching for a Hunter Wolf form, a lycan, anyone.

"Gray." Agent Logue's voice sounded distant, rough, and rattled.

What would rattle a Blood Rain lycan? She didn't want to know. Macy checked the aisle, and finding it clear, started toward the agent. "On my way."

Agent Logue didn't respond, the silence bringing the concern in his voice to the forefront of her thoughts. Images of Hunter Wolf forms and their victims played freely as she ran the last twenty feet while trying to keep her instincts sharp. Skidding to a stop, she waited at the narrow entrance for her eyes to adjust. Once she could see the beam from a flashlight shooting straight up, she used it to find her way. The small room felt tighter with the tall walls, thick darkness, and the heat seemed to increase by degrees as it closed around her. She shook herself as the bright LED light glittered against a grimy container, casting a burnt white halo into the room. Her instincts came in a rush and warned her of danger. A lycan. A human. With controlled movements, Macy stopped beside Agent Logue, picked up the flashlight, and holding it at an angle, cast enough light to see the body.

"No," she mumbled. The heavy air invaded Macy's mouth at the same time the seeping wounds and broken body of a woman joined the cache of horrors in her head.

"Keep your distance, Detective Gray, she is suffering from multiple infections and her wounds are bleeding," Agent Logue warned. "I think I sense the contagion, but cannot be sure."

Macy backed up three steps. The woman's battered body created disgust and anger while death's icy hand touched her, its chill slipping through the fibers of her clothing to touch bare skin. The woman was going to die. Negative. Ignoring the feeling, she clung to her anger. The woman's lifeless form slumped between the side of the container and concrete floor, and resembled Mrs. Barrette. Dry blood sat on her swollen, spilt lips, more of it matted her dirty blonde hair, and dirt covered what wasn't bloody. What was left of her shirt hung from one shoulder, revealing claw marks and scratches from human nails while around them swollen, white skin puffed up and tore, giving way to spiderwebs of red lines seeping fresh blood. From the middle of the deepest cuts, buttery liquid oozed its sheen of sweat gleaming on her pallid skin and looked as if someone had poured oil over her. At first look her symptoms resembled someone suffering from shock, but if Macy risked touching her, she would feel a fever. The woman was losing her fight with the contagion while fighting the infections from her contaminated wounds. Macy frantically searched the woman's shoulders, legs, any exposed skin for a Death Bloom. None. Yet.

Equal parts of anxiety and rage coursed through her when the images of David's prone body on the warehouse floor plagued her at the same time Sergeant Mayco's accusations tumbled through her decisions, making her second guess herself. Sweat beaded on her forehead and her clothing felt tighter as the heat wrapped around her. *I killed it.* And would do the same when she found the lycan responsible for hurting the woman.

"I can feel your anger. It will not do her any good if we cannot get her out of here and find who did this. All of this," Agent Logue stressed.

Macy repositioned the flashlight, taking its beam from the woman. "You need to get her out of here," she ordered. "Now." She exhaled slowly, counted to ten, and tried to tear her gaze from the woman's wounds. Purplish-blue bruises circled each of the woman's eyes, erasing the definition of her facial structure. If it weren't for knowing she had eyes, it would be hard to tell where they started and where her chin ended.

"If I leave, you will not have backup," Agent Logue argued.

Detective Ramirez was somewhere, could she depend on him? Didn't matter. "It's not up for discussion, Agent. Get her out of here," Macy ordered.

"You don't have the authority to give me orders, Detective Gray. There is a werewolf loose somewhere in this maze, and if you run into it, you could end up like her. Or dead." Agent Logue held her gaze.

The lycan agent cared for her wellbeing. "You are going to take her out of here. *Because* there is another lycan in here with *your* agent. I'll remind you, Agent Logue, no one knows how long Agent Sinclair has been here. It's hot, he's hurt, and I'm searching." Macy checked the entrance and faced the agent. With each shallow breath the woman fought for, her chances of survival grew slimmer. "It's clear. You can go."

When Agent Logue looked up at her, his frustration showed in his wolf's bronze glare, like stones set in a human-oid face. "Agent Sinclair can take care of himself. Agent Pixley will never allow the risk you are taking."

"I could report to Commander Wilson you're trying to in-timidate me by using your animal, for the third time. You know it's against the rules, lycan," Macy threatened.

With his eyes gleaming in the dimly lit room, she under-stood he was powerful and embraced his otherworldliness. You wouldn't find him sulking somewhere and crying about being a lycan. She shoved her fear down and embraced her anger, and reaching for a semblance of compassion, Macy knelt beside Agent Logue, proving she wasn't a complete bitch, but she wasn't going to back off or give in to his lycan games.

In a calmer voice, she said, "She needs medical attention. She needs Sanative, and you can easily take her out. Besides, there are plenty of us, calling for backup won't be a prob-lem." She then gave him her Detective Gray smile. "Like you said, I don't have the authority to give you an order, but on the flip side, Agent Pixley doesn't have the authority to give me orders. I'm BPI. I'm asking Sergeant Mayco."

"This is a DOJ investigation. My people are in charge." A low growl laced his words.

"I'm not arguing with you. I'm reporting it to Sergeant Mayco."

"Not good enough."

She was finished with him. Macy held his gaze, then looked at the woman, her breathing slowing as they wasted time. "Agent Logue found a woman, she's alive, and is bringing her out. I'm continuing on my own," she reported clearly into the radio. She wasn't going to stop searching when there was a violent lycan on the loose.

They were staring at each other in the hazy halo of the flashlight while they waited for Sergeant Mayco to reply. Seconds ticked one by one, giving her the feeling his bronze eyes stayed on her for hours. She was sure he would burn holes into her face if he could. Macy kept her breathing level, her temper under control, and her desire to find the lycan responsible for the woman's beating dampened to a small fire. Agent Logue shifted his weight, and his stare changed to an outright glare, the same one he used when he put Agent Kriss in his place. Clearly, he wasn't used to having his orders challenged.

*Too bad.* "You can't intimidate me into going with you. I'm not part of your dominance game," Macy stated.

"Negative, you are not. You are mortal and it shows." Suddenly, he seemed older. His voice taking on age while his eyes grew darker, and she knew he wasn't the thirty something he appeared to be.

"Then it shouldn't surprise you," Macy responded matter-of-factly.

"You cannot fight the werewolf. You do not know what form it is using." His voice was low, the growl in it thickening with his deteriorating patience.

"Negative, I can't, but I can shoot it." Macy stopped. Damn, she said more than she should have. Her stomach rolled as tingles danced across her skin and adrenaline coursed through her veins. She was going to find the lycan responsible.

"I know who you are, Detective Macy Gray of the Bureau of Paranormal Investigations. Killing the werewolf will not make it easier to deal with shapeshifters." The growl was gone from his voice, and his eyes slowly eased into a rich caramel with honey undertones. He leaned closer, and she thought he would touch her. "Revenge will not take away the pain or the past. It will not end what you are feeling."

His words blasted through her wall, going straight to her bones, damn him. Macy guessed they all knew who she was. It didn't take a genius to figure it out, not when her file was in their team leader's truck, but she didn't expect to have it thrown in her face. The DOJ's Blood Rain team was in town for a reason, which case took priority was anyone's guess.

"Save it, Agent Logue." Macy's voice held an edge of anger. It didn't give away her insides were crumbling, and she was trying to bluff a lycan.

If the DOJ knew her by Officer Murphy's death, they knew about the investigation of negligence, and she had disobeyed a direct order that put her team in danger. What they couldn't possibly know was Macy was being blackmailed by her commander, she was looking for a spy, and the BPI detectives weren't sure if she was on their side. Her silence was going to be the end of her. Macy stood, backed away from them, and creating distance let the guilt over the Barrettes and David run through her veins as freely as her blood. She wasn't going to lose control. She needed to go forward. She had a target.

As a precaution, in case Agent Logue thought about taking her, against her will, Macy backed farther away, telling herself it was enough he couldn't reach her. She could have laughed. If he wanted, his lycan speed would make it easy for him to catch her, even with the distance she was creating. If she made it out of the small room, where would she run? Would she hold the bottlenecked entrance until agents and detectives wanted to know what the hell she was doing? Negative. Her own damn agency would arrest her. Poor plan.

"As you said, there is backup. You have no reason to put your life in danger," Agent Logue challenged. "On purpose."

Did Agent Logue imply she was taking an unnecessary risk? Maybe attempt suicide by lycan? The idea wasn't unfamiliar to her or anyone else. Law enforcement officers had been killing themselves on the job for years. The average BPI detective worked for ten years before the kills and the threat of infection weighed on their conscience and haunted their dreams, then the injuries, stress, and PTSD forced them into medical retirement. It messed with your head, gave you nightmares, and poisoned the family living with you and anyone who cared. As much as you wanted to, you couldn't check-out by committing the ultimate sin of suicide. Not when you would be mocked, forgotten, and a statistic. Not much thought went into that. Death in the line of duty gave your family protection from law enforcement, an insurance cash out, and was considered a sacrifice that would turn you into a legacy.

Macy didn't consider dying an option. She was too proud, too vain, and had too much to do. And dying at the hands of a shifter was an insult. "Agent Logue—"

Static filled the air, cutting her off, and staring at each other, they waited. "Negative, Detective Gray, stay with Agent Logue," Agent Pixley ordered. Her voice crackled over the radio as the static corrupted her words.

Agent Logue's eyes no longer held his disapproval. Instead, his entire body expressed his satisfaction and said he won the round. "I told you she would not allow it. The threat to human life is real. If the rogue wolf shapeshifts and turns into the beast we are here to investigate, your life is in danger. They are hard for another werewolf to defend themselves against."

Investigating Hunter Wolf forms and not the BPI spy, he wasn't telling her the truth. She shook her head, her life was always in danger, it was part of the job. "Like I said, I didn't ask Agent Pixley. I know about the files in Agent Sinclair's truck. I know there is suspicion of a spy, a pending investigation, and I'm on the suspect list. It doesn't begin to explain the gravity of the situation, Agent Logue. You have no idea what's going on. The woman needs medical attention immediately. Agent Sinclair is still missing, and the warehouse is too big to lose another body."

Agent Logue watched her, his eyes moving over her face and down to the woman. She was right. They were there to investigate them. By admitting the BPI had its problems, did it make her look guilty? Either way, Macy wasn't walking out of the warehouse with him, not until Sergeant Mayco ordered her out. She would bet her life, he wouldn't.

"Detective Gray, keep searching," Sergeant Mayco ordered.

"We're waiting for you, Agent Logue," Agent Pixley followed.

Killing the grin of victory, she could imagine the agent's green eyes narrowing while her disagreement with Sergeant

Mayco's decision creased her forehead. "I told you, there are things you don't know. I'll cover you." It wasn't a real win on her part when Sergeant Mayco was *testing* her, maybe hoping a Hunter Wolf form finished her off. With the scene at Agent Sinclair's truck fresh in her mind, and Sergeant Mayco telling her he didn't want to die, Macy prepared to find her target.

Agent Logue's irritated gaze landed on her, making it difficult to keep her face neutral. "I guess I have my order." With a low growl, he turned from her to the woman.

He wasn't happy, and there wasn't much she was willing to do to change it. Agent Logue didn't know what game Sergeant Mayco was playing and how it had been going on for weeks. If Sergeant Mayco saw her now, would he think she knew shapeshifters? The woman couldn't have weighed more than a hundred pounds, but Agent Logue carefully lifted her broken body off the concrete floor as if she weighed nothing. While Agent Logue waited, Macy grabbed the flashlight, clicked it off, shoved it in the right-side pocket of her BDUs, then made her way to the entrance. With the woman's limp body cradled in his arms and her bruised face against his tactical vest, he stopped in front of her.

"I am against this. You do not understand what this place smells like. There is old death here. Life was corrupted and left to die without respect. It is a threat," Agent Logue cautioned. "Whatever is going on, keep your thoughts straight and watch your back."

Macy didn't have a reply to his statement, "watch your back," when there was too much truth in his words. Agent Logue was wrong though. She knew what was lurking in the warehouse, had witnessed the chaos behind the dead, and knew what it smelled like. It was death, many kinds, and in multiple ways. She took her gun from its holster and followed in silence, keeping a watch on them, the front of the aisle, and behind her. At the entrance of the next aisle she stopped, deciding it was the end of the line. Sergeant Mayco and Agent Pixley were two aisles over—it wasn't a long walk—and there were other detectives and agents. Agent Logue stopped, met her eyes, held the stare as if he was going to say something, then stalking away disappeared in the maze. Macy released the breath she had been holding, pushed the agent's remarks from her thoughts, and scanned the area.

The wall of containers continued for several yards like a continuous river of metal that radiated heat. Holding her gun, sweat seeped between her palms, forcing her to stop, wipe her hands on her pants, and start again. Behind her, a trail of wet, dark dots punctured the sand-dusted concrete. Listening to the wind rattle the roof, she struggled to keep her *thoughts straight.* They were straight. She had a target.

"Oh, hello," Macy mumbled.

She paused at the mouth of the narrow opening as memories from Harper's warehouse ate at her confidence. *Not the same.* Slipping between the ends of the containers she scooted to the other side. It opened to an entirely different setup. Damn, it was going to take them longer if random gaps, to narrow for the larger agents and detectives to squeeze through, were the only way to get to the other side. Macy backed out, checked the aisle for detectives or agents, and considered updating Sergeant Mayco of her position when a cold wave of warning slid over her shoulders and danced along her spine. Her target was close. With her back against metal, she scooted through, took her helmet off, and setting it by the gap, marked the entrance. After a quick search of the space, she headed toward her target.

# CHAPTER SEVEN

TWO stainless-steel tables—bolted to the floor, and equipped with chains and manacles—flanked Kayne. He grazed his fingertips across the smooth metal as he stared at the stack of blue plastic crates with medical emblems stamped on their sides, their numbers taking up most of the far wall. Beside them sat a table with a small incubator, and farther down, with its motor running softly, was a commercial-size refrigerator. On the opposite wall, a desk contained a computer, notebooks, a camera, and a microscope.

"Experiments," Kayne mumbled. What the hell were they doing to their victims?

Echoes of voices from the approaching invaders didn't sway him from his thoughts and he continued to scan the lab. Rubbing his neck with his right hand, he wanted to know why the BPI hadn't investigated. From the outside, the warehouse appeared abandoned, he would give them that, but the inside—with the dead, empaths, ersatz, the containers, and lab—should have been found. *If* the BPI was investigating other warehouses, they should have known about this place. Not to mention connecting the dead with the missing persons reports. Using the edge of the stainless-steel table, he steadied himself and allowed his mind to accuse one person of the failure. Every file he had read concerning the surge in shapeshifter crimes had one detective associated with them ... Detective Gray. She should have known about the warehouse.

*Detective Gray.*

For weeks, her face sat in his head, her presence a weight in his thoughts, and then at his weakest Kayne convinced himself she had arrived to save him. Why? Because she was guilty. He pictured her finding the files, searching for him, finding the Hunter Wolf's body, and then Grace and Henry. What would he say to her when she found him? He shuddered. It's the damn empath.

*Focus.* Forcing his thoughts back to the case he remembered Grace had told him the BPI kidnapped them. Was the spy keeping the BPI from investigating? It was a possibility. Still, he hoped he hadn't compromised the investigation by entering the warehouse and killing the Hunter Wolf.

With anxiety running wild, Kayne rummaged through the desk drawers, finding files, notes, pens, but nothing identifying the people involved. He finished searching the lab, and leaving the contents behind him, looked for a way out. There was nothing. A solid wall made up the back of the warehouse, and staring at it then at the lab, indecision weighed on him. If he wanted backup, he needed to go to the front. It meant facing whoever was there, and somehow keeping Grace's presence a secret until he could get help. Kayne zeroed in on Grace's weak heartbeat, concentrating on it until it pulsed in his ears. She was alive. Time was slipping from her.

He started maneuvering out of the lab and toward the containers to make his way into the maze when a wave of energy riding the heated air stopped him as the stronger crux of others swept over him. Left with little choice, he had to try his senses and trust his instincts. Opening himself to his wolf, Kayne searched for Henry the same way he had

Grace, let his wolf follow the link created by their shared power, and felt the new wolf's feel. It vibrated, evened out, and Kayne felt Henry's heartbeat. Calm. Good. Suddenly, Kayne stopped mid-step; Henry's heartbeat thundered as if in warning.

Someone found the wolf. He ran, using his senses as a guide and not paying attention to the haphazard path he was taking. Running back into the maze, the crux of were-wolves, therians, and mortals flooded the warehouse, their essence saturating the air. In the mix was another, its search went beyond the capabilities of shapeshifters. He knew the feel of their rough invasion, had dealt with it all damn day. There was another empath. A stronger one. He didn't need another one. Swiftly, the weight of his gun reminded him he had one remaining bullet, and no way to defend himself if confronted.

*Get to Henry.* Kayne stalked carefully back to where the wolf waited when the sharp scent of a mortal drifted on the air. He slowed, letting the smell fill his nose, his mouth, and his head. There was something different about it. It wasn't mortal and it wasn't werewolf, but a weak combination of both. And it was dark.

Adrenalin fed excitement and dread fought for dominance as Kayne quickened his pace and jumped to the top of a container. He was desperate to get to Henry as he ran across the stacks, and jumping over breaks, he knew he couldn't risk staying on the containers when they might see him. He leapt, landed on the floor, and quickly headed down another aisle. If they saw him, if Elijah saw him, he would see a half-crazed, paranoid man, without a shirt and covered in grime. He would see his creation. Kayne blew a breath out, and raced down another aisle, passing rooms.

Mortals and shapeshifters.

Their presence continued to grate against his instincts and push on his senses. If he felt them, Henry knew they were there. Their presence grew stronger, closer, driving his worries into a frenzy while his imagination fed him scenarios he didn't want to think about. Did they find Grace? Did they have Grace? In answer to his worry, her weak heartbeat disappeared, and he knew she was gone, and in its place was defeat. He didn't get her out. He didn't get help. There was no help coming. It was another failure added to his growing list.

*Fight it.* Damn the effects of syn silver poisoning, dehydration, and being driven crazy in the warehouse was destroying him. He had to focus on his priority—saving Henry.

Kayne pushed through the haze sitting in his mind and reached for the new wolf. Henry responded by using his senses to search for him, and the link lit up with stirrings of fear, its ends reaching out to him, and poisoned with terror, polluted his mind. The backlash left Kayne dazed, weakened, and caused his knees to buckle. Stumbling, he fell face first to the floor. He barely choked out a groan, placed his hands on the warm concrete, and pushed himself to his back. With a string of growled curses, he looked up at the ceiling, his senses going wild over the approach of the enemy. He couldn't stay where he was any longer. Rolling to his side and finding his footing, he stood, and with a sideways gait headed down the aisle. He needed to get to Henry. Together they would get to his truck and call for help, and if he had to use his wolf against Elijah and fight his way through, he would. Consequences be damned.

Macy followed the uneven trail of bloody handprints and greasy smudges the woman left in her wake and let them guide her to another room created from the never-ending sea of containers. Keeping in mind she didn't have backup, she used caution, wanted to tell the lycan agent she was being careful, and went deeper into the warehouse. She made a right; the woman's prints lead to another stack, where they stopped. She searched for any indication there had been a fight—blood, debris, or evidence the lycan was still there. Maybe it was the same one who wrecked the agent's truck.

*Yes. The perfect target.* With her thoughts, responsibility reared its ugly head, telling her the agent should be her priority, not hoping to find the lycan. But, like Agent Logue pointed out, Agent Sinclair could take care of himself, and the agent would know. She wanted the lycan to pay for what it did to the woman. And David. Mrs. Barrette. The death in the warehouse.

In the open space, the containers had been reinforced with thick, steel bands at the tops and sides, fresh metal shone where they cut a door into the side, and each wore new locks. Why the difference? Were they using each container for something different? A different prison. God, how many were there? Macy walked down one side, checking the locks of the ground level containers as she went, all of them secure. She tried the next row—locked, locked, locked. Frustrated, she backed up to check the top row and saw more new locks. All but one. The door stood open, letting limp, dirty yellow straw peek out from the corners, while faded material hung from the rail. Taking three steps backwards, she struggled to see anything.

Not taking any chances, Macy raised her gun. "I'm Detective Gray with the Bureau of Paranormal Investigations.

Show yourself," she ordered. *Let it be the lycan.* Above her, the roof rattled, its metal clanging, the sharp sound adding to her nervous energy. With a deep breath, a warning slithered down her spine and instinctively she stepped farther away. *This is not Harper's warehouse. I'm in control.*

"This is Detective Gray with the BPI," Macy repeated, her barrel pointed at the entrance.

No answer.

"I order you to show yourself. If you do not comply, I will use excessive force," she warned.

Silence.

Macy blew a breath out, trying to calm her nerves, and lowered her gun. Everywhere there were victims, bodies, and shapeshifters, it didn't mean *her* target was in the container. Agent Sinclair might have helped the woman escape her prison, and if he had, he would know who beat her. Could Agent Sinclair have found the lycan? She didn't know. However, she did know she needed to report her location. Staring at the open container, she held the mic clipped at her shoulder. Static buzzed, and she waited for it clear. The wind died down, the radio cleared, and she stopped, instinct driving her back several more feet. A low growl rumbled. Backing up, she raised her gun and tension tightened across her shoulders and sent tingles into her wrist. The pounding of her heartbeat in her ears drowned out the lycan's next growl.

"I found the lycan. Repeat, I found the lycan," Macy reported. No response. She waited. Still, no response. "I'm at the back of the warehouse. Repeat, I found the lycan."

A shuffling noise chased a growl as the muzzle of a lycan in wolf form appeared with its flaxen eyes nailed on her. At least it wasn't a Hunter Wolf form. The lycan straightened to its full height, and standing at the rail of the container, its huge paws covered metal while its long nails reached out over the edge. From its nose to its ears flecks of cinnamon, sable, and white blended into its massive chest and down to its paws. Another low growl sounded across the space, creating pressure through her shoulders in anticipation of squeezing the trigger. *It wouldn't jump thirty feet.* As sweat beaded on her forehead, rolled down her temples, to her cheeks, it added misery to the situation.

"This is Gray, I found the lycan. Repeat, I found the lycan. Need backup," Macy ordered with urgency in her voice. "Backup, at my location."

The radio mocked her with silence and her thoughts went to pulling the trigger. Was she going to shoot it? Macy visualized the woman's eyes, broken body, and the contagion as it tore through her body, and she tightened her grip on the gun. Negative, she couldn't shoot it. She wanted to, desperately. It would be murder, and while she might blame it for every paranormal crime in the county, she wasn't a murderer. Clicking the button on the radio, she watched the lycan move its head in the direction of her hand, then it inched closer to the edge of the rail, its claws clicking on metal, and its lips lifted, revealing a set of canines.

Three walking, talking lycans in humanoid form and she couldn't get one of them to answer the radio and help her. Macy couldn't walk away from a lycan in wolf form, it was against policy. Her saving grace was the pale yellow assuring her it wasn't very powerful, and the absence of red meant it wasn't near Blood Rage. She held her position. Powerful or not, she wasn't going to make herself prey, and after what it may have done to the woman, she wasn't going to provoke a defense response. Still, she would be damned if she was going to wait for it to jump and attack. Macy's only choice was to shoot it while it was in the container.

That's weak.

*What the hell am I thinking, weak? It's a lycan. My target.*

Caught in the conflict of her thoughts, she watched the lycan watch her. She tried the radio again, and again was denied. In response, the lycan growled and pawed at the metal. Shoot it, wound it, get help. It tried to kill the woman. The woman's face reminded Macy of the truth. Shoot it and kill it. The truth was Macy hated all shapeshifters to a point, but this one, the wolf growling at her, destroyed a human being.

Kill it.

Macy gripped her gun, wrapping the fingers of her left hand around the fingers of her right, and took aim. With a quick motion, the lycan jumped from the container and landed hard in front of her. Instinctively, she slipped into the place in her mind where calm prevailed, told her to squeeze the trigger and shoot the target. The moment lasted a heartbeat. A shadow swept across her, and ignoring it, her focus stayed on the advancing lycan. Her breath caught when long fingers found the contours of her thinner wrists, and holding them restrained her as if they were steel bands. She fought the hold, struggled to find the lycan, and squeezed the trigger. The gunshot echoed, pieced her ears, and dulled her hearing. When the resonating echo started to clear, she heard a deep growl accompanied by sharp clicks on concrete.

Someone trapped her.

The lycan was free to attack.

Macy struggled to get loose, jerking in his grasp. His fingers squeezed, sending fire rushing through her elbows, tracing hot pain into her shoulders. Her hand loosened on the gun, she felt it slipping from her sweat-damp grip, then it made a clanging sound as it hit concrete, driving panic into her fight. She lost her only defense. This was worse than Harper's warehouse, way worse, her fear screamed. The assailant was in humanoid form; she didn't see his face and refused to look up at him. There was no way she was going to give him the satisfaction of seeing the panic in her eyes. Gathering what nerve she could, she stared at his hands, his naked chest, and shoulder holster. With another failed jerk, he easily drew her toward him using his strength to trap her wrists and forearms against his chest. It left her no place to go and put her face too damn close to his bare skin covered in grime and blood, while behind them the growling lycan paced back and forth, its nails clicking. The man's deep rumble of a voice brought her head up, and she caught glimpses of his determined dirty face and fixed amber eyes. Amber like jewels. His wolf's glare stared straight through her. Macy's strength plummeted with her struggle as she stared up at the lycan holding her against his body.

*Hold tight*, she told herself. She stopped struggling against his strength; she couldn't out muscle him, but she could feign giving up. With the heat and their skin-to-skin contact, Macy waited for sweat to soak her hands and arms, and when drops slid between them, she gave a sharp jerk. Her right hand slid free, and she went for the knife in her vest and pulled it from its sheath. With her next breath, she allowed him to twist her around, his amber eyes staring with mild surprise, as the point of her knife threatened the soft skin of his throat. Putting pressure on the blade, she gave him a quick tease, the sharp bite of silver drawing a breath from him. With her threat realized, he tightened his hold on her left wrist.

He looked volatile and unhinged, and the idea her defense—against a lycan who could turn into a Hunter Wolf form—was a knife made her tremble. Macy did not, under any circumstances, want to die by shapeshifter. With his violent countenance and his tightened grip on her wrist, he knew she was scared, as if he was sensing it, and it drove her crazy. Neither of them were going to be the first to give up, then their gazes locked on one another, and she prayed he did something, anything, to give her a reason to shove the blade deep into his throat then she was going to shoot the lycan.

Where the hell did the knife come from?

Several feet behind Kayne, the new wolf growled, closed the distance, and began circling them. He wouldn't risk taking his attention off the woman as he leisurely scanned her features, watching intently as the soft lines around her eyes deepened with her expression. The creases caught the scabbed over cuts and the muted colors of yellow and purple staining the right side of her face. Bruises. Didn't surprise him. With her struggle, he tightened his grip on her wrist and watched her cinnamon eyes narrow. In response, she nudged the blade to the underside of his jaw, the silver tip like a torch to his skin.

It became a standoff.

Not much of one when Kayne wasn't accustomed to hurting women, let alone detectives, which created a pang of guilt that simmered in his middle. Not only was he hurting her, but he also knew he was scaring her. She recognized what he was, and his closeness was feeding into her fear and causing it to grow into a physical wall around her. The wicked glare she shot him told Kayne everything he needed to know. When she had the chance, she was going to slit his throat, watch him bleed out, and would calmly explain to her commander it was justified.

When she stopped fighting his hold, Kayne risked breaking eye contact to see the patch on the front of her vest. BPI. Law enforcement had arrived. He didn't have a patch, a badge, or a shirt, and he could only imagine that he must look crazy. Having already survived syn silver, he had zero desire to feel it again. He took a breath, and she pushed the blade closer to his skin, its sting slicing across his nerve endings, promising more pain. It didn't, to his dislike, quench the heat radiating from her. Like bullying her was going to stop her from tormenting him, his fingers tightened around her thin wrist, fitting into the curves as if made for them.

The knife touched his skin for a second time, sending razor blades of fire into his core. She might be scared, but she wasn't going to let it stop her, and she knew what she was doing. Anger flowed freely as Kayne looked down at her lashes dusted with sand, her face gleaming with sweat as light brown dirt tinted her cheeks, the fading bruises, and braided hair. For a moment, familiarity touched his mind, its hold making him dig into his memories of her, and the effect was enough to scare him. He quickly shoved it down, not wanting another round of hallucinations polluting his mind and actions while he held a BPI detective.

Her harsh inhale broke through the panic, and ebbing, the rush allowed Kayne to think clearly. Detective M. Gray, sharpshooter with the BPI stood in front of him. Her file and picture were in his truck. How many times had he read her file? One dozen? Two dozen? It didn't matter what he told himself, the nagging feeling he knew her, recognized her from somewhere else ate his thoughts. Like the information was just beyond his reach. Detective Gray had been in his head all day, despite this being their first meeting. As he studied the files, he learned her record had been immaculate, making it easy to reject the idea she was part of the group behind the ersatz, and helping Elijah. So it didn't prove she was guilty but it didn't prove she wasn't. Then again, he didn't have evidence against any of the detectives, hence the investigation ... the one he was screwing up by manhandling Detective Gray.

Macy hated being the first one to break the silence, but the standoff couldn't last all day, or until another detective saw her in the arms of a lycan. She did not need that added to the list. "I'm Detective Gray, with the Bureau of Paranormal Investigations. If you don't release me, I'll use extreme force." Her voice was breathy and embarrassing and didn't hold the threat she tried to convey. She pushed the words through clenched teeth, ignoring the way they sounded.

In contrast to his tanned skin, her white knuckles gave away how tightly she held the hilt and how badly she wanted him to move. He blinked, amber to brown, and she saw con-flict—or maybe confusion—pass in his eyes. How long had he been in the warehouse? Was he going to push her to use force? Macy held her breath while he stared at her with his dark chocolate human eyes. Heat flooded her insides, and she knew it wasn't from the warehouse. *Embarrassment,* she told herself, *absolute embarrassment.*

*Let her go.* Kayne didn't respond, nor did he release her. He couldn't make himself when there were questions about her, and he wanted answers.

Pretending she had it all together, Macy asked, "Do I need to repeat myself?" She guessed the man, bare chest and all, must be Agent Sinclair. He could have taken her gun, her knife, and her life. He hadn't. He also hadn't answered her. He remained silent like he wasn't comprehending what she was saying.

Kayne grudgingly let go of the detective's wrists, splayed his fingers, and stepped back from her. "Agent Sinclair," he stated, his voice husky. "Department of Justice."

"Do you have a badge?" she asked. *And a shirt?*

Macy checked on the lycan in wolf form, and finding it was several feet from her, she took several steps from Agent Sinclair, creating more distance. His face changed from serious to irritated, and she couldn't stop the heat from spreading out from her core and over her already sweaty skin. His eyes darkened as his hands went to his hips, and his body relaxed. His bare chest shone with sweat, highlighting the dried blood, dirt, and the crimson flakes that fell from shiny scars marking his toned stomach. Following the line of dark hair, smears marring his hips disappeared into the waist of his filthy blue jeans. More scratches, cuts, and scrapes riddled his body, none of them matching the amount of blood or the damage done to his clothing. Damn lycan must have shapeshifted after the fight with the Hunter Wolf form.

Kayne watched her watch him and saw fury in her gaze. "The badge is in my truck. It's parked in front of the warehouse. You must have seen it."

"The black wreck with no windows?" Macy asked. *With files on the floorboard?*

"Affirmative."

"We all saw it." Macy wanted to ask him who his commanding officer was, and maybe three, four more questions as retribution for restraining her. But the approaching lycan and its clicking nails took her attention. "I don't know what protocol you follow being part of Blood Rain, Agent Sinclair, or if there is a protocol for a lycan DOJ agent when dealing with a loose lycan in wolf form, but there are humans inside of the warehouse, and *that* will have to be given a tranquilizer." She started to take the tranq from her vest. "Per BPI protocol the lycan needs to be sedated."

"Not necessary, he's under control," Kayne assured. He lowered his right hand, and the wolf stopped. Detective Gray, spy suspect, followed protocol.

"Maybe you misunderstood. I didn't ask you if *it* was under control, I stated there are humans in the warehouse. Per protocol, the lycan gets sedated." Macy shoved her authority into her eyes and held his stare.

*Are you going to carry his limp body out of the warehouse?* "Negative. It's not necessary. He isn't going to do anything," Kayne insisted. *You're armed with a gun and syn silver,* he wanted to point out.

Not believing him, Macy kept her eyes on the lycan as she left the tranq in her vest and reached for the mic. "This is Gray, I found Agent Sinclair. Repeat, I found Agent Sinclair and a lycan in wolf form." Silence followed as she waited to hear someone. At this point, she would take anyone, even Agent Kriss and Detective Ramirez. "I repeat, there is a lycan in wolf form. Prepare transportation."

*A syn silver lined cage, nice.* "The wolf is the husband of a woman. I lost track of her. Did you find her?" Kayne asked.

"The one beat up so badly she might not survive, and if she does, she'll live the rest of her days as a lycan? Affirmative, we found her." Macy turned with the last of her words, not wanting to look at him, and waited for someone to respond.

Did she have to counter everything he said? Affirmative. Kayne bet she challenged everyone. The tension in Detective Gray's shoulders was obvious through the body armor and tactical gear she wore. Rather than argue with her—he would never win—he forced himself to ignore her comment.

"They were locked in the container he jumped from. Every container will have to be searched."

*No shit.* "We are aware. Agent Logue took the woman out," Macy replied in an exasperated breath, as if she had explained it a thousand times. *Calm down.* She was going to put her hand on the butt of gun when she noticed it was still on the floor and she had a death grip on the knife. *I'm losing it, in front of a DOJ agent, who will report everything to Sergeant Mayco. Great. Add that to my file.* Macy quickly slid blade into the sheath, picked up her gun, and holstered it with as much dignity as she could muster.

"Agent Logue is here," Kayne mumbled. Knowing his team was there changed the direction of his thoughts. "Who else is here?"

"Agent Pixley, Agent Brecht, Agent Lyrick, Agent Flynn, Agent Kriss, and Commander Wilson. Your Blood Rain team came looking for you, Agent Sinclair," Macy answered, facing him. *Your mistake blew your investigation, didn't it?* "They're calling in White Rain."

The entire Blood Rain team and White Rain. Damn. Something must have happened because the team wasn't supposed to be there for two more days. The plan, which he was destroying, was to meet with Commander Arden, offer the BPI Blood Rain's help, and have his team work side by side with the BPI detectives. He hadn't told anyone when he left Feather River, not even his pack, and when he was supposed to meet with Commander Arden, he didn't. Today was not one of his better days. Commander Wilson was going to have a field day with him for putting the investigation at risk.

"When you didn't check in and there was no communication, they sent Blood Rain and two teams from the BPI." Macy's voice sounded strained. She was barely keeping her frustration under control, and she decided she hated Agent Sinclair. Damn lycan. "To find you they felt an interagency relationship was more effective."

"You've met Commander Wilson," Kayne replied, trying for a lighter tone.

There were too many questions hanging between him and the front of the warehouse. She said they all saw his truck, did that mean she found the files? Did he destroy his opportunity to investigate the BPI while pretending to help them investigate the Hunter Wolves? Kayne hoped not. As quickly as possible, he needed to get to Commander Wilson, without jeopardizing himself, the investigation, and his team. In the off-chance Commander Wilson had given him an excuse to be there, eliminating BPI's doubt, he might as well start the investigation with Detective Gray.

"Affirmative." Macy checked the lycan.

There was no humor in her tone and her eyes turned darker with her anger. With the tension between them thickening, Detective Gray wasn't going to answer any of his questions. He would have to wait.

"Did anyone call medical or whatever agency serves as shapeshifter support?" Kayne asked.

Macy met his gaze, and with an irritated edge, like he thought she didn't know how to do her job, and responded, "Without going into detail, affirmative, Agent Sinclair, everyone who needs to know does. We're wasting time." She remained where she stood, clearly wasting time and trying to think of a way to get the lycan out of the warehouse without Sergeant Mayco finding out she didn't sedate the animal.

With Detectives Gray's hostility, Kayne didn't want to ask her any questions ... hell, he didn't want to talk to her. But she was right when she said they were wasting time. He needed to get to Commander Wilson, have the proper care for Henry, and check on Grace. Detective Gray shifted, looked like she was searching the room, while whatever caught her attention cradled her face for an instant, then it was gone. Her eyes went back to the wolf and silence thickened between them. It was then he understood the radio silence was causing her apprehension. Good. He hoped she was miserable.

"There might be a deadener in here," he offered.

A team of damn shapeshifters and not one of the super-power group had heard the gunshot with their heightened hearing. They were worthless. Macy's ears were still ringing. "It appears that way. The deeper you go, the less the radio works. It might be simple interference. Hopefully, once we get close enough to the others the radio will feed from their signal," Macy explained through a breath and looked around. "Until then, what about the lycan? Need I repeat protocol and there are humans present?"

"He isn't going to attack anyone." Kayne could say it a thousand times and it wouldn't change the mortal's mind. Especially BPI.

"How can you be sure? You found him in here, God knows what happened to him, and I saw what he did to the woman. His wife," Macy countered.

The wolf whined, and Kayne drew a slow breath, letting it calm his frustration. He wanted to tell Detective Gray he was going to take great pleasure in investigating her, and after that, he wanted to explain as the alpha of the Garrick pack, he could keep Henry in check. He wanted to assure her that she and her fellow mortal detectives were safe. Not all werewolves were killers, and while Grace looked like death's next victim, she was alive. But Detective Gray, a mortal, wouldn't believe anything he said. It didn't matter if she knew thirty werewolves with clean records; as a BPI detective, she saw the evil in all shifters. *Cautionary. Has expressed prejudice toward all shapeshifters, paranormals.* He hadn't made things better when he restrained her, forcing her to struggle in his grip.

"As team leader of Blood Rain and an alpha, I think I can handle one wolf," Kayne assured.

*Like you handled the Hunter Wolf form*? Agent Sinclair, alpha and team leader, was lost in a warehouse and refusing to take orders. She wasn't impressed. Macy looked toward the front, carefully considering her options. All zero of them. It didn't change BPI protocol, which stated they needed—she was sure there was a *shall* in there somewhere—to tranquilize the lycan and carry it out in a cage with the appropriate agency in control. There was no agency present. She shook her head, imagining the lycan running free through the warehouse, Agent Sinclair chasing it and Sergeant Mayco waiting for her. Agent Sinclair's impatience drifted over her as he waited for her to make a decision. If she agreed, she was allowing the lycan to walk freely and giving it a chance to harm others.

Humans. Detectives.

It would be another mistake. Sergeant Mayco would see it as agreeing with a lycan about a lycan. How the hell was she going to get the lycan and Agent Sinclair to Agent Pixley and Sergeant Mayco when they would meet other detectives? It was obvious Agent Sinclair wasn't used to anyone questioning him and his authority. Still, it didn't change her instincts and the warning screaming in her head. She didn't trust him and trusted his skills as an agent even less. After finding her file in his truck, she didn't like him at all. The BPI was there to rescue him, not the other way around.

Macy met his glare. "If it attacks, I'll kill it." It wasn't what she planned to say, and wasn't the appropriate thing to say, but it was the truth and too late to take it back.

"Wouldn't expect anything less." Kayne's voice vibrated through the space between them.

Unlike Agent Logue and the growl he had allowed to roll through his words, Agent Sinclair was careful. There was no growl, just his authority and otherworldliness.

The wolf whined louder as it sunk to the ground.

"Lead the way," Kayne insisted.

Of course he couldn't find his way out. "Fine." Macy wanted to laugh—long, hard, and loud. It would have eased the tension coiling in her body from finding the lycan, Agent Sinclair, and the little chat she had with Agent Logue. *Going to pay for that one.* She met Agent Sinclair's dark eyes, paused, and couldn't help noticing his bare chest, the blood spoiling his tanned skin, and the short pink lines standing out over his ribs, arms, and sides. Under his skin, as if they were fading webs, gray lines traced throughout. Somehow, he had been poisoned with syn silver, survived, and fought the Hunter Wolf. *Fought and won*, she thought. *Stop, get to the front of the warehouse where human detectives are waiting.*

Eyeing the lycan, she opened her mouth to once again tell him she didn't like it was free, when his narrowed gaze blazed amber, turned from her, and he gave her his back. His dismissal of her burned through her; he had no idea what was going to happen when Sergeant Mayco found out she agreed with him. Agent Sinclair's muscles flexed down his spine, his shoulders bunched with anxiety, causing his holster to tighten around him. The leather crisscrossing his back didn't hide the blackened skin surrounding the four jagged holes puncturing the skin over his shoulder blade. Syn silver. It explained why he wasn't wearing a shirt, and why he shifted when he knew it was against the rules. Not only against the rules, against the law.

Damn, she didn't need this. She didn't like lycans ... hell, she didn't like shifters in general, and wasn't going to feel sorry for one of them. Macy blew a breath out and stared at the line of runes in black ink following his spine, to his jeans. It wasn't uncommon for alphas to have tattoos representing their beginnings, the pack, their strength, and their history. By the look of Agent Sinclair's, his life had been extensive. One peeking out from the cross strap of his holster made her think it was a sign of death. He lost someone. A wife? A family member? She did not care. Nope. She didn't care what the symbol meant.

"Commander Wilson and Captain Dixon need to know you're alive, Agent Sinclair. We have to join the team," Macy demanded.

"Wait." Kayne raised his left hand, telling her to be quiet.

Macy rolled her eyes. "We need to join the team."

"I thought I heard something." He tilted his head, his eyes staring at nothing. "Who do you have specializing in paranormal welfare?"

His anxiety was palpable and something about it deterred her attitude. "Sanative. It's a trauma center and recovery unit. Doctor Locke is a lycan, alpha of the Gawain territory, and head of the hospital. He's either here or will be here as soon as possible."

Kayne considered her answer, figured it might be the reason for the uneasy feeling, and stared at the back of the warehouse. "Does he deal with empaths?"

"Affirmative. Agent Pixley said there was one in here, and the other agents have felt its influence. How are you?" Macy asked.

"Fine. It's weaker now. Could be the amount of people." His instincts hummed with a warning. "Are there agents outside?"

"Detectives and agents are patrolling the perimeter. One human and one shapeshifter per pair, safer that way." Macy gauged him. What the hell was he thinking?

"We need to go. I have to talk to Agent Pixley." Kayne paused to listen and tried to understand the cause of his hesitation. If his instincts were stronger, he would know exactly what was tripping him up.

*Very good, Agent Obvious.* Macy looked at the lycan and the agent and knew it was a bad idea to walk into a group of BPI detectives with them following. There was no other choice and whatever fallout happened when Sergeant Mayco saw her was going to be rough. Inwardly, she threw her hands in the air like she was giving up, turned, and started toward the narrow break. Each thump of her boots exaggerated the growing distance stretching out in front of her. After rounding the corner, and confident Agent Sinclair couldn't see her, her ramrod straight back curved, beginning with the slumping of her shoulders. As she walked, the feeling of his fingers wrapped around her wrists and his arms holding her against his chest teased her, taunted her. *It's because he's a lycan. A damn lycan.*

Macy's pace quickened. All she had to was get the lost agent to the DOJ and he would be their lycan babysitting, shirtless problem. The warehouse would be investigated, and he and his pet would be nothing but a memory. As she refused to turn around to make sure he was following, the nagging feeling something wasn't right dug in. It was Agent Sinclair and his nervous energy; it caught her in its morass and had her on edge. She doubted the reliability of his instincts but couldn't dismiss him completely. There was something wrong. Besides death saturating the warehouse and the evidence of prisoners, White Cell, and Hunter Wolf forms, there was something calling her.

*It's natural to have reluctance in an environment mirroring the catastrophe at Harper's warehouse*, she heard the therapist's voice assure her. As quickly as the voice had taken shape, Macy shut it down. A warehouse on the outskirts of town, Hunter Wolf forms, shipping containers ... although Harper's didn't have prisoners, the idea behind it was the same. She took a deep breath, grudgingly checked behind her to see if Agent Sinclair was following, and saw he wasn't. *Nice.* Bending down, she grabbed her helmet and waited.

It was Harper's warehouse on a bigger scale, and the BPI didn't have any witnesses, leads, or anyone who knew anything about the condition of Pennsky. They had nothing. In a world of reports, cameras, cell phones, social media, linked computer systems, and plain nosy people, they had nothing. Maybe Agent Sinclair had found something. Maybe the couple would be able to identify who locked them up. Maybe they'll find out who's trying to destroy the city and the relationship between paranormals and humans. Those were a lot of maybes left up to shapeshifters and a bureau that didn't trust their detectives. The fear Macy might not be there to work on the case haunted her. Sergeant Mayco would make sure Captain Dixon knew she found Agent Sinclair and the lycan, and it wouldn't be because she simply ran into them.

"Damned if you do, damned if you don't," she mumbled. Clicking the mic, she prayed the radio worked, and reported,

"Advise, Agent Sinclair is safe. I repeat, Agent Sinclair is safe." One second. Two seconds. Static. "I'm working my way to the front."

*Come on.* Macy watched the aisle for the agent while continuing to think about the repercussions and Sergeant Mayco when she heard movement on the other side. If it was another DOJ agent, she was going to tell him exactly where they could find their man. Her job was done. And when she finished with him, she was going to find Detective Ramirez and explain how he should have been her backup. She slid between the containers, anger fueling her, and her mind racing with creative diatribes.

On the other side, she anticipated seeing a detective or agent, and with her anger ready to explode, she stepped into the empty space. Total let down. She exhaled her disappointment, her patience thinning, and leaning against the container, rubbed the back of her neck and the knot of muscles. After wiping her sweaty hand on her pants, Macy inhaled, and figuring she needed go back through and wait for Agent Sinclair started into the gap.

*It can't be easy, can it?*

Halfway between the containers, pain erupted where a hand/claw gripped her upper arm, its sharp nails tearing through the sleeve of her BDU top. A tighter hold and it threatened to rip the thick compression undershirt. The claw shook her back and forth, making her shoulders hit each side, her helmet clanging as her head bounced off the containers. Struggling to stay on her feet, her nails grated on metal as she fought to grab the container and stop herself from slamming into their sides. When she feared losing consciousness, it yanked her out of the gap, tossed her into the aisle—its strength sending panic coursing through her—then it growled, and stalked toward her.

*I'm trapped,* Macy thought as she scrambled backward.

---

# CHAPTER EIGHT

Blasts of light exploded in her head and eyes as a haze crowded the edges of her mind. *Stay awake.* Just as she was getting to her knees, her assailant pushed her hard on the back, making her fall forward. She threw her hands out to protect her from the concrete, and her helmet went spinning across the floor. Her heart pounded in her chest as she stopped herself from skidding and half crawled to the closest container. With her pulse rushing in her ears and fear gripping her heart, Macy turned around, putting her back against metal, and pulled her gun from its holster.

*Dear god.* She had looked at his picture for days, and for days wondered where the hell he had gone. Despite the half transformation disfiguring his body, she recognized Mr. Barrette. Rather, what was left of him. His barrel chest rose and fell with each labored breath, and his cat-shaped eyes glared from sunken sockets as he stood in front of her. Sweat soaked the remains of his shirt and slacks, and dirt stuck to fabric, making dark, wet spots. Through the strips of cloth, she could see bleeding wounds swollen with infection.

"Mr. Barrette, stay where you are," Macy ordered, thankful her demand sounded forceful. With slow movements, because she didn't want to provoke him, she started to stand. "Stay where you are."

Mr. Barrette's head lolled to one side in confusion, but he didn't move. He studied her with gold eyes, his uncertainty sitting in their depths. How many days and he couldn't complete the crossover? Had he been in the warehouse the entire time? And if he had, what had the empath done to his mind? His eyes skated over her to the containers behind her, and slowly came to a rest on her gun. With her left hand, Macy reached for her mic, desperate to reach someone, grabbed pieces of black plastic, and the shattered remains fell to the floor, leaving her on her own.

Without the mic, the cord dangled from her waist, its end hitting the back of her legs. If he attacked and caught the cord, he could strangle her with the damn thing. She hesitantly reached for the end connected to the radio unit at her side when Mr. Barrette took a step forward, inhaled, and roared. The primal cat mixed with human vibrated off containers, and the painful pulsation flooded her ears. His roar ended and he wavered back and forth, unbalanced by the distortion of his body, and his mismatched feet. He wore one brown loafer on his left humanoid foot while his right foot— a bare, misshapen, bloody mess—flexed, forcing his semi-humanoid toes straight. Macy cringed at the sight of long, dirty nails jutting out from his flesh.

"Mr. Barrette, go to your knees," Macy ordered. "Help is here." *He's as good as dead, like his wife.*

His back straightened and he stood as a man. For a breath, he held the position, then his shoulders slumped, his spine curved, and he continued to ignore her. Macy watched him while cautiously returning her gun to its holster, then she yanked the cord from the radio unit, dropped it, and carefully eased the tranquilizer from an inside pocket on her vest. Good thing she hadn't used it on the lycan. The palm-sized syringe was for attacks when you had exhausted all other options. It was nothing more than a false sense of security. If you were close enough to stab an attacking shapeshifter, you were as good as dead, and should use it on yourself to spare yourself extra pain. The BPI needed answers. She needed to clear her name. With the cylinder clasped in her sweaty palm, she told herself she could get close to him without him attacking her. Sure, she could.

Wet wrinkles scrunched his clammy, buttery yellow skin that covered twisted webbing of his pulsing veins, while tight muscles stood out like sinuous cables, bursting from under flaccid flesh. Macy couldn't stop from holding her breath, like it was going to save her from seeing his deformity in her dreams, and slowly approached him. It was a sight from a horror movie, one with a mad doctor who had made a cruel mistake. Mr. Barrette stood five feet from her with his head bowed, his shoulders slumped, and his claw/hands clenched into fists. She searched his body, wondering how he was alive. Shards of human were left untouched by the shift. His sun-bronzed face stood out against his black hair sticking up from his skull in thin patches. A torn, dirty, white button-up shirt hung from bulky shoulders while its ripped sides revealed a protruding rib cage. His soiled, black slacks were missing material around his knees and hung off misshapen hips. Uneven, his left side sat higher than his right, and she could see crimson dots peppering his face.

Taking another couple of steps, Macy held the syringe tightly in her left hand, regretting holstering her gun. The BPI needed answers. Mrs. Barrette. David. Sergeant Mayco. The woman. The people responsible were going to pay. Mr. Barrette raised his face to her, his cat-shaped eyes narrowing on the syringe, and she felt fury emanating from him in waves. She stopped and considered tossing the tranquilizer, grabbing her gun, and ending him, when a roar thundered in the warehouse. They both looked toward the back as another roar joined the first and dread flooded her stomach.

"Mr. Barrette, look at me. Help is here," Macy assured, trying to keep his attention. "I can help you."

Mr. Barrette's claw/hand came as a blur. The hit sent her stumbling backwards, the syringe bounced off the concrete with light metal clicks, and she hit a container with her shoulder. She rounded, her back against metal, and pulled her gun from its holster. Her vision blurred. In a heartbeat, it focused, and she meet his gaze. His face softened into the handsome man he had been, and then he blinked his gold cat eyes and they melted into dark velvet brown and the depths of his pain bled into them. She didn't want to know how she knew or why she understood, but she did. Mr. Barrette knew his wife hadn't made it out of the house alive, and it was a matter of time before a Death Bloom took his life. He had come to terms with his death. Mr. Barrette wanted to die. His animal was killing him. *Damn it.* Gripping her gun, Macy knew she was going to pull the trigger because he was going to force her.

"St-Stay where you are. I c-can get you h-help," she stammered. *God, stay where you are.*

He looked down at his body, then back at her, as if showing her the monstrosity he had become. His chest heaved with his rapid breathing. Macy waited, and hoped he believed what she said.

"I can help you," Macy pleaded. "Please let me help you." *Don't make me shoot you. Don't make me kill you.*

Mr. Barrette's howl bellowed at the same time he raised his claw/hands, his lips pulled back, showing a combination of humanoid and cat teeth, then he charged her. Damn fool. He became the target. Three long strides. He growled as the shift rippled through his body, gold engulfed his cat's eyes, and strings of ruby slid from his mouth as his lengthening teeth punctured his lips. Blood splattered the concrete, leaving a trail behind him.

*Bastard.* Macy inhaled, raised her gun, met his golden gaze one last time, and pulled the trigger.

With mumbled curses, Kayne stalked from the room in the direction of the aisle Detective Gray hurriedly marched toward. Keeping the wolf safely behind him, he assured himself it was going to be worth it, as soon as he made it to his team. *Sure.* If the evidence wasn't enough for the Council, he would have to look harder for Elijah, but it would be enough for the DOJ. Kneading the tension in his neck, he adjusted his stiff holster to keep it from rubbing his sides and back raw. *It's going to be worth it.*

He rounded the corner, entered an empty room and fury shot through him when he realized Detective Gray left them on their own. Kayne glanced at the containers, his eyes blurring, making the end-to-end rows seem to go on forever. He swore if he made it out of there, he never wanted to see another shipping container, warehouse, or anything resembling the desert. And he hated the damn heat. When his eyes focused, he checked his anger—it wouldn't do him any good—and kept his mind from wandering.

Detective Gray could have met up with another detective and slipped through a break between containers. *Right* ...

If she had, she would be on her way with a tranquilizer and a cage for Henry, per protocol. Or she went ahead to report to the mortals there was a lycan coming in their direction and they needed to get the tranquilizer and cage ready. With her promise to shoot Henry, Kayne needed to reach Commander Wilson before the BPI intervened. The eerie sensation continued, and infecting his instincts they hummed with warning. He knew he couldn't trust what he was sensing, but if there were Hunter Wolves coming, Detective Gray was safer with him. Because Kayne would protect her. After she threatened him with a knife to the throat, he would protect her? It had him shaking his head. When he stopped, lowering his left hand, Henry brushed his leg and stopped at his side. He waited, his nerves jumping under his skin, as alarm crawled over him, dug in, and spread out.

*What's happening?*

A roar thundered. Not from a Hunter Wolf, or a werewolf ... no, it was a therian-lion spliced with human. The aching cat sound made Kayne jerk his head in the direction he guessed Detective Gary had gone. If he had full use of his senses, he would be able to find the therian. Another deep roar bellowed but it wasn't the therian's hurting mewl. Twisting, he searched the tops of the containers and anticipated seeing a Hunter Wolf. With the next roar, Henry lifted its head, let a guttural howl free, and lowering his muzzle, he gave Kayne a shadowed look and darted off. Without hesitating, he followed, hoping to find the detective before the Hunter Wolves and the therian-lion. Running ahead of him, Henry wove, made a sharp turn as if pulled by strings, and disappeared between two containers and out of sight.

The therian-lion's wail rode the air, the Hunter Wolves' barking overtaking the crying, and he struggled to isolate the direction it was coming from. His senses were improving, but they weren't good enough to keep up with the commotion in the warehouse. With no other options, he continued down the aisle, following it until it ended in another empty room. Detective Gray wasn't there, hadn't been there. The therian's sorrowful cry ended, and turning into a furious roar, its deep bellow promised death. Kayne needed to find it.

With his next step, a gunshot blasted, echoed off the containers, and died. He stopped, waited, and felt the emotion in the warehouse embrace chaos. Using the link to try and find Henry, he felt its weakness and gave up. The need to get to his team grew urgent, and if he needed another reason, an invading Hunter Wolf roared. Feeling crazed, he knelt and prepared to jump to the top of the nearest container when a second growl responded to the first, creating a corrupted chorus, and they roared as one. Kayne reminded himself he wasn't alone anymore, and his one round would turn into dozens with Blood Rain's presence. To push the urgency, barks tangled in growls exploded from every direction.

Hunter Wolves were flooding the warehouse, their wild insanity saturated the air. It surrounded him as their darkness bullied through to touch him. He didn't have a choice. Kayne jumped, landed on the top of a container, crossed it, when in mid-stride he caught a ribbon of Detective Gray's scent. Leaving his perch, he landed on the ground, inhaled, breathing more of her in, and recognized her fear as it rode beneath the threads of syn silver. Her scent, her fear, and syn silver tangled to make a toxic potion. He exhaled to get the strongest trace from his nose, cursed, and stepped back. Sprawled out on his stomach, the therian-lion, half shifted, remained motionless on the concrete while a pool of scarlet laced with black blood spread out and soaked the tattered material of the man's shirt. He growled. The low rumble vibrated his chest as he knelt beside the body and his thoughts went to Detective Gray and her actions. She intentionally left him to find the therian, not a Hunter Wolf, and then shot the man in his most defenseless state. In the midst of shifting.

Like a coward. Like a fucking mortal.

What did he expect when she was prepared to shoot Henry? *Per* her file, while at Harper's warehouse she was confronted by Hunter Wolves and proved she would down a shapeshifter. After a Hunter Wolf attacked and killed an officer, it turned its attention to Detective Gray, who shot it twice in the head, killing it. The coroner pronounced Officer Murphy dead at the scene, while a doctor—he knew now as Dr. Locke—transported Detective Gray to Sanative Hospital. An alpha werewolf took a mortal cop to a paranormal hospital to treat her wounds. Why?

The reports from detectives, officers, and Internal Affairs convinced Kayne someone knew about the search warrant for the warehouse and planned a trap for the BPI and DRPD. No one knew why. Kayne stood, made a note of where the body was, and continued. Had Elijah planned the trap? He knew someone in the BPI or the DRPD was giving Elijah information. But why would Elijah target the agencies his spies were working for when attacking law enforcement made the investigation a top priority? It would guarantee whoever was orchestrating the betrayal was going to be found. The questions continued to multiply; who was the spy, why did he think Detective Gray was part of it, and how were the ersatz involved?

Kayne took a left, jumped to the next container, and began running down its length, a repeat of the entire day. A twisted case of déjà vu. Jumping to another container, he searched the aisles for Detective Gray, Henry, and the Hunter Wolves. Several gunshots screamed through the air. He skidded on the toes of his boots, dragging on metal to slow down his momentum, and went to his knees. When he stopped, he lifted his face and smelled syn silver and blood. Another round of gunfire followed by mortal yells, enraged shapeshifter roars, and the warehouse went silent, save for the sharp ringing in his ears. Without his consent, his thoughts focused on Detective Gray. She might be able to defend herself against a half-shifted therian and maybe hold her own against a werewolf, but a werewolf in Hunter Wolf form and an ersatz?

They would kill her. They would kill the entire BPI team. And put Blood Rain in danger.

He raced along the tops, heading to the area where he left the dead ersatz. Detective Gray said she saw it, meaning everyone had. He leapt to another container, and another, each time landing with a thud. When shots rang out, he stopped and dropped to his stomach, not wanting to be caught in the crossfire. Yells sounded, the firing ended, and he waited for the aftermath. Orders echoed, trailed by more roars. After getting to his knees, he crouched and watched a Hunter Wolf jump from one to another, and trailing behind it a second followed, and together they sprinted toward the front of the warehouse. Giving them distance, he waited, then started to follow when Detective Gray's yells stopped him, and her voice swirled in his head. Her tone dredged up the memories he had fought throughout the day to forget and were better off in the past. He couldn't fight them and the Hunter Wolves at the same time. *It's the warehouse, nothing more*, he told himself. *Forget them.* He continued trailing the wolves, because he had the sickening feeling they were headed to the same place. Detective Gray.

*"If we face Hunter Wolf forms, I don't want to die."*

With the scene in front of her, Sergeant Mayco's words came back as a freaking foretelling of the future. He had known where they were headed and hadn't told her. Two

Hunter Wolf forms had him cornered in the remains of the office and were quickly closing in, while the open door mocked his retreat. Failure sat inside of her. Macy hadn't done anything to prevent it from happening. *No, because I was busy killing Mr. Barrette. A witness.*

A growl jerked her back to reality, and turning, she pointed her gun. Inches separated the tip of the barrel from the lycan's head, and she considered moving her finger to the trigger. She didn't know when the animal found her but was sure it should have been with '*I'm an alpha and team leader*' Agent Sinclair. It was one of them, a lycan, a Hunter Wolf form, loose to kill one of her team. Macy risked a glance at Sergeant Mayco, and saw he wasn't watching the encroaching lycans but was watching her. Of course he was. Priorities.

The lycan barked, getting her attention, then lowered itself to the ground, its belly grazing the concrete, whined, and acted like it was going to pounce. Macy watched it, wondering what she was going to do with it, when it sprang to its feet and rounding her it ran straight toward Sergeant Mayco. It was running at a team member.

*Shoot it, take the damn shot!* She stopped herself and tracked the animal while aiming her gun. When it covered several yards, it turned around, and pinned its flaxen eyes on her. One look and she felt its unspoken thoughts sink into her head as its desperate need for revenge burned a line between them. For a moment, Macy stared, stunned, a part of her understanding the lycan while part of her rejected the thought. Was she being influenced by the empath? Affirmative. Negative. It doesn't matter, lives were at stake.

"Go."

When the lycan turned away, she met the confused gaze of Sergeant Mayco. *Join the club,* she wanted to yell at him.

She pushed it aside and decided maybe later when there was time, she would think about what happened. After the Hunter Wolf forms were dead and everyone was safe. Sure she would. Next Sergeant Mayco would explain to Captain Dixon she was talking to lycans and when she was fired, she would have plenty of time to think about it.

*"You know shifters like you have a connection with them."* Negative. So why was the lycan with her and not one of the shapeshifter agents? She didn't want to know. She knew his reason for fighting—his wife and his transformation—because she understood revenge. Who didn't?

Macy skirted debris as she made her way to the left side of the room in search of a clear shot while to her right Agent Logue and Agent Kriss chased a Hunter Wolf form across a row of containers, all of them disappearing out of sight as they ran toward the back. Agent Pixley, Captain Dixon, and Commander Wilson were missing, including the woman. During the eruption of chaos, she hoped they had made it out before the attack, or the woman was as good as dead. In the center of the room, she watched the lycan stalk around the right side of a Hunter Wolf form.

*No. No. No.* For one wild second she fought the urge to yell, but she had no idea what the hell she would have said. How do you warn a lycan in wolf form? It leapt at the Hunter Wolf form, and dread sank inside of her knowing it wasn't going to succeed. The Hunter Wolf form on the right rotated its upper body in plenty of time to swing its long arm, swatting the lycan like it was a fly. The forced caused it to twist backwards in the air, and it landed with a sickening thump on the concrete floor.

Even with surprise on his side, he wasn't quick enough to beat the Hunter Wolf forms. Their speed added to their aggression and was another testament to what the BPI had been dealing with. There was something happening to all the shapeshifters. Negative, there was something happening to the humans who had taken White Cell. The BPI was investigating the outer fringes of the problem, not the real reason for the crimes. Someone was kidnapping humans, forcing them to take a corrupted version of White Cell, and it was turning them into something else. Like the Barrettes.

Macy checked the lycan. *Come on, come on, come on, get up.* She had no doubt he had been taking White Cell along with his wife. So, what made him different? Agent Sinclair. He said he was an alpha. The lycan obeyed him as if Agent Sinclair was its master, and when she confronted the lycan, Agent Sinclair mysteriously showed up. She knew after a crossover the new shapeshifter had a connection to its alpha and would obey, which meant he used his power as an alpha to force the lycan's wolf from him, saving him from Mr. Barrette's fate. The wolf was unconscious, and she regretted letting it try and fight the Hunter Wolf form on its own.

Quickly dismissing them as a threat, the Hunter Wolf forms turned their attention back to Sergeant Mayco and the open door. Neither rushed forward, neither attacked; they stalked as if they were corralling him. Sergeant Mayco was one human with an empty gun, making him defenseless. She needed to do something. Going to the far left where the background was clear, she raised her gun, fired, and hit her target. The syn silver round created a hole, and instantly blood welled to stain its massive chest. The wounded Hunter Wolf form stumbled into the second, and after gathering itself, turned its body and narrowed its gaze on her. Together they stalked toward her, making her heart seize in her chest, her lungs fighting for oxygen, and her mind reliving Harper's warehouse. And if they attacked at one time?

She didn't have enough rounds for both and wouldn't have time to reload; there was no way she could miss a shot. Targeting the wounded Hunter Wolf form, she fired. She hit it in the neck, and its grating howl echoed as blood flowed, and coating its thick fur, its claws fumbled to cover its throat. While it swayed back and forth, the second one continued approaching, then the wounded Hunter Wolf form fell like a heap to the floor.

*That's one.* Excited she may have finally killed one, Macy aimed her gun at the second and fired. A hit to its side; bad shot. If it noticed the wound, it didn't act like it ... rather it stopped several feet from her and considered her. She waited. Its pale yellow eyes showing no signs of Blood Rage narrowed at the same time it tilted its head, then it turned around and started in Sergeant Mayco's direction. She stood, stunned. She had never witnessed a Hunter Wolf form, especially the new breed, consider a threat or not, and move on. They were killers, plain and simple.

When Agent Flynn and Agent Pixley appeared, Macy stalked after the Hunter Wolf form, raised her gun, and prepared to fire, but then cursed and lowered her weapon. They moved into her background, and she wasn't going to risk firing. Everyone watched two more Hunter Wolf forms charge through the door behind the agents, then advance through the warehouse. There weren't enough curses in the world to express her frustration over the situation. Macy's breath left her lungs at the same time a surprised cry left her lips and she tripped ... no, was pulled down by the fallen Hunter Wolf form who gripped her left ankle and was trying to drag her. She thrashed to get free from its hold. It tried growling, the low rumble forcing blood to pour from the ravaged hole in its throat, its jerking movements making the first wound tear open. The closer it pulled her to the pooling blood the more she kicked at the claw with her right boot, then it squeezed her ankle harder, sending a burning pain into her calf muscle and knee. She stopped struggling, sat up as much as she could manage, raised her gun, and fired. Fur, skin, and brain matter sprayed out from behind its head, its grip loosened enough when she kicked its claw it fell to the ground allowing her to scramble to her feet.

Its large eyes stared at nothing as black filled them and tainted blood continued seeping from its wounds. Backing up, she checked her pant leg. No holes. No contagion. Clear of the dead lycan, her attention went back to Sergeant Mayco. The Hunter Wolf forms had corralled him, Agent Pixley, and Agent Flynn farther from the door and deeper into the office area where the warehouse walls met a container. When two more Hunter Wolf forms surrounded them, it was like water filling the room, the beasts were everywhere. Sergeant Mayco and the agents walked down the wall, creating a greater distance from the door, and from the new intruders. What was she going to do when she was on the outside? Macy's head throbbed from being hit and from the heat, her muscles screamed, her arm grew heavy, and her shoulders burned from holding her gun at the ready. It was making focusing difficult.

If she shot one of them, she would piss it off, and then what? There were a half a dozen others to take its place. Macy couldn't help them. She felt beaten. *Trapped.*

The word sank into her mind. Was it a trap? It might answer the question of why Agent Sinclair was in the warehouse. Was there more to his investigation than the BPI and the Hunter Wolf forms? With their retreat, the lycans were able to enclose the others, and her mind whirled around Agent Sinclair. Where the hell was he? Macy could use some help from the alpha agent. She felt time escaping her when one of the beasts broke the pattern, loped swiftly to the right, and targeting Sergeant Mayco, closed in. The second stayed in the middle, and flanked by the others, was confident no one would challenge their position. Helpless to do anything, she watched them do nothing more than intimidate the trapped agents, then images of torn bodies resting in scarlet pools haunted her.

"Not now. Not again," she whispered and gripped her gun. She ignored her doubt and fear and let her instincts take over. Getting rid of one of them was better than watching them destroy her world. With resolve driving her actions, she started toward the thick of them.

"This is not happening," Kayne growled and was quickly reminded of his one round.

The Hunter Wolves were working together, one charging forward, another darting back and forth, and changing with swift movements they circled the group, then repeated their steps. With each taunt, Detective Gray lost footage, having to retreat farther from Agent Pixley, who was kneeling on the ground and covering someone with her body. The wolf struck out, letting Detective Gray gain a foot, only to have it taken back with the advance of another Hunter Wolf. He watched while the detective attempted to get close enough to guard the others, and he tried to figure out how he was going to help. It made his chest tighten with panic thinking about them being ripped apart. Thinking about Detective Gray dying at the hands of an ersatz. Why? She did the ultimate disgrace by shooting and killing a half-shifted therian.

Detective Gray darted in, and chancing firing a shot, hit one in the chest, as another advanced, forcing her back. Did he believe the detective risking her life to protect Agent

Pixley and a wounded man would purposely shoot a defenseless therian? He believed the evidence, and it proved she would go to any length to kill a shapeshifter. Was part of her drive for revenge the officer's death? The investigation into her conduct? He didn't know, but if they made it out of there, he was going to find out. Kayne's thoughts bounced between the BPI investigation, and the rage and hate from the Hunter Wolves and their twisted insanity. Their lack of a wolf spirit, conditioning from the warehouse, and the empath's mental torture made their violence endless, the need for death working like an addiction they could never slake. They wouldn't hesitate to kill her, Henry, or the agents and detectives. They would plow through them as death's swift hand before he made it across the room. He would watch them die. Or watch as they were infected and fought the contagion the same way Henry and Grace had. Detective Gray would turn into the monster she hated.

Another attempt and Detective Gray failed to breach the wall of Hunter Wolves to join Agent Pixley. It didn't mean he couldn't use her as a distraction to get close and get them out of the damn warehouse. First, Kayne needed a gun. He saw the man Agent Pixley was holding wore the same uniform as Detective Gray, and as a BPI detective he would have a loaded weapon. Doubt slithered down his spine, chilling his heated skin and cooling the abrasions from his holster. Unless the detective was out of ammunition and he had to depend on Pixley. Kayne needed to get to them and get them out at all costs. Gauging the row of containers and their closeness to Agent Pixley, he started his plan.

Macy stole a quick glance to measure the distance between herself and the wounded Sergeant Mayco. The sickening feeling she would never gain enough room ate her resolve and made the ground the Hunter Wolf forms gained a painful retreat. All she was doing was stalling for time because she knew if they wanted to kill them, all the Hunter Wolf forms had to do was rush them and take them down with their claws, speed, and strength. If Macy, a detective, or an agent fired at the charge, they would risk hitting one of their own. She didn't have the energy, the time, or the ammunition to kill them all. The lycan raced forward into the center, and darting between the Hunter Wolf forms tried to separate one of them from the group. One dead was better than nothing. The Hunter Wolf forms closed in, blocking and then defending themselves, their actions stunning her. There was a method to their madness. They weren't attacking when they could—like rushing them—they were holding them in place, and waiting as if they were being directed.

"Holy hell," Macy mumbled. *They have a leader. Are they keeping Agent Pixley and Sergeant Mayco for their master?*

The lycan retreated to stand beside her, his bark making her cringe when his jaws snapped, and she turned to see another Hunter Wolf form approaching. *Shit.* How many were there? The lycan stalked forward, gaining ground on the new arrivals, and ran back to give her room. Macy took the opportunity, fired on the newcomer, and hitting it in the chest the shot created a glistening bloom. Firing a second shot, she watched another Hunter Wolf form reinforce their advance. How many shots? She lost count of her ammunition, lost ground, and they forced her farther from Agent Pixley and Sergeant Mayco. No way was she going to gain the ground back.

A short burst blasted through the air, sending her to the ground as its stream of fire cut through the Hunter Wolf forms, the spray of bullets ricocheting off containers. Commander Wilson leaned against the door frame in his torn vest, dirty and ripped BDU pants, and his face wet from sweat and beige with sand. He tucked the stock of the M-4 machine gun in his shoulder and fired another jet of bullets. The M-4 beat the hell out of her pistol. She knew tactically, her pistol was more efficient for the warehouse, its close quarters, and for the precision, but it didn't change the fact that she was thankful. Several Hunter Wolf forms stopped, their chests torn open by the bigger caliber of syn silver, their inhales sounding like oxygen seeped from their lungs, while crimson spilled from multiple holes. Macy held her breath and prayed the wounded fell.

They didn't fall.

The wounded howled and bayed as they limped and staggered, leaving a glittering black trial of tainted blood behind them. Finding the weakest one, she prepared to fire when it fell to its knees, and then to its stomach. One by one the others fell, hitting the concrete, breaking bones, and blood gushing from their wounds. Win. The group appeared confused as they looked at the dead, then bellowed as one, the deafening thunder ringing in her ears. She was staring at Commander Wilson, like he was their savior, and meeting her gaze, he nodded. He was going to give her cover. Taking advantage of their confusion, she stepped over the bodies, raced through the wall of Hunter Wolf forms, and felt the first stirrings of victory as she skidded to a stop in front of Agent Pixley. From his perch, Commander Wilson blasted another spray, sending her back to the ground, and destroying the rest of her hearing. Another one down. She craned her head, watched Commander Wilson empty his magazine, and disappear. In front of her the Hunter Wolf forms regrouped, sighted their prey, and started a new assault.

"Detective Gray," Agent Pixley yelled from behind her.

Macy hurriedly stood, half listening, the words a messy string around the ringing in her ears. The agent's yells drummed as she concentrated, and picking a Hunter Wolf form, aimed low. She wished she had the M-4 instead of her handgun, killing it would have been quicker.

*Focus.* She fired at its legs, trying to cripple it before it reached her and the others. As the shots tore through its knees, its jaw dropped open, it sucked wet gulps of air, and stalking closer showed no signs of pain in its yellow eyes. Her stomach rolled, her brain throwing images of David at her. She wanted to scream to release the explosion of chaos consuming her nerves and tightening her muscles.

Macy gripped her gun, fired another round of direct hits to its knees, and watched it stumble. Seconds later, it lost its balance, and its corded legs gave out, sending it to the floor. She released the breath she was holding, ran over to it, and in a panicked hurry, fired two rounds into its head, to have its skull burst in a spray of red and black against the floor. The threat of infection from the contagion and their poisoned blood were all forgotten as the drive to kill them engulfed her. Fury gripped her, and she struggled to contain the frustration as she took the empty magazine from her gun and replaced it with a new one. With her eyes on the group, she checked her vest ... damn, she was down to one magazine.

The group of Hunter Wolf forms retreated several feet, and for the second time, Macy felt a hint of victory. Both the BPI and DOJ appeared to be winning, but she was a human and didn't know how much longer she was going to be able to continue. Her lungs burned, her head pounded from the gunshots and dehydration, and her muscles burned from exhaustion. Part of her wanted to give up, but then she met

Sergeant Mayco's wounded gaze and heard the ragged cry escape his mouth. Stuck staring at him, she ignored Agent Pixley's yelling. What was she going to tell her ... another Hunter Wolf form was entering the warehouse? Nothing new. Where the hell did Commander Wilson go? *Please, God, let him be all right.* With each step, the agent scooted inches and fought to drag Sergeant Mayco to a safer distance.

Armed with a fresh magazine, she shot at the newest Hunter Wolf form before it could join the others and create a complete wall. If she kept them on the edge of confusion, she might be able to deter them from their plan. *I'm delusional.* Its angry howl made her shudder, and the constant bellow was driving her crazy, but keeping it separated from the others did exactly what she wanted it to do. It turned its attention from Agent Pixley to her. Macy shot again, hitting it in the side. Sharpshooter for the team and she couldn't make a shot. She was failing and letting Sergeant Mayco and the lycans get inside her head. She needed to calm down. If she missed, her plan was going to have a price, and it wasn't going to come cheap.

Another step backward, the Hunter Wolf form followed, and she gripped her gun, getting ready to shoot its legs out from under it. A growl alerted her to the lycan right before it leapt at the Hunter Wolf form. It swung its arm to deflect the attack and missed, allowing the lycan to land safely. The lycan skidded around the Hunter Wolf form's side and repeated the attack. With a hit, the lycan knocked it off balance, and the Hunter Wolf form landed on its side, its wounds opening and seeping black blood. The lycan retreated, she raced over to the fallen beast, and fired two shots. Taking two uneasy steps back, exhaustion threaded through her as she gazed at the Hunter Wolf form while the others regrouped. How long was she supposed to last?

The lycan barked, and readying to fire, Macy turned to see Agent Sinclair jump from a pile of fallen containers and silently land. Standing frozen, she watched the shirtless agent assess the situation before him, his amber eyes blazing from his stern face, and he found her and held her gaze. The determination in them told her he knew what he wanted, and when his eyes left her and found Agent Pixley, he started in her direction. Agent Sinclair's speed and strength were superior to her human traits, and he didn't fear the contagion, making it easy for him to evade the Hunter Wolf forms. Agent Pixley waited for him, and when he was close enough, she tossed him her gun. Without slowing, he made for the door and another advancing Hunter Wolf form. The entire charge took seconds where her attempts to do anything besides risk all their lives felt like hours. At least he was there, because there was no way she could have fought the remaining lycans and those entering the warehouse.

Agent Sinclair's presence pushed the Hunter Wolf forms to change their tactics. They stopped keeping them corralled and advancing on them, time sped up with their aggression, the anger showing in their jerky movements and guttural roars. One broke from the group and stalked closer, the lycan swiftly darted in, and Macy raised her gun, as the lycan leapt. Repeating their process, she hoped he knocked it off balance so she could shoot it. With a quick swipe, the Hunter Wolf form hit the lycan, sending it skidding across the floor, his limp body careening into the side of a container. The Hunter Wolf form didn't watch the lycan, it raised its arms, howled at the ceiling, chipping a shard from her sanity, and crossed the last few feet separating them. Macy squeezed the trigger, sweat dripped from her palms as the first shot rang out, then she fired a second and third time, each echoing around her and bringing a howl of anger. It didn't stop. Cursing, she backed up out of its reach and fired.

*Fuck.* Gasping for air, her arms dropped to her sides, and her eyes closed against a blast of white sparks. Needles of fire spread out from the back of her head, and wrapping around her skull drove into her eyes. *Stay awake.* She fought the darkness, forcing herself to keep her eyes open and her grip on her gun, then swayed as the Hunter Wolf form blurred. With fear building up, she couldn't stop her muscles from weakening and turning into wet noodles. Her eyes skated down the length of its body as she sank to the floor, her knees hitting the concrete with a crunch, and in a desperate attempt to save her face, she twisted to land hard on her right shoulder.

*Get up.* Macy struggled to roll to her stomach, she needed to her hand out from under her weight in order to push herself to her knees. Hard footsteps faded as her attacker retreated, leaving her under the scarlet gaze of the wounded Hunter Wolf form. *Shit.* She mumbled prayers hoping it died before it went into full Blood Rage. Black mixed with red blossomed and oozed from new bullet wounds as blood flowed freely from the older holes in its chest. The last shot she fired hit it above its ribs, its flesh melting where syn silver liquified everything it touched.

"How?" Macy whispered. How was it alive? Terror teased her as she watched it close in, her thoughts circling the idea the altered Hunter Wolf forms were the future.

Exhausted and scared, Sergeant Mayco's words played, his accusations deepening with the pain and failure to do her job. Macy got to her knees and risked looking at him, faced watching him die, the same way she watched David.

She didn't bother pushing the worries away, she didn't have the strength, and didn't want to fight herself. Holding her gun, she knew if she didn't make the shot and kill it, she was going to end up like David.

*You didn't lose your mark.* Affirmative, she didn't. And she didn't give up. Rage radiated from the Hunter Wolf form, threatening her determination and feeding her fear, making her fight feel pointless. If she could feel its rage as a human, how much fury was boiling inside of it?

Unsteady on her knees and with a haze closing in on her thoughts, she lifted her gun and squeezed the trigger at the same time the Hunter Wolf form swung its arm. Its clenched claw connected with the side of her head, the force throwing her backward, sending her skidding. When she stopped, she wasn't sure where she was, and any sounds died under the pounding inside of her skull. Automatically, she balled both hands into fists and felt more than understood her gun was missing. She didn't have the tranquilizer or her gun, and without a way to defend herself, she stopped fighting and rested her head on the cool concrete. Attempting to reassure herself, she struggled to remember where the rest of the agents and detectives were, and her mind went blank, but not before tears threatened to fall.

With her weakness, the salty water seeped from the corners of her closed eyes, tracking wet paths down the sides of her face. Their warmth faded on her hot skin, as the fog of unconsciousness closed in and took her into oblivion. She couldn't stop the spy, she couldn't stop the Hunter Wolf forms, she couldn't protect Sergeant Mayco, and she couldn't stop from drowning.

*Damn.* Macy gave up fighting and let the darkness take her.

---

# CHAPTER NINE

One. Two. Three. *Die already.*

In answer to his plea, it stumbled over its clawed feet, fell and crashed to the concrete with the weight of the dead. With one last roar, Kayne watched and waited, and when the Hunter Wolf didn't get up, a small amount of tension eased from his shoulders. His werewolf hearing had taken a beating with every shot, while the warehouse echoed with additional gunshots and angry howls. Turning around, he faced Agent Pixley, saw her face twisting with her words, and the worry lighting up her emerald eyes. At the same time, she was trying to tell him something he couldn't hear. She shifted the detective with impatient pushes, and finally raised her left hand, and pointed to the center of the room. While he tried to control his breathing, he searched the area, then stopped, the oxygen leaving his lungs in rapid exhales when he saw a Hunter Wolf near Detective Gray's body. He couldn't hear anything except the ringing in his ears, making it impossible to listen for her heartbeat. Was she alive?

*How many shots?* Kayne asked himself. *How many shots did she fire?* Not enough to kill it. When the ringing faded and the noises of the warehouse grew distinct, he dissected the various sounds and focused on Detective Gray. In his mind, he saw a shadow drift over her, covering her in darkness and making its home inside of her. The void reminded him of the ersatz—empty, spiritless—and Kayne stopped. Can't be the same. Detective Gray was a mortal. It had to be the empaths. He didn't have time to argue with himself when he needed to know she was all right.

The soft beat of her heart joined the weaker whimpers, and they sent the smallest ripple of relief through him. She was alive. With relief came rage. The warehouse was under siege, and he stopped to watch *her*. A sheen of blood covered the right side of her face, her hands were dirty, scratched, and bleeding, and despite having injuries, she tried crawling away from the Hunter Wolf. Kayne's wolf surged, his humanoid features morphing, his skin turning hot under the veil of sweat covering his chest and arms, and he knew he was going to lose control of his wolf in front of the DOJ and the BPI, and risk losing his badge. Why? For a detective who didn't hesitate to kill a therian. *She didn't kill the wolf,* he reminded himself. Maybe the therian attacked her, sure. Making excuses for a mortal was beneath him, and he hated himself for it. Still, he couldn't stop his wolf from wanting, needing to save her.

Kayne's body shook with the force it took to fight for control over his wolf, and when he dominated the beast, he shoved it back to its depths. Detective Gray's hair, free of the braid, fell to her shoulders as she clawed the concrete, her fingernails slipping and tearing from her skin, as the toes of her boots skidded and lost traction. Her mumbled curses fell under the raspy sound of the Hunter Wolf's harsh breathing, then it grabbed her ankle and pulled her backwards. She twisted to meet his gaze, fear darkening her eyes. They didn't hold the panic Kayne expected to see in a mortal. Detective Gray targeted the Hunter Wolf with a glare. Gripping

Agent Pixley's gun, he raised his hand and aimed it at the Hunter Wolf.

"Hey." Kayne's yell thundered across the warehouse.

Its massive head swiveled on its thick neck, and looking at him, its yellow eyes were overtaken by its saucer-size black pupils. *Head shot.* Kayne fired, the hammer slammed back and clicked empty, the echo of metal louder than any gunshot. Roaring in victory, it jerked Detective Gray, making her cry out, and stalked away from Kayne. A growl tightened his chest before working its way up his throat and stirred his wolf once more. He held onto the growl, forced his wolf back, and let his anger have freedom.

"Sinclair, she dropped her gun," Agent Pixley yelled. "To your right." She tried sitting up and pointing with her right hand while using her left arm for leverage.

Kayne met Agent Tippi Pixley's worried gaze, then the wounded detective as a heartbeat of time slipped by and he saw pain and raw dread churning their gazes. He did this. He was responsible for the entire mess. The detective fought Agent Pixley to look at Detective Gray, and she immediately stopped him and held him tighter. The wounded detective didn't care about his injuries, he wanted to check on Detective Gray. She risked her life for his, for theirs. While Agent Pixley talked to him, his brows knitted, then he glared at Kayne with accusations in his ice blue stare, as if blaming Kayne for the Hunter Wolf attacking him and infecting him with the contagion. *Get them out of the warehouse.* Turning away, he left Pixley and the detective and ran toward the abandoned gun. It wasn't a DOJ issued Glock, it was a BPI issued H&K .45, with a twelve-round magazine, thirteen with one in the chamber. How many times did she fire? No fucking clue. He needed one round, one shot to the head.

The Hunter Wolf heaved Detective Gray backward, flipped her to her back, wrapped a clawed hand around her throat, and lifted her off the concrete. Worry enveloped Kayne, shaking his resolve, and threatening to derail the shot. If he missed and hit Detective Gray, he would kill her. If he shot the Hunter Wolf, its contaminated blood would infect her. If he didn't do anything, she was going to die anyway. Gripping the gun, he ran at the Hunter Wolf, letting the growl free from his chest and a roar explode from his throat. The Hunter Wolf turned lazily to give him a challenged stare, begging him to come closer for the show. *This is it,* Kayne thought as he skidded to a stop. It was either going to snap her neck or let her fall.

While holding his stare, the Hunter Wolf squeezed, as if teasing him, lowered her to the ground, the tips of her boots grazing the concrete, and lifting her again, her weight added to the strain, making her cheeks blaze purple. Kayne took a step, only a few feet separating them, it squeezed, he stopped, it barked a laugh, and he cursed. His face held his surprise, which he rapidly masked, as Detective Gray's left hand, gripping her silver blade, slice deep into its wrist, causing blood to hit its muscled thighs and her pants. With a staggered jerk it let go, Detective Gray hit the concrete, her cry turned moan, and her knife skidded out of reach. It held its bleeding wrist, and taking several steps back, its glare narrowed on the fallen detective.

*Perfect.* Kayne raised the gun and fired. One. Two. The force from the shots drove the Hunter Wolf's battered body back and farther away from Detective Gray. It stumbled, to Kayne's surprise, gained its balance, and standing straight faced him. *Time to end it.* He aimed for its head, pulled the trigger, and its sickly eyes rolled back and out of sight as a combination of bright scarlet, thick, black liquid stained its fur. Kayne walked up to the fallen monstrosity, pulled the trigger until a metal click echoed, and with sweat sliding down his cheeks, he continued to slam the hammer before loosening his grip and lowering his arms. The gun hung freely from his hand as he gazed at the warehouse, the detectives, the agents, and saw the aftermath of his actions.

It had to be worth it.

The chaos from yells, gunfire, and roars stopped, and plunged the warehouse into an eerie silence. Kayne remained standing over the Hunter Wolf, looking for any signs of life. With the continued silence, he assumed the invasion had ended and the last of the attackers were in front of him. To be sure, he risked using his battered senses and searched for others. Threaded through the air like strands of energy were the signs of his team, the crux of werewolves and therians, and the crux of mortals, their anxiety easing and replaced with calm. It was over. As his senses let go, his mind grasped onto the frail beat of Detective Gray's pulse. The shadow he sensed, while weaker, remained. It could be from fear and pain. After killing the therian, she worked to protect the wounded detective and Agent Pixley, then faced saving herself from a Hunter Wolf. Whatever it was Kayne didn't like the way it felt and how it resembled the ersatz. It was another unknown about Detective Gray. He told himself he needed to check on her. *Not yet.* Was it panic holding him where he stood? Negative. He was staring at the Hunter Wolf, making sure it was dead.

The image of its thick fingers around Detective Gray's throat with its ashen nails pressed against her skin flashed in his mind. One scratch would release the contagion into her blood stream, and she would face becoming a werewolf. If she didn't get the antiserum in time. *It didn't scratch her.*

And if it had? They weren't werewolves. They were ersatz. Spiritless. Bloodthirsty. In the melee of fighting for his life, finding the lab, and finding Grace and Henry, he forgot about the White Cell. Henry hadn't been infected by a werewolf or an ersatz and didn't show signs of wounds from an attack. Kayne had found vials of the illegal version of CD4-T antiserum. Were the ersatz a product of contaminated White Cell? If they were, what did they infect their victims with?

His theory about the wolf spirit and the mortal spirit dying during the transformation fell apart with his overthinking. He was wrong. What made them remain in their animal form? Kayne wished he had the answers. Knowing he would get them eventually wasn't helping his patience. First, he needed to get out of the warehouse. Detective Gray's heartbeat reminded him the detectives needed medical care and they all needed the antiserum. He hung his head, closed his eyes, listened to the rhythm of her heartbeat, and his exhausted body relaxed into a quieted peace.

"Agent Sinclair," Tippi yelled, the words grating from her sore throat. She hated yelling at the team leader—the scars she wore from challenging a desperate werewolf were physical proof there were consequences—but she had to get his attention. "Agent Sinclair."

Tippi adjusted Sergeant Mayco, then pressed a rag, with God only knows what on it, over the gaping gash in his chest and stomach. After a Hunter Wolf wounded him, she had used her empath trait to ride his emotions and absorb his pain, but it left her trapped, and all she was able to contribute to the fight was yelling orders at the detectives and agents, who promptly ignored her. Believing the unnerving silence meant the warehouse was secure, the sergeant needed medical attention, STAT, because she could smell the contagion taking its hold on the human's body. She needed Sinclair's help.

"Agent Sinclair," she repeated.

The man wore cold detachment like a cloak, radiated power and authority with his six foot, six inch height, board shoulders, taut muscles, and if you met his amber gaze the rawness in them sent you back several steps. She guessed he worked his lean body day in and day out, and it was probably the reason he survived the warehouse, the empath, Hunter Wolves, and was still standing. Despite her yelling at him, he ignored her, and stayed standing over the dead beast, his head bowed, his shoulders hunched, and his wounds caused by syn silver seeped thick liquid. How bad had he been hurt? How long had he been in the warehouse with the empath? Unknown.

If the empath fed him his nightmares, his thoughts would be fighting for their places between reality and his imagination, and combined with his injuries, she feared for him. Tippi had watched him repeatedly pull the trigger, and when the gun clicked empty, he hadn't stopped. Hadn't checked his surroundings, his team, or the unconscious female detective. He remained standing over the body, acted unemotional and beaten, but it didn't match the ferocity with which he fought and the determination to save the detective's life. The sergeant shifted his body, his weight pinching her knee between him and the floor, and she budged him to free herself. Fighting the sergeant, Tippi repositioned him, and cringed when her hand dipped into the wound. He needed medical.

"Let me up, dammit," Sergeant Mayco groaned.

"Negative." She held him down, and when his fight weakened, she turned her attention to Agent Sinclair. "Snap out of it, Agent Sinclair."

Agent Pixley's voice sounded distant and unfamiliar, and he didn't want to listen to her, or anyone else for that matter. Kayne left the dead Hunter Wolf, checked the area for signs of others, and after finding it clear, approached Detective Gray. Scattered on the floor was the aftermath of the attack. Spent shell casings, blood, flesh, and the bodies of the dead Hunter Wolves, all of them in pools of their poisoned blood. Each of the half dozen steps felt as though he was walking through thick mud with weighted feet. His thoughts and concerns twisted inside of his mind as every fiber of his body told him to hurry, pick her up, and get her out of the warehouse. Once safely outside, Dr. Locke and his medics would take the victims to Sanative. Detective Gray wasn't paranormal. She was a mortal and her fragile body required mortal medical treatment. He didn't know the extent of her injuries, and if he moved her, he could turn those injuries fatal. With frustration a constant companion, he didn't want to wait for mortal medical to arrive, he didn't want to wait for backup, his team, or anyone or anything. With his muscles screaming in protest, Kayne knelt beside Detective Gray.

Agent Sinclair's callous behavior faltered as he knelt beside the detective and his narrowed amber stare bled to rich brown. Tippi didn't know why. "Do not pick her up. You cannot help her. Do not touch her. Agent Sinclair, you're covered in blood," she frantically ordered. *Gods, let him hear me.*

*"How far are you willing to go?"* Michael's question had irritated him. Kayne had looked at his third as if the man had asked the question, he knew the answer to, in order to annoy him. He answered, with the confidence of a selfish man, he would go as far as he needed. How easy it had been. Now it haunted him. This was too far, and it was his fault. If not for

his selfishness, she wouldn't have been attacked, none of them would have. This is the end. If there wasn't enough evidence to prove to the Council Elijah was alive, and he was responsible for the ersatz, and the kidnappings in Desert Rock, Kayne was finished. The DOJ would investigate, and he would happily go back to Feather River, the Moonlight Territory, and casting off his absentee alpha role, take his place with the Garrick pack. He would be the leader they needed, they deserved. Kayne accepted his decision, his resolve, and to his surprise, it eased his nerves.

With his thoughts consuming him, he absently reached out, his hand bloody from the fights, his arm bloody from his wounds, and it hovered her. Mortal. Nearly touching her, he realized his mistake, and stopped himself. With his hands on his thighs, he gazed down, knowing there was nothing he could do to help her. Couldn't check for a pulse, damn it, couldn't do anything because she was mortal, and he was a werewolf. The divide between them wrapped in polite equality, lycan, mortal, as long as nobody was hurt. With no other way to help her, he listened to her shallow breathing and faint heartbeat, the combination tightening his chest with helplessness.

A blossoming bruise edged the torn skin above her right eye, its curve reaching into her cheekbone where the Hunter Wolf had hit her while fresh scarlet seeped from the center of the deep cut, spread out, and mixed with sweat. The liquid blend created a crimson veil on the right side of her face, its fringes already drying in the heat. In places where there was little fatty tissue, white bone showed bright against red. There was blood in her hair and across her nose and lips, where it created a web, ending in thick lines down her neck. Despite Detective Gray's strength and willpower, seen when she used her knife on the Hunter Wolf, she was lucky to be alive.

"The warehouse is clear," Agent Logue reported through a breath. "Here, use these."

Kayne tore his gaze from the detective and looked up at Chayton, Agent Logue, to see him holding a pair of black gloves. Sand dusted his familiar face, dark hair, and uniform, and taking the gloves, he saw cuts and scratches scored his hands. In silence, Kayne started with the first glove, sweat making it impossible to pull on.

"The other detectives are safe, and the wounded are not in danger. The agents are unharmed. I can hear her heart-beat. It is weak, but it is there," Chayton commented.

"She's been out for at least two minutes," Kayne answered. "I think she has a concussion."

"If she has a concussion, she escaped a worse end," Chayton replied, his eyes landing on Agent Pixley and the wounded sergeant. "The cut looks deep."

*Yes, she did.* "Affirmative."

Kayne didn't explain how she received her wounds ... why when the details were meaningless, and they wouldn't help her. With both gloves on and his contaminated skin covered, he leaned closer to carefully sweep loose hair from her face and neck. No cuts. Gently moving his hand under her neck, he cradled the back of her head and slowly turned it to one side, searching for signs of fresh blood and scratches. When he found her skin unmarked, he changed hands, and again, slowly turned her head in the opposite direction. A purple and red bruise bloomed under suntanned skin, the edges of it speckled with bright red flecks where the Hunter Wolf had tightened its grip. Inside of the darker combination of colors, thick lines showed him how much larger the wolf's clawed hand had been compared to her thin neck. It hadn't scratched her. She was missing a couple of fingernails and there were scratches on top of her hands from fighting and hitting the floor—they looked superficial—while the black blood splatter dotting the left side of her body wasn't enough to soak through her BDUs. Her torn sleeve revealed her long-sleeved undershirt, which hadn't been compromised, and he didn't know who had attacked her and ripped her sleeve. It didn't matter when her tactical gear saved her. His worry eased, if only a little.

"Medical is waiting for someone to clear them so they can enter," Chayton reported hesitantly. "It is your call."

"Did any of the Hunter Wolves live?" Kayne asked, his attention remaining on the detective.

"Negative."

"Are there any in the immediate area?"

"Negative."

"How can you be sure?" Kayne asked roughly.

"Russell and I worked our way to the back of the warehouse, turned around, and searched as we headed here. If there were ersatz, we would have seen them," Chayton explained.

Kayne didn't look at him. "I want to make sure medical doesn't walk into a trap, no one else needs to get hurt. Do a thorough perimeter search and check for vehicles or anything looking out of place. When it's clear, you can let them in."

"Out of place?"

"They didn't walk here. Someone brought them." And released them after the BPI and DOJ entered the warehouse. Like a trap. The DOJ held their own, but the BPI, mortals, didn't know what they were up against. Kayne stared at Detective Gray's chest as it rose and fell with her shallow breaths and wondered if she was the spy. If so, why hadn't she known the ersatz were going to attack? And what about the therian? Who the hell was he?

"Affirmative, sir," Chayton answered.

He lingered beside Kayne with his hand on the butt of his gun and staring over his shoulder. Chayton Logue served as fourth in the Garrick pack, had witnessed Kayne's obsession with finding Elijah, and selfishly leaving the pack in search of evidence. Repeatedly. As he kept his gaze on the detective, he could imagine Chayton thinking he had completely lost his mind. He would worry about it later. Kayne physically checked her pulse, finding it stronger than it had been, its beat sending a feather of response into his fingertips. It wasn't good enough, not when he wanted her to wake up, look at him, and tell him she was all right. He held his breath when she whimpered, her head lolling to the left, her brows drawn in pain, but her eyes remained closed, and his worry spiked when her face paled. With his exhale, he drew his hand back, rested it on his thigh, and touching the dirt and blood staining the denim, knew if he wanted to touch her again, he would have to change his gloves.

Mortal versus werewolf. The great divide.

Chayton exhaled an exaggerated breath, catching Kayne's attention before he turned, his boots scraping the concrete floor, and he stomped off at the same time yelling orders. Kayne listened, Chayton's forceful steps and harsh commands telling everyone exactly what he thought of the situation. Whether it was his attention to Detective Gray, or being ordered to do a perimeter check, he wasn't sure. Either way, the Hunter Wolves had to have come from somewhere. With a quick look behind him, he saw Russell, Agent Kriss another member of his pack, join Chayton, and the two men left the warehouse. Jealousy snaked through him with a vengeance, knowing they were walking out of the warehouse, out of the rot, and the death saturating the air, and out from under the influence of the empath.

Kayne looked up, gauging the time of day by the dusty sunlight filtering through the broken windows, its dim glow failing to reach the darkest parts of the warehouse, making it impossible for him to tell. Damn, he wanted to be the person leaving. His lungs burned for clean air, and he longed to feel the wind that had thrashed the roof, on his skin, but he wouldn't, not yet, not when he was waiting for medical. He had been there for hours, he could wait minutes. Detective Gray and the other BPI detectives needed to get the hell out of the warehouse and needed the antiserum as soon as possible.

His eyes drifted from the broken glass to the closed door and over to Agent Pixley. She was sitting cross-legged on the floor with the male detective resting against her, her left arm hooked under his left arm, allowing her hand to rest on his chest. Her right arm was the same way, except her right hand held a piece of blood-soaked cloth. Kayne took a closer look and saw the detective suffered from a dozen cuts along his arms and chest and all of them bleeding. His long sleeve compression shirt—the last defense against the claws of a shapeshifter—hung in loose strips from his arms while thicker pieces of material rested against Agent Pixley's leg.

The detective was in good hands. Thankfully, Agent Pixley, like the entire Blood Rain team, had a trait, or gift as the Otherkin called it. As an empath she was able to absorb physical feelings like hunger, anxiety, and pain. The disturbing part, the one making him respect her, she could take those physical sensations from the body and intensify the feelings to the point of causing death. He saw the look of concentration and anguish on her face, and assumed she was easing his pain and taking it into herself. The BPI detectives weren't the only victims the day brought ... no, besides Detective Gray and the wounded detective, there was Henry and Grace. His eyes glided over Detective Gray to find Henry. His hind end and legs were up against a red container, his front half limp on the floor. The position left his body twisted, like the hit broke his back. The sight made Kayne cringe. They kidnapped him and his wife, then gave them White Cell knowing they would take it to protect themselves against the Hunter Wolves, then locked them up and waited for them to die. Very slowly. An image of the broken, bloodied face of Grace flashed in his head. Thanks to Detective Gray and Chayton, she had made it out. Hopefully.

While the warehouse wasn't the lab Kayne wanted and needed to prove Elijah was behind the ersatz, it was an example of his intent. Had Henry and Grace stayed and lived, they would have been subject to a cat and mouse game as the ersatz hunted them while fighting the empath's influence. Brutality was an understatement and used as an instrument to break the mind and body and then with a victory over their victims it would rewire their minds. The warehouse was meant to shape pain and fear as it made death their companion. Through the network of containers cruelty pushed them, terrorized them, forcing them to maneuver around the empty holes inside of their somas and inside of their minds. Elijah was creating werewolves devoid of emotion and reason without the primal insanity of Blood Rage.

Over the years, his hunts for Elijah had given him nothing, and had exhausted Kayne's reach and authority. As an alpha, he had to state the reason for travel in his requests to cross through territories while carrying mandatory documentation and pacts of protection promising he wasn't looking for a new territory. Those documents needed to be signed by someone in the Council. His last request had been denied, and Kayne realized he couldn't do it on his own. That was when the DOJ offered him a place with Blood Rain, and he knew it was the perfect answer to his problems. With the state of the warehouse, the evidence, and the Hunter Wolves, it looked like he was getting exactly what he wanted and would be spending weeks away from home. Absent from his pack. Encouraged by the confidence he was getting closer, despite blowing his cover and hindering the investigation, Kayne was going to change tactics and start over. It was clear the BPI detectives didn't know about the warehouse and what was going on.

*How could they*, Kayne thought, *when no one made it out alive?* If a victim escaped, they wouldn't have enough of their mind left to tell anyone what had happened, if they were in humanoid form.

His thoughts tangled in his head as he watched Detective Gray and thought about his earlier declaration when he decided he was going to end his search after putting innocent lives at risk. Was he going to give up? With conflict weighing on him, the irritating itch wouldn't end, making it impossible to stop the feeling she was hiding something from him. Kayne wanted to question her about the void living inside of her, the ersatz, the BPI detectives kidnapping victims, and Elijah. When she ditched him, she knew where she was going, like she knew the layout of the warehouse. And the Hunter Wolves. In the chaos of the attacks and the fights, and all their violence, they hadn't hurt her. They hadn't attacked *her*. They savagely attacked the detective, infecting him and leaving him. Was there a chance Detective Gray was the spy Captain Dixon suspected? He didn't know.

Kayne listened to her faint moan, her hand leaving the concrete and going to her stomach, resting on the curve of her waist and hip. The slight motion held his attention, and he couldn't stop staring when her head turned toward him. His chest clenched with need as he waited for her to open her eyes. *Detective Macy Gray.* She met his gaze through swollen lids, causing dried flakes of blood to fall, her brows drawing together in pain, while her face didn't pale, rather scarlet crept up and into her cheeks. The mortal detective he suspected as a spy, invaded his mind, had him worrying about her, and it scared him. Because he put her life at risk. Because she risked hers to protect Agent Pixley and one of her team. Nothing more. She did her job. Kayne inhaled, the tension in his shoulders tightening his wounds and sending pain down his spine when his breath caught.

Negative. No. It couldn't be. Kayne denied the memory. It was a lie, he tried convincing himself as he stared into familiar eyes the color of cinnamon and ringed with silver. Like precious metal.

Voices tagged along with consciousness, and creeping in dragged Macy from the haze, and giving her blurred images confused her worse. She didn't know where she was, how she got there, or why she wanted someone to cut her head from her body. The pressure exploding behind her eyes, the ringing in her ears, and the smell of blood said enough. Something bad happened. Emotions bubbled up, giving her fear, so much fear, and death, and images of Hunter Wolf forms. God, she was surrounded by them. Macy clenched her fists, had lost her gun, vaguely remembered losing her knife, and struggled to raise her arms which sent white fire to engulf her body forcing her to stop.

No matter how hard she tried, she couldn't make her arms or legs move, and trying rendered her defenseless against the blasts. Her gun was gone. Her knife was gone. She couldn't get off the ground. She was defenseless. Macy promised she would stop thinking if it kept the heated wave of nausea from rolling in her stomach and the panic simmering in her middle. The Hunter Wolf forms were there, stalking her, she needed her gun, at the same time she wanted to cry from the pain racking her body. *Don't panic.* She had to relax, assess her injuries, and start over. Inhaling for a calming breath, that was quickly denied, her chest tightened, and fighting harder, panic raced.

*Breathe.* She tried pulling her vest from her chest, her hands ached, and with each successful tug she gulped air, then her throat burned and her lungs collapsed. *Calm. Calm.* She plunged deeper into terror when the hard blade of suffocation intensified, her chest heaved and with shallow breaths, she couldn't get enough air. Macy's fingers dug into the vest, more pain, slipped on the stiff material and she struggled to tear it from her neck. She needed to get off the ground and out of her gear before she hyperventilated and passed out, again. Completely defenseless. Fighting to sit up, her head swam, her stomach rolled, and she forced herself to swallow, hard. Almost there. When hands gripped her upper arms, held her, and pushed her back, a moan of defeat escaped her, and she painfully willed her eyes to focus.

"Let go of me. I can't breathe," Macy ordered. Her mouth too dry to make a sound, and using what oxygen she gained, her lungs caved in once more. "Can't. Breathe."

"Relax," Kayne replied, using his steady voice to calm her. "I will help you after you answer a couple of questions."

Negative. She needed to sit up, the pressure was getting worse, and the haze was coming back. "Can't. Breathe."

"Detective Gray, calm down, I'll help you." Kayne felt her muscles contract in his hands, her left eye wide, staring at nothing, as if she couldn't see.

Macy wanted to scream she didn't need a lycan's help, and didn't want him touching her, but didn't think her voice would hold. Instead of wasting energy she didn't have and yelling at him, she struggled in his grip, and for a minute thought she was gaining. Then he drew her closer to him, pining her back against his chest for the second time.

*Shit. Shit.* The BPI detectives would see her, Sergeant Mayco, and Captain Dixon, and they would say she sided with the shapeshifters. Her job was already at risk, add her wounds and the BPI would use the combination to fire her. They would graciously show her to the door under the guise of a medical release. Early retirement. Damn Agent Sinclair, DOJ agent and lycan. With the feel of his skin, Macy used her anger to fuel her fight, but it didn't last long ... the pain in her head drummed, making her stop. Blinking back tears from frustration, failure, and the increasing pain, she let him hold her.

When she stopped fighting him, he eased his grip but kept his arms around her. "What is your name?"

"Macy Gray." She gave up. Damn if anyone was watching them. "Detective Macy Gray." Her rough voice grated her throat and she tried to swallow spit to ease the burn.

"What day is it?" Her muscles relaxed and she leaned into him, his arms cradling her, and he should have stopped her. He should have been wearing gloves, but the moment she opened her eyes, he had to stop her from hurting herself. *Keep telling yourself that. Silver, like metal.*

At her ear, his voice remained low, calm, and stern. Macy understood why he was keeping her still and why he was asking her questions. He suspected she had sustained a head/neck injury and a concussion. If the pounding and confusion was any indication, she knew she did. "Day?" The series of questions always seemed too easy ... what day is it? What's your name? What city do you live in? Being the one on the wrong end, she hated it, and didn't know what day it was. "I don't know," she admitted, her training slipping in and out. What was next? Raging emotions. Please God, no. Macy would embarrass herself.

Kayne eased her to a sitting position, urged her to turn around, and when she obeyed, they were facing each other. Her right eye had swelled closed, a bruise marred the side of her face under blood and grime. Soon, her inhales came easy and her left eye focused, not wild with confusion. "Where do you work?"

Macy inhaled and exhaled, sitting up had lifted the weight from her chest. "The BPI. Southern California division of the Bureau of Paranormal Investigations." Her words lacked their usual firmness but didn't give into the depth of confusion and pain she was having a hard time thinking through.

Kayne knew he was asking the question for his own reasons, and the pang of guilt, for the deception when she was obviously confused and in pain, wasn't going to stop him. "What's your position?"

Macy hesitated. Not one of the usual questions. Agent Sinclair was starting his investigation with a detective that couldn't remember what day it was. Most honorable. She lifted her chin as much as she was able and met his gaze. "Junior team leader." He didn't want to know that. "Sharpshooter."

Detective Gray sat upright, her shoulders back in defiance, and the knowledge of what he was intending narrowed her gaze. Kayne closed his eyes, not wanting to believe he was going to investigate her after she saved Agent Pixley and the other detective by risking her life. "Do you remember what happened?"

*He's going to investigate me.* Macy could only hold onto her self-assurance for so long with the drumming in her head. She closed her eye, hoped for relief, then her shoulders caved in as his voice tumbled down to her, lending its weight to her already fractured brain. She had to relax, couldn't let confusion muddle her answers. The questions weren't going to stop, she knew that much, and neither was the pain. Her head felt like it was splitting in two, if it hadn't already. When she opened her eye to stare into the depths of Agent Sinclair's dark gaze, she saw more emotion than she wanted. More than she needed. Did he feel sorry for her because she was a broken human? Or because he knew what happened and like Agent Logue, he thought she was on a suicide mission by Hunter Wolf form. Macy knew the threats against her, and he was one of them. *Too damn soon. Sergeant Mayco should have sent me home.*

Home.

The word sent bitter pain through her, and another wave of nausea rolled higher, toward her throat. *Feather River.* It's the concussion. Head trauma.

"Detective Gray, do you remember what happened?" Kayne repeated. Her eye went glassy, and he thought he was going to lose her to the effects of the concussion, when what he assumed was an endless reserve of determination kicked in.

Holding his gaze, she confessed, "I shot Mr. Barrette. He's dead." Her mind felt splintered and raced in a million directions, but Macy remembered, how could she forget? When Agent Sinclair's eyes hinted at amber, she wanted to turn her head from him to hide the uncontrolled emotion welling up inside of her. And she wanted to tell him to leave her alone.

Alone. She was always alone.

It nagged her at times, hurt her at times, but now it was playing freely with her head while she was defenseless. As if sensing her loss, he leaned closer, gripping her arms, and repeated the question. Sensing her loss, what was she thinking, the bastard is a lycan. He's mocking her weakness, and knew she hated shapeshifters for the pain they inflicted. Macy thought about her file, bowed her head, and wanted to go to sleep and disappear. Agent Sinclair didn't let her go, his body tensed, and he tightened his hold.

"I understand. Do you remember what happened to you? How did you get hurt?" Kayne held her, couldn't let her go and didn't comprehend the admission and why it was relevant to her. Why did she tell him?

To put emphasis on his question, her head throbbed, the side of her face ached, and her shoulder felt like a truck hit her. She was going to have to answer the damn questions if she wanted him to leave her alone. *Think. What happened?* Macy strained to remember what sent her to the ground and tried harder to hold onto the images as they drifted from her and into the broken part of her mind. Thrown into the mix of memories was Harper's, David, and the Hunter Wolf forms. Those turned into flashes, quick pics of the past but didn't help her remember what had happened.

"Blurry, not sure," Macy mumbled.

Agent Sinclair asked another question, and when she didn't answer it, he asked again. And again. Macy thought she answered, when she realized it wasn't her voice. David was warning her ... you don't work close to the monsters without one of them getting the best of you. Without one of them infecting you. She saw his face twisted with pain, the clicking of his empty weapon, his blood, and the Hunter Wolf form standing over his ravaged body. It was bound to happen to her.

"Calm down, I'm right here," Kayne assured. "Help is coming." Before Detective Gray closed her eye, it had glassed over, her one-eyed stare going empty. Her skin crinkled, trying to fight against the swollen wound, and it made him cringe.

Fear slid through her, warning her if she kept her eye closed for too long, David's ghost was going to finish the job the Hunter Wolf form started. Macy forced her eye open, only to see Agent Sinclair a sliver from her face.

"Are you with me?" Kayne asked.

"Yes," Macy groaned. "Affirmative."

"Good, stay with me."

Every time she closed her eye, he tightened his grip, like squeezing her arms until they burned was going to keep her from slipping into numbness. With her confusion getting worse, she figured it would be easy to ignore how close he was to her, his attention, and the way worry was carving itself on *his* face. It made her head swim. And looking in the dark depths of his eyes, she watched as they changed, giving way to smoldering amber. Macy wanted to scream while every instinct told her to run from him. Held in place and physically unable to move, she watched the change in eye color with grave fascination. There was no escape. She wasn't going to outrun him, her job, the spy, shapeshifters, or the mistake with David. His amber eyes narrowed as he searched her face and stopped when their eyes met. She should be yelling for help, scrambling to put distance between them, and the fear from it all driving her from his touch and in search of a human.

"Macy?" Kayne asked, holding her gaze. "Macy, stay awake."

Her name. The sound rang inside her head, bringing the sight of treetops, the clear cerulean sky behind him, and she felt the heated summer wind on her face. She saw Feather River. It was more than awareness feathering her thoughts and dreams from her past while she stared at him; her memories were in the lines fanning out from his eyes, the creases of worry across his forehead, and the thin scar tracing down from his left ear. Agent Sinclair inched closer as wisps of dark brown strands of hair fell forward, grazing his dirty cheek.

God, she knew him. *Negative. No. No.* Not possible. She had been living, surviving on anxiety, investigating her team, watching every word she said, second guessing her actions, and taking verbal abuse from Sergeant Mayco. It was her imagination. That was all. She lived through a warehouse filled with Hunter Wolf forms, watched her sergeant get attacked, was suffering from head trauma, exhaustion, and dehydration. Swallowing hard, Macy tried to believe her denial when Agent Sinclair's eyes were not the eyes of a stranger, or the eyes of a lycan ... no, they were the eyes of someone who had tried to save her once before and failed. The pain sat thick in them, old pain like it would leak out and spill down his cheeks in a cascade of broken pieces of him. His haunted stare drew her in and embraced her.

In the middle of the chaos and the fight, Macy hadn't understood why his presence had changed her, making her feel safer with him near. *Not true.* The warehouse was a concentration of emotional suffering and death. She shot Mr.

Barrette, was helpless to stop a Hunter Wolf form from attacking Sergeant Mayco, and watched her team defend themselves against countless attacks. Agent Sinclair was another gun. Period. Macy didn't believe whatever lies drifted through her head. Sitting heavy in his eyes was the truth, she saw it in him, leaving no doubt he recognized her. *This isn't real.* The entire day was playing with her head. *It can't be real.* Closing her eyes, she gave into the haze as a chill tightened her skin and sweat rolled down the sides of her forehead. *I'm in shock.*

"Macy," Kayne whispered in her ear, his lips moving against the curve of her earlobe. "Stay with me. Please, stay awake for me. Help is coming."

*He keeps saying that,* Macy thought.

Kayne wanted her awake. Needed her awake. He hoped by using her name, he would be able to reach her and keep her attention. He needed to know if what was happening between them was real, or—like he hoped—it was the effects of having been poisoned with syn silver and manipulated by the empath. When her eye slid closed, her head lowered, and she slumped into him, he nearly gave up, then her body stiffened, she raised her face to his and met his gaze. Her lips curved around a silent word, and for an agonizing heartbeat of time her past sat in their cinnamon depths, while silver streaked them, and he understood she recognized him and his failure. With a blade of sorrow sticking in his heart, Macy exhaled, and closing her eye, cut him out. Kayne tried rousing her by repeating her name, and when she didn't respond, he said it louder, all the while kneeling and holding her. Each time he repeated her name, he prayed it would force a memory from his mind. The next time he tried saying her name, he failed as it crumbled under his irritated growl.

He wanted answers. He needed answers. When her tear-damp lashes rested on her bruised cheeks, and her body went limp in his hold, he had to accept Detective Gray wasn't going to give him any. He had to wait. With regret, Kayne gently eased her to the concrete while behind him, Agent Pixley's voice grew louder, forceful, demanding his attention. He didn't care. The Hunter Wolves were dead, the agents were checking the perimeter, and help was minutes from arriving. There was nothing he could do to help Agent Pixley, the man she held, or Detective Gray. Nothing. Kayne let her rising voice go unnoticed as his attention remained on the unconscious detective.

"Tell me who you are, dammit," he mumbled.

While he selfishly wanted her to tell him who she was he knew his investigation and the chance to question her depended on her recovery. Her wounds would give her time off, at least three weeks, if not longer. *Good job.*

On some level he noticed Agent Pixley's voice no longer sounded in the background and the warehouse gave into an unnerving silence. How long was it going to take Agent Logue and Agent Kriss to check the perimeter? The answer came quick enough when his senses twisted around the arrival of others, their presence announced by the hair on his neck rising and a faint vibration skidding over his skin. He wanted medical, backup, and Commander Wilson. In place of the familiar feel of the DOJ agent's crux, came anger mixed with a heavy amount of anxiety. He growled with frustration at his damaged senses and couldn't tell if the new arrivals were mortal, shifter, Otherkin, or more ersatz.

He would find out soon enough. A loud crash echoed through the warehouse as metal slammed against metal and heavy footsteps followed. Kayne picked up Detective Gray's empty gun, his wolf rising with its weightlessness, and standing, faced the door and waited to see what was entering the warehouse. Would shifting be worth the risk? Wasn't Agent Pixley, the wounded detective, and Detective Gray's lives worth breaking the rules? Kayne cursed with indecision when the risks involved included lives. With his next breath, warmth from his wolf flowed under the surface of his skin, readying for the shift. A slow breath calmed his heartbeat, and let his mind catch up with the scene in front of him.

The first figures to enter weren't paranormals and they weren't ersatz. The team rushed in as shadows, spreading out to flank the right and left sides, all wearing black helmets, ballistic goggles, black masks, and armed with high-powered rifles. The darkly clad figures moved like gears to an engine as they took their positions in front of him, guns at the ready. Kayne watched them mirror one another's actions, and swiftly, as if they were ribbons of smoke, shifted in silence. He knew them, remembering the briefing Commander Wilson had given, and he recognized their uniforms. Detective Gray was wearing one and was one of them. They stalked silently, the only sounds coming from their boots scraping faintly against the concrete. If he wasn't a werewolf, he never would have heard them. Chancing a glance at Detective Gray, he had to face she was trained to do the same thing. Dozens of BPI detectives flowed into the warehouse, and taking their points, were everywhere, surrounding him, and every black eye of death pointed at him.

The cavalry arrived.

# CHAPTER TEN

"Do not move." Creating a black wave, they blended, making it hard for Kayne to recognize the leader. "Put the gun on the ground," a male ordered, his deep voice breaking through the wall of silence.

They were exactly how Grace described them. Black on black BDUs, helmets, goggles, gloves, and black masks hiding their sex and identifying features. They weren't wearing name tabs or patches identifying them as BPI. A ghost squad. Detective Gray wore patches, but nothing else the others wore. Where was her equipment?

"Put the gun on the ground," he repeated.

Without argument, Kayne bent down, knowing he was more of a danger than the empty gun he held. Mortals saw guns as weapons with minds of their own, inanimate objects willing to kill indiscriminately while they erased the mortal responsibility from the equation. Kayne was a killer in his humanoid form, his wolf form, and his Hunter Wolf, if he chose. He didn't need a weapon. He *was* the weapon. Metal scraped concrete as he purposely, in order to look at Detective Gray, placed her gun beside her thigh, his fingers brushing her pants so he could feel her. The tactical vest she wore sat high on her torso, allowing her hand to rest on the black undershirt between it and her hip. He watched her chest rise slightly with her labored breath and the instinct to protect her from the intruders burned. Pushing it down, he straightened and faced the black clad wall.

"The gun in your holster. Put it on the ground."

Kayne deliberately pulled his gun from the holster, held it up to prove he wasn't going to point it at anyone, and set it beside Detective Gray's. Again, his fingers feathered her leg.

"Raise your hands and walk toward the sound of my voice." Closer than before, the voice deepened.

As if someone had sliced his tie to Detective Gray, Kayne's mind cleared, the sharp end making him dizzy. *They found the empath.* He wavered and caught his balance while his instinct to protect her became corrupted as his need to touch her felt dirty and wrong. Their moment was over. Kayne took solace in knowing he would be back to reality and real investigations, as Agent Sinclair. Whatever he and Detective Gray might have seen in each other was nothing more than exhaustion and desperation fueled by the empath's influence. While he recovered, the detectives surrounded him in their practiced silence, and he imagined what he must look like to them. He wasn't wearing a uniform—he almost laughed; he wasn't even wearing a shirt—and didn't have his badge. *It's in the black wreck.* The wounds from the Hunter Wolf's nails, cuts, blood, sweat, and sand covered his upper body, and his jeans were torn and stained. *If* the BPI asked him who he was, he was going to have a hard time proving it. With their advance, he recognized their anxiety. One unarmed man didn't concern them. It was the injured and unconscious BPI detective behind him, provoking them.

"Walk toward the sound of my voice," the male demanded, his words louder than before and clipped with his anger.

With his mind straight and his senses working, Kayne easily found the masked detective giving him orders, and felt the overwhelming feel of mortal excitement, anger, and violence. The energy wrapped around him and brought the wolf within closer to the surface. Its feel flowed into his arms and legs as each of their actions thrust him on the defense.

"Walk toward the sound of my voice. Now. Extreme force will be used."

Their excitement vibrated through the air like quick firing sparks emanating good, bad, violent, and calm. The calm and good faded under violence as their patience with Kayne's hesitation thinned. With his refusal to obey, he felt their unrest, and sensed they knew what he was, because a mortal wouldn't have survived the wounds crisscrossing his chest. They were examining him, gauging his response, his body language, and if they thought he was the enemy, they wouldn't hesitate to take him down. He would become a 'taken with extreme force' casualty.

Physically and mentally exhausted, the last thing he had patience for was playing submissive to a BPI detective and his orders. Except he didn't have a choice. It was comply or get shot. Kayne raised his hands, took three steps toward the sound of the male's voice, and stopped. His instincts were warning him of the detectives sweeping to surround him and others stalking behind him. As they closed in, his heartbeat sped up, and his wolf weaved restlessly inside of him. They were at his back, their excitement seeping into his skin. The chaos weakened Kayne's control over his wolf, and he frantically grasped at the remaining splinters. Without thinking, he turned around to see who was there and to ease the crawling feeling of the detective's presence.

A detective holstered their weapon, then knelt beside Detective Gray, while allowing their anger to infuse the air. As if Kayne wasn't there and with careful movements, the detective turned Detective Gray's head side to side then checked her tactical gear, and the condition of her uniform. When they finished, they slowly removed their helmet and goggles to reveal bright, azure eyes framed by long lashes, while her nose, mouth, and throat remained covered by a black mask. Meant to camouflage her face, it also protected her from the contagion. When she looked at Kayne, he lowered his hands and glared down at her with amber wolf eyes. Satisfaction rested in the fear her gaze embraced, for an instant, then dismissing him, and her attention returned to Detective Gray.

"Status. Code red has been suspended. Update, Directive Six. Report, there is a code blue, I repeat, code blue. Requesting medical." She held the mic as she stared at Detective Gray, and then gazed at the bodies in the warehouse.

"Copy." Static buzzed over the radio while in the background, rushed orders were given. "Sanative or Rapid Response?"

Kayne waited and listened as the question hung in the air. Would Sanative help her again or would mortal medical take her out? He wanted to know who Dr. Locke was and why as alpha of the territory he was helping Detective Gray?

"Sanative or Rapid Response? Charlie Thirty-six, respond. Sanative or Rapid Response?" the static voice asked.

"Rapid Response, cautionary. Sanative is yet to be determined," the female detective answered.

The BPI called in Rapid Response—an armed, specialized medical unit trained to extract victims—under dangerous conditions. As he listened, he figured out the directive; the warehouse was clear, and the code, detective down, medical needed. He was watching the female beside Detective Gray when he was given another warning.

"Last chance, lycan. Ready the tranquilizers," the male ordered. Kayne heard the dull clicks of a half dozen guns priming. "Walk toward the sound of my voice."

He didn't need tranquilizers added to his list of problems, and his delay was stopping medical from entering the warehouse. Kayne followed the order and taking a relaxed step stopped when he heard Detective Gray's supple moan and her struggle to breathe. When she was on her back with all of her gear, she had a hard time. Could she be waking up to the same panic and pain? Without thinking, Kayne was going to turn back—he had to check on her, her confusion making him worry—when the clicking of a gun made him pause. The barrel, close enough he could smell the stringent scent of the tranquilizer they were planning to use on him, overpowered the smell of the woman pointing it at him. A spark of anger burned brightly, and proving one thing never changed, and maybe it never would, departments like the Bureau of Paranormal Investigations were better at killing paranormals than saving them. Detective Gray was one of them.

A sharpshooter for her team. Possible spy. Murderer.

She wasn't his problem. He needed to focus on saving the investigation. Giving the woman and Detective Gray his back, he took several steps when the male ordered him to go to his knees. He obeyed and waited for the next. The order came from a different detective, and following it, Kayne went to his stomach, his right cheek against the concrete.

Soon, dull black boots stepped in his line of vision, blocking the others from view. He held his breath as the deepest of foul fumes invaded his nose and lungs. Without moving his cheek from the concrete, he looked up and met the black hole of a gun barrel. It was a careless move to be that close, Kayne could take the weapon. The detective's confidence in his backup gave him the boldness to get as close as he wanted. He wasn't fooling himself, even with his state of mind, Kayne knew if he moved an inch, he wouldn't have to worry about a tranquilizer ... no, it would take the BPI seconds to blast him with syn silver. The flicker of anger from following orders had him wanting to bet money he could rip out the nearest throat before they fired.

"There are two agents declaring they're with the DOJ's Blood Rain team. They have badges, and they're claiming the man on the ground is Agent Sinclair, their team leader," a detective reported.

The warm tip of the barrel touched the back of Kayne's neck, stopping any chance to respond. "Paranormals. We'll see." The male detective pushed the barrel again, its tip digging into his tendons. "He's not moving until I get confirmation from Captain Dixon."

"What do you want me to do about the agents?"

"Keep them outside. We don't need any more help from the DOJ."

"Affirmative, sir."

No, he guessed they didn't. It wasn't going to be easy to question them when they blamed the DOJ for their wounded and the warehouse. The accusation stole the fuel from his anger. Kayne would have to work through their resistance, but first he needed his team. His wolf sank into his depths when the detective removed the barrel and stepped back.

He remained silent, cheek on the floor, hands even with his head, waiting for someone to tell him he could get up.

The heightened anxiety descending on the warehouse eased to a mild alertness. Above him, voices rose and fell as conversations started between the detectives. Selfishly, he wanted to hear Agent Pixley or Agent Logue, but wherever they were, they were not in the warehouse. *Today it paid to be in uniform.* Damn, if he had a shirt and his badge.

"At ease, Detective, this is Agent Sinclair." Authority oozed from the voice he recognized as Commander Wilson.

Without responding, the detective made no move to allow Kayne off the ground. Instead, he took a step closer and shoved the barrel into his neck. "Negative. Where is Captain Dixon?"

"Occupied. I'm in charge here, Detective. I'm ordering you to back off and allow my agent to get up from the ground," Commander Wilson snapped.

One. Two. Three seconds and the detective removed the barrel and walked away. A different detective remained behind, watching as Kayne stood up and brushed flecks of grime and dust from his chest and jeans. It was more out of habit than necessity; there was no way he was going to be clean or free of the stench until he spent an hour in a shower and his jeans were going into the trash at the earliest opportunity. Ignoring the detective, he flexed his arms and back, then placed his hands on his hips and waited for Commander Wilson. *This is going to be bad.*

"You look like shit, Sinclair." Commander Wilson motioned Kayne, and they distanced themselves from the detectives. "Who did you fight?"

"At what point?" Kayne asked. He noticed the commander's uniform was dusted in beige, sweat soaked through his T-shirt and the waist of his BDUs, and sand sat in the creases of his face. Everyone witnessed the destruction of the Hunter Wolves.

"Don't push me. The one who tried kicking your ass," Commander Wilson replied.

"An ersatz. You'll find its body an aisle over from here."

"I was hoping you weren't going to say that," Commander Wilson seethed. "Did you have to kill it?"

"It was either me or him. It wasn't possible to take it alive," Kayne replied in defense.

Commander Wilson shook his head. "Ersatz. It doesn't change the fact you killed a Hunter Wolf. By the way you look and the lack of clothing, I'm assuming you shapeshifted."

Kayne hated admitting he needed to, but he would have died if he hadn't. "Affirmative, there were extenuating circumstances."

"I'm sure there were, and I believe it's self-defense which is why the DOJ is keeping this in house. You'll be explaining your actions to the homicide agent when you go in for questioning, and it's going to be a rough one. Trespassing. Breaking and entering. Use of force. Shapeshifting. Every agent here is going to be interviewed."

*Hours of interviews.*

Commander Wilson's attention went to the werewolf in wolf form. "What do you know about the lycan over there?"

Homicide. Kayne would be held for hours describing what happened while keeping certain details like the vampire Jaxyn and the Council, a secret. "His name is Henry. I found him in one of the containers, but he isn't a threat." He helped Detective Gray keep the Hunter Wolves from harming Agent Pixley. "I don't believe he was infected by a Hunter Wolf. It looks like the White Cell he had been taking gave him the contagion. The Sanative team will be able to take care of him." Kayne turned to the nearest detective. "Detective Gray assured me it was their job."

"Detective Gray is unconscious," the detective replied. "Maybe she didn't tell you at all."

It wasn't the response Kayne expected, and he fought to keep the surprise off his face. "The wolf is a potential witness for the Department of Justice. You will see he receives the proper care."

"We'll do what we can," the detective responded half-heartedly, as if he was bored from talking to a lesser being.

The insult didn't go unnoticed. "Detective, you will make sure Doctor Locke's team is aware of the lycan, and make note, his name is Henry," Commander Wilson ordered. "If there is going to be a continual problem, you can discuss it with Captain Dixon. Better yet, I will take it upon myself to discuss it with your commander."

"Affirmative," the detective snapped. He glared, his hate beaming from his eyes before turning and leaving.

When the detective was out of hearing, Commander Wilson's mask of calm fell, and he wore his irritation as he directed his attention to Kayne. "Nice bit of trouble you got yourself into." He looked around the warehouse, his questioning gaze stopping on Detective Gray and the detective helping her to sit up. "Remember the plan to infiltrate the bureau and get close to them in order to question the detectives, yes? This is going to be a cluster fuck, Sinclair. You were supposed to investigate the BPI, not get their detectives killed."

He knew that. "I parked out front and was attacked."

"Why were you parked out front?" Commander Wilson demanded.

"I had a lead," Kayne answered. He refused to confess it came from Jaxyn, not that anyone would believe him. Before the Requiem, vampires had watched the death, hunts, and fires burning in the night as mortals searched for shapeshifters and the Otherkin and decided to remain hidden. They were part of the Veiled, the concealed paranormal population, the Council protected.

"Who gave you the lead?" Commander Wilson asked as he tossed a crumpled T-shirt at him.

"Thanks. It was an anonymous call from a burner cell. They reported there was suspicious activity in the area, including unaccounted for traffic at an abandoned warehouse, and there had been sightings of Hunter Wolves. Since I was in the area, I figured it wouldn't hurt to look." Kayne bent down, retrieved his gun, holstered it, and then handed the combination to Commander Wilson. After pulling the T-shirt with DOJ agent written across the back over his head, he took his holster, hated the way it felt, and put his arms through. The blue tee fit snug through his shoulders and chest and covered the stifling smell of his own stink, along with the blood, and the smell from the warehouse. He inhaled an easier breath, saw the warehouse teaming with law enforcement, and exhaled some of his worry.

"What did you tell the BPI?" Kayne asked.

"It was reported you were investigating warehouses where White Cell and Hunter Wolves were allegedly present. Your GPS confirmed what was reported. Not my first rodeo," Commander Wilson explained as he eyed Kayne. "As soon as the crime scene techs arrive, you'll turn your weapon over, and spent magazines, they're evidence. You'll be given another one, so you aren't unarmed. Once you're cleared, your property will be returned to you. Do you understand?"

"Affirmative." There was one round in his gun, and he didn't have any extra magazines. They were in his truck. Untouched.

"Good. This lead knew you would be in Desert Rock, and you figured you would disobey an order, go without backup, without a search warrant, and without any authorization whatsoever to check it out?" Sarcasm dripped from every word, as did Commander Wilson's self-assured arrogance.

"I wasn't going to do anything but confirm the address. There wasn't a person in sight, and I couldn't sense anyone inside. From the outside, the place looked abandoned. It does raise the question how they knew I would be here."

Trap. Someone knew he was going to be in Desert Rock besides Captain Dixon and Jaxyn. Was Jaxyn working with Elijah? He teased Kayne with Hunter Wolves, possibly Elijah, and off Kayne went, bent on finding evidence. Like a damn fool.

"You didn't clear your presence with local law enforcement, or Captain Dixon. Do you know how surprised he was when I called him?" Commander Wilson met Kayne's eyes with an unimpressed look in his. "I do remember ordering you to notify him."

It was impossible for Captain Dixon to be surprised when he knew Kayne was going to be in Desert Rock. Fearing being trapped by the captain, his questions, and the investigation, Kayne explained he was going to the motel, dropping off his luggage, and would get a feel for the city before going to the office. Captain Dixon knew. It was possible with the alleged spy and steady calls he forgot. Still, whoever it was—Jaxyn, Captain Dixon, or the spy—someone had warned Elijah of his arrival. The Hunter Wolves knew him ... hell, Elijah told Henry about him. *"You kill your own."* His response to Commander Wilson stalled with his thoughts, then the noise level escalated, getting his attention, and they both turned toward the door.

Several paramedics wearing biohazard suits and weapons, then agents and detectives filed through the opening, while the last team, wearing green BDUs, shoulder holsters, and carrying medical bags followed. Their presence brought a ripple of awareness skidding across Kayne's skin, leaving a tingling wake behind.

*Must be Sanative because they're all shifters.* It didn't end; the power trailing the team turned static, and a new force sizzled the air, its sharp bites on his skin alerting him to who was entering. An alpha on alert. Kayne didn't turn from the team as they walked through the cluster of people and made their way toward him. A man took the lead, dressed in the same uniform as the others, only brown, his confidence telling Kayne it must be Dr. Locke.

The air changed at the same time as his eyes—mortal to wolf, and back to mortal. He was the alpha of the territory, and with the simple reminder between them, Dr. Locke didn't stop to talk. Behind him was a woman with blonde hair and yellow/green eyes, and she did not make eye contact, cats rarely did. She kept her eyes locked on Dr. Locke, like he might turn and leave her behind. A therian-cat of some kind, her nervous energy and sharp actions giving her away. The two others, men and shapeshifters, broke from them and went in Henry's direction, each carrying a medical bag.

Dr. Locke hadn't acknowledged Kayne's presence, other than the display of power. The snub sent a current of anger through his exhausted body, but at the same time he was thankful he didn't have to play visiting alpha. As a government agent it gave him the freedom to expel with the time-consuming ordeal of pack policy. He wouldn't respond to the display of power when Dr. Locke was in charge of Sanative and Kayne needed his cooperation during the investigation. The situation made the doctor's help imperative. He could be diplomatic when he needed to.

"I said, after breaking into the place, what did you find?" Commander Wilson asked, oblivious to the doctor, his power, and the therian-cat.

"I didn't break in. After the Hunter Wolf attacked my truck, it opened the door, and I walked in." *Ran in without my badge, extra magazines, or backup.* "There's a small lab at the back. The warehouse itself is set up so the front is opposite from the back. The two meet up in the middle, creating two different sides."

"And all the cargo containers?"

Kayne's eyes narrowed, his wolf rose, the need to protect Detective Gray threading through his muscles, and even as he tried to break the influence, he couldn't stop watching Dr. Locke approach her. What was he going to do? Dr. Locke couldn't help her, because he couldn't touch her any more than Kayne. But he had, and held her to his chest that was covered in his own blood and ersatz blood.

With a medical bag slung over one shoulder, and continuing to ignore Kayne, Dr. Locke talked causally to the therian, and scanned the warehouse. Right away she nodded, and after responding, turned and left. He continued to close the gap between them, while taking a pair of gloves from his side pocket, and before reaching her pulled them on. Happy to see Detective Gray awake, alert, and sitting up, watching her eased tension through Kayne's shoulders and the instinct to protect her waned, but it created trails his mind freely chased. With it came the memory of her cinnamon eyes ringed with silver. Their familiar feel came rushing back, smashing the illusion and blaming it on the empath became harder than he wanted to admit. Was there a connection between his twenty-three year old memories, and the mortal detective? Negative. He stopped himself. When they found the empath, the connection snapped its force like whip across his mind. *No connection.*

"... the containers. Agent Sinclair, are you listening?" Commander Wilson asked.

"Affirmative. They're using the containers to hold their prisoners. If the containers are used as cells, there are going to be more victims. We'll have bodies. I don't want to guess how many. I caught glimpses of remains in the containers the Hunter Wolf pushed to the ground."

"This has been going on for a while then. If the décor is any indication, we have serious problems," Commander Wilson replied. "It's bad if I can smell the death in this place. We're looking at more bodies than either agency and the coroner's office will be able to handle. We're going to have to set up a base." He looked at Kayne before continuing. "That's just what I wanted, a low-key investigation turned to shit," he mumbled with the look of disapproval on his face. When someone passed, the expression was gone and replaced with his mask of professionalism. "I'll get the California Highway Patrol to set up a checkpoint at the entrance, no one except DOJ and BPI allowed. I don't want the local PD anywhere near this place. Then I'll get a team together and have our crime scene techs work with the BPI's crime scene techs. The more help we have, the better chance of retrieving evidence and getting the people responsible for this mess."

"Why the CHP and not the PD?" he asked as he watched Detective Gray and another detective talk. He tried listening but couldn't understand what they were saying over the commotion and the other conversations.

"Recent events have added tension between the DRPD and the BPI. And I don't need trouble from either one of them," Commander Wilson explained, his attention split between Kayne and what the other agents were doing. "You're sure they're ersatz?"

"Affirmative," he answered on auto.

Captain Dixon hadn't said anything to him about the discord between agencies, which would have been nice to know. When the other detective nodded her head and seemed content with whatever Detective Gray had said, she left, allowing Dr. Locke to kneel beside Macy. A mortal paramedic—wearing a white biohazard suit, thigh holster, and gun—joined them, but she didn't greet either. Instead, she raised a palm-sized tablet over the patch identifying Detective Gray as BPI, and scanned the electronic chip hidden inside. The paramedic would receive Detective Gray's medical history, including blood type, prescriptions she was currently taking, the last time she went to the hospital, and past injuries. The paramedic would then upload Detective Gray's treatment to Genesis, an interactive program and the ambulance medics would receive the information and treat Detective Gray accordingly. With a scowl, the paramedic met Detective Gray's gaze, and began talking. Or lecturing. Not a good medical history.

"Agent Sinclair?" Commander Wilson repeated. "Were they resistant to syn silver?"

"Affirmative. One of them took more than six shots to the chest, with a .45 at point blank range," he explained. "Another had its knees shot out, it continued to attack." And Detective Gray killed it.

"Do you think they're not susceptible to the silver?" With his brows drawn, Commander Wilson watched detectives and agents bring in cases and set up equipment.

"Negative. I don't think they feel pain. They are without senses, instinct, and they fight until they're dead." What the hell was Dr. Locke doing?

"That's the last thing I wanted to hear. At least they're not resistant, especially since syn silver is our only defense. With the deaths, this has escalated to serial killers. We have to get this contained before word of it spreads and panic starts in." Commander Wilson ran his hand through his hair in frustration. "This is a small city, its population is split between paranormal and human. When the humans find out law enforcement isn't able to stop the ersatz or the contagion, it'll increase the demand for White Cell. Not to mention put innocent paranormal lives in danger."

Kayne hadn't thought of that. "I told you Henry hadn't been infected by another werewolf, he was taking White Cell, and tried to shift within a week. It's the White Cell." Where did Elijah fit into this? And why did Kayne feel his theory was being shot to hell? "Grace, Henry's wife said, BPI detectives took them from their house because he wasn't keeping up his side of a deal. What deal, I have no idea. She said Henry used to sell White Cell." And the spy? His mind roamed over the pieces as he stared at Detective Gray.

"Let's hope the couple survives so we can question them. Until then, I'll have agents reach out to law enforcement agencies in the area and see if they have received reports of crimes associated with White Cell and the ersatz," Commander Wilson explained.

"And dealers. We need names," Kayne added.

While the paramedic lectured her about taking time off work, being careful, and putting herself in harm's way, she stripped Macy of her tactical vest and had cut most of her compression shirt from her right arm and shoulder. Without the thick material, the warm air quickly dried the thin layer of sweat coating her exposed skin. Free from the vest and shirt, Macy relaxed, inhaled, and slowly tested her arm. It hurt and was going to be sore, but she didn't think anything was damaged. She flinched when the paramedic, completely covered in her biohazard suit, mask, and gloves began cleaning the wound above her eye and scrapes on her forehead. Macy was convinced whatever she was using was liquid fire as it burned her skin, the germs, the contagion, and specks of sand to ash. Then she watched Dr. Locke cringe when he saw her face, making her want to shrink into the concrete. She stopped worrying about him and the paramedic when Sanative's paramedics circled Sergeant Mayco and started working on him.

"Detective Gray, Sergeant Mayco will be taken to Sanative," Dr. Locke assured. Kneeling beside her, his hazel eyes searched her face, arms, neck, then met her gaze.

"He was sliced open by a Hunter Wolf form, the kind that don't return to their humanoid form. Six rounds of syn silver didn't stop the damn thing," Macy explained, her voice sounding exhausted and strained. She did not share his confidence. Adding weight to her lack of confidence was the bodies and blood staining the warehouse floor. "It's been hours since the attack."

The window for fighting the contagion was two hours, maybe less, maybe more, depending on the person and the way they responded to the contagion. Sergeant Mayco had been infected by a Hunter Wolf form, an altered Hunter Wolf form, and it put his recovery at risk. Would he survive as a human or a lycan? And if he crossed over, would he blame her, like he blamed her for Officer Murphy's death?

"I understand, and I'll make sure he receives treatment and has the help he needs. That's all we can do," he stated.

Macy wasn't going to argue with him while the paramedic was listening. She flinched when the first butterfly closer stretched over the cut, increasing the pain, if that was possible. To distract herself, she looked from Dr. Locke to the warehouse. With an attempt to control the fear and her emotions, she watched BPI detectives work only to increase the pain behind her eyes and the pressure of tears wanting to fall from frustration and anger and her head trauma.

*Hold it together.* She didn't know who was behind the White Cell, the Hunter Wolf forms, or the warehouses and might not have a chance to find out. The spy was out there, and if the DOJ and BPI thought she was guilty, and she took the blame, the spy was getting a free pass. Taking a deep breath, she let the pain from her head to her toes invade her thoughts and stop her tears.

"I didn't stop them." Macy sounded weak and felt weaker.

"There was nothing you could have done. I see nine Hunter Wolves here, and that's more than any human, with any gun, can stop. It is what it is. You're alive and so are the other detectives and agents. Sergeant Mayco could have been killed," Dr. Locke tried convincing her. By the expression on his face, he knew he was failing.

What was she doing confiding in him? Macy was desperate and wanted assurance Sergeant Mayco was going to be all right. It didn't change the need to burn holes through him with her eyes. Not only was she talking to him, knowing everyone was watching them, including the paramedic, but he *was* reassuring her. Like they were friends, and he knew what she wanted. Fuck, needed. And he wasn't holding her responsible the Hunter Wolf form's death, like he had at the Barrettes', when he thought she shot Mrs. Barrette. Maybe she should tell him she *did* shoot Mr. Barrette? *His body is somewhere over there.* Then she would pray he got mad and left her alone. Frustration ate at her. She needed someone, even Dr. Locke, to understand Blood Rain was there, an entire team of shapeshifters and empaths, who were stronger, faster, with enhanced abilities and they could have changed things. Deep down, she knew blaming the DOJ and Agent Sinclair wouldn't change what happened to Sergeant Mayco. It wouldn't change what happened to her, and it wouldn't fix her career. It was guilt.

*"I don't want to die."* No, he wasn't dead, although he might wish he was when he crossed over.

The moment Macy remembered the name of the warehouse, she should have confirmed it with dispatch. She could have saved them all. Somewhere in her mixed thoughts, she convinced herself David had investigated the claim there was White Cell, and if he cleared the damn thing without contacting the BPI, it made him look guilty. Accusing a dead officer of a crime. Macy was digging herself a hole. What if he didn't? What if he did, how had he missed the mess inside? Because he was helping the spy. Stop, negative, no way. It's head trauma, shock. Macy was guilty of not telling Sergeant Mayco because she didn't want to listen to another tirade. He created a volatile working relationship, turning him into the liability. *Blame the wounded.* She turned her head and met Dr. Locke's stare as silence built on the tension sitting between them. She was finished talking to him. The paramedic, working silently beside her, could tell her friends, Detective Gray, above all else, wasn't a friend to lycans.

"What kind of injuries does Detective Gray have?" he inquired.

Macy heard the paramedic's inhale of surprise and saw her visibly hesitate. Human paramedic, lycan doctor. The hesitation spanned several seconds, causing her to question whether the paramedic would answer him. She didn't have to. She could order him to leave and force him to watch the humans take care of the humans. The paramedic ignored Dr. Locke, and tapped information into her tablet, and after several seconds of silence, she shrugged.

"Detective Gray has contusions on her right shoulder, most of her right side, actually most of her upper body, and she'll have to have X-rays. Her head wound needs stitches, and she has a concussion. She'll have to have an MRI confirming there are no other injuries. There's blood loss from the lacerations on her face, hands, she's missing fingernails, and she's a touch dehydrated."

"Missing fingernails?" Dr. Locke asked. "What happened to you?"

"Hunter Wolves," Macy answered. She wanted to roll her eyes but stopped when it hurt.

Dehydrated. She figured that out when she stopped sweating and her head felt like it was splitting open, all before the Hunter Wolf form clocked her. Relief, as brief as it was, sank into her and strengthened her. She remembered what happened, and by the way, Agent Sinclair, it's Wednesday. The memory had Macy thinking Agent Sinclair had asked her who she was. Hadn't she told him her name? She thought she heard him repeat the question but couldn't be sure. Preoccupied with the returning memories, she watched Dr. Locke as the paramedic began putting used gauze and instruments into a contamination bag and started taking various equipment out. Along with her memories, the images of Sergeant Mayco and Agent Pixley trying to escape the group of attacking lycans vexed her. It was all coming back. Maybe she didn't need all her memories. Absently, she reached up to touch the split above her eye, wanting to end the pain. With his gloved hand, he grabbed her wrist, and she met his stare.

"Don't touch it. We don't know what's on your hands. What's left of them." Holding her hand, he showed the paramedic.

Dr. Locke let go of her and she raised her left hand. "What's wrong with my forehead?" Macy asked, not wanting to look at her hands.

"I'll clean your hands, wrap what I can, but the tips are open. Like your forehead. Touching the wound puts you at greater risk from contamination," she explained. "Don't touch it." Her eyes darted over Macy, Dr. Locke, and the condition of the warehouse. The entire area was a giant contamination zone.

"Do you remember what happened? How you got hurt? And your hands?" Dr. Locke asked.

"Do you want a play by play?" Macy couldn't control the frustration and exhaustion clipping her words.

"Yes. I would appreciate it."

"Me too," the paramedic added.

*Fine.* "I was focused on the Hunter Wolf form in front of me when I was attacked from behind. The hit sent me to my knees, that's when I was punched. Then it started dragging me and I tried saving myself by clinging to the concrete," Macy answered. *I remembered.* "It stopped when ... Agent Sinclair yelled at it, then it tried strangling me." He saved her life. *That sucks.*

"You were attacked twice. If either of them had hit you with their full strength, you could have been killed. They could have easily broken your neck," Dr. Locke cautioned. "Not to mention crushing your sternum, ribs, lungs, or heart."

Macy could see the gears grinding as he tried picturing a Hunter Wolf form dragging her and her fingernails being ripped from her fingers. Then nearly strangled. Yeah, the violence had been extreme.

"I shot it a couple of times first. What about the blood?" she asked. Macy saw it glittering on her vest, pants, and the arms of her shirt. It covered her, and if it was her blood ... damn, no wonder she was out of it.

"The cut is deep," he replied. With an exaggerated inhale, like he felt defeated, he said, "You're alert, answering questions, and you're steady. It's a good sign."

Because she had been out like a light for God knows how long. "What about my eye?" Macy ignored him, as she carefully turned to the right and tried to look across the warehouse. With a slow breath, she steadied herself and carefully turned to the left. Her right eye was swollen shut. She couldn't see anything on that side and was having a hard time focusing. Her blurred vision spawned a swirl of nausea that captured her head at the same time it reached for her throat. Inhaling, she swallowed the worst of the pressure and stilled.

"Are you all right? Detective Gray, is something wrong?" Dr. Locke asked. He was watching her when she wavered.

"Affirmative. Dizzy. Negative," she whispered, trying to keep from getting sick. "My eye?"

"The side of your face is swollen, your eye is swelled closed, but there will be nothing wrong with your sight.

When properly treated the cut will heal, and the swelling will go down." He was trying to comfort her, and it was irritating her.

The paramedic gave him a sideways glance. "You're not going to have to worry, I've called for a gurney. I've alerted the paramedic on board, and once you're with her, she'll give you a shot to help with the nausea."

"Negative. I'm walking," Macy insisted. She had to stand. She could do it without getting sick and making a fool of herself. Sure she could, because limping out was better than being caught lying on her back if anything happened. The warehouse might be full of law enforcement and guns, but she wasn't taking a chance.

"Cancelling the gurney." The paramedic gave Macy a stern glare through her goggles and from under mascara-covered eyelashes. "I'm telling the ambulance medic to radio ahead to Mercy Summit's trauma unit, stressing one detective from the BPI with injuries. It's not a case for Sanative. I'm also advising advanced treatment of CD4-T. You will be en route in twenty."

Mercy Summit's trauma unit was code for a quarantine room consisting of three concrete walls, with the fourth being made of ballistic glass in order to observe the patient. Inside the sparse room was a bed and whatever equipment was needed. There they would give her larger doses of the antiserum, CD4-T, with less time between treatments, and monitor her condition. Like if she lost her mind, became suicidal, had an adverse reaction to the CD4-T, or shifted. Macy was looking at staying in the hospital overnight with needles in her elbows and the back of her knees and the thought had her stomach rolling and her throat tightening. A concussion and CD4-T guaranteed she was going to be sick all night. There was no question she was thankful for the antiserum, the thick liquid injected by an even thicker needle, hurt when it went in and burned as it traveled. That, at least, was bearable. Being sick caused her grief. She hated feeling helpless, hated waiting to recover, and hated it happened every time.

Every time ... it was twice in a matter of weeks as the paramedic reminded her. The doctors would put the needles in the same holes like they were plugins. The BPI had a policy regarding how many times you were injured and exposed to the contagion resulting in the treatment of CD4-T before they considered you a hazard to the job and a casualty. *A liability.* Macy's mind went straight to her earlier thought—her medical history was going to force her into retirement before Captain Dixon, Agent Sinclair, and Sergeant Mayco could file their reports and have her fired.

As the paramedic checked Macy's shoulder for more wounds, she cleaned blood from her neck, the sharp smell of cleanser making her eyes water, and turning her head from the source and the smell she tried for a breath of clean air. Her attempt was stopped when a hand feathered over her skin, continued to skim across her shoulders, and down her right arm. It stopped on the frayed edge of her sleeve and held her. *It's not the paramedic's hand.* Someone was touching her.

The paramedic was an average height woman, fit, like she ran, brown hair, and equally brown eyes. While she was lecturing Macy about CD4-T, her injuries, and not ducking from a Hunter Wolf form's fist, her stare held an edge of sadness in it, as if she was tired of seeing and dealing with what waited at the end of every call. And her touch through her gloves was light, hesitant, and cold despite the heat, not the warm, overpowering feel against Macy's shoulder. Bare skin on skin. Power. Otherworldly. Macy brought her eyes up, ready to meet Dr. Locke's gaze, and prepared herself for the worst, when he wasn't looking at her. He was staring over her. Her heart skipped a beat, and she closed her eyes. She didn't want to know who was touching her, ignorance was bliss.

Ignorance was fleeting. She knew who it was. *No. No. No.* He wouldn't dare touch her.

*"Tell me who you are."* He thought he knew her. She knew him, recognized him from where? Nowhere. Her mind raced as she tried to think of way to escape him. Them. Both men. Both lycans. Macy needed her gun. With the hand holding her, she searched, her stomach fell, and her heart raced, when she saw the paramedic had shoved her gear, gun, and weapons out of her reach. An empty, naked feeling crawled over her at the same time Agent Sinclair feathered his hands over her shoulders, leaving a tingling sensation in their wake. She tried easing her nerves by convincing herself he wouldn't do anything stupid in a warehouse teaming with human law enforcement detectives and agents, and he would protect her. His little, human friend.

Then she attempted to convince herself Dr. Locke was the most controlled lycan she had ever met. They had known each other for years, worked together, had been at some of the worst chaotic scenes together. Macy doubted her own words when Dr. Locke's eyes were not human, but a lycan's shape, held in his human face. She had never seen his eyes change. Was he going to lose control? In contrast to Agent Sinclair's amber lycan eyes, Dr. Locke's were a pure sun yellow, almost white. His power and strength never occurred to Macy, but now, the gleaming in his stare proved why he was the alpha of the Gawain pack.

The energy from them became tangible as it wove around them and through her. Did Agent Sinclair want something from Dr. Locke? Negative. The image of his heated amber eyes and the feeling she knew him came roaring back. No, it was the concussion. Head trauma. Blood loss. Macy turned as far as she dared, despite the pain, and saw dirty, torn jeans hugging muscled legs that ended in dirtier boots, and she closed her eye. His closeness surrounded her as his power grew, skidding along her skin, causing heat to rise into her cheeks. Its thickness increased between them, invading every empty pore, and feeling as if he was touching her entire body. Inhaling, she pushed herself to confront them both, when Agent Sinclair's hands glided up and down her arms, in soothing strokes, then stopped on her shoulders. Her heart pounded, ice filled her veins, and she knew both lycans were pushing her panic. As if sensing her unease, Agent Sinclair tightened his hold, his fingers digging into her shoulders, and clenching her teeth she stopped herself from gasping from the pain. They were destroying her and destroying the shred of confidence the other BPI detectives might have had in her.

What did she have to do to free herself of shapeshifters?

She needed to kill them.

# CHAPTER ELEVEN

*Calm down*, he wanted to yell at her.

Detective Gray's head turned to the left, he saw she was struggling with her eye, as she frantically searched for her gun. When she found it beside her gear, she tried reaching for it. Wasn't going to happen. He tightened his grip, stopping her, and pulled her back toward him. He barely registered the skin of her right shoulder and arm was already colored with bruises, when she whimpered, and he repeated the process of sweeping his hands up and down her arms in a relaxing way. He hoped. He had no idea if it worked. Up, down, up, down, up, down, he rubbed his hands over her warm skin to her shoulders, where his thumbs kneaded the strained muscles in her neck.

When he tightened his grip, she futilely sank away from him while under his palms, he felt Detective Gray recoil, her muscles tightening as she continued to struggle to get out from his hold. Yes, she was fearless when armed, fighting the Hunter Wolves, and defending herself against them, but defenseless and hurt left her exposed and losing herself in fear. Her heart rate spiked as fear boiled inside of her, and guilt slid through Kayne. For the second time in one day, he was scaring her, but it wasn't going to stop him. He had to know. He needed to see for himself. If he didn't, he would do something he regretted.

Kayne forced his mind to the task, and ignored her eyes, the feeling he knew her, and the instinct to protect her. He realized he was hurting her when she stifled a cry and covered his right hand with her bandaged one, silently begging him to release her. He wasn't going to let her go, but he did ease his grip, and her hand left his. He couldn't stop from losing himself in the feel of her heat, the sound of her whimper, all while keeping eye contact with Dr. Locke. Knowing his eyes reflected his wolf and with the change came its rolling power as if his wolf knew his mortal skin was the only barrier before it felt freedom and the feeling of tearing into the alpha standing beside her. His silent challenge fed the chaos and pushed his lack of control.

When he approached them, Kayne thought he made his motive as plain as possible, hiding nothing from the doctor. He was a DOJ agent, they were in a warehouse surrounded by mortals and paranormals, every one of them law enforcement, and he wouldn't put their lives at risk. He wasn't sure when the situation turned into a challenge but felt he needed to explain that he wasn't there for the alpha's territory. He had his own and his own pack. He didn't need another, nor did he want it. The gods knew he wasn't at home taking care of those in his pack.

The doctor's reaction made him question why the alpha was ignoring the truth and acting like a jealous, overprotective male? And why was he possessive over Detective Gray, a mortal with the BPI, and enemy? Damn the consequences. If he was right, and he knew he was, because he saw its black lines after the paramedic removed the fabric from her shoulder. There was no mistaking the tattoo.

And if the doctor knew, he owed Kayne an explanation.

Kayne watched for Dr. Locke's reaction as he drew his fingertips over Detective Gray's shoulder and across her neck, causing her to tremble and her entire body to sink under his touch. He gripped her and they watched her struggle and search for someone to help her. When she twisted, she saw her fellow BPI detectives, acted like she was going to call out to them, then stopped. The mortal needed one of her own kind to rescue her from the werewolves, but she remained quiet, unmoving, while the others stared at her. Kayne didn't know what it meant, didn't care, he wasn't going to quit when he felt the doctor's power increase.

Her pain and fear drifted to him, and he regretted his actions, knowing he was adding to her already heated hatred of werewolves, paranormals, and her fragile state. *Let a detective come and save her*, Kayne thought with defiance. Throughout the day, his suspicions of her grew, and when some died where they started, others formed solid questions. He forced himself to keep control as his fingers slid over her skin—he couldn't stop from touching her—and pushing her shirt to the side, he exposed the lines and curves of the image inked into her flesh. Black and crimson for an eternity. *What the hell?* He fought the impulse to turn her around, forcing her to face him so he could yell at her until his throat was raw, all while shaking her brain loose.

He would accuse her of being part of his nightmare, for fueling it and making him crazy, and reminding him he yearned for forgiveness, redemption, and anything else he could think of, repeatedly. Kayne lived for hearing her excuses and the lies she would tell to keep her secret safe, then he would take her from Desert Rock and haul her ass back to Feather River and deliver her to her master. In the center of the tattoo were six swords, their hilts butting one another and merging into a solid circle. The blades reached out, forming a ring, above them six dragons with their necks extended, created a second larger circle. The blades and dragonheads were outlined in black, while the necks of the dragons reaching out beyond the blades were crimson, as if the razorblade edges had scored their outstretched throats and their blood had dried on their scales. The tattoo, a mark of possession, represented the power of Casa di Daeland, or house of Daeland and his *Kindred*. The dragon was his crest, the image holding the past, present, and future for those wearing the symbol. The outstretched dragon necks were a sign of faith and sacrifice, the stark red ink a sign of power, and the two together told of their unyielding courage. Each dragon head represented a campaign won, the blades telling of promised brutality, and the loyalty they worshiped. The blades were also a warning—if you harmed her, if you threatened his Kindred, he was going to take pleasure in making sure you wished for death.

In the years Kayne had known Daeland, he had heard of six vampires to wear the Kindred blood mark. Four of those had been dead for hundreds of years, leaving two, and they didn't live in the US, their responsibility was taking care of his businesses abroad. The thousand-year-old vampire hadn't marked one of his Kindred in hundreds of years, and yet Detective Gray, a mortal, brought the count to three. He knew the mark of dragons and swords personally. Daeland, Lord with the Council and the vampire headed toward the Affliction, was the person he was trying to convince that Elijah was alive. His territory in Feather River, Amarnath, bordered the Garrick's pack territory of Moonlight. Kayne succeeded the fallen Alpha Garrick Grayson when Elijah murdered him. As alpha, the years had shaped an unlikely alliance between them, and seeing Daeland's blood mark on

Detective Gray, binding her to him for eternity sent chills down Kayne's spine, and fury through his veins. The vampire known to some as Death Dealer, had lied to him. Or used him. Or both.

He stared at the tattoo, realized she never tried stopping him from seeing it, never tried to keep it hidden, like she didn't know it was there. With his gentle grip, Detective Gray continued her struggle to escape the wolves trapping her between them. Did she know the tattoo blood bound her to a vampire and marked her as his Kindred, his property, and gave her his protection? Negative. Detective Macy Gray, sharpshooter, mortal, was living in complete ignorance of the existence of vampires. By marking her, Daeland made Detective Gray a target in the paranormal world, at the same time he gave her status and protection with those living in the open and the Veiled. Even the Council would be forced to recognize her.

*Why?* Kayne's need to hold her faded into the memory of her silver-ringed eyes and the feel of her skin under his palms. He didn't stop her. He didn't hold her. He didn't let go of her. Rather, his fingertips trailed over her bare skin, what was left of her braid fell down her back, and the remnants of the compression shirt covered her tattoo. He had pushed the limits of her patience, the doctor's, and continuing to force her to stay with him would add to his mounting problems, and the questions surrounding her. Detective Gray slipped from his hold, hastily crawled, on her bandaged hands and knees, to the waiting paramedic. When she was safely out of his reach, the paramedic held her and helped her to stand. Her heartbeat remained in his ears, its rhythm like a song, and her fear wrapped around him. His wolf demanded freedom to protect. Kayne fought the instinct. *She's nothing to me.*

"Detective Gray, I can help you," Kayne offered. *With what?* His professional veneer, a false showing. "Detective Gray?"

"Stand down," the paramedic ordered. Holding a tranquilizer gun, her brown eyes blazed with her anger and the dare to defy her order.

Macy should have risked calling for help, she wasn't sure why she hadn't. Was she scared the detectives who doubted her would have refused? Maybe. Fury raced through her with her doubt in her fellow detectives as she stood beside the paramedic, willing her to shoot Agent Sinclair with the tranq. Embarrassed, shamed, and made a fool of by Agent Asshole, he single-handedly risked her job. If she had her gun, she would shoot him and redeem herself. She held her right shoulder, battled nausea, and looked around the warehouse to see they had become the center of attention. *Shit. Good job, Agent Asshole.* Getting angry had her heart pounding, her pulse echoing in her ears, and it was making her dizzy. She swayed. Dr. Locke took a step toward her, his hand out, and reached for her.

"Do not touch me." She was shocked he would even think she wanted to be anywhere near him after what he did. With accusations in her good eye, Macy nailed him with her glare, as much as she could with one eye, and backed out of his reach.

The paramedic urged her behind her, pointed the tranquilizer at Dr. Locke, and warned, "I suggest you back away. I have enough rounds for you both."

"I was going to help her," Dr. Locke began.

"You can't, lycan. You're not going to do anything with her," the paramedic warned.

*Lycan.* Kayne saw surprise cross Dr. Locke's face with Detective Gray's rejection, and the paramedic's order, but the alpha quickly masked it and lowered his hands. They stood in a half circle with more than a dozen eyes on them, judging them. Another paramedic and a BPI detective emerged from the crowd, armed, and walking between Kayne and Dr. Locke, they shoved them out of the way. Reaching Detective Gray, the paramedic held her left arm, and acting like her protector, shot a glare at Kayne. The BPI detective stood beside the female paramedic, gun at the ready.

"I'm sorry." Mortals versus shapeshifters. They all knew who won the round. It wasn't Kayne.

"Are you ready?" the male paramedic asked.

"Get me the hell out of here," Macy demanded. Agent Asshole could take his apology and shove it up his ass, the damage had been done.

Kayne didn't expect Detective Gray to reply, but the hurt in her eye, as if he had wronged her, burned him, and left him watching in silence and holding onto her crux. As the paramedic helped steady her, and with their assistance, she met his gaze again. A dark cinnamon eye narrowed on him, giving him a view of the vehemence tangling in hate, while deep purple bruises with scarlet centers marred her face. Her lip was bleeding and crimson seeped through the white strips holding the cut above her eye closed. Detective Gray continued to glare at him when two more paramedics arrived to help. Both were men, and both wore guns. With her safely tucked between them, the four paramedics escorted her through the crowd and out of the warehouse. His hands were on his hips, he hung his head, and listened as the warehouse gradually returned to a mass of conversations and noise.

"Detective Gray left here wounded, scared, and angry," Tippi accused as she narrowed her green eyes. Her red cheeks gleamed with sweat, the front of her uniform was dark and stiff from blood, sweat, and dusted with sand. "If that was your purpose, to scare a BPI detective after she survived multiple Hunter Wolf attacks, I will be sure to include it in my report." Her glare flicked from Agent Sinclair to Dr. Locke and back again. "Agent Sinclair, your actions will be discussed later and in private. Doctor Locke, while I don't know you, and this is your territory, and you are the head of Sanative, it doesn't change the fact you've tainted your reputation because of your behavior. I would think having someone fight for the shapeshifters in this area to the extent Detective Gray has, you would have swallowed your pride."

"Excuse me? My pride?" Dr. Locke protested. "I have every right to speak with Detective Gray."

"Negative," Tippi countered. "You do not."

"Agent Pixley." What was Kayne going to say? *I needed to see her tattoo.* Negative.

Raising a blood-stained hand, Tippi gave them her palm to stop them from talking. "Enough. There are empaths in here, Agent Sinclair, maybe you can use their influence as an excuse for your behavior. Part of me hopes they are taking great pleasure in your agony. However, we need to find them and make sure there are no other victims held prisoner in those containers. And may I remind you this warehouse is teeming with mortals." With her last words, she gave them each a scowl, turned, and left, ending the conversation.

Kayne watched Agent Pixley's back and her red hair as she waded through the mass of people and disappeared. Despite her reprimand, he would do it all over again. With his imagination ruling his thoughts, he had to see the tattoo.

*Haul her back to Feather River and give her to Daeland then demand answers.* If there had been time, he would have looked for fang marks, but that would have been harder to explain. The paramedic would have shot him if Detective Gray didn't beat her to it. When she glared at him, her cold intentions filled her eye, and he knew she was thinking about killing him.

"Agent Sinclair, I offer an apology for my actions. They were a far cry from correct protocol as the head of Sanative. As alpha, it lacked a decent welcome to my territory," he stated.

Kayne faced the other alpha and met human eyes. "You are not the only one to blame. I, too, owe an apology. More so as I'm here with the DOJ, and not as an alpha."

"Agent Sinclair, then you know Desert Rock has seen its share of death and violence because of shapeshifters and the Otherkin. And whatever they're turning into. The mortals have accused me and my hospital, where I employ paranormals and give them sanctuary of protecting those responsible. This isn't good for us or the paranormal community. We cannot let this divide us," Dr. Locke began, then looked past Kayne to the expanse of the warehouse. "Let's not give our alliance to the list of victims."

"Indeed," Kayne agreed. The doctor never said anything about the tattoo, and neither would Kayne. He needed to talk to Dr. Locke alone, but there was no doubt the other werewolf knew it was there and knew about Daeland.

"You may be here in a professional compacity, still I welcome you, Alpha Kayne Sinclair of the Garrick Clan, from the Moonlight Territory." Following the greeting custom, he gave Kayne his forearm. His diplomatic words soothed over the situation while covering his strength boiling just beneath the surface.

"I accept your welcome, Alpha Landon Locke of the Gawain Territory," Kayne replied. With strong grips, they stared into each other's eyes while a soft vibration skidded along Kayne's skin, as if it was a slow flame reaching out from the alpha's hand. He knew his touch felt the same way, but knowing didn't absolve Dr. Locke's intention of another display of power. The vibration faded, leaving skin against skin. Their shared power meant their argument was over and would never be repeated. If it were brought up again, it would be a show of disrespect.

His hold tightened at the same time his eyes brightened with his wolf and he leaned closer. "Let it be known, Detective Macy Gray is under my protection, and I have enacted my right as alpha and claimed her as one of the Gawain pack. No one from the shapeshifter world or the paranormal world goes near her," he threatened. "That includes you."

*No, it doesn't.* "Does your pack agree with this?" Kayne asked, as he tightened his grip. *Protection from an alpha and a vampire lord, interesting.*

"Yes." Dr. Locke didn't back down, didn't ease his grip.

Did Detective Gray know the alpha of the territory was protecting her? By her reaction to him after their faceoff, he guessed not. "Your wolves allow you to protect a mortal? A mortal, who wouldn't hesitate to kill one of you given the chance."

Without hesitation, Kayne called Detective Gray a cold-blooded killer. Murderer. She admitted to shooting the therian, Mr. Barrette, and then when held by the throat, she used her silver blade to cut the Hunter Wolf's wrist. Her lack of fear in the wake of bloodshed and danger proved he was right. Why, then, did he feel the betrayal of his words in his bones? Because she had gotten inside his head and hadn't let go. The tattoo. If the doctor knew what it meant, was he using her to score points with Daeland?

"Like I said, there have been accusations against Sanative. And the death of Officer Murphy further fractured the tentative relationship between Sanative and law enforcement," he explained, the stress in his words. "The violence of these crimes and the crossovers are creating a divide between mortals and paranormals, and this area is too small for such a division. Detective Gray is an asset to the hospital and my pack. With her, we have an ally in the Bureau of Paranormal Investigations. My pack understands her worth."

"Is that all she is to you, an asset? A tool?" Kayne asked. Dr. Locke's challenge made jealousy rip a hole inside his emotions; her heartbeat drummed in his head, and her whimper drifted. He stopped from shaking his head, attempting to dislodge her presence.

"Anything else is none of your concern, and you have no jurisdiction over my territory, Agent Sinclair."

They released their hold on each other, and immediately put distance between them, leaving Kayne standing by Detective Gray's abandoned gear. He remained silent and stared at the pile while the tattoo, the investigation, and the doctor's protection over her fed his future accusations. If the doctor didn't know about the tattoo, why would he claim her? Why not another detective? It infuriated him. But the doctor was right, Kayne had no authorization for his line of questioning. Dr. Locke was within his rights to conduct business any way he saw fit, as long as it followed mortal law, pack law, and the Council's law. But it didn't mean Kayne had to like him, his claim of protection on Detective Gray, or the rules. In fact, he hated them.

"Understood. This is your territory and your rules, but if Detective Gray is involved with what is happening to the

Hunter Wolves, I will be well within my rights to ask as many questions as I want. You don't want to put yourself or your pack at risk for obstruction of justice, or have the Council inquiring about your actions, do you, Doctor Locke?" Kayne asked. His challenge plain on his face.

"You're investigating the wrong person," he replied and easily ignored the threat to himself and his pack.

"Time will tell," Kayne countered as he casually swept the area, making sure they hadn't become another spectacle.

"There is no doubt," Dr. Locke began. He inhaled and exhaled, and gathered his patience before saying, "I would be failing the Hippocratic Oath, if I didn't offer you medical treatment for your injuries."

Kayne faced the doctor when a man approached, dressed in the same green BDUs as the other Sanative medics and carrying a medical bag resembling Dr. Locke's. Clearly the mortal paramedics weren't going to give him medical aid. He was a walking contagion. Before he could refuse treatment, someone announced they found a survivor and it activated a variegated of uniforms, including Sanative medics, to rush for their gear.

"Meet Jason, he'll take of care you. Now, I'll leave you, Agent Sinclair, this is where my job begins," he advised as he turned to Jason. "Give him whatever he needs then join me."

"Yes, sir," Jason replied as he lowered his bag to floor.

"Doctor Locke, I'll expect an appointment with you to talk about the empaths, and the victims I found. I do know the Hunter Wolves are not our natural counterpart, and any information you have would help in the investigation. It may work in your favor," Kayne explained, his eyes showing his intent. A threat to Detective Gray and her relationship with Dr. Locke was low, even for him.

With drawn brows, Dr. Locke understood exactly what he was saying. "After we find them and get them secured at Sanative, I'll make sure you know. Right now, allow my medic to look at your injuries." He ignored the refence to Detective Gray's innocence, and after nodding to his medic, turned around and walked away.

"I don't need my injuries looked at," Kayne protested.

"I figured." Jason leaned toward him, inhaled, opened his mouth, and closing it bent down to his red medical bag. Opening a side pocket, he checked several bottles before choosing two and standing. "Syn silver. I'm assuming its secondary exposure, and you shifted. Two things, the first is a combination of vitamins and minerals. The vitamins will help your immune system and the minerals will break down the syn silver and will continue to help you over time. I'm recommending you take the vitamins and minerals then shift again. The second is a sedative, to help you rest."

Kayne was hesitant about taking the bottles and was prepared to tell Jason no, but the medic knew what he was talking about. *Can't hurt.* "Thanks." Kayne took the bottles from him and watched him close his bag, and slinging it over his shoulder, left to find Dr. Locke. Kayne replayed the doctor's words over and over, and his confidence with her innocence. How could she be innocent? The web he created was unraveling like the investigation.

"What the hell was that about?" Commander Wilson asked.

His sharp question instantly grated on Kayne's nerves, and he shook his head. He wasn't going to tell Commander Wilson the truth, when he evoked pack tradition over a challenge, and in front mortals. Plus, it was against the rules. It was another reminder of the problems with being a werewolf and working side by side with mortals. The situation reminded him of Detective Gray and how hard it was going to be for him to question her.

"Doctor Locke is the alpha here, I greeted him," Kayne answered. Simple and true. "We're going to need to question him."

"That might be true, but I'm not talking about you greeting the local alpha. The paramedic explained how you trapped Detective Gray. The same BPI detective that saved Agent Pixley's life and the life of her sergeant. Not to mention she's a person of interest in the investigation you blew wide open," Commander Wilson reminded him.

*The mortal caring about the mortal.* "I didn't know who he was, and a werewolf cannot give medical attention to a human. Naturally, knowing the extent of her wounds, I believed he posed a threat to Detective Gray." *Not a bad lie.*

Kayne scrubbed his face with his hand, felt sand grate on his skin, and exhaustion sat heavy in his muscles. Damn he was tired. Just for a moment, or at least until he was able to begin the actual investigation into the BPI, he wanted to forget Detective Gray, the mystery surrounding her, the tattoo, and Dr. Locke. *One thing at a time.* Commander Wilson barked an order, and Kayne watched as agents responded and detectives followed. He put himself in the middle of three investigations, the first being the warehouse, the second being the BPI, and the third being Elijah's connection to both. He couldn't kick the image out of his head and struggled to figure out how to best deal with Detective Gray and her tattoo. He would call Michael about Daeland. And then risk calling Daeland directly. *Lord Daeland, I found a mortal who hates paranormals with your blood crest inked on her back, and the local alpha has laid claim on her.* That'll go over well. *Oh yeah, even with her blatant hate, they all think she protects paranormals.*

"Agent Sinclair, I'm not going to repeat this ... keep your tone professional and your shapeshifter politics the hell out of your job. And if you see another lycan posing a threat to a human, how about not acting like an animal and ask about their intentions, instead of having a standoff?" Commander Wilson mocked.

"Affirmative, sir," Kayne responded.

Was he going to allow an over thirty-year-old mortal to call him, a two-hundred-and-seventy-six-year-old alpha and werewolf, who had served as a solider with the Coterie and Lord with the Council, an animal? Affirmative. Commander Wilson's tone continued to grate on his nerves, and his pride, and it left the bitter taste of frustration coating his mouth. Was it worth it? Was it worth dealing with Commander Wilson? Despite his anger and damaged pride, the answer was again, affirmative. He was too close to finding Elijah to care about anything else.

Above her, the golden sun started its decline, bringing garnet and honey sweeping through azure and across the scattered clouds. Macy loved the desert sunsets, admiring them from the comfort of her patio with wine and music, a little on the blues side, and her job faraway.

*Sharpshooter.* She had answered Agent Sinclair's question with arrogance, and it served as a warning to him. Cringing, Macy told herself she needed to stop thinking about him. With her mind busy trying to forget Agent Sinclair, she barely stopped before she touched the strips across the wound currently beating in time with her pulse. Then she looked at her bandaged fingertips and winced when scarlet had soaked through the white gauze. She was missing fingernails, had been punched, strangled, and had a concussion. What was next? How far was she going to push herself? How much more damage was she going to endure?

Macy heard Agent Logue's doubt and saw it in his hard gaze. She wasn't a suicide by Hunter Wolf form candidate. She would be the first to admit this one had been the worst. There had been lives on the line, and she was going to find out who was behind the Hunter Wolf forms. The paramedic beside her checked on her and she pushed the thoughts down. At least her throbbing head eased when a heated breeze feathered her skin, and she inhaled a breath of fresh air. Soon the worst of the tension from the warehouse began wearing off and she wished she was at home and locked away.

Two of the four paramedics remained beside her, the others leaving when they were safely out of reach of Dr. Locke, Agent Sinclair, and the Blood Rain team. The remaining two were escorting her toward a Rapid Response ambulance, its diesel engine rumbling while its red, blue, and amber lights cut through the tranquil hues of the evening's sunset. Her heart sank when among the evidence coaches, SUVs, and patrol cars, one of two Sanative ambulances, with its authoritative green and blue emergency lights warning drivers what was coming, drove over broken asphalt and toward the highway. *Headed to Sanative*. Macy heard it had taken three shifter paramedics and an empath nearly an hour to stabilize and properly sedate Sergeant Mayco for transport. She wondered what his medical records revealed, and what they said about his injuries and treatment. *Guilt*. Sergeant Mayco didn't need an hour drive in an ambulance, he needed a medical airship to take him to Sanative's trauma center.

That would never happen when his condition included critical wounds from an altered Hunter Wolf form, an unknown contagion, and he had spent hours in a hostile environment. It made him a hazard, and if he shifted and went into a frenzy inside the airship, the crew and Sergeant Mayco would be lost. He was getting his first taste of the difference between human and lycan.

*More guilt.* No one was talking about the contagion, because they knew it was going to be polluted, like the Hunter Wolves, and you could be next.

Dread pulsed in her veins, racing straight to her heart where it wrapped around the sliver of hope she cradled. Hope, a forbidden word in the BPI life. You didn't *hope* for anything—either you had a solid strategy securing a win, or you didn't, and you lost. Yet it didn't stop Macy from holding onto it with all her strength, even knowing hope played like a bitch and rarely let you win. She prayed they filled Sergeant Mayco's veins with CD4-T and he survived and continued to live as a human. Not a lycan. Not an abomination, and he didn't go through the same torture Mr. Barrette had. Half shifted and losing his humanity. With regret, she understood if the antiserum worked and he remined human, Macy would never work with him. She failed to protect him and then the catastrophe Dr. Locke and Agent Sinclair engineered to destroy the shreds of confidence the detectives had in her. And that said nothing of her own injuries. Head trauma, missing fingernails, and another round of treatment meant her time in the BPI was quickly coming to an end. It wasn't as bad as Sergeant Mayco. If the antiserum failed and he crossed over, his career with the BPI was instantly terminated. Medically retired due to the lycanthrope virus. Humanoid identification rejected.

"All right, Detective, Sergeant Mayco is on his way to Sanative. You've waited long enough, it's time for you to leave," the paramedic urged and nudged her, his voice soft.

*So much guilt.* Macy watched until the lights disappeared, and she was staring at the open desert. "My gear is in the warehouse. My gun." She wanted her gun knowing she wouldn't get it. It would be tagged as evidence and sent to forensics, the same with her gear. Agent Sinclair and the DOJ were there to investigate the BPI, she didn't want them having her things. Mainly her gun. Screw the chip in her vest, Agent Sinclair already knew. "I need to talk to a detective."

"Negative. You're going to the hospital. I'll make sure a *detective* retrieves your belongings," he assured as he placed his hand on her back, urging her to walk.

She stopped and feebly faced him. "I have to tell a detective not to let the DOJ have it. I'm going back," Macy ordered, and caught her sharp tone.

The paramedic's hazel eyes held regret and sympathy. "No. I will tell a detective no DOJ. Especially Blood Rain."

He looked at her like she was trying to hold onto water. *Don't feel sorry for me,* Macy wanted to say. Instead, she gave a fake smile, that must look horrific with her wounds and the blood covering her. "Especially. And I want another gun."

"Understood."

*I want another gun. I sound like a lunatic.* Having to accept he was going to do what he said, Macy forced her stiff muscles to obey and limped beside him. When they reached the open doors, a female paramedic was waiting and wearing a white biohazard suit and gloves, her hair pulled back from her face. Stepping down the first stair with a booted foot, she held her gloved hand out. "Let me help."

Macy let the woman take her left arm and help her amble up the two stairs, and into the cabin where she sat on a gurney. She had no idea her legs were so sore.

"Cobi, the details of Detective Gray's injuries have been uploaded to Genesis," he reported. Remaining outside, strands of brown hair drifted with the breeze and Macy caught him inhaling, no doubt relieved to be out of the warehouse.

Without acknowledging Macy or the paramedic, Cobi sat on the bench seat and touched the screen mounted to the top of a storage compartment. "Affirmative, Jake, I have it."

"Perfect. Closing it up." Jake nodded to Cobi, gave Macy a half smile, and closed both doors of the ambulance, then hit the side twice.

"Initiating sentient Genesis. Recording treatment of patient two-fourteen, BPI Detective Macy Gray. Please, Detective Gray, lay down and we'll start. Are you still having problems with nausea?" Cobi asked, and continued tapping the screen, only pausing to give her a quick look.

*Affirmative.* "Negative," Macy answered. She didn't need anything else added to the cocktail they were about to give her. Easing back on the gurney, her body relaxed into the padding, her breathing coming in small gasps while the air-conditioned interior sent chills spreading across her skin. A blast of purified air caused her to jump. She tried fisting the sides of her BDU pants and was reminded she couldn't. Out of the corner of her eye, she watched Cobi narrow her gaze, like she was gauging if Macy was going to lose her mind, and if it happened, how fast could she sedate her. "Sorry, took me by surprise."

"Understood. I'm going to touch your arm," Cobi warned, and reached for her right arm. Turning it palm up, she rested it on the gurney. After cleaning dirt and blood from the bend of her elbow with another dose of liquid fire, she warned, "There will be a pinch." The first needle slid in, and securing the catheter, Cobi removed the needle and unrolled clear plastic tubing to a waiting bag. Efficiently, she repeated the process on Macy's left arm. "Another pinch, Detective Gray."

Cobi finished with the IV, tossed the used needles into the biohazard container, and facing the screen tapped it several times, and then turned her attention back to her. "Patient two-fourteen, BPI Detective Macy Gray, has multiple surface abrasions on her hands. The right hand is missing fingernails and partial nailbed from the ring digit, middle digit, and index. Left hand is missing fingernails, nailbed intact, from the middle digit, ring digit. Surface abrasions to the face as well as a deep laceration across her forehead. As stated, the deep laceration is consistent with the diagnoses of a concussion. Patient two-fourteen is alert and responding to commands. As recommended by Medic Reed, I'm starting a line of NS for dehydration and antibiotics for possible bacterial infection. With shapeshifter presence and the evidence of blood on her face, exposed skin, and clothing, a line of CD4-T, precautionary for therianthrope and lycanthrope contagions, is authorized."

After Cobi finished listing her medical conditions and treatment, making her thankful she didn't get into anything airborne, because they would have put her in a bubble and shipped her to the hospital, Macy closed her eyes. *It's over.* She could relax until they arrived at the trauma center. Her head began throbbing and she tried to force the world to stop spinning and the confusion from taking over. She didn't fight the bank of hazy fog closing around her thoughts, and it left her with the feel of Agent Sinclair's hands on her skin. They had been rough, calloused, and his sun-kissed skin meant he spent a lot of time outside. *Sun-kissed.* Head trauma and blood loss. She changed the path her mind wanted to wander by concentrating on Sergeant Mayco and the CD4-T headed to her veins.

"Detective Gray, what is your date of birth?"

*Here we go.* Macy opened her eye, stared up at the ceiling noticing the camera, and answered, the date tumbling from her lips. Tasting blood, she raised her left hand to wipe it away with her cuff when Cobi held her arm.

"Sorry, I'll take care of that." Cobi took a germicidal wipe and cleaned the blood from Macy's lips, igniting flames. She threw the wipe into the biohazard bin and began arranging the transfer straps. Cobi watched her reaction as she buckled the first restraint across her chest, hesitated, then continued with her hips and legs. "Your work phone number?"

Again, Macy stared up at the camera. *See, I'm normal, not a spectacle on display.* She answered the question.

"Excellent. Lance, we're clear. Let's get out of here."

"Affirmative," Lance replied from the front.

"Initiate live stream. Mercy Summit will watch her."

"The patient has a concussion, you need to stay with her," Lance advised.

Macy clung to the conversation, using it to battle her wandering thoughts of Agent Sinclair and the weight of his voice in her head. There were mere feet separating them and the driver sounded distant, like he was mumbling. No, whispering.

"After the effects of the initial dose have passed, the CD4-T will put her to sleep. I'm not worried about the concussion. Anyway, Medic Reed reported she has anxiety, PTSD, and after an altercation with Doctor Locke and a lycan DOJ agent, feared it may have triggered her. Right now, she's calm. Plus, she's missing fingernails down to the nailbed ... I've never seen a BPI detective with missing fingernails. If her wounds are any indication of what went on inside of that place and what happened to her, there's no doubt she needs the rest," Cobi explained.

"Copy," Lance responded. The engine rumbled, eased into motion, and he maneuvered the vehicle through the maze of emergency trucks and law enforcement cars. "This is transport eight, en route to Mercy Summit."

*PTSD. Anxiety.* Macy could hear her therapist. *An altercation, my ass.* The radio buzzed, and her mind went to Agent Sinclair and he might have been right when he said there was deadener in the warehouse. *Stop thinking about him.* Would explain why no one escaped the place, they couldn't make a call to get help. Dispatch responded, and she listened as they relayed that they were waiting with a quarantine room on standby. The ride smoothed out telling her they were on the road, and she drifted back to the warehouse, back between Dr. Locke and Agent Sinclair and it made her mind and body ache. They had disrespected her, embarrassed her, and she wanted payback. She would have to wait until she was healed. Macy needed to go to sleep and forget about Agent Sinclair. *There's nothing I can do to him. But Dr. Locke ... I'll take care of him later.*

"Is she asleep?" Lance asked.

"Detective Gray?" Cobi called. "Appears so. I'll add the dash screen." A second of silence ticked by, the ambulance slowed, then sped up. "She's out. Go ahead."

"What did Doctor Locke do?'"

Macy fought the urge to fall into the deep end of her mind and the nothing inching closer, but she needed to hear their conversation. She wanted to know what had been reported. *So they can add it to my stellar career file.*

"From what the report states, he challenged the agent when he tried to talk to Detective Gray, but no one said anything, and neither of them asked a question. When Detective Gray crawled out from between them, Medic Reed pulled a tranq gun on them. She also said Doctor Locke wouldn't leave Detective Gray, and watched her treat the detective's wounds. Like he could help her when he isn't allowed," Cobi explained.

*Crawled.* Another strike to her pride. Macy wanted to argue but couldn't because it was true, and it left her without a defense. She didn't make a sound or act like she had heard them. And really, she didn't care. For the first time in hours, she wasn't defending herself, caring what someone saw, and as sad as it was to admit, she felt protected.

"Doctor Locke, of all people? He has the most to lose by threatening a BPI detective. If they wanted, they could investigate him and shut down his hospital."

"Maybe they should investigate him. Say he's responsible for what's happening. Hunter Wolf forms? And he's a doctor. He could have a mad scientist lab," Cobi mused. "Think about that."

"I don't want to. Did Medic Reed find out what the DOJ agent wanted?" Lance asked.

"No, but that's what you get when you have to work with paranormals and have them for friends," Cobi answered. "You can't escape them."

*No truer words, damn lycans.* It was the same reason Sergeant Mayco doubted her and didn't want to work with her. She consorted with the enemy. Losing the battle with exhaustion and the drugs, she felt her muscles relaxing as images slipped before her eyes. Perfectly good eyes. She could see their faces and the hate saturating their bodies like a disease as they stared at her. David, Sergeant Mayco, and Agent Sinclair. She didn't want to see Agent Sinclair again, ever. Macy had the feeling he was going to be the one to hit the final nail into her coffin. Worse than that, she didn't like the way he looked at her. His eyes alone made her feel things she shouldn't, like she needed him. That made her feel like a traitor.

"Doctor Locke and the agent better be glad Detective Gray didn't shoot them. I've heard she has never hesitated to down a shapeshifter," Lance continued.

*Let the damn conversation die*, Macy prayed.

"Medic Reed moved her gear and gun out of reach, or I think she would have," Cobi teased. "I would have loved to see it."

*I hesitated.* Mrs. Barrette entered the game. *Turn it off.* She made it out and wasn't going to Sanative. The thick veil of unconsciousness crowded her as the CD4-T continued to slide from the bag to the line, and burned as it coursed through her veins. She hated this part. How was she going to sleep when her circulatory system was on fire? Tears slipped down her temples from the pain, then excruciating seconds ticked by when an artificial numbness, which Macy eagerly embraced, saturated her bloodstream. Drifting further, the sound of Agent Sinclair's voice as he said her name tangled within her, and the unnerving feeling she knew him took root. Macy didn't want him invading her dreams. She wanted the darkness all to herself.

Two Sanative medics, carrying a stretcher with a black body bag, walked by Kayne and out of the warehouse. With the help of Agent Pixley and an empath from Sanative, three empaths had been found, their emaciated bodies making it look like they had been dead for weeks. But with the heat and imprisoned in a steel container it could have been days. The one survivor, a female, fighting for her life, had to wait for the BPI sergeant to be transported—which had taken over an hour—before it was safe to transport her. Once she was out of the warehouse, the emotionally-charged atmosphere cleared, letting the paranormals do their job without her influence.

Kayne watched a detective holding a tablet walk the warehouse, making notes. The information would be wirelessly transmitted to the BPI office where a team of detectives and forensic technicians would watch the video feed and read the reports. Afterwards, they would conduct interviews, then recommend charges against the empath, which would be extensive since she used her trait to manipulate her victims. The investigation would include the owner of the warehouse, the dead, the Hunter Wolves, Henry and Grace, and a search for other suspects. Elijah could have kidnapped the empath, like Henry and Grace, and forced her to do whatever he demanded. It would help her case. If she lived. Kayne cringed with the influence one woman had been capable of creating and didn't want to know what it would have been like to have the four empaths manipulating him. He would have gone insane. His mind instantly went to Detective Gray. What the hell was he going to do with her?

Lost in thought, he looked at the sun's honey glow breaching the sand-crusted windows and realized it was early evening and he spent the entire day inside of the disgusting warehouse. Mumbled voices from a dozen different conversations buzzed, creating a distinct difference from when he first entered the building. The mortal BPI detectives and DOJ agents were dressed in protective biohazard suits and collected evidence while the shapeshifters, Agent Logue and Agent Kriss among them, continued to search the containers. Kayne shifted his feet, taking weight off his side—he was going to have to shift—and half listened to Commander Wilson's cell phone conversation.

When he ended the call, he groaned, put the cell in a side pocket, and rubbed his neck. "After they're finished checking the containers, the crime scene techs will be here for hours cataloging the perishable evidence from the lab."

"How long will we be able to hold the place?" Looking at the stacks of containers, Kayne felt the hours multiplying, and his stay in Desert Rock turning into months.

"This isn't staying local. The state of California is planning to take control of it indefinitely. The attorney general is filing an affidavit based on the Requiem Preternatural Act as we speak. As soon as the judge signs it, we'll have it until we're done," Commander Wilson explained. "Then it will be turned over to a state controller and most likely auctioned off."

When a string of territory fights resulted in the deaths of mortals, destruction of property, endangerment, and created a contagion hazard, the federal government created the Requiem Preternatural Act, or RP Act. It worked as an ongoing, open-ended search warrant, giving law enforcement agencies the right to search compounds, meeting grounds, or anywhere packs, clans, prides, or factions were present without the need of a judge-signed search warrant. Unless the state was absorbing the property, then a signature was required, like now it gave the state the authority to take whatever land or property they wanted ... indefinitely. The RP Act worked as a hostile, exaggerated, and corrupted version of eminent domain.

*If there's an ongoing investigation.* "That was quick. And aggressive."

"Affirmative. I asked about that. The state is confiscating the property because of the problems involving shapeshifters the area is known for. And the owner of this little piece of heaven disappeared from his house several days ago after a confrontation with DRPD and the BPI. During the call the husband and wife shapeshifted into lions," Commander Wilson explained.

"All right, they were therians. It doesn't explain why they can enforce the RP Act," Kayne countered.

"No one knew they were therians. They identified as humanoid and were registered as human, which was why the DRPD was first on scene. Neither applied for the screening process for inclusion and a controlled crossover. Both had been infected and refused medical attention. Mr. Barrette owned this warehouse, as well as Golden State Shipping Company, one of the biggest in the state. He broke state and federal laws. The RP Act is just one of many laws they will enforce to seize all of his properties and assets."

Infected against their will, maybe. *If* they were infected by another therian and not given the contagion through White

Cell. Kayne would have to ask Dr. Locke about the autopsy. "Did you say Mr. Barrette?"

"Correct. He was a suspect. Mr. Barrette is the therian Detective Gray shot. Sanative is taking care of his body as we speak," Commander Wilson answered.

*Damn.* "I saw the body. He had been trying to shift for a week?" Kayne asked. Like Henry, he couldn't complete the transition, and was probably losing his mind. He had to accept the therian attacked Detective Gray, and she knew who he was. She told him as much when she confessed to shooting him.

"Affirmative." Commander Wilson met Kayne's gaze.

"The BPI was at his house? Was Detective Gray present?" he asked, knowing the answer.

"Affirmative. Both Sergeant Mayco and Detective Gray were there. The wife died from a Death Bloom. It's being blamed on White Cell, of course." Commander Wilson's usual arrogant tone faltered under his frustration.

Kayne felt his unease and didn't know if it was over the crimes, the warehouse, or both. "White Cell?" he asked, needing confirmation. What was it doing to the victims?

"The BPI found bottles all over the house. It appears the couple had been taking it for an unknown amount of time. It's assumed, because they were actively taking the drug, they believed it would stop them from crossing over. It didn't. It didn't stop them from redecorating to suit their new selves either," Commander Wilson answered. "I would wait before adding that information to our investigation, until you have read the entire report."

"Affirmative. Was Doctor Locke at the house?" Of course he was. Why did it piss Kayne off?

"Affirmative. The woman died before being cataloged as therian, so the BPI denied him entrance. He took control over the body after the coroner gave him permission. He wasn't allowed in the house, so he might not be any help with those specific details," Commander Wilson replied.

Someone told the doctor no. "Who denied him entrance?" Kayne asked. *Let me guess* ...

"Detective Gray."

He knew that. "Doctor Locke might be able to answer some questions about the White Cell. Hopefully he has tested the Hunter Wolf's and Mrs. Barrette's DNA and has an idea of what's altering shapeshifters into ersatz."

"Maybe. It'll be a stretch," Commander Wilson responded absently. "Someone else can talk to him. Captain Dixon wants his people questioned about this warehouse. It came under investigation several months ago by the city's Building Division. An officer from the DRPD and a BPI detective oversaw the investigation. The report states the applicant, Mr. Barrette, was a humanoid, proved by DNA testing, and the warehouse came through as clean, ending the investigation. We'll have to find out who the officer and detective were and if they physically inspected the warehouse. Also, I want any report connected to this warehouse. There has to be something."

"Copy. A BPI detective was involved, and the captain doesn't know who? That's another element added to their growing list of problems. They seem to be putting their detectives at risk," Kayne added.

"Which was why there was a quiet internal investigation planned. Since you singlehandedly made it impossible, I want you and Agent Pixley to do the questioning. I'll be back and forth between here and the office." Commander

Wilson's face twisted with the thought he was going to spend hours and days inside the warehouse.

"Absolutely. Like I said, I didn't see evidence a werewolf infected the victim, I believe it's White Cell. At least for Henry. I want the Hunter Wolves checked for it, too," Kayne requested.

"Affirmative. FYI, Detective Gray insisted the White Cell from the Barrettes' house was tested, and had a rush put on it, so the BPI are aware of the ersatz and the connection to White Cell. The tested version had the same characteristics as White Cell, without the degraded CD4-T. The tested vials won't stop the contagion or anyone from crossing over. If our suspicions are correct and someone is spreading the contagion by saying it's White Cell, they're purposely infecting people. Purposely turning them into ersatz against their wills. We're in trouble," Commander Wilson replied.

Kayne wasn't surprised Detective Gray and the BPI knew the shapeshifters were different. How were they investigating the crimes? "It's not White Cell. It's the contagion, and something else, what if there's an accelerant? Henry infected his wife days ago and it had already started to change her humanoid features. The contagion from a natural lycanthrope would have given her the ability to heal, and she wasn't. There's something wrong."

"Mutating its victims. White Cell is on the street and there's no way to stop it. It would be like trying to eliminate drugs." Commander Wilson put his hands on his hips. "Days. The usual time frame, in a perfect world, would be?"

"Perfect time frame. Weeks with the assistance of the full moon, and an alpha," Kayne replied.

Commander Wilson studied him, looking as if he had destroyed the slim chance they were going to figure out who was behind the polluted White Cell, and the spy in the BPI.

"You said the wife died from a Death Bloom, and the BPI was present when it happened. Who witnessed her death?" Kayne asked, trying to change the subject. He was surprised they hadn't shot her. Shoot first, kill your witness, the BPI had a lot to learn if they wanted to solve the case. Suddenly, the reason Detective Gray was still working after the internal investigation of negligence in Officer Murphy's death made sense. There wasn't anyone else to take her place. The detectives were plagued by covering anything related to paranormals.

"This is where I'm going to remind you, if you had checked in with Captain Dixon, and read the complete report, we wouldn't be having this conversation." Commander Wilson gave Kayne a sideways glance. "Per the report, Mrs. Barrette ran toward the BPI team. The sergeant called for tranquilizers, and when they failed, he ordered the sharpshooter to put her down. Before a shot was fired, Mrs. Barrette collapsed and died."

"No one shot her when she attacked?" It was hard to keep the tone of surprise out of his question.

"Don't be shocked, Agent Sinclair. Not all humans think shooting shifters is the answer. There are some law enforcement officers who believe the term 'innocent until proven guilty', or some variance of it, applies to paranormals, too." Commander Wilson gave him another slightly irritated glance, took a slow breath through his mouth, and exhaled. The heat in the warehouse was stifling, and the smell even worse. "The BPI has been dealing with the increasing violence as best they can. If they had one witness, one break of who or why this was happening, I think they would use it. It just so happens, Detective Gray was ordered to take the shot and refused."

*Sharpshooter.* "Why her and why did she refuse?" Thoughts raced in his head while accusations, questions, and her tattoo fogged his concentration.

"Captain Dixon says she has an uncanny way of tracking her target and that makes her the best marksmen for the team. That's why she's active, despite the mess with the officer. But they're not saying why she didn't take the shot. Just that she refused."

"Who is saying?" Damn, if he had checked in, he wouldn't be missing information. Important information.

"The other BPI detectives. She's good at her job, sometimes too good. If I didn't know better, I would say they're a little jealous or maybe fearful. So much so, they test her for lycanthropy and therianthropy every couple of months. Interestingly, they failed to point out they test everyone every couple of months, per BPI policy, and depending on the cases worked. Sounds to me they have a grudge."

"Like Officer Murphy. It doesn't explain why her fellow detectives are turning against her," Kayne mumbled. When he held her, she searched for another detective but didn't ask for help. Was it out of embarrassment because she needed help or because she didn't think they would have helped?

"Murphy and Gray had been seen together in public and some of the DRPD officers and BPI detectives thought they were seeing each other on a personal level. Then Doctor Locke overrode Rapid Response and took her to Sanative after the attack at Harper's warehouse. And his actions today did not help her. Nor did yours."

Choosing a werewolf over a mortal would make her a traitor. "You said the doctor transported her to Sanative?"

"That's right. She had been banged up pretty good, although not as bad as today," Commander Wilson answered. "Why?"

*It gave Dr. Locke the opportunity to have an unhindered view of her tattoo.* "Detective Gray refused a direct order to take a shot, was transferred to Sanative for injuries, and returned to work. Did the BPI reprimand her for disobeying a direct order while under duress? And don't they have a mandatory medical leave?" Kayne asked.

"There is no paperwork about a reprimand. And I don't know about the medical leave, you'll have to ask. Are you worried about questioning her?" Commander Wilson nodded in the direction of two detectives.

Kayne watched them approach. "Affirmative. Detective Gray's injuries are extensive, she could be out for weeks. And if they have protocol concerning the emotional repercussions, she'll have to complete the required counseling. If she chooses to take leave, her absence could be longer."

"If Captain Dixon approves the leave, which he won't, it'll turn into an administrative hearing," Commander Wilson lowered his voice, "and she'll be forced to come in. Albeit every convenience will be made to accommodate her needs."

Without saying anything to Kayne or Commander Wilson, a detective knelt, and with gloved hands, started to put Detective Gray's gear into a plastic bag marked evidence.

"What are you doing?" Kayne demanded. He had planned on the DOJ collecting her things.

"What does it look like?" the detective countered. He picked up her gun, checked to see if it was loaded, and after clearing the weapon, placed it in another evidence bag. Both bags had the BPI emblem, and Bureau of Paranormal Investigations Evidence on their sides.

"This is a DOJ investigation." Kayne lowered his voice, emphasizing his statement.

"Affirmative. The BPI assisted," the second detective explained, his brown eyes narrowing when they met Kayne's gaze. "In order for Detective Gray to remain armed, her weapon has to be turned in to evidence."

"Armed?" Kayne asked. She was demanding another gun.

"Affirmative. I don't blame her." His eyes blazed with his hate toward Kayne.

Must have watched the standoff. "It was a simple question." Sensing the unease and anger from both detectives, he enjoyed the feeling. He was almost back to his normal self. *Have to get out of the warehouse.*

"It was a simple answer," the first detective shot back at him. After securing the items in the bags, they gave Kayne and Commander Wilson scowls, then turned and started in the direction of the door where a female crime scene tech waited.

"Looks like your stunt got their attention. They might have their internal disagreements and problems, but they'll protect their own. When the truth comes out and the spy is revealed, I'm curious to see how they recover." Commander Wilson watched the men. "They don't like you."

"Not surprised. Do you think they're *against* her?" Kayne asked, watching the working detectives with new eyes. Any one of them could be the spy. And still his mind went to Elijah, Detective Gray, and their connection to one another.

"Maybe not against, but like I said, cautious. I'm sure they are all wondering who the spy is and the Hunter Wolves are an added threat. The little things, like Doctor Locke, add up and pollute the truth. Besides, Detective Gray's actions today won't be ignored. She saved their sergeant and Agent Pixley and didn't escape unharmed. If she's playing for the wrong side, I don't know why she would put her life at risk. It'd be a shame if she's guilty, I'm going to hate arresting her." Commander Wilson's voice was thick with agitation.

True, Detective Gray hadn't given up the fight. Kayne didn't have a reply when his body and mind were exhausted and thinking about the case had his thoughts going in circles. He was too close to the detectives; he needed to read the files, and he needed time to think about the questions he was going to ask.

"Agent Sinclair, why don't you get out of here? Tomorrow is going to be busy, and you need a shower. That's an order." Commander Wilson gave him a once over.

"That's putting it mildly," Kayne mumbled. "Affirmative, sir." He checked the warehouse, the agents, detectives, and the evidence. He got what he wanted. Whether it was going to lead him to Elijah or not he didn't know, but it was start. It made the ersatz real, and with the BPI they would be able to prove it. In silence, he turned from the wall of containers and started toward the door and freedom.

"Agent Sinclair, wait," Commander Wilson ordered.

Kayne hung his head. *So close.* "Sir," he replied, and slowly faced the commander.

Commander Wilson closed the distance, and when he stood in front of Kayne, he stopped and handed him a stainless-steel vial, the plunger at the top unused, the needle hidden in the chamber. Behind him a forensic detective held an evidence bag with a helmet, goggles, and a black coiled cord. "Doctor Locke wanted me to show this to you."

"Why?" Kayne asked. What did a vapor tranquilizer have to do with him?

"Standard BPI issue and holds enough sedative to knock out a shapeshifter. It was found not far from Mr. Barrette's body. Looks like Detective Gray tried tranquilizing him."

Not possible. She had reached for a tranq when she was stating protocol over Henry. Kayne didn't believe it and handed it back to Commander Wilson. "How do you know its hers?"

"It's an assumption right now. They also found pieces of a mic and a cord. She was missing her radio, and it's assumed to be hers. The BPI has her gear, they'll check to see what's missing, and back the information with matching serial numbers. Plus, Detective Gray was the only person to see him. Mr. Barrette would have been an excellent witness. Why would Doctor Locke want you to see it?" Commander Wilson asked.

*Would have been an excellent witness.* A broken mic? Mr. Barrette attacked her. "To prove she isn't the hardened sharpshooter her reputation would suggest," Kayne replied. *Maybe not the spy.* If the serial numbers matched, the doctor was going to be Detective Gray's savior, for the second time.

"I see. You questioned him before or after the standoff?" Commander Wilson gave it to a detective, who dropped it into an evidence bag.

Kayne looked at the containers and never wanted to see another one in his life. "After, sir."

"Don't make an enemy out of him. We need his help," Commander Wilson warned. "Now get out of here."

"Sir." Dreading another distraction, Kayne quickly wove around evidence containers, gear, and personnel, and made it out of the warehouse.

The clean breeze brought fresh air swirling around his face and a crisp chill across his skin, which swiftly vanished as the warmth of the desert's wind took its place. The parking lot was a different scene than it had been when he chased the Hunter Wolf hours earlier. There were vehicles everywhere, and industrial lighting was being set up in anticipation for nightfall. Kayne spotted his truck and ambled an easier path as he made his way through the network of vehicles. He tried focusing his thoughts on the investigation, came up short, and had to admit the Hunter Wolves proved their point. They were stronger, they were getting organized, there could be dozens of them, and they weren't opposed to killing law enforcement. Several BPI detectives had been wounded and were on their way to hospitals. One of them was heading to Sanative for treatment for wounds and the contagion, while the others were heading to mortal hospitals. Like Detective Gray.

When he stood in front of his truck he stopped, exhaled and inhaled, and stared at the wreckage. *The black wreck.* He wasn't going to be driving it anywhere with missing windows, a bent axel, and the hood, caved in by the Hunter Wolf, hid whatever damage had been done to the engine. Under the truck he could see puddles where its fluids had drained. *Damn.*

"Sir, I can take you back to Desert Rock," Agent Lyrik offered. "We have three more agents waiting at the BPI office." His blue BDUs wore beige dusting from being in the warehouse, and his usually combed sandy blond hair was sweat soaked and stuck to his skull.

"Thanks. Let me get a tow truck out here," Kayne replied as he walked around to the driver's side.

How he was going to get it fixed, he didn't know. Metal squealed when he tugged the door open, the movement sending shards of glass to the ground. Shaking his head, Kayne climbed behind the wheel, sat back, and for the first time in hours, relaxed. The weight on his shoulders brought the sting of syn silver to reach into his neck, then it skated down his spine. He didn't change positions to ease the pain; it reminded him he almost died in the warehouse. Yes, he was satisfied with what he found, and relieved it hadn't been a lost cause, but it meant more. He couldn't lie to himself and blame the warehouse and the empath when the truth nagged at him.

"Redemption," Kayne whispered. "Forgiveness." His heart clenched with the admission at the same time his emotions amped up. "Stop." Syn silver, near death, and fighting were going to make his emotions erratic. Made sense. Straightening, he grabbed his cell phone from the center console and found he had service. There had been a deadener. After a couple of phone calls, he reached a woman whose thick voice, from years of smoking, assured him she would send a truck and sure, towing it to the BPI office wouldn't be a problem. With a shaky hand, Kayne replaced his cell, and without thinking, fearing it would cause damage, he leaned on the seat and reached over to the files on the floorboard. Intending on taking them with him, he noticed the shuffled papers and photos weren't as he had left them and weren't in the folder.

Detective Gray's picture had been sitting on top with her file and medical records; now, it sat under the stack, hidden. Kayne leaned farther, trying to reach the farthest report, when he caught the slightest aroma. He didn't have to guess it was her. His senses began eliminating the odors and targeting the scent. It wasn't the sweat, dirt, fear, and rot from the warehouse clinging to them all, but a vanilla spice tangled with the harsh desert air. Detective Gray had been in his truck, saw the files, and rifled through them. She knew why he was there when she found him. She knew and hadn't said anything to him or the other DOJ agents. Anyone else would have tried to prove their innocence, and maybe tried to excuse their guilt. Detective Gray hadn't. He didn't know if her silence made her look innocent or guilty.

Kayne sat up, and keeping a hold on her scent, let it linger in his head. He had smelled her when he held her, and when he had shoved her shirt to the side to see the tattoo. He inhaled the threads of vanilla while his hands held her warm skin against his and it quickly gave him images of Detective Gray and her cinnamon eyes ringed with silver. *It's my imagination.* She was as much a suspect as Elijah. Closing his eyes, he opened them to see the parking lot. The poisoning and exhaustion were causing him to see things that weren't there. Cinnamon eyes ringed with silver meant nothing but guilt, his need for redemption, and revenge.

Crawling out of the murky depths of the sedative-induced sleep, Macy felt the familiar sting of heartbreak when she saw their faces and their voices played. Her weakness amplified her pain as she watched her mom's red/brown eyes, holding worry, narrow and searching Macy's face, her lips curved around silent words. A warning? Was she saying I love you for the last time? She didn't know, its worth lost in her imagination and the years her mother had been gone. *Years*, Macy reminded herself, *and here you are*. Carefully testing her aching body, she rolled to her back, and not wanting to see her blurred bedroom, her eyes remained closed, allowing her to watch her parents come back from the dead.

The need to understand what her mother had said bit down on Macy like a steel trap with teeth. How? It was an unknown she couldn't investigate. There was no one to answer her questions. Her grandparents said it was an accident. There were no leads. It left her without a target. Time forced her to accept the unsolved case, what caused the crash, and the details of her parents. Lost inside her dream, she turned to see her dad, his height put his head close to the roof of the car, the ends of his dark hair near his ears and skirting his collar, while his broad shoulders made the seat look narrow. He was driving fast and struggling to control the car while beside them the mountainside grew ever closer. His eyes glanced to the rearview mirror, locked on her, his fear holding his dark gaze, then to the road, his face twisted with dread.

Macy couldn't stop herself from watching him struggle and continued to when his eyes, midnight black, slowly bleed into an icy silver, like fear had taken a physical form in his gaze. The image had her heart pounding inside of her chest. It wasn't real, none of it was. Her father's eyes and her mother's missing words were all imaginary like they had been for twenty-three years. A hot tear escaped her good eye, slipped down her temple, and following the curve of her head slid into her hair. Macy refused to touch it when the nightmare wasn't new. How could it be when it was always the same?

*No, God, no.* Panic threatened her, and she wanted to scream to block out the noise and the smoke, and when she thought terror would stop her heart, everything went silent. No crunching metal, screams, or growls. It felt like an eternity before she woke to black smoke pouring in through the air vents, dirt and rocks through the broken windows, and she fought to see through the thick cloud. As the fire quickly spread, a cold sheet of sweat covered her, and fighting a cough, she ignored the burning in her lungs and jerked on the safety belt. It wouldn't budge, making her struggle against its hold as she fought to get to the front of the car. She had to see her parents, save them, get them out, but the seatbelt held her tight, she couldn't move, and didn't have the strength to fight. Through the fractured windshield she watched a rush of flames sweep over the hood and heard the crackling paint, the searing hiss of oil and fluids sounding louder than her thoughts. When the blaze swallowed the front end and reached through the windshield, she pushed against the seat as orange/red tips inched toward her, licking her knees and moving up their heated ends kissed her face. She was going to die.

Macy stilled, knowing what she was going to do and knowing it was going to hurt, and crying from sorrow and pain, she wasn't leaving her parents behind to burn. *My family.* Held in the memory's grip, she yanked the flannel blanket to her face, was reminded of her missing fingernails, inhaled, and smelled the familiar lavender of fabric softener and rolled to her side. No fire. She was in her house, living her life, and good or bad, those were the cards dealt.

"This time it's different," she mumbled into the blanket, her split lip catching on the fabric.

A gust of wind swept inside the car, clearing the thickest smoke, and facing the window she saw David had joined the cast of ghosts. She blamed the warehouse, the concussion, and the painkillers, it didn't change seeing him waiting for her, through the haze and flames. With no way out, she met his gaze and watched his empty eyes narrow on her. Slowly, like he knew her life story, knowledge sat in their dead pits, bringing unspoken accusations to life. Did he know she had been investigating him? That she didn't love him, and their closeness had been a lie? Did he suspect she wasn't capable of loving anyone? The truth sent another hot tear down the side of her face. Macy investigated a fellow cop, betrayed the people she worked with, and the people who thought she believed in them. Could he see the betrayal in her eyes?

*"You're the cause of this."* When he spoke, his mouth remained closed, his blue lips unmoving, and his bruised face didn't react to his charge. He stood with one shoulder lower than the other, his shredded uniform hanging on his boney frame as blood seeped from claw marks, and he stared at her with black eyes.

Guilt never played fair. She knew she failed to protect him, and David died while she was investigating him. Macy executed the ultimate betrayal. As for her parents and the memory, they were more fiction than reality, a truth hurting more than their deaths. The regret and pain were pointless when there was nothing she could have done. Even in the aftermath of the nightmare, she understood saying sorry wasn't going to change things. It wasn't going to change her. She escaped the flames and wreckage, and they didn't.

Rolling to her back, she stared up at the blurry ceiling fan and watched the blades until they merged into one. Damn, she hated being hurt. It let the memories she worked to bury and keep under control have freedom.

With determination to get over her aches and pains, she pushed herself up, ignoring the stings of scratches and the thundering in her head. Macy sat up to stare out the window at the cool yellow sun as it warmed the day and crossed the sky, moving everything along, like the investigation, without her. She didn't care. Cared less she would miss Agent Sinclair. Nausea swam in her stomach, her sight blurred, and she eased back to her pillow, snuggled into her covers, tugged the soft blanket to her face, and feigned sleep.

Images of Agent Sinclair's amber eyes brought the feeling she needed him back. No, she resisted the urge to keep him in sight, as if he would protect her from the car crash, David, and the future, she forced her thoughts to the hospital and the quarantine room. She needed a heavy dose of reality. After a doctor treated her hands and nailbeds, he stitched her laceration closed, and when the MRI confirmed there was no other damage, they transferred her to the cold, concrete room with a window. She had settled in wearing a cotton gown and rested on a bed covered by a thin sheet, while two IV hooks reaching out from the wall held bags of CD4-T. With catheters at her elbows and the back of her knees, Macy drifted in and out of consciousness, unable to stop the scenes from the warehouse from playing for hours.

Finally at dawn, in her opinion, she was alert and ready to leave, but they denied her request, forcing her to wait. There were tests she had to pass. Blood tests verifying she was human. During her stay, she half expected Commander Arden to visit her in the hospital or at least check in with her to find out what happened. When he didn't, she felt like he was ignoring her, and she was on shaky ground with him. Like he would believe Sergeant Mayco over her. Anybody over her. Commander Arden left her on her own to deal with Blood Rain and Agent Sinclair, and their accusations leaving her alone.

*I have no one.*


With coffee in hand, Kayne paced between two stucco columns in the front of the Bureau of Paranormal Investigation's office. As he waited for his rental, he considered calling Michael, to question him about Daeland, and to tell him to keep an eye on Amaranth, the vampire's estate.

He decided against it. He needed more information before he accused Daeland of marking a mortal and knowing what was going on in Desert Rock. If Kayne was wrong—no way he was—the vampire would twist Kayne's words, making him look crazier than he already did, then add his ravings to the growing list. He couldn't screw with Daeland, he needed the vampire's authority with the Council to secure the authorization to hunt for Elijah.

Raising the paper cup to his mouth, he sipped the coffee, the bitter bite a mild comfort after having spent an uncomfortable night dealing with the wounds left behind from syn silver and the Hunter Wolf's contagion. He had doubted the effects from the ersatz, believing he was strong enough to purge the contagion before it did any damage. He was wrong. It forced him to take the vitamins the medic had given him, shapeshift, more vitamins, and another shift. His wounds had completely healed with the third shift, but the lingering, foggy feeling of syn silver remained. It was close to dawn before he slept, and even then, his sleep had been riddled with images of the warehouse, Detective Gray, her eyes, and her tattoo. In the midst of the mirage playing in his head, the investigation he blew to hell fell from the list of priorities. Giving up on sleep, he showered, dressed, had breakfast—food enough for six mortals—and with his mind clear of his dreams, he reevaluated the priority list. The investigation returned to the top. At least close enough.

Kayne sipped the coffee, checked the time on his watch, and looked up and down the street. The constant threat of contamination to mortals, shapeshifters, and the Otherkin made collecting evidence and bodies tedious. Both the DOJ and the BPI teams had worked through the night and managed to dismantle the lab, and load everything on a truck to transport to forensics. Kayne didn't want to wait for forensics, he wanted answers now, and in the throes of his frustration it latched onto Elijah and the BPI. Elijah wasn't going to sit by after finding out the warehouse had been taken from him and there were witnesses. Which led to Henry and Grace, and the irritating fact he hadn't heard anything from Dr. Locke. *Surprise*. Kayne wanted to know what was in the White Cell to create the ersatz and made them crossover in record breaking time. If Henry and Grace couldn't identify who kidnapped them, gave them White Cell, and monitored the warehouse, it was a lost opportunity. Without stopping himself, Kayne's thoughts went to Detective Gray, and the images of her in his dreams, and the way his wolf wanted to protect her. His wandering thoughts proved he was losing control over the situation.

From the street, the rumble of traffic grew as the sun crested over the office building and he made another pass by the column. He arrived early to get a feel for the office and the reactions of the detectives after they found out about Sergeant Mayco, Detective Gray, and the others wounded in the warehouse. He didn't get far when they knew he was a shapeshifter with the DOJ's Blood Rain team, was there to question them, and had been the reason their teams had been sent to the warehouse. Since no one was willing to talk to him, it gave him several hours to *hang out* at the office until the questioning at eleven o'clock. Another pass, another sip, and he wondered if Detective Gray would be able to attend. Damn, he didn't want to wait to question her, and damn, he needed to see her.

He looked at his watch. The hospital released her four hours earlier, after a night of CD4-T, MRIs, antibiotics, and steroids, and a negative test result for lycanthropy. He knew because he checked. Kayne left the warehouse, got cleaned up, and wearing a button-up shirt, tie, slacks, and his badge, went to Mercy Summit. While he watched her safely from the observation room, he questioned her doctor. Detective Gray suffered a concussion, bruised ribs, but no facial fractures or strained tendons in her arm and shoulder. Nothing broken or permanently damaged. He was more concerned with the deep cut above her eye that followed her eyebrow and stretched down to her temple and to her cheekbone. It had taken twenty stitches to sew the gap closed. Her right eye remained swollen shut, the bruises turned her bronzed complexion into ugly shades of purple and green, and the pastel blue gown she wore made her skin color look ashen. The hospital staff, worrying Detective Gray would become combatant from the antiserum and having a history with Post Traumatic Stress Disorder, kept her under constant observation. She didn't react, rather she relaxed in the bed, as much as she was able, and let them work freely. Kayne witnessed her fight the Hunter Wolves, and never would have expected her to survive, at least not with the injuries she sustained. Detective Gray should have been dead, or in the same condition as Sergeant Mayco.

He took another sip of coffee, saw brown residue clinging to the sides and covering the bottom of the cup, flinched, and turned his back to the morning sun.

The few pedestrians walking by didn't notice him, didn't turn their attention to him, they continued on their way without remark. Why? Kayne looked natural standing there, outside of the BPI office, in black slacks, dove gray, button-up dress shirt, and silver and red tie. His tie wasn't by accident. As alpha of the Garrick pack, Kayne wore the color representing the Moonlight territory—silver. A simple reminder of who he was. He completed his outfit with his soft brown, leather shoulder holster, another gun, badge, and his cell phone. He held an air of authority, and yes, he looked the part, professional and competent, as a DOJ agent should. Not at all like the disaster he had been the day before when the BPI arrived at the warehouse. Covered in blood, dirt, and having various wounds where the ersatz's claws caught him, he resembled a madman. A madman who had been standing over an unconscious BPI detective. With the influence of the empath bringing his regrets to life and his hesitation, he was lucky they hadn't shot him on sight.

Fidgeting with his tie, he stared out at the street, memories of dealing with the empath reminding him how close he had been to losing his mind. Detective Gray, her eyes, the nightmares from his past ... he never wanted to experience mental torture like that again. *Torture.* Sweat beaded on his forehead and he contemplated going into the office, for the air conditioner, when his cell phone came to life, sending a soft, silent vibration across his belt.

"Good morning, Michael," Kayne greeted.

"My liege." Michael's smooth voice didn't give away his seventy plus years.

"To what do I owe the honor?" Kayne asked, knowing what to expect. He didn't tell Michael he was leaving and put off calling him. He must have heard about the warehouse from someone else.

"As third in the pack, I stand behind my alpha. However, I hate when the DOJ calls to say they don't know where you are, or when they find you, you've been fighting Hunter Wolves and have suffered syn silver poisoning. I don't like learning you have taken the pack's fourth, Chayton, and our strongest sentinel, Russell, with you. It leaves the pack vulnerable. No, don't worry, I will explain your absence ... again.

And I will because you are my alpha and I do not question my alpha, I serve," Michael elaborated in a mocking tone.

If Kayne was the kind, he would have rolled his eyes at Michael's diatribe. "Your loyalty is much appreciated. As is the concern for my health. I'm sure it isn't the reason for your call."

"As always, you're correct. I called to tell you Daeland isn't at Amaranth, he left Feather River."

Kayne straightened, stared at the passing cars, and not seeing them, his imagination fired into gear. "Why?"

"The vampires aren't saying."

Before he dropped it, Kayne placed his paper cup on the decorative ledge around the column beside him, and then with his free hand, rubbed the back of his neck. "Figures. I might know where he's going. Or coming." Daeland traveled only when the Council required it, or when he wanted to see the woman who wore his blood mark. "I think he's headed to Desert Rock."

"Why would he go there?" Michael asked. "Have you finally convinced him Elijah is causing problems?"

"The warehouse is loaded with evidence of the ersatz. There are witnesses stating Elijah had been there, kidnap victims, and the owner of both the warehouse and a shipping company is dead. Whoever set it up knew I was going to be in town." *Jaxyn.* He forgot about the vampire. And didn't notice the remark about convincing Daeland. "Not to mention there's a detective here with his blood mark tattooed on her back."

"Part of his kith, maybe his coven?"

*Don't I wish.* "Negative." Kayne stopped when recycled air drifted to him and Agent Pixley stood at the door, one black high heel inside, one high heel outside. "Hold on." He held his cell to his chest to muffle the conversation. "Can I help you?"

Tippi stepped out of the office and walked in the direction of a column, her heels clicking on the concrete, and stopped where his coffee cup sat. Brown sludge sat at the bottom, making her stomach twist, and turning she met Agent Sinclair's questioning gaze. "Detective Gray isn't coming in today."

Kayne squeezed his cell, wanting to crush it. Not what he wanted to hear. He eased his hold when an audible crackling sounded. "Why?"

His clenched teeth and his low growl didn't surprise her. It did cause her to pause. Old wounds. Tippi pictured them trapping Detective Gray, and her resolve returned. "You of all people should know. You were at the hospital for hours and had spoken to her doctor."

*Guilty.* "I needed a time frame. Detective Gray is part of the investigation," Kayne explained. He hadn't been there to see her.

"I don't know what your motives are, Agent Sinclair, or why you have decided she's guilty, when the investigation hasn't started. Rest assured, she will be in tomorrow. I talked to the doctor a minute ago, he advised she wasn't coming in." Tippi wasn't going to explain herself, or wait for an explanation from him, when she figured he wouldn't give her one.

"You talked to her doctor? Did you call him?" Kayne asked.

"Affirmative," Tippi flatly stated.

"A conflict of interest is against DOJ policy." Kayne reciting policy, that's a good one.

Tippi faced him, her green eyes narrowed, and her hand squeezed the worn, black handle. "This coming from the agent found in a warehouse without authorization, which, initiated a homicide investigation and sent said detective to the hospital." She looked away from him, her anger getting the best of her, inhaled and exhaled, then met his eyes. "Detective Gray protected me. If not for her, I would be dead." Tippi had faced death one to many times, alone, and having someone at her back, fighting for her, whether bad or good, left an impression. "It was a trying day for law enforcement, lives were at risk, and we go on as if nothing happened. A man's humanity has been taken from him."

Kayne's eyes went to the ground. He felt like an ass, especially when Agent Pixley was right. "My apologies. I'm wrapped up in the case. I want to stop whoever is doing this so what happened yesterday isn't repeated." Kidnappings. White Cell. Hunter Wolves. The last thing they needed was a fight between paranormals and mortals.

Agent Sinclair's emotions were all over the place and she couldn't nail them down to decipher them and understand why. It didn't help he was blocking her like the alpha he was. "Your apology is accepted. I will ready the files for the questioning."

"Copy." They stared at other for a second, then she went inside.

Before the door closed, Commander Wilson stepped through and greeted, "Agent Sinclair." Wearing a set of clean BDUs, thigh holster, and his badge, he stopped at the opposite column.

"Commander," Kayne returned. *This can't be good.* He lowered the cell and slipped it in his pocket. If Michael hung up, he would call him back ... maybe.

"You aren't doing the interviews." Commander Wilson raised both hands, stopping him from interrupting.

"Commander Arden denied the DOJ. The BPI's review board will interview the BPI detectives involved with Pennsky warehouse."

"Commander Arden, no one has seen him. When did this order come down?" Kayne turned in a circle. Being on the outside of the questioning wasn't going to help him. Inhaling, he faced his commander.

"This morning. I'm warning you to stay away from the detectives. When the DOJ is allowed to resume their investigation, I'll let you know," Commander Wilson explained. His hands were on his hips, his stance tense. "This could delay it by weeks."

Weeks. He didn't have weeks. "I have to question—" Kayne stopped. He had to question Detective Gray. No one else. Everyone else.

"You have your orders. Try to follow this one." Commander Wilson turned, hesitated, and faced him. "Command has justified your actions at the warehouse because of the evidence. This wasn't what we planned, but having the BPI as witnesses worked out for you."

Cleared of any wrongdoing. All he needed to do was wait for the authorization to investigate the BPI. "Affirmative, sir." Kayne held his gaze. Commander Wilson turned, reached for the handle, and with a shake of his head, pulled the door open and entered the office. Kayne waited for the smoky glass to close behind Wilson before taking his cell from his pocket. "Michael?"

"Sir. What the hell is going on?"

*Besides all my plans going to hell?* "A detective has Daeland's Kindred blood mark, the one with the dragonheads and swords," Kayne explained.

"That would mean they shared blood, and she's blood bound. And she's a detective? Wait, she's a BPI detective, yes?" Michael's question was more to himself than to Kayne, but he said it aloud, and Kayne heard it.

"Affirmative." He rubbed his neck, then his shoulder, the ache and tension coming back with a vengeance. Daeland drinking from her set his anger on fire, and Detective Gray drinking from him made Kayne's stomach turn. A vampire feeding off you was disgusting, but feeding off a vampire was worse than the primitive act of shifting into a wolf.

"Maybe she's a set of eyes," Michael offered. "She has authority as a detective and investigates paranormal crimes."

"I don't think so," Kayne replied with Agent Pixley's words ringing in his ears. *Don't get caught up in her sentiments.* There was too much Detective Gray didn't know, like her tattoo, Dr. Locke's protection ... and those were not small details. She was missing big pieces of the puzzle.

"She has eyes and ears. She sees and hears things, stores the information without knowing it. Daeland comes to town, takes a trip through her head, and retrieves what he wants. He's probably powerful enough, when she sleeps, he does it from the safety of Amaranth. She lives too far away for his threat to be effective, so he protects her. Did you see any bite marks indicating the Ascension?"

*Ascension.* A mortal's conversion into a theow, a vampire's servant. The process started with the vampire drinking from the mortal, nearly draining them, and when in a weakened state, the vampire feed the mortal its own blood—repeatedly, if necessary—to establish a link. Once the connection proved true, the vampire shared its power, like placing an enchanted sliver into the mortal, which allowed the vampire to control the theow.

With the Ascension complete, the theow wouldn't age, was resistant to illnesses, and healed the same way their vampire master did. If the vampire had weaknesses, like not being able to heal quickly, the theow had the same weaknesses. Basically, a theow was a vampire's half-turned clone and daytime underling. The theows were always mortals. Vampires couldn't turn a shapeshifter into theow because of the animal spirit, and the divide between them blocked out the vampire's control. If Daeland was her master and Detective Gray was a theow, she would have healed from her wounds, instantly, and she didn't. Damn, she never would have gotten hurt if she shared Daeland's power.

"She's mortal, and no, I didn't strip search her," Kayne answered bitterly.

The notion Daeland was sitting in Amaranth and using Detective Gray as if she were his personal puppet burned across his skin. He considered the bites, purposely scarred on the theow's body, and near the tattoo, and couldn't remember seeing any. It didn't mean anything when his mind had been twisted from the empath. He didn't think the vampire lord, who never left Amaranth and considered himself an elitist, would sink his teeth into a mortal woman, give her his crest of protection, and leave her ten hours south on her own. Anger swept over him, thick and heated. He couldn't imagine what Daeland was thinking by marking her. She was a detective with the BPI and the damn tattoo put her in danger with everyone, including Dr. Locke. The line went silent, and he assumed Michael sensed his anger; it left him with his third's inhale and exhales.

"I'm not saying she is, my liege," Michael started, "but it is possible. Whatever you stepped into this time has Lord Daeland traveling, during the day, of all times. The scouts saw him leaving before dawn this morning."

That convinced Kayne that Daeland was headed to Desert Rock. It left him with seven hours before the vampire arrived and made his ETA the middle of the afternoon. Where would he go until dark? The doctor's place? As part of the Veiled population, vampires didn't do anything during the daylight hours, for fear of being exposed or a victim of the sun. Which, for some unknown reason, burned them until they drifted on the wind as ash. Kayne thought it was a gift straight from the gods, the sun. The older vampires whose powers increased with their years built a tolerance to the ball of fire in the sky, but most often waited for darkness to cloak themselves, and night made it easier for them to blend in and move among the mortals on which they fed.

In the good old days of horse and carriages vampires didn't travel during the day, but times changed and brought new technology, making it possible. Daeland rode in an expensive, silver, full-size SUV with blacked out windows made from polycarbonate, polyester, polyvinyl, and polyurethane that protected him from the sun, gunfire, and explosions. His life spanned a thousand years, and while he might be powerful, and amassed friends, all those years had given him an equal number of enemies. In the world of vampires, the differences between friends and enemies were clouded and hard to separate. To say his vehicle was the typical truck you would see driving out of a small, mountain town, where the windshield and paint job might fall victim to the harsh winters and debris from logging trucks, was wrong. Daeland didn't sacrifice comfort. The inside of the SUV met his every need, and those of his coven. The accommodations included leather seats, internet connection, a space for a laptop, a security window between the back and the front, and a safe to store blood.

As one of the originals who created the Council and the Coterie, a unit of specially trained soldiers employed to uphold the laws of the Council, his power extended further than most. Just how far, Kayne didn't know, but he was quickly realizing he was about to find out. Grabbing his empty cup off the column, he crunched the paper in his hand and started for the door when a small, red compact pulled into the parking lot. In white lettering around the license plate ring was the rental company's name and logo.

"Nice," he mumbled under his breath.

"What?" Michael asked.

Kayne forgot about Michael. "My rental just arrived. If I see Daeland, I'll call you, and if you hear anything, call me."

"My liege, did you say rental?"

"Michael, don't call me liege."

Kayne hit the end button, missing the days where when pissed off, he could slam the phone down. If he took his anger out on his cell it would shatter into a million expensive pieces. He took a step, drew his lips back in a half smile, and greeted the mortal sitting behind the wheel of his shiny, red car.

# CHAPTER THIRTEEN

**One** full day of sleep and uninterrupted rest and no phone calls had gotten rid of the nagging exhaustion and restored the vision in her right eye. Macy sipped coffee as she considered the reflection staring back at her in the mirror. *Not going to get any better.* Mascara, coverup, eyeliner, and eyeshadow containers sat beside her prescription bottles on the smoky gray concrete counter. The makeup softened the hues of red, yellow, and green of the bruises, while the black stiches running from her eyebrow to her cheek resembled train tracks from a road map. At least it didn't look like she used a spackle tool to apply the makeup.

Dressed in low rise jeans and her bra, she twisted to see the extent of the bruises darkening her ribs, going along the contours of her abs, and farther down where they stopped at her waist. *They're going to be there a while.* Sighing, she grabbed her white blouse, and slowly slid her right arm through the sleeve, then her left, the action causing her bra to rub against her sore ribs. Unable to make the slightest move without prompting aches and pains to riddle her body, she sucked in a breath, and gingerly worked the buttons with scabbed over fingertips. The last button made her sigh in relief and Macy left the bathroom for her bedroom. The sunlight slipped through the blinds, giving it an easy, airy ambience which lightened her mood. Then the black duffle bag sitting on the end of her bed stared at her, reminding her of reality, as if mocking her career. She wouldn't be surprised if they medically retired her. *It's called being fired.* It didn't matter how you said it, it amounted to the same thing.

When Macy checked her cell for messages, half expecting to see a blank screen, she was surprised to see Commander Arden had contacted her. He assured her the DOJ wasn't going forward with their investigation and ordered the BPI 's review board to conduct the interviews. It nearly made her cry. Macy immediately reported the suspicions she had about the warehouse and David and updated him on her findings. He replied that the DOJ would remain stalled until the evidence was completely removed from the warehouse, and the review board had cleared the detectives involved. The DOJ's investigation into the spy and Hunter Wolf forms would resume and the BPI and DOJ would investigate the warehouse. No one said the spy was BPI, when it could easily be DRPD, or anyone else. In theory, it would give her time to come clean about secretly investigating David and the others, and she wouldn't be living under an umbrella of secrets. Macy would be able to clear her name.

Commander Arden's assurance didn't stop apprehension from drumming through her. Macy considered calling and telling Dr. Harrison she was feeling sick, and the pain was too much, she couldn't drive let alone sit for several hours. One call and she would change her clothes, crawl back in bed, and let the day move on without her. She nearly laughed. She didn't believe one more day at home was going to help her, when she would sit around stressing about what was happening, her imagination filling her head with what-ifs, and then there was the chance they would order her to the interview. She would become a hostile suspect.

The upside, she wasn't going to have to see, talk to, or deal with Agent Sinclair.

"It's a review board interview," Macy mumbled. A simple interview to establish the scene and then they would turn it over to the homicide detectives. Her part would be over.

It wasn't going to be an interrogation, an internal investigation, or an administration hearing. Standard questions and the details surrounding the death of Mr. Barrette. Doubt. If they didn't believe her the shooting had been in self-defense, she would be facing another interview with Internal Affairs. Death by cop. *Damn Mr. Barrette.* In an antique chair, Macy sat heavy and with her worries weighing on her she put on her running shoes. The evidence concerning Mr. Barrette spoke for itself, and Dr. Locke would have the autopsy report confirming her statement. Sure. Standing, she grabbed the duffle bag and headed for the stairs.

The thirty-minute drive was hell on her body, her head hurt, her muscles ached, and the sunglasses she wore made her entire head throb. The throbbing radiating out from her face by far beat out the sun's burning rays into her retinas. She shifted in her seat as she rolled her Jeep to the security gate that separated the public parking lot from the BPI's secured parking. Macy lowered her window, and leaning over, pressed the number code into the pad and waited for the triple beep. Seconds ticked by, and when she didn't hear anything, immediately thought they may have locked her out. When the high-pitched trio finally sounded, she released a breath, her shoulders caved, and she sat back in her seat. *Won't lock you out when they want you to come in.* She moaned and squeezed the steering wheel, which invited an army of sharp needles to march out and trample along her spine and around to her ribs, where they started stomping.

The heavy gate topped with razor wire rattled, jerked, and rolled along the rail, cutting its path across the single lane to disappear behind several overgrown oleanders. Macy watched the chain link glitter in the sunshine until there was clearance, then slowly drove through and to the back of the office. Opening to a large parking lot, SUVs, crime scene vans, and patrol vehicles were parked on the left side while across the lot personal cars sat in silence. A fueling station with four pumps—two for gas and two for diesel—took up the center while mechanics walked around an attached garage, carrying equipment to an SUV, while others opened the hood of a car. Continuing to the far back, she headed to where her parking spot sat empty.

*Damn.* Agent Sinclair's truck, dents and all, sat beside her space, and she knew he put it there on purpose. What his truck was doing at the BPI office and not the local DOJ was beyond her. The sight of it made her heart pound and sent a line of fear down her spine and over the bristling pain. A numb feeling snaked up her legs, blazing through her hips, to her waist, where it fluttered in her stomach. It felt as if someone cut her in half and left her without legs. Even knowing he was going to be there, Agent Asshole, the living, breathing lie detector, hadn't prepared her to see his truck. It meant she was going to see him because the office wasn't that big. Macy gripped the steering wheel, turning her knuckles white and making the muscles in her forearms scream with pain. She had to calm down or she was going to lose her mind before the interview. Taking a deep breath, then another, she eased her grip, exhaled the breath she had been holding, and headed to the parking spot.

*I'm not the spy. This isn't the end.* Spy or not, they had the authority to terminate her. Macy would be forced to leave Desert Rock and live somewhere else. With nothing anchoring her to any one place there was always somewhere else. Where the BPI and shapeshifters weren't her problem. Sure thing because she accidently stumbled into law enforcement. Macy parked the Jeep, killed the engine, at the same time remnants of the dreams from the night before plagued her and lingered.

She was prepared to accept David as another ghost she would see every night, but she wasn't prepared to live with guilt for crimes someone else committed. What had changed? If she faced Mrs. Barrette, months ago, she would have shot the woman, no guilt, no hesitation. *Maybe I don't have it anymore.* And Mr. Barrette, had he been a victim of the same person who kidnapped the couple? Macy shouldn't have shot him. *I should have let him beat me to death.* Staring at the fence, the links blurred with her thoughts, and she had to admit things had gradually changed. The violence increased, the Hunter Wolf forms became braver with less fear of law enforcement, while investigations concerning shapeshifters had decreased. That's when Commander Arden had handed her a list of names of the people, he wanted her to watch. Damn shapeshifters created her problems and were threatening the world she was fighting to protect.

What was she going to do about it? Go to the interview. Get in and get out. Macy looked at the bag sitting on the upholstered passenger seat of her Jeep, its crumpled sides waiting for her to fill it with the things from her desk. She reached for it, hit the black strap with the bare tips of her fingers, sucked in a breath, and held the strap in her scratched hand. No. She let it go and it fell to the seat. Taking it inside would be admitting defeat. It would be admitting she did something wrong. And she didn't. With decisive motions, Macy took her sunglasses off and set them in the cup holder, and avoiding looking at the duffle bag, got out and closed the door. Before heading to the office, she checked her reflection in the window and tucked a stray strand of dark hair behind her ear as she considered the person staring back.

It didn't scare her, although she thought it should, and there should have been a part of her hating what she saw. The cut above her eye, the black dots lining it, and the gross rainbow of colors flooding her skin. They should have been the wakeup call she needed to push her to quit the BPI and find something less dangerous. What was it going to take before she realized her life was at stake? She stared and knew she didn't hate it. Bruises heal. What she hated was the way her face revealed her fear, worry, and stress. Macy didn't want to be at the office, nor did she want to lose her job, and she didn't want Agent Sinclair to convince her team she was the traitor. *Stay in control.* The review board needed to complete their reports and Agent Sinclair wasn't going to be involved. She inhaled as the coping mechanisms she relied on to keep her demons under control began crumbling under her worries.

*Because I'm drowning in lies.*

Cool air stirred the varied scents in the breakroom while a slight hum from the air conditioner drummed above the lower sound of electricity. Captain Dixon insisted on sequestering Kayne from the BPI detectives, so he didn't intimidate them, and he found himself alone with his files. The small room, the only one in the building not equipped with cameras and listening devices, had pale cream walls, tan tiles, and held the smells of reheated food, stale snacks, and burned coffee. The dark table, stained from years of use, with matching chairs, enough to seat six, dominated the center. Along the far wall was a countertop, complete with coffee maker, paper cups, mugs, tea, and a basket overflowing with condiments. At the end, sitting side by side, was a soda machine and snack machine.

He lifted the porcelain mug, sipped the hot, black liquid, its bite causing him to think twice, and set the mug down. With his elbows on the table, the files scattered from his impatience, and his eyes staring forward he tried to listen to the detectives talking. The closed door muffled their conversation but wasn't enough to keep him from understanding them. They were all relieved the review board was nearing the end of their interviews, Detective Gray being one of the last, and it was clear even without her statement, the actions taken by the BPI were going to be justified. They were acutely aware the DOJ and Blood Rain weren't leaving and understood when the confirmation came back from Commander Arden, the investigation into the spy would resume. That meant no one was voluntarily talking to him. Which was why he was eavesdropping.

Kayne scooted a file, pushed another, and stared at Detective Gray's. The investigation couldn't start quick enough for him. She hadn't been heard from in twenty-four hours, not one call, and no one called her to find out how she was doing. Or if she was coming in. Not seeing her and not having a good reason to talk to her made him crazy. And where the hell was Daeland? The vampire, like Detective Gray, hadn't been seen or heard from. He wasn't sure if Daeland was in Desert Rock. This is one time he hated the silence. Kayne sipped the coffee, regretted the taste, and set the mug down.

"Agent Sinclair, Detective Gray has arrived," Tippi reported as she entered the room. Her straight shoulders could be seen under her black blazer and white blouse, and he could make out the lines of her shoulder holster. Her red hair grazed the collar and made her emerald eyes gleam in the florescent light.

"Noted. It doesn't have anything to do with me," he lied. Not yet. His heart pounded in his chest knowing she was in the office.

"You're lying. You're staring at her file. Her picture," Tippi pointed out as she walked around the table. When she reached the counter and the coffee maker, she took a mug and poured coffee. Its stringent aroma drifted, and she thought about pouring it out, then reminded herself she was going to be there a while and needed the extra kick. Turning from the coffee maker, she leaned against the edge of the counter. "When we started working together you were cold, calculated, and distant. I get it, you're an alpha and maybe you keep yourself separated from the rest of us because of your status and responsibilities. But now, I know you're blocking me, I feel your walls. This means I've had to watch you. This woman, Detective Gray, is someone to you and not just a suspect in the BPI investigation. At the warehouse, you treated her differently. Alpha Sinclair, I believe you have your own agenda and reasons for being here."

*Alpha?* "Agent Pixley, I have no interest in Detective Gray besides the investigation." Kayne didn't turn to face her. Instead, he placed Detective Gray's photo in the file, closed it, and chose another one. Despite his lie, he saw himself sipping scotch and holding her picture while gazing at his territory from his deck. Zero interest.

She accused Agent Sinclair of having his own agenda, causing her to hesitate and second guess the confrontation.

Then his blatant lie, and the way he ignored her and wouldn't look at her, proved she was right. It also added fuel to the fire that was his mysterious past.

Paranormals considered empaths, a group of the Otherkin, part of the mortal world because physically they were human, didn't belong to covens or packs, like the shapeshifters, witches, trolls, fairies, and vampires. Instead, they belonged to classes, each specific to the talents of the Otherkin. Unlike paranormals, empaths didn't have a hierarchy, there wasn't an alpha, or master. They considered themselves equals, which meant there were no rules when traveling or when one wanted information. Tippi's class networked throughout the US, which allowed her to find an Otherkin close to the Moonlight pack, now known as the Garrick pack. A couple of messages and a phone call later and she had details of Agent Kayne Sinclair's past.

Before becoming a lord with the Council, Kayne Sinclair, then married to Eryin Sinclair, was a soldier for the Council's Coterie, the law enforcement to the paranormal. As an active solider, he proved his loyalty and rose through the ranks to work beside the most powerful lords. The Council noticed his increasing power and influence and gave him the first rank of master, with hopes he continued to strengthen and would eventually become a lord. At first, Agent Sinclair refused, stating he was a soldier, and unaccustomed to the refinement of the Council, preferred working in the field. *He refused the Council, that's cute.* The Council let him have his rejection until Lord Daeland, a vampire with status, offered him a position as a sentinel for his Kindred, the vampires under his authority, and to rule over the shapeshifters at Amaranth, his estate.

Agent Sinclair, hating the politics of the Council, and believing the Council would leave him alone, promptly accepted, and with his wife, moved to Feather River, California. It was there Garrick Grayson, a new alpha with a growing pack, petitioned the Council to recognize his land as the Moonlight territory. Because Alpha Garrick's territory bordered Lord Daeland's, the Council sent Lord Daeland and his sentinel, Agent Sinclair, to determine whether the alpha was strong enough to control a pack and keep a territory. Both agreed Moonlight and its alpha were an asset to the Council and approved the petition. Both were present at the enthronement ceremony.

The Council continued to keep track of Agent Sinclair's increasing strength and ordered him to work closely with Alpha Garrick in order to help him establish the pack. After Alpha Garrick passed the required probation period, the Sinclairs joined the Moonlight pack. With his presence and relationship with both the alpha and Lord Daeland an advantage, the Council ordered Agent Sinclair to accept the authority of lord and end his time with Lord Daeland. Newly appointed to lord, Agent Sinclair obeyed with the stipulation he would remain in Moonlight and with the pack. It didn't take him long to gain the respect and trust of Alpha Garrick, and Agent Sinclair became third to the alpha as well as the protector of the Grayson family. *Family.* Tippi's thoughts drifted to the memory of Agent Sinclair holding Detective Gray, and it started to take on another meaning. She needed to know more, and refusing to wait for an email, she called Abbie, an Otherkin with magic powers, and her contact in Feather River.

"What happened to Eryin?" Tippi asked. She couldn't believe he had been married.

"Before I answer, you aren't allowed to take notes. Everything I say is property of the Feather River class of Otherkin."

Tippi had placed her pen on the notebook, reminded herself to delete the emails, and sat back in her chair. "Done."

"Mrs. Sinclair had an affair with Elijah Northrip, another pack member. They were charged with treason for conspiring against and attempting to murder the Grayson family. Both were found guilty and sentenced to the paranormal prison Devil's Peak," Abbie explained.

Devil's Peak, a frozen prison in the wilds of Alaska, where torturing and punishment were frequent and death preferable. "Why would they risk exposure and punishment from the Council, by murdering the alpha and his family? They could have easily challenged the alpha. Or reported the dispute to the Council."

"Garrick and his mate, Sabine, had a daughter. It was the reason Alpha Garrick chose Lord Kayne. The alpha knew about the years Lord Kayne had spent with the Coterie and wanted a soldier to protect his daughter."

Tippi inhaled and exhaled. "A Pureblood."

"Correct. It's believed Mrs. Sinclair and Mr. Northrip were part of a radical group rallying against the family because of the girl. Without proper medical care, Purebloods were few, rarely lived through the difficult birth, and if they survived, they were put down due to their physical mutations. If the Pureblood didn't display said mutations, and lived through puberty, it served as proof of their power and were seen as a threat to the pack. The old ones thought they were primeval, and considering them an abomination, would hunt them down and kill them."

"Agent Sinclair protected this Pureblood. Did the Council know about her?"

"Yes. They were well aware of her. With the changes the Requiem brought, like equal rights and freedom to live in the open, the Council felt it was time to cast off its old ways and start anew. And they couldn't kill anyone without getting attention from mortals. Purebloods became part of the future. There are thousands now," Abbie said as if she was giving a history lesson.

"If they were imprisoned, what happened to the family?" Tippi asked. "What happened to the Pureblood?"

"Mr. Northrip and Mrs. Sinclair were being held awaiting transport when the Grayson family was involved in a car accident. When the vehicle caught fire, it took Alpha Garrick and his mate. However, Lord Kayne found the wreckage, pulled the girl from the burning car, and she died in his arms on the side of the road. He failed to protect the family, and with his grief, he disavowed his lordship. The Council allowed him to recede with the requirement Lord Kayne would succeed the position as alpha."

"He failed and didn't fight for his place. They handed it to him," Tippi mumbled. Werewolves fought for their stations to prove their strength, power, and worth. Anything less was an embarrassment and a shame. Tippi knew Agent Sinclair was a proud man, and werewolf. He saw himself as a coward.

"Yes. Lord Kayne tried disputing the Council to no avail. He said he viewed it as a punishment for failing. As if to add to the open wound and his grief, mortal law enforcement reported there were pits in the body of the car matching bullet holes and believed there was foul play. After an investigation, the sheriff's department filed the accident as a homicide. Lord Kayne is convinced Elijah is responsible for the car crash and continues to appeal the Council for authorization to hunt him."

Tippi caught the use of *hunt.* "You said Mr. Northrip and Mrs. Sinclair were imprisoned. How could he be responsible for the crash?"

"Hours earlier, Mr. Northrip escaped, leaving Mrs. Sinclair behind. After the deaths, her punishment was accelerated, and she was sentenced to death. Mrs. Sinclair served out her punishment alone. As their newly appointed alpha, and with his status with the Council, Lord Kayne was required to serve as her executioner."

After she had an affair, then found guilty of being a traitor, Agent Sinclair killed his wife. "There weren't others?"

"No. Anyone associated with the group, Mr. Northrip, or Miss Gunn disappeared. Some speculate the Council deployed the Coterie. Others, and this is purely speculation, say Lord Daeland used his power and resources."

The Coterie. Lord Daeland. "Wait, you said Miss Gunn. Who was she?"

"My apologies, it's Mrs. Sinclair's maiden name. The Council dissolved the marriage between Lord Kayne and Miss Gunn, leaving him free to pursue a mate and second for his pack."

A pack is only as strong as its alpha. "He has never married? Dated?" Tippi couldn't imagine what it would feel like to live with your ghosts as your lovers.

"No."

Strong no. "How long has Agent Sinclair been an alpha?"

"A little over twenty years. Let me see ... twenty-three, to be exact. His anniversary is coming up and will make it twenty-four."

"He's been single for almost twenty-four years?" No way. Agent Sinclair was handsome, strong, motivated.

"Yes."

"How old was the girl?" Tippi asked. Was it possible Agent Sinclair saw Detective Gray as a replica of the girl?

"Eleven. There is little information about her and what I have is hearsay. I've heard she was beautiful as a child, taking after her father and her Native American mother. I do know, Alpha Garrick and his daughter shared the same wolf eyes, and at a young age she ran with him and then the pack. Some say she could have been as powerful as her father," Abbie answered, her voice softening as if she was lost in thought. "The grief Lord Kayne experienced and the force in which it plagues him is proof the two were close."

"Close?" Tippi wasn't fluent in werewolf traditions, customs, or the like, and didn't know what Abbie was going to say.

"With the threats coming from within the pack, Lord Kayne was her bodyguard, and would have been the girl's shadow. He would never have left her alone. And she would have depended on him the same way she depended on her parents."

He lost what he considered a daughter or sister and failed the alpha. *Focus.* "How old is Agent Sinclair?" Did she really want to know? Tippi would have to maintain a working relationship and see him every day as long as the investigation was active, and again if there was a need for Blood Rain.

"Two hundred and seventy-six."

If he was as powerful as the Council believes he was, he hid his power well. In a life spanning hundreds, maybe thousands of years, twenty would feel like a day. It made the pain of losing an alpha and failing the family he swore to protect fresh in his mind and heart.

"What is your interest in Lord Kayne?"

*He spent an unknown amount of time having an empath bring his nightmares to life, was attacked, suffered from syn silver poisoning, has a weird fascination with a female detective, and I don't want to be there when he loses control of his wolf to Blood Rage.*

"I need to know what I'm dealing with."

"He isn't the same." Abbie let silence stretch out. "The paranormal world sees us as mortal. The mortal world sees us as paranormals. It's this displacement that binds us. Tippi, we brought our numbers together, drew our power, and held you in its nucleus. I'm glad you're healed. That said, don't take your past out on Lord Kayne. You'll regret it."

Ruby eyes blazed like stars as his body shifted into a humanoid with animal features, a roar thundered from his jaws, and the man she knew lost himself to Blood Rage. She watched the fury and primal instincts rip his mind apart, then he trapped her. Tippi shuddered with the memory. "Why?"

"The Council watches him. Lord Daeland watches him. His pack protects him. He has their respect and their empathy. If they feel you pose a threat, they won't hesitate to take you out of the equation."

She wasn't in the equation. "I'm not a threat. If he hates everything he is, why protect him from himself?"

"He's powerful and an asset to the Council. And they believe he will break through his grief."

She didn't know that kind of grief. She did know fear. "Why do you refer to him as lord?" Tippi asked.

"The Council gave the decree," Abbie replied.

Sipping her coffee, Tippi stared at Agent Sinclair over the rim while the conversation repeated through her thoughts. He looked to be in his late thirties, early forties, not a two-hundred-and-seventy-six-year-old disavowed lord with the Council, who retained his title, an alpha werewolf who resented his position. And was his wife's executioner, and remains a close acquaintance to Lord Daeland, an influential vampire. Why the hell was he a DOJ agent? *"He appeals the Council for the authorization to hunt Elijah."* Maybe she was wrong, and Detective Gray wasn't in the crossfire of his past. Wrong place at the wrong time.

"You're using your authority as an agent to search for Elijah Northrip. You think he has something to do with the ersatz?" Tippi accused. "Or maybe you don't care about the ersatz at all."

Her accusation broke through the silence and forced him to give the agent a real answer. Not a vague lie. He scooted the chair back, turned in his seat, and met her narrowed gaze. Kayne controlled his reaction, keeping his eyes human, and his anger a low burn so she wouldn't sense him. Agent Pixley's fear of aggression changed her behavior, and if she knew he was chasing Elijah, he needed her on his side.

"I care about the ersatz, and affirmative, I want Elijah. What would you know of it?"

Agent Sinclair stood and faced her. His six foot, six inch height towered over her five foot, seven inches, making the room feel small while his board shoulders and bearing ignited a flame of fear to heat her insides. *He's a good man.* Broken from the pain in his past, but good. *Not evil. Not like—*

She let the thought slip from her and fought for control. "I made some calls. I know what you believe he's responsible for, but I don't know how he's involved with the ersatz," she replied

*Neither do I anymore.* Kayne didn't care who Agent Pixley talked to when his past wasn't a secret. "*Why* he's involved, I have no idea. Henry, the wolf I found in the warehouse, said Elijah was the one who locked him up. There's something here he wants. Whether it's the ersatz, the corrupted White

Cell, or a fight between mortals and paranormals is anyone's guess. But he is here."

"What other information have you kept from me?" She didn't know Henry had said anything or was able to talk.

"I haven't kept anything from you. I gave my report to Commander Wilson." Kayne looked at the files and back at Agent Pixley. "Henry had been a White Cell dealer, then the BPI showed up at their place and someone told him he wasn't keeping up his end of the bargain. Grace said that's when the BPI took them," Kayne explained.

"You could have told me the BPI was directly involved." Tippi was going to have to reevaluate her questions.

"I don't believe they were. And I don't believe they are. I think someone wants us to think they are." *Like Elijah.* "Grace reported they were dressed like the BPI, but couldn't identify any of them," Kayne clarified.

"Would Mr. Northrip go through all of this to get revenge?" Fighting the feeling to slink from him and sit at the table, Tippi sipped her coffee, her eyes barely over the edge.

"Negative. It involves too many people and is to elaborate for revenge. Anyway, if he wanted me, or Moonlight, he knows where to find me. I've been in the same place for nearly seventy-five years. This is about something here," Kayne replied. What the hell did she find out? He leaned against the edge of the table and stared at the coffee maker. *He found what he wanted.* What the hell did Elijah find?

Tippi set her mug on the counter, harder than she expected, and the porcelain hitting the tile created a sharp click. She looked at the inside and saw a dark brown stain from the coffee and wondered what it was doing to her stomach. She had enough, and leaving the coffee mug on the counter, she walked to the opposite end of the table from Agent Sinclair.

"The Hunter Wolves blatantly attacked law enforcement at Pennsky warehouse. This case has changed from investigating the possibility of ersatz to confirming they exist. While we wait for forensics, we have to assume someone is injecting the lycanthrope and therianthrope contagions into White Cell. This person, maybe your Mr. Northrip, and maybe he's kidnapping humans, forcing them to take White Cell to infect them. Those who crossover shift into their Hunter Wolf forms. Those who are too weak to complete the shift are used as emotional triggers for the ersatz. Whoever is doing this is a serial killer. If you are convinced Mr. Northrip is behind this, we have to get his name and description to the public. Not only that, we also have to warn them about White Cell."

Kayne was getting what he wanted. Granted, the Council wasn't giving him the authority, but did it matter? "Agreed. You need to understand, Elijah has connections to the Council and his actions have the potential of exposing the Veiled. The Council isn't going to let that happen. We have to approach this accordingly."

Protecting the Veiled. It explained his hesitation. "Understood. Now about Detective Gray?" Tippi questioned. "How does she fit into this?"

Her eyes are like molten silver, and she wears a vampire's blood mark. If Kayne confessed that he knew her eyes, he would sound like he was losing his mind. And if he confessed she wore Daeland's mark, it would further expose the vampires. No one needed to know about the tattoo. Kayne was prepared to be honest with Agent Pixley to a point.

"I have read and reread the reports. She's in the middle of everything, but her actions are the opposite. Detective

Gray hasn't tried to defend her conduct, and why would she risk her life to protect the sergeant if she was the spy giving up intel to purposely put her fellow detectives in danger?" Detective Gray didn't tell him she found the files in his truck. Acted like she didn't care. Just like the tattoo.

"She protects him to divert attention. Or, just maybe, she isn't the spy," Tippi suggested.

*Dr. Locke said as much.* "Detective Gray is keeping secrets, I sensed it and so did you. To find out, we need to question her," Kayne said with exhaustion in his voice. He needed to be near her to prove there was a darkness inside of her.

"Even if Detective Gray does, it doesn't mean she's lying about the spy. Anyway, everyone has secrets." *Like you.* "Your attention on her and the reasons for the tracker are weak," Tippi stated, and before he could argue, she continued. "Captain Dixon took your advice and sent the warrant to the judge. I understand it's signed and waiting."

*No shit.* "Did he hesitate?" Kayne asked. He wasn't giving in under the agent's scrutiny of his ethics or lack thereof. For an empath, she was letting him feel the chill of her disapproval and it felt like a cold front raging around her. He might have started out abusing his authority, but his hunt for Elijah led him to the warehouse and the ersatz, and there was a spy. He needed to find out who. Detective Gray was his only connection to the warehouse and Officer Murphy, he had to start somewhere. The question threading through every thought was, *Is my focus on the detective making her look guilty?*

"Negative, he didn't. It seems he was waiting for someone to suggest it. The paperwork was waiting. Captain Dixon is of the same mind you are." Tippi waited for him to defend himself. *No.* "I also requested the DNA test. To not add *anymore* unnecessary attention to Detective Gray, I had them run several detectives. It's believed the test results will be entered into the BPI and DOJ reports for the investigation."

It's happening. In hours he would know if his suspicions were correct or if he let the empath from the warehouse influence his sanity. "Excellent," Kayne replied absently.

"I'm not going to question your intentions, Agent Sinclair, this is an investigation. Be warned, if she is innocent, and I feel you're threatening her career for your personal gain, I'll step in," Tippi cautioned.

"Agent Pixley—" Kayne started to defend himself and stopped. He turned to watch the door open and waited to see who was entering.

"Agent Sinclair, Agent Pixley, I'm glad you're still here. First, let me say, regrettably, I have agreed with your advice for the tracker on Detective Gray's vehicle. The reason I'm here is Commander Arden ordered the investigation to resume. You've been authorized to start the questioning," Captain Dixon explained as he stood with the door against the toe of his boot. "Detective Gray has completed her report and will be available. We need to question her today, immediately."

The smug expression he wore wasn't of a man who was dealing with one of his own at Sanative fighting for his life, and several others recovering, and a detective under investigation. Captain Dixon didn't seem to mind an outside agency invading his territory. In fact, he looked satisfied.

"Affirmative, sir. Give us ten minutes," Kayne requested. It took one night, while Detective Gray was in the hospital, and another day while she was at her house recovering, for Captain Dixon to make her the focus of the investigation. Wasn't he doing the same thing? Negative.

"Captain Dixon, why today?" Tippi asked.

"The use of force and the death of Mr. Barrette have been justified. It gives her clearance for medical leave," he explained. He raised his left arm, placing his palm on the door to keep it open, the movement stretching his tan, button-up shirt across his thin chest.

Can't lose her. Kayne caught the anger he didn't understand, which the captain was trying to cover with his false indifference. "Ten minutes and we'll be ready."

"Affirmative." Captain Dixon left, letting the door slowly close behind him.

Tippi skirted Agent Sinclair on her way to the counter for her mug and more coffee. "You got your wish."

# CHAPTER FOURTEEN

With a frail handle on her nerves, Macy left the interview, having explained everything from their arrival time, the code red, to when the Hunter Wolf form knocked her unconscious. She didn't explain Sergeant Mayco's refusal to tell her who or what Agent Sinclair was or how he overrode Agent Pixley's order, allowing Macy to search on her own. The details of Mr. Barrette's attack, his inability to complete the shift, the lycan and his wife, and the Hunter Wolf form attacking Sergeant Mayco poured from her like an open spout. She had to explain everything to justify her actions and hoped the smallest detail made a difference in finding who was responsible for the Hunter Wolves and the spy.

*Cause, I might not be here.* Macy snuffed the thought and started down the hallway, not noticing the pictures of her fellow detectives, their awards, or the plaques of excellence.

When she was out of sight and halfway down the hall, she wanted to stop to rest and to relieve the worst of the nagging pain in her side. Her ribs didn't feel bruised ... no, they felt broken, and every step felt like they were grinding against one another. One second. She couldn't take it anymore and stopped, right by her picture and plaque, the award for becoming the first female sharpshooter in the Bureau of Paranormal Investigations Southern California division. A sad reminder of the life and successes she was going to lose. Leaving her accomplishments behind her, she headed toward the end of the hall where she inhaled a small breath, trying not to ignite a flare from her side, and prepared to face the office. A right turn and the area opened to desks, neatly lined in rows, computers sitting on top of each, while printers lined the far wall. A hush swept through the room, as detectives stopped talking and watched her enter. She kept up her façade of strength and control, even with the pain and bruises, and smiled as she wove through detectives, desks, and chairs to finally make it to hers.

Macy sat down, slowly to not incite pain, all while keeping the smile on her face when people walked by, then replied hello when needed. Waiting to be ignored and to appear normal, she opened a file, pretended to shuffle through the papers inside, while chancing glances around her. The chatter went from low whispers to full-on talk and the work resumed as if she wasn't there. When she was confident no one was paying attention to her, she pulled the drawer open, to see pens, paperclips, blank forms, and several Tic Tac containers sitting next to a micro voice recorder. No one used tapes anymore, everything was digitally recorded, or live streamed to any console mounted in a BPI vehicle or computer in the office. The ease of use made a tape recorder obsolete. Macy had kept it, and the tapes, like they were a diary of her career. She reached for it and stopped.

"Detective Gray," Detective Gaines greeted. Dressed in her black-on-black BDUs, and thigh holster, she stood at the end of the desk, her fingers splayed on the top.

Startled, Macy looked up. "Gaines." She met the icy azure stare lined with blue liner and braced herself for the onslaught of accusations.

"I can't believe you still have one of those," Detective Gaines said with a slight smile.

No accusations. No hate. Macy's fear subsided, a little, but didn't stop her from being guarded. She trusted Kinsie Gaines, the detective had her back more times than Macy could count, and she considered her a friend, and someone she could trust. Then her life turned upside down in a matter of weeks, and Macy didn't know who to trust. Faking a smile, no one would know she faked because of the swelling and bruises, she replied, "Right. Nothing like the past staring you in the face."

"About your face ..." Detective Gaines smiled in return. "You're supposed to kill them before they hit you."

"That's what I did wrong. Thanks. Next time you can be there to remind me." They weren't going to talk about Sergeant Mayco, he was a jarring example of what could happen to them. You can't play with the monsters day in and day out, and walk away unscathed. Uninfected.

Detective Gaines laughed an uneasy sound and looked away. "I don't like this, but an order came down from Commander Arden. The investigation is resuming for the spy. Blood Rain is waiting for you in the breakroom."

*Shit. Shit. Shit.* "Where is Commander Arden?" Macy asked as she stood, her side erupting in pain, and she held her ribs. She had to face Agent Sinclair without gathering evidence to clear her name.

Detective Gaines' eyes darkened. "No idea. He gave the order to Captain Dixon, who fears you won't come back from medical leave. I was told to get you. You're first."

*Captain Dixon is a coward, and Gaines agrees.* This was Agent Sinclair's fault. He wanted to pin a S for spy on her like the fucking scarlet letter. Macy ignored the throbbing in her head, the electric currents of pain shooting down her side, and looked at the micro recorder. "All right. Can you give me a minute?"

Detective Gaines slowly nodded. "Sure. I'll tell them you're on your way." Giving Macy her back, she took a couple of steps, then turned. "I call bullshit. Commander Arden ordered the DOJ to leave us alone, so we could regroup after Pennsky, and now, the order is changed, and he's nowhere to be found. But Captain Dixon has talked to him."

*Arden is missing and Captain Dixon is in charge, great.* "The DOJ's investigation is a cluster, and their presence is making all of us doubt ourselves and each other. If command isn't going to protect us, then we protect each other." Macy leaned back and took an exaggerated breath.

"You're right. White Cell, Harper's warehouse, the Barrettes, and Pennsky, it's no wonder we're on edge. I'm good, I just needed to vent. I'll let them know you're on your way." Detective Gaines nodded and left.

Macy caught how Detective Gaines didn't mention Officer Murphy or the Hunter Wolf forms, and their changes, when talking about Pennsky and Harper's warehouses. Exhaling slowly, she took the micro recorder from the drawer, and pushed the cover for the battery compartment off. Where there should have been batteries, were two memory drives. She turned it and they dropped to her open palm, and she quickly shoved them into her jean's pocket. Replacing the cover, she set it beside a handwritten note, paused like she would never see her belongings again, closed the drawer, and stood. *This is going to be bad.*


**Kayne** took the folder, opened it, stared at the picture, and then placed it under the stack of papers. "This includes

Internal Affairs report on Harper's warehouse, Officer Murphy's death, and the BPI's investigation into her actions. I see there's also Detective Gray's report on the Barrettes but nothing about her refusing a direct order. Is this what we're supposed to base our questions on? There's no indication there's a spy except for the presence of Hunter Wolves at Harper's. DRPD agreed with the BPI it was a setup. None of this means anything."

"It's the same with the others. I can't imagine official reports would lead to the spy. He, or she, would have been exposed and there would have been no need for the DOJ," Tippi replied. She flipped through Sergeant Mayco's file, finding the same information. "DRPD agreed with the BPI about Harper's. They believe someone tipped off *whoever* before they served the search warrant. You would think *whoever* it was would have left the warehouse, not stayed to confront law enforcement."

"Agreed." Kayne sat back, frustration nagging his patience.

The scene at Pennsky warehouse bugged Tippi. Sergeant Mayco ordered Detective Gray to continue the search despite not having backup. It could be nothing. It could be something. "This case is a mess." Tippi looked up from the report, Sergeant Mayco's dispute with Detective Gray's refusal to take down Mrs. Barrette drifting through her thoughts. "You're right about the Barrettes, there's no report stating Detective Gray refused the order. As team leader, it's Sergeant Mayco's responsibility to file a disciplinary action against Detective Gray. There's nothing."

"Maybe the report is with our elusive Commander Arden." Kayne closed a folder. "Why don't we have their personnel files? I want to know who they are, not a grammatically correct retelling of a scene," he said with annoyance running through his words.

"Do you want all of them? Or Detective Gray's specifically?"

Kayne met her gaze. "All of them."

"Sir." Tippi stood.

They both stilled when the door opened and Captain Dixon, with an air of confidence, strode into the room and took his seat beside Kayne. "In preparation for this questioning, I have several more folders. You'll find past cases, background information on Harper's, Pennsky warehouses, and Mrs. Barrette's autopsy." Captain Dixon placed the folders on the tabletop. "I've been assured by Detective Gray's doctor that her wounds will prevent her from leaving town."

"What about Mr. Barrette? Where is his autopsy?" Tippi asked.

"Doctor Locke is working on it," Captain Dixon replied absently. He looked at Kayne, his brown eyes glowing bright with humor. "I haven't seen Detective Gray, but I heard she doesn't look well."

An image of her in the quarantine room, her sun-bronzed skin pallid under the fluorescent lights, and lines of CD4-T in her elbows, flashed before him. "Negative, she doesn't." Kayne fought to control his anger. She wasn't going anywhere. She was, however, walking in front of a firing squad.

"The BPI thanks the DOJ and your Blood Rain team. We aren't used to investigating one our own," he explained as he handed Kayne a folder, Detective Gray's name printed across the top along with her ID number. "The tracker will allow us to monitor her while she's on medical leave."

"Affirmative, Captain. If there was another way, I would have suggested it long before this drastic measure, rest assured," Kayne replied.

He didn't need his senses to feel the man's eagerness in his words or the energy coming from him when it told a different story. The captain was reacting to having Detective Gray under guard and watched, and he liked it. Kayne stopped thinking about Captain Dixon and said her name, Macy, then repeating it let it ease from him. Macy.

*Focus.* He needed to find out what he could from her and the BPI, use it to find Elijah, and the person responsible for the White Cell. That was his priority. Nothing else mattered. *Lie.* He was going to find out about Macy, her past, and her connection to Daeland, and his instincts were telling him her DNA was going to expose her. A sharp knock jerked Kayne from his thoughts and the folder he held dropped to the table.

"Detective Gray is on her way, Captain," the detective reported. She leaned in through the opening, its pale maple clashing with her black uniform, blue eyeliner, and black hair.

Kayne watched the woman's cool blue gaze carry her reaction to seeing Detective Gray. There was a mixture of emotions coming from her, a strong sense of respect, strength, and loss. He read Detective Gaines' file and found she recommended Detective M. Gray for a promotion to sergeant and put in for the position of second. The two of them would have created the first female BPI team. If this hadn't happened, Detective Gray would have been promoted to sergeant, making her career. The one, in the eyes of her captain, she was going to lose.

"Thank you, Detective Gaines," Captain Dixon responded.

"Sir," Detective Gaines answered.

While Kayne spent the morning eavesdropping, word spread about the warehouse and the fight, but their concern was concentrated on Macy and Sergeant Mayco. The implications and Blood Rain's presence showed in Detective Gaines' eyes and the cold stare, raw with rage, she gave him. They knew it could have been any one of them sent to Sanative, to the quarantine room, and urgent care for wounds inflicted by shapeshifters. With cases increasing, the violence threatening their lives, and a spy among them, they didn't know who to trust. It sure as hell wasn't him. Detective Gaines wasn't upset because he was DOJ, or Blood Rain, she didn't like him because he was a werewolf, and liked him less, because he was there to investigate her family. He was in her home and on her turf, questioning her kin. Sadly, Captain Dixon should have been displaying those very traits not willingly trying to convict one of his own. Kayne understood territory. Walk into his and attack one of his wolves and see where it gets you. With appreciative understanding, he respected her anger.

Detective Gaines turned and the door closed, cutting off the chatter from the other side. Captain Dixon waited, then faced Kayne. "Is there anything I can get you, before Detective Gray arrives?"

*Her personnel records would be nice.* "Negative, I believe I have everything." Kayne didn't hold his gaze, couldn't, and taking the report continued reading.

The BPI review team was using the formal interview room, which left the interrogation rooms, and the briefing room. He refused to use either. The breakroom was comfortable, clean, and non-threatening, and wouldn't make the detectives feel intimidated, like they would have been in one of the rooms they used for interrogating suspects. Kayne sat on the right side of the table, facing the door, Captain Dixon to his left, sat one seat away from him. Between them, several manila folders cluttered the tabletop and sat on top of Kayne's original files. Agent Pixley sat at the left end of the table with a pen and pad of paper. Far enough away she could face the door and was able to observe their body language, facial reactions, and nervous habits. Being an empath with the DOJ, she was there to feel their emotions as they answered a series of questions, and their answers would be compared to Kayne's senses. Instead of one person's opinion of whether someone was lying, there were two.

The detectives faced the wall during questioning, their backs to the door. The door meant freedom and was a mental image reminding them they could leave at any time. Kayne didn't want them thinking about freedom, he wanted them thinking about the questions. If they were going to charge a BPI detective with being a spy and responsible for the deaths of law enforcement officers, and the innocent infected by the corrupted White Cell, the evidence needed to be infallible. As agents with the Department of Justice, and being part of Blood Rain, their testimony would be admissible in court, he couldn't leave anything to chance.

When Commander Arden delayed the investigation, Kayne felt Detective Gray and the opportunity to question her slipping through his fingers. If the delay lasted, it would have left him inventing reasons to talk to her. With nervous shoves, he placed a report back in the folder and took another. Knowing she was on her way had tension racing across his shoulders and his imagination creating dozens of scenarios. It wasn't as if he didn't know what he was going to do, he had a plan. Had obsessed over it the day before, he had time, and over the night and most of the morning.

His questions repeating through his mind while her answers matched what he knew about her.

Absently, he shuffled papers, grabbed her file from Captain Dixon, opened it, and scanned the pages. He continued reading through cases when a soft knock interrupted him, causing his head to jerk up, and the file to fall soundlessly to the table. His heart jumped to his throat, his nerves bounced under his skin, and he heard his pulse in his ears. What the hell was happening to him? One woman. A mortal. A detective with paranormal kills. He wanted her past to act as cold water and quench his heated emotions. To cover his unease, he lifted Detective Gray's file from the table, flipped through, and taking a page, pretended to look over it once more. Luckily, Captain Dixon hadn't seen his reaction and didn't wait for anyone else to respond.

"Enter," Captain Dixon ordered. He opened the file in front of him, peppered with handwritten notes, and spread several pages out.

*Intimidation tactic*? Kayne was giving the captain a shielded glare when the glossy maple door slowly opened, her voice, a sultry sonance he remembered from the warehouse, entered before he saw her. Someone was telling her it was good to see her, and the door closed an inch, she laughed, making his heart pound. The seconds ticked by when the opening widened, and finally, he saw Macy standing sideways, her left hand, missing fingernails, bruised, and scratched from the fight, resting against her white shirt and over her ribs. The stark contrast reminded him of her strength, and the way he treated her when he forced her to stay still so he could see the tattoo. His attention remained focused on her as she laughed, said thank you, and turned to face them. He didn't waste time searching with his senses, he knew the conversation cost her when her eyes darkened from the pain.

Kayne watched her shoulders straighten as she did her best not to show her discomfort, then using measured steps, she walked to the table where she pulled a chair out and sat down. With a slow exhale she scooted the chair in and sat back. This was the first time he saw her. Macy Gray. The woman. She wasn't in uniform, her curves weren't hidden under body armor, and she wasn't armed and fighting. He gauged her height at five feet and a couple of inches, and she was fit, her jeans hugging toned legs, her tapered shirt accentuating her narrow waist. Her dark auburn hair was up and away from her face, leaving the black stitches, yellow and purple smearing around her eye and down her cheek clear for everyone to see. Her thick lashes shielded eyes lined with black, and lids dusted in brown, and he could tell she tried to soften, not disguise, the bruises with makeup. The escaped strands of hair curled and sat softly against her neck, nearly hiding the scarlet pinpricked skin where the ersatz had held her. Is this who he was going to interrogate? An injured detective who had put her life on the line for her team and agents of the DOJ?

"Good to see you up and about, Gray," Captain Dixon began. "How are you feeling?"

*Gray?* "All right. Thank you, sir," Macy replied. Ignore them. Ignore him.

First lie of the day. Kayne waited to meet her eyes, and when she refused to look at him or Agent Pixley, it was clear she wasn't happy about being there, and wasn't going to play their game.

"You remember Agent Pixley and Agent Sinclair?" Captain Dixon asked. "They were at the warehouse."

"Affirmative, sir," Macy answered. *I didn't hit my head that hard.*

"I'm glad to see you're doing well," Tippi offered.

Kayne looked at the agent. She hadn't spoken to anyone since Captain Dixon told them about the questioning. Not the detectives relaying messages. Captain Dixon. No one. Not one word. He wasn't the only one who noticed; Captain Dixon turned to give her a questioning look that Agent Pixley easily ignored.

Macy met the agent's eyes for a second, gave her a small, fake smile, and quickly looked away, still refusing to acknowledge him. She was blatantly ignoring him, and she hoped he noticed.

Kayne imagined the possessive look in Dr. Locke's eyes and the need for her to look at him, for her to acknowledge him, surged through him. She stared forward, and he knew she wasn't going to yield, and the emotion of her rejection wrapped around him and had him clearing his throat and sitting back. The force brought a squeal from the chair at the same time Agent Pixley gave a narrowed stare, reminding him of his role. He was there to question her about the warehouse, Hunter Wolves, and the spy.

Macy refused to speak, she didn't trust her voice, or what she would have said with the thousand thoughts racing through her head. Damn Agent Asshole. He was going to interrogate her and make her look guilty, even after the rescue and losing Sergeant Mayco. It infuriated her. Like leaving her cell in her Jeep, but she feared they would demand to see her messages and she wouldn't risk Captain Dixon or the DOJ bringing Commander Arden into the interview. On the other hand, she wished she had it to check for messages and to send a message to him. She would ask him if this was really his idea, and if it was, he could have at least warned her. Why wasn't he there protecting his bureau? Commander Arden's silence left her with nothing. She was on her own. As usual.

"Let it be known, Detective Macy Gray is here by her own accord. This interview is part of the investigation into the alleged spy within the Bureau of Paranormal Investigations. Observing as an unbiased agency is Agent Sinclair and Agent Pixley from the Department of Justice, and team members of Blood Rain. Agent Sinclair is a lycanthrope and Agent Pixley is an empath and their combined testimony will be an addition to the report. This session will be video recorded, and voice recorded. Do you understand?"

*My own accord?* "Affirmative, sir," Macy answered. Walking, talking lie detectors. She kept her eyes on Captain Dixon while his were drilling into her as if it wasn't an interview but an interrogation and he knew the questions were a formality. He knew the outcome and was going to be the person who placed her in handcuffs.

"Very good. Let's get started." His eyes narrowed on her before shifting to the paper. "There is evidence leading to the conclusion that over the past couple of months, someone from this bureau has been leaking information. This alleged spy has used this information to warn suspects of the Desert Rock Police Department and the BPI's combined mission to serve a search warrant at Harper's warehouse. The questions will focus on the cases where there have been joint operations. We suspect the person responsible is either a BPI detective or with another law enforcement agency, such as the Desert Rock Police Department. Do you understand the following questions will pertain to those issues?"

"Affirmative, sir." Uncertainty wrapped its cold fingers around Macy's confidence and proved she should have brought her duffle bag. While she was asleep in her house, what information had they collected to find her guilty of being the spy?

"For the record, please state your name, employment, and status on your team," Captain Dixon ordered.

"Detective Macy Gray with the Bureau of Paranormal Investigations. Junior team leader and sharpshooter," Macy answered. She continued to stare at Captain Dixon, refusing to give Agent Sinclair the satisfaction of seeing her weakness.

"I want you to explain why you took a piece of evidence, a vial, from the scene at the Barrettes' house and then gave it to Forensic Detective Brindos," Captain Dixon demanded.

*What?* The question has nothing to do with the spy. "After making entry into the Barrettes' home, we found substantial amounts of White Cell throughout the residence. When we found the suspect, Mrs. Barrette, her behavior was erratic, she appeared panicked and unsure of her surroundings. I felt it was imperative the contents were tested immediately."

"Without cataloging it, you took evidence from the house, why?" Kayne asked.

"I requested authorization from Sergeant Mayco, which he confirmed. I took the *evidence* to the *evidence* van where Forensic Detective Brindos cataloged it. The Barrettes were wealthy. They could have gone to the hospital and received CD4-T to fight the contagion or could have requested inclusion and a secure crossover. They didn't. I wanted to know why." Macy saw the statement register with Agent Asshole ... Captain Dixon, not so much. "The new Hunter Wolf forms are unpredictable, violent, and don't shift back to their humanoid forms. They don't react to the tranquilizers or synthetic silver. If the White Cell is the reason, it would explain Mr. Barrette's inability to complete his transformation."

"The case concerning the Barrettes is ongoing. I warn you, Detective Gray, don't get off topic. I want to know about the White Cell, and confirm you gave it to the proper personnel. What were the results of the White Cell?" Captain Dixon asked.

Kayne watched Macy flinch from the captain's remark, shift slightly, taking pressure off her right side, and he couldn't stop himself from tracking her movements.

"Forensic Detective Brindos stated since it was a field test, he could only confirm if it was CD4-T. It tested negative. It didn't mean the other vials were going to be the same. He advised me, he would have to wait until he was at the lab to test the rest of them," Macy explained. She reported her actions, Sergeant Mayco authorized it, and Rick stated it in his report. While forensics continued their work, testing the other vials in the house, a homicide detective was sifting through the Barrettes' life, and working the investigation. With a paper trail, it wasn't a secret. The captain wanted what? The DOJ to doubt her character.

"Detective Gray, you admitted you thought Mrs. Barrette might act the same as the altered Hunter Wolf forms, yet you watched her attack you and your team. I have a statement given by Detective Gaines reporting Sergeant Mayco ordered you, multiple times, to take the therian, Mrs. Barrette, down. You refused the order which should have resulted in termination. However, since there is no record of punitive action, pending disciplinary stages, or a written warning from Sergeant Mayco, you were cleared to continue working." Captain Dixon was staring at her, like he had caught her and was waiting for the DOJ to arrest her. "Care to enlighten us?"

Commander Arden has the paperwork. Macy took a deep breath, her chest tightening as she made every effort not to look at Agent Asshole as he sat waiting, his fingers playing over her file, her picture sitting on the table out for her to see. She knew every manipulation tactic for an effective interrogation and felt the first stirrings of panic. Clearing her throat, she struggled to focus.

"I reported Mrs. Barrette wasn't trying to attack the team, she was trying to escape. She had been confronted by the DRPD, then her husband. She knew Mr. Barrette left the scene, therefore leaving her by herself to face law enforcement. The refusal to follow the order was based on Mrs. Barrette not being a threat. She was trying to shapeshift by herself and had a Death Bloom." Lying to the DOJ. They had her and they knew it.

"You saw it?" Captain Dixon asked. Doubt sat in the question, and his certainty she was going to lie to get out of the situation etched itself on his face.

"Affirmative. She was naked." Macy's insides collapsed. *I saw it.*

"Detective Gray, while I believe you might have seen the Death Bloom, it isn't the reason you didn't shoot," Tippi started. "Please tell us the entire truth."

What the hell was she going to say when lying to a lycan and an empath would get her arrested? "Ma'am."

Kayne heard the tremble in Macy's voice and knew she was going to lie to them. "Tell me what happened. We need to know about Mrs. Barrette," he urged.

Macy couldn't do this. *Breathe. Answer the questions and get the hell out.* "Sergeant Mayco ordered Mrs. Barrette to stop. She didn't. We were at the end of the hallway, her only way out, and she continued to approach the team. Sergeant

Mayco ordered the tranquilizers, and when they failed to subdue her, he ordered me to take the shot." *Easy shot.* "The target was wounded. It made her gait wrong, weak, and it appeared she might be responding to the tranquilizers."

Macy was back in the house, surrounded by sweltering heat the rancid smell of blood, while the decaying concoction pushed on her like the walls of the hallway. White powder hung in the air as chunks of drywall fell to the ground to land beside broken picture frames. Mrs. Barrette's weakened heartbeat pulsed in her ears while darts riddled her blood-stained body.

"Mrs. Barrette, the target, jumped to the wall and ran down its side on all fours. When she leapt from the wall to the floor, she landed in front of me, that's when I saw she had been bitten, clawed, and coloring the wounds was the Death Bloom. It wasn't the tranquilizers. Mrs. Barrette was sick, bleeding, and dying from the inside out. I've been doing this job long enough to know she was as good as dead. I didn't have to add a bullet to it." Macy stopped talking and stared at Captain Dixon. She wasn't going any further, and she wasn't going to tell them about Mrs. Barrette's failing heartbeat in her ears.

"You didn't know what condition Mrs. Barrette's mind was in, if it was animal or human, and you didn't know what she was planning to do. She was a therian, unknown cause of infection, by instinct she would be violent and pose a threat to you and your team. By refusing the order, you put the welfare of your team in jeopardy. And because you have been doing this job as long as you have, Detective Gray, you should have taken the shot," Kayne lectured, his voice becoming a low rumble. The disfigured therian fighting to shift and survive possessed the strength to kill them and infect them. Macy risked her life.

Where the hell did he get off saying anything? Anger fired a small blast into the unfairness of his statement, but it wasn't enough to override her guilt. Not when he was right. Macy put her team at risk. The pain from her injuries joined a new panicky kind, and together they worked into her arms and legs. Its ache spread out from her core, quickly becoming a throb and sinking deep into her bones and pulling back like a vice grip. She lowered her eyes to the table, where she had shared meals with her friends, fellow detectives, and stared at nothing, barely noticing the fading coffee stains, dents, and wood grain. She wasn't going to defend herself to Agent Sinclair, not when Sergeant Mayco was at Sanative and it wouldn't have happened if they hadn't been in Pennsky. Her eyes slowly glided across the expanse of the table and up to Captain Dixon's gaze. Acting as if he was unfazed, he wore a mask of indifference, but his eyes accused her of not taking the damn shot and it was her fault there was an investigation into a spy.

"Why didn't you take the shot, Detective Gray?" Tippi repeated the question.

The refrigerator hummed to life, the coffee maker wheezed, as if they were listening, and begging to hear how she was going to spin her lies. Grudgingly, Macy met the agent's narrowed, emerald stare. *She knows I heard the heartbeat.* "The BPI needed to know why they were in possession of White Cell, where they got it, and Mr. Barrette was missing, we needed a witness. I wasn't going to kill her if I didn't have to." Not a complete lie.

"Thank you, Detective." Tippi gave Agent Sinclair a 'your turn' look.

"Did you know Mr. Barrette or Mrs. Barrette before entering their house?" Kayne asked as he ignored Agent Pixley.

*Half lies pass.* "Negative," Macy answered. With her eyes on the wall behind Captain Dixon, she wasn't going to look at Agent Sinclair. Not going to look.

"When did you learn their identities?" Kayne leaned forward and shuffled pages, creating a rustling whisper as he tried to get her attention and force her to look at him.

"Sergeant Bailey of the DRPD informed us before we entered the house. Per BPI regulations a detective from the backup team, Detective Cutler, confirmed while we were searching for Mrs. Barrette." Ignoring Agent Sinclair was harder than it should have been. His presence was like a damn weight in the room demanding her attention.

"Were you aware Harper's warehouse and the Pennsky warehouse were both owned by Mr. Barrette?" Kayne continued. With an exaggerated flair, wanting her attention, he made a note.

"Negative," Macy answered. Her brows drew together in confusion, and she struggled to keep her reaction off her face and out of her eyes. The Barrettes had been in deep. Whatever it was.

"In Officer Murphy's report it says you helped with the background investigation into the owners. And yet, you say you didn't know who they were?" Kayne asked with doubt in his voice.

It's a witch hunt. "Officer Murphy was assigned to a drug task force. Southern California Drug Interdiction, their purpose is to find dealers who sell and transport White Cell. Officer Murphy would not have been able to start a background check. It's the Building Division's duty to collect the required paperwork, and initiate the investigation, that takes at least six months to complete. If asked for assistance from a BD agent, about a paranormal, I can add information from a case file, or the National Chronicle of Anthropomorphism, a database of every registered paranormal, to a specific report. As a BPI detective, it's illegal for me to go to the location and do an inspection. Without the initiation of a formal investigation, I cannot make an inquiry of any kind. It's an infringement of rights," Macy explained as she recited policy. "If the applicant has been classified as a biological human, the police department provides the requested information. As a BPI detective, it's illegal for me to initiate or conduct an investigation into an applicant who is a biological human, identifies as humanoid, or their DNA is that of a humanoid."

"Did you give the Building Division agent information about Mr. Barrette?" Kayne asked. He made a note to check into Officer Murphy's records.

"Negative, I didn't have anything to do with Mr. Barrette." *Except for killing him.* "When Harper's was investigated, a Mr. Stiles, classified biological human, owned the property." It was in the report and written down in her notebook. "Because he identified as humanoid, my involvement ceased. It's public record. It wasn't until the DRPD's search warrant team called the BPI for assistance that I revisited Harper's warehouse." Macy took a deep breath and stared at her file sitting in front of Agent Sinclair. The information he was demanding was right there.

"When did the PD suspect Harper's warehouse was important to the trafficking of White Cell?" Kayne asked as his fingers tapped the page.

"I understand Officer Murphy and his team had an active wiretap on an informant and were in contact with the individual. The DRPD would have records confirming the wiretap, and the request for the search warrant. I can't be positive, but I believe the warehouse had been under investigation for several months," Macy answered while watching his fingers. *Not going to look at him.*

"I'm confused. The warehouse changed hands, and no one knew about it? And had been under surveillance for several months. You didn't think to check," Kayne charged.

It wasn't a question it was an accusation and Macy caught the smirk on Captain Dixon's face and held his gaze. "It's not the BPI's responsibility. Mr. Barrette had to have purchased the property as a biological human, making it the DRPD's responsibility to investigate the calls concerning the warehouse," Macy replied as if she was explaining it to Captain Dixon and not Agent Sinclair. *This has nothing to do with me.*

Macy's eyes never met his. They darted from the captain to the file and Kayne's hand, and he stopped drumming his fingers on her picture. "I understand. When did the PD call the BPI?"

"Mandatory two weeks before the search warrant is to take place. We have to make sure we have a team available. You have my report," Macy pointed out. *Stop asking me stupid questions.*

Plenty of time for the spy to make plans. "I would rather hear it from you," Kayne replied, easily covering his impatience with her. "Prior to entering Pennsky warehouse were you aware Mr. Barrette was the owner?" Agent Logue informed Kayne none of the containers were reported stolen and the cartons in the lab belonged to Renew Pharmaceuticals and the company had secured contracts with Golden State Shipping. It tied Mr. Barrette to Renew. Did it mean Renew was behind the manufacturing of White Cell and was storing it at the warehouses? Did Macy know about it?

*Of course they want to hear it from me,* she thought. *Easier to know if I'm lying.* "Negative."

"When you reported activity at Pennsky warehouse, Commander Wilson informed Sergeant Mayco, Mr. Barrette owned the warehouse and explained the connection to the scene at the Barrettes' house." Kayne waited for a retort.

*Activity ... Like finding your wrecked truck.* "He neglected to relay the information."

"You were given a code red and ordered to wait for the DOJ's Blood Rain team before entering the warehouse. Sergeant Mayco didn't give you background information?" Kayne sat back, folded his arms across his chest, and waited for her to counter. He wanted to hear her quick wit about why they were there to begin with. *To save my ass.*

Mr. Barrette hadn't been there by accident. Was he looking for someone? "Negative."

*"I wanted to see your reaction,"* Sergeant Mayco had said. The idea was simple and stupid at the same time. Sergeant Mayco didn't trust her, and Agent Sinclair was angry with her. The lies tightening around her neck were becoming her noose.

Negative, she didn't take the shot.

Negative, she didn't save David from the Hunter Wolf form.

Negative, she didn't save Sergeant Mayco from the Hunter Wolf form.

Affirmative, she was lying to the DOJ.

Damn lycan was going to make her the spy. Her skin crawled over her as the urge to run drove through her. Agent Sinclair was going to destroy her given the chance, and she had the feeling Captain Dixon was helping him. The bureau would hail Dixon a hero for finding the spy. They would hang her for turning her back on law enforcement, humans, killing humans, and working for the shapeshifters. Macy couldn't ignore Agent Sinclair any longer and met his dark tawny eyes, their intensity lit fear that burned inside of her as she watched rage pass inside his forced composure.

Kayne stilled, like stone, when her cinnamon eyes narrowed on him. Her face softened for a split second, and if he hadn't been waiting for her to look at him, he would have missed it. Holding her stare, he hoped the cinnamon melted to molten silver. It didn't. In its place he saw red lines spiderweb her right eye, where blood vessels had burst, and scarlet flooded the corner. *Maybe I'm wrong.*

"You're saying Sergeant Mayco, your sergeant, withheld important information from you." *It's not a question.* "Key information concerning an active case," Kayne reiterated as he sat forward in his chair. He rested his forearms on the table, making his thick shoulders pull his stark white, button-up shirt tight. "Am I correct?"

Macy diverted her attention from his gaze to his muscles and the strength he held, to his sports watch, which probably told you the time for a dozen different places. On the average man, it would have covered the entire wrist, but on Agent Sinclair it looked small. Its glittering, black plastic side made the softest click as it hit the table. "Affirmative." Turning her glare to Captain Dixon she expected him to deny it, confirm it, to say something. *Silence.* The truth she didn't want to face, she didn't want to explain, was out in front of the Blood Rain team. Macy was going to look like an incompetent detective.

"I find it hard to believe Sergeant Mayco, a seasoned detective, and team leader, would have purposely misled you, his junior leader. He would deliberately put you in danger. Not to mention his entire team. Why would he do that?" Kayne asked. Macy saved his life and he lied to her. What the hell was going on with the BPI?

*To teach me a lesson. No one chooses shapeshifters over humans.* "I don't know," Macy weakly mumbled. For every question she answered, he would add another piece of information, repeating them, twisting them, and waiting for her to make a mistake. Or for Agent Pixley to confirm she was lying, and she would stop the interview and arrest Macy. Icy fingers started at the base of her neck, their nails reaching out across her shoulders.

*Lie.* "Officer Murphy's report states you were at Pennsky warehouse as part of the background investigation. Did you assist him?" Kayne asked. There had to be a reason the officer kept mentioning her.

*Back tracking.* "Negative. I cannot inspect a property. Legally I cannot be included in an investigation concerning a being classified as biological human," Macy repeated. It appeared David spent more time falsifying documents than he did investigating claims of White Cell.

"Are you saying he lied in the reports?" Kayne's voice evened out and grew lower. "Sergeant Mayco excluded you from information and Officer Murphy lied. That is what you are saying, Detective Gray, and those are serious allegations. What would make two officers of the law, one of whom you had a relationship with, lie to you, endangering you, and put the future of their careers at risk?"

"I don't know." Damn if she wasn't investigating David for Commander Arden and he turned around and played her. She was a fucking fool and was going to pay the price.

"Detective Gray, I don't appreciate you trying to tarnish Officer Murphy's record by accusing him of lying. I don't think the police department would like what you're saying about their dead," Captain Dixon chastised.

"My apologies, sir." Macy looked down at the folders and the lies scrawled on files and felt defeated. There was nothing she could say about David or Sergeant Mayco without making the dead look bad and the wounded look like a liar.

*They trapped her.* "You see how this doesn't make sense. All the while, Officer Murphy and Sergeant Mayco lied or kept the truth from you, you didn't do anything," Kayne accused. With his elbows on the table, he leaned in to level his stare at her. "Why?"

Sergeant Mayco made his point, she had nothing left to say. But David. Macy hadn't had a plan when she started watching him. Commander Arden told her to pay attention to the way he treated his informants, find out if they were human or paranormal, check his cases, and if he told her anything out of the ordinary to check it out. "I had no control over what Officer Murphy wrote in his reports and I have nothing to do with the DRPD. I didn't do anything because I didn't know what was going on."

With her silence, the charges were starting to mount, and the pile was becoming a mountain. Macy's mind scrambled for something, a shred of anything, to defend herself without making herself look guilty or like she was trying to blame the dead or the infected. After David's death, she told Commander Arden about the evidence, explained David's relationship with his informants, the connection to the sale of White Cell, and the cases he had been working. All of it a haphazard investigation because she wasn't convinced there was something going on. As if to remind her of the evidence, the memory sticks dug into her hip. She needed to go home and read over the reports, she had to have missed a detail. *Think.* Harper's warehouse. Her mind raced as pieces of the puzzle refused to fit together with what she knew.

The Barrettes.

Hunter Wolf forms.

Harper's warehouse.

White Cell.

David.

*Fuck me.* David knew about Mr. Barrette and who was responsible for the White Cell in Harper's warehouse. A simple detail, the BPI doesn't handle cases involving biological humans, and it excluded them from the investigation. No one in the BPI would have had a reason to investigate. Macy saw the Hunter Wolf form coming at her and fired one round, hitting it in the shoulder when it pushed her to the side to get to him. They murdered him. David knew and they murdered him. She needed Commander Arden because Agent Sinclair and Captain Dixon weren't going to believe her. Don't want to tarnish Officer Murphy's immaculate record.

"Detective Gray, I asked you, what was your relationship with Officer Murphy?" Kayne raised his voice, attempting to reach her. He watched her eyes clear, she sat straighter, and he waited to catch her lie and feel her heartbeat react to her guilt.

"Acquaintances," Macy stated absently. Dysfunctional. *We were spying on each other, and because I wasn't paying close enough attention, he tagged me in his mess.* Macy wasn't going to explain the sympathy she received from the police department and the BPI at his funereal, thinking they had been dating. No doubt someone had told him. That's why Agent Sinclair asked the question.

Her heartbeat spiked. *Lying.* "That's all?"

"Acquaintances." The line of questioning, combined with her thoughts, had her shoulders stiffening and her light blouse hanging on her like it weighed hundreds of pounds.

Macy knew she was staring at him with bloodshot eyes, the force from holding back hot tears from frustration. There was more than one spy and from multiple agencies and they were killing their own. And if she dared to confess her accusations, they would make her look crazy. Please bring in the men in white coats. She could live in PJs.

"I was led to believe there was more going on. In fact, several people have confirmed the two of you were in a relationship," Kayne added.

Tawny. Amber. Did his eyes change? "That is my personal life. It has no bearing on the case or this questioning," Macy answered quickly. Her heart pounded, making pain radiate through her.

"You'll answer the question, Detective Gray," Captain Dixon ordered.

"It does when the officer in question is dead. Your reluctance to answer has me assuming you were more than acquaintances," Kayne quickly said on the tail of the captain's order. *Tell me you weren't.*

They sat across from her like a firing squad. Outnumbered and alone, Macy felt heat creep up her throat and over her wounds, sinking into them as if trying to get back inside of her. Right then would have been the perfect time for Commander Arden to breeze into the room like a superhero and explain everything. She waited. Negative. "Interagency relationship."

Kayne dismissed her answer. He couldn't sense her anymore. The chaos of her emotions whirled around her like a storm, taking definition from him and destroying the edges of the void he felt. "Did you know Henry or Grace Taylor?"

"No. Negative," Macy answered. Her strength was draining from her like her body was a sieve.

"Do you know how they ended up at Pennsky warehouse?" *Convince me you weren't involved.*

"No." Macy saw the woman's battered face and wondered if she was alive. And the lycan, what happened to him? *Don't ask me about the lycan.* "Negative."

"Mrs. Taylor said they had been kidnapped. Are you aware of how many kidnappings have been reported?" Kayne asked as he took pictures from a folder.

Macy stared at Agent Sinclair's hands, free from wounds, as he placed the photos in front of her, then his long fingers separated them. "Negative." She glanced at them and up at Agent Sinclair and his rich, tawny gaze.

"Missing persons?" Taking more pictures from a folder, he lined them up in front of her.

"Affirmative."

"Could you elaborate?" Kayne pushed. He was losing her. Whether it was the questions, her guilt, her secretes, or the pain seizing her body, he didn't know.

"Missing persons in the desert area are sixty percent higher than the average," Macy began. She spoke slowly as she began reciting statistics. "Of the sixty percent, half are homeless. They come here seeking the mild winters, and the encampments along the river. A quarter of those have a mental illness, and if they have a medical history, it makes it easier to track them. A quarter are transients that move on and those are hard to keep track of. Sometimes there's a report if the missing has a family, but more often than not there isn't. The others are underaged runaways. The established homeless rule the encampments, chase the off runaways, and they head to Los Angeles or Las Vegas and from there they're lost. All missing persons are kept in the system until they're found. If a human is reported missing it's DRPD's responsibility to conduct the investigations, not the BPI. We don't investigate humans." Her attention went from the pictures and the faces staring up at her to Captain Dixon, where there was no help, and back to the pictures.

"How do you know about them?" Tippi asked. She met Agent's Sinclair's gaze, and understood Detective Gray was falling apart.

"The Hunter Wolf forms don't transform back to their humanoid form. If the missing persons have medical records, we would have access to their DNA. If they have been arrested, their DNA is in the system. We've tried to crosscheck missing persons with the unidentified Hunter Wolf forms. For that we need DNA from the Hunter Wolf forms. However, their behavior and unwillingness to standdown means their bodies are damaged by synthetic silver. The times we've recognized the differences in them it was too late." Macy placed her hands in her lap, and squeezing them, started twisting her fingers.

"Correct me if I'm wrong, Sanative is responsible for the autopsies. You assist Sanative?" Kayne asked. If Macy wasn't having a relationship with Officer Murphy, could she have been in a relationship with Dr. Locke? Kayne saw the look of confusion, maybe hurt on his face when Macy rejected his help at the warehouse, and then heard him say, "Claimed her as one of the Gawain pack." Fury erupted inside of him, feeding his jealousy.

"Assist, negative. The BPI does work with the medical facilities in the area," Macy answered. Agent Sinclair's demeanor changed, he tensed, and relaxed in the same breath and the quick switch spooked her.

"Are you part of those investigations?" Kayne demanded.

"No," Macy slowly replied. "Negative. Forensics and homicide are in charge."

Captain Dixon reviewed reports turned in by every detective on the bureau, which gave him information on the cases she had worked on, their conclusions, and her active files. Macy's head throbbed, warnings went off provoking her panic, and she felt trapped. Captain Dixon knew the details of the cases, the homeless, the runaways, and he was close to the sergeant in charge of homicide. Paranoid much. Her secrets were making her look guilty. Maybe she should give up the charade and point a shaking nub of a finger at Captain Dixon and tell him the truth about David and then throw the memory sticks at him. Or she could hand them over to Agent Sinclair. Sic the lycan onto the captain. She would turn her back on the BPI, and the humans, like they believed she had.

Macy sat back in the chair, a barely there squeal sounding, her thoughts becoming a mess of accusations and lies and it made her unaware when the room went silent. Without Commander Arden to back her up, all she had were her allegations, and she doubted the lycan was going to believe her. Shutting down her thoughts, her emotions, and her instincts, she wanted to cross her arms over her chest in defiance and would have if the pain wouldn't have been too high a price to pay. If they wanted her to confess to being the spy, they were going to have to do a better job besides tossing questions into the air to see which she would field, and which she would lie about. They needed physical evidence and if the questions were any indication, they didn't have any. The silence thickened as the minutes blew in the air and disappeared into the past. The strength and anger she was desperately trying to hold onto began falling apart. *I have to leave.* A couple more questions and she would end up staying in a cold cell marked traitor.

His rage subsided when Kayne noticed he was losing her. Damn. Doesn't matter. He would push her as far as he could. "Before Doctor Locke transported you to Sanative, had you been there before?" Not part of the investigation.

Macy looked at him, confusion in her eyes, and disbelief on her face. Why didn't it surprise her neither Captain Dixon nor Agent Sinclair could stick to a line of questioning? "Negative."

*Good.* "At Harper's warehouse the Hunter Wolves came out of several containers. Officers from the warrant service team reported it looked as if they were expected. Do you know why?" Kayne asked, continuing his interrogation.

"Negative." *Here's some information you can think about.* "The intel from Officer Murphy and his team said the warehouse was abandoned. Lack of traffic made it possible for the dealers to use it to store White Cell." Abandoned like Pennsky. And like Pennsky they were attacked. "In cases where shapeshifter presence is expected, the BPI assists and acts as security while the DRPD seizes the White Cell and prepares it for transport. Once the DRPD is done the BPI is relieved of their duties. We were ambushed. I'm not the only person to add it their report. Both agencies conducted an investigation and both review boards stated it appeared to be a setup."

"No one believed it could have been bad intel? Or you walked into their operation and they retaliated?" Tippi asked. Detective Gray bounced back and forth between giving an articulate answer and completely shutting down.

Macy heard David's gun click empty as the Hunter Wolf form tore him apart and warm blood drifted on the air. "Negative."

"Why?" Kayne asked. Her eyes grew haunted and darkened, her face twisted in a grimace, and her lips pressed together, causing beads of scarlet to fill a fine line.

"The night before and that morning the DRPD had been doing surveillance on the warehouse. They had an active watcher." Macy met Agent's Sinclair's gaze. *I'm not the spy.*

"I agree with the statement it had been a setup. But what you're alluding to, Detective Gray, is one of the DRPD gave up information. That's an accusation you don't have evidence to prove. I blame it on simple human error. It's difficult to have a perfected operation when there are so many moving parts," Captain Dixon explained. "I would like to keep this questioning about the spy within our number. The DRPD can take care of themselves."

"Affirmative, sir." Macy stopped herself from physically shuddering. She proved there was more going on than the spy in the BPI, and Captain Dixon wasn't going to listen. None of them were going to listen.

Captain Dixon wanted Macy delivered to him as the spy. Not going to happen. Kayne needed her and he knew what he had to do to get her out of the office and on the road. He wanted her to show him her secrets and believed the tracker was going to do the job. "Detective Gray, your answers have proven you're in the middle of this case. Deflecting attention isn't going to help you."

Desperation. Run. "That's not a question." Macy stood. Her sudden movement shoved the chair from the back of her legs, the metal bottoms screeching against the tile. Her ribs screamed with new pain, her head throbbed with her racing heartbeat, and her knees felt weak.

"Detective Gray, Macy, sit down and we'll talk about this. I want to help you," Captain Dixon weakly pleaded as he stood.

His voice slithered over her. He was lying. Macy couldn't shake the feeling and took a step back. "Negative."

"If you leave like this, I'll be forced to take the past cases into consideration and it will make you a suspect," Kayne warned. He was bluffing and playing a dangerous game, one he didn't know if he was going to win. Damn Captain Dixon. Kayne wanted Macy but was risking her future worth it?

*As if I wasn't a suspect. See the scarlet S for spy on my chest.* "I'll take my chances," Macy countered, her words breaking from the desperation riddling her body. *Keep it together*, she thought as she took another step back.

With Grace in a medically-induced coma, it was easy for Kayne to keep the information she had told him about the BPI kidnapping them and with Henry in wolf form, his involvement with White Cell was another secret. He wasn't going to divulge the details to the BPI until Agent Logue and Agent Kriss were finished checking the list of known White Cell dealers. There had to be someone who knew about the spy and the rogue detectives. If they were detectives. It clearly wasn't Macy.

"Stay and talk to me." *Please*. Kayne used every ounce of control he had to remain seated and not jump up and block her from leaving. Which went against his plan.

"Negative," Macy quickly answered.

"You were allowed to return to work after the Internal Affairs investigation because they didn't find you at fault for Officer Murphy's death. It's true, there's no report of punitive action after the Barrettes, however, Sergeant Mayco requested to be transferred to a different team because he didn't want to work with you. With your allegation that he didn't tell you information, I would understand if you wanted revenge." Kayne's thighs hurt with the strain to stay still, and he was losing his false show of calm.

Agent Sinclair's fingers pressed against her file so hard they turned white. "Revenge?" Macy whispered and shook her head. "Negative." She raised her hand and touched the cut above her eye. She wouldn't risk lives because Sergeant Mayco was angry with her. How did her reputation as a proficient detective, that took years to achieve, turn to dust? What did Agent Sinclair think of her? Macy didn't fucking care and wasn't wasting anymore time. She turned around and headed for the door.

They all saw the bright red tips of her fingers and the scratches scarring her hand as she shoved the chair. "Wait. Can you confirm your whereabouts for the last couple of weeks?" Kayne asked, grasping at anything.

Macy stood within feet of escape. She didn't face them and answered, "Affirmative." With no warning, Agent Sinclair was suddenly standing in front of the door. She slowly twisted enough to look at the table, his seat, and the distance he covered in absolute silence. He moved with a lycan's speed, grace, a human was incapable of having and was in *her* office. "I'm leaving," she whispered. Reaching for the door handle, she waited for him to move, and when he didn't, she took a slow breath.

"I'll check the records. But if you leave now, like this, you will put doubt in our minds about your intent," Kayne softly threatened. Did he want her to stay? Negative. He needed her to leave, but if she gave him the answers he wanted, she could stay, and he would protect her. "You could change my mind if you told me the truth."

A threat delivered by whisper. "I told the truth. I'm not saying anything more to you or anyone else," Macy replied to him in the same soft tone. "If you're going to arrest me then do it, and I'll call my authorized representative and my lawyer. I'll explain your intimidation tactics and this charade of an interview to them," she threatened louder, in order for Agent Pixley and Captain Dixon to hear her. The shiny brushed nickel stared at her from behind black dress slacks, and she prayed he bought her line. She didn't look at him, choosing to concentrate on the door handle, for fear he would see her doubt.

Kayne didn't budge, he stayed close to her, inhaled the harsh scent of her fear and acted as if he hadn't heard her. Her false strength crumbled under her panic while her racing heartbeat thundered in his head. Macy's scratched hand reached for the handle, her wrist, marred with bruises, brushed his hip, making him inhale.

It was an audible hiss when Agent Sinclair's breath caught, the sound driving through the scant space to strike her nerves. Inside a storm of thoughts, Macy pictured several scenarios. First, Agent Sinclair tried talking her into staying, and second, Captain Dixon called her fellow detectives in to arrest her. When she wore a shiny set of handcuffs, the men in white coats would arrive to take her away. And those were the good ones. Reality was crueler than her imagination. Macy waited for him to start the bargaining with 'we want to do what's best' speech, except Agent Sinclair didn't say another word. He acted like he was just as puzzled as she was. Like at the warehouse. They stood letting silence reign while she stared at the door and he stared down at her.

"Agent Sinclair, let her leave. I don't believe she's physically strong enough to sit and answer any more questions. And quite frankly, Captain Dixon, this questioning has turned into an interrogation," Tippi stressed. "Detective Gray, you need to rest. Please don't go anywhere in case we need to contact you."

Kayne looked at Agent Pixley to find her standing, hands on her hips, her green eyes glowing with anger while her white blouse made her short, red hair blaze against the pale walls behind her. He used the time to punch down his anxiety and turned his attention back to Macy. "You aren't going anywhere, are you, Detective Gray?" he asked, his voice, while being low, carried his frustration.

"Negative." Macy had to clear her throat to give the word sound, making it nothing more than a humiliating whimper. Where the hell would she go? Agent Sinclair unnerved her with his speed, strength, and otherworldly bullying. If he wasn't a DOJ agent, and she had a gun, she would have shot him, more than once.

When Agent Sinclair ended the standoff and hesitantly took a step backwards, Macy gripped the handle, turned it, and slowly pulled the door open. No one said anything and the space between them stretched out into the rest of the breakroom turned interrogation dungeon. When the door nudged him, Agent Sinclair took another forced step. He continued staring at her, his eyes a dull amber as if he was holding back the edge of his power as he watched everything she did. Like he was processing her. She could feel his magic, like a warm wind, flowing around her, over her. Damn lycan. Agent Sinclair was riding the energy her body was pumping out the same way he had at the warehouse.

*Do you get off on scaring me?* Macy pulled the door another inch and squeezed through the opening, leaving them behind her. Successfully escaping Captain Dixon and Agent

Sinclair, she walked as fast as she dared around desks, her desk, detectives, and their gazes.

*Get ready, you're next,* Macy thought as she dabbed at the blood on her lip with the back of hand. With the double doors in sight, she headed straight to the parking lot.

# CHAPTER FIFTEEN

"Captain Dixon, I apologize if I've overstepped my authority," Tippi began. "With most of Detective Gray's attention on her injuries and dealing with the emotional repercussions of Sergeant Mayco's physical condition and her fellow detectives, it's hard to judge her answers."

"That's unfortunate. I wasn't aware of how extensive her injuries were. Were you able to sense anything from her?" Captain Dixon asked. He stared at the door, like Detective Gray would appear and confess.

Tippi wanted to argue and point out he knew exactly how extensive they were, Detective Gray had been punched in the face by a Hunter Wolf, ersatz, but knew it was a moot point. "Detective Gray was here to report to the review board. Our interview came as a surprise and quickly turned into an interrogation. Between her injuries and your endless accusations, it made it difficult to understand her reactions. As I said, she was preoccupied. The questions were the least of her problems," Tippi explained.

Kayne held the door open and watched her until she disappeared while struggling to understand his senses and why it was hard to distinguish her reactions. At the warehouse he blamed it on exhaustion, the empath, and syn silver poisoning ... now he didn't have an excuse. It's as if Macy's high emotions blocked everyone out, which for a mortal was impossible. Returning to the table he looked through the next file, his mind on the DNA test and Daeland, while Agent Pixley argued with Captain Dixon. With frustration eating him, Kayne shuffled papers, looked over several, put them back, went through them again, and listened to the captain.

"Was she lying?" Captain Dixon demanded. "This is about a spy. I need confirmation."

"I can't give you confirmation and I'm not going to put my reputation as an agent with the DOJ at risk by making a bad recommendation. If I said yes or no at this point, it would be unfair to her, and I would be lying to you. I need her healthy, not fighting to sit through questions while suffering from bruised ribs and a concussion," Tippi insisted. Guilt sank inside of her knowing she was delaying the inevitable and there was nothing she could do to help Detective Gray.

Kayne fought his wolf's instinct to follow Macy and make sure she was all right, and to apologize to her. Apologize. It was an investigation. He stopped himself, choosing to shuffle the same papers while Captain Dixon and Agent Pixley went back and forth about the questioning. With his frustration simmering it made the smallest details aggravating, like the breakroom smelling of mortals, sweat, stale food, and Macy's fear. Under it all was an unbridled passion, its presence giving her secrets life, while its stringent edge called his wolf. Kayne told himself he needed air, and he wasn't going to track her down to talk to her. She was probably in her car and headed home. And if she wasn't, he would know.

Hitting hard, but not as hard as the questions, was the pressing heat of the desert afternoon and the glare from the sun. Macy shielded her eyes as the comfortable chill from the office slid from her skin and faded, letting the heat quickly invade her clothing and her skin. Like a vessel of safety and means of escape, her Jeep sat across the parking lot. All she had to do was get to it. Easy.

Macy considered running, or at least speed walking, and knew it was out of the question when thinking about it had her muscles tightening with anxiety, and her head pounding with each pained step. Like a mantra, she kept telling herself to keep the tears, from dread and anger, from falling until she was safely on the 15 freeway going eighty miles an hour in the opposite direction of the office. She didn't need witnesses to her breakdown. Halfway there, she left the pump station, and heated fuel fumes to fade in the breeze, as well as the evidence van, several other cars, a truck, and Detective Gaines' sports car.

Within yards of her Jeep, Macy believed she was home free. The pressure from her tears eased, the tension retracted its claws from her shoulders, and she walked an easier pace. The strain drained from her muscles, and she allowed herself to breathe a long inhale, a longer exhale, her worry lessening. Then, she heard the familiar squeal of the door. She cursed, her hope for escaping instantly killed, and she knew someone was behind her.

*Shit. Keep walking.* Nearly stumbling from the eerie sense of awareness crawling up her neck and into her shoulders, she knew it was Agent Sinclair.

What was he doing to her? Macy hurried her steps, tripped, sucked air as it stretched her ribs, and felt her tears threatening to spill down her cheeks. She gained her balance, quickened her pace, and knew it was pointless to try and outrun him when she could hardly out walk him. Hell, the lycan beat her to the door of the breakroom. Why was the lycan lie detector following her? Macy knew the law, upheld the law, and lived on the right side ... until now. It was as if they tossed her to the other side, the wrong side, and left her there to drown.

"Detective Gray, wait!" Kayne yelled from behind her.

Why wouldn't he let her go? His voice drifted through her, around her, inside her head, as if he knew she lacked the control to stop them from taking her career. Pushing forward, she told herself she was close, so close to escaping. He yelled again, and this time he didn't use Detective Gray, he called her by her name. He said it the same way he had when they were at the warehouse. The damn warehouse. It had been a couple of minutes, maybe he wanted to tell her how he connected her to every crime in Desert Rock.

"Macy, stop," Kayne demanded. Ignoring his order, she kept walking and it grated on his nerves. How was he going to convince her he wanted to help her? *Should not have taken Captain Dixon's side.*

Agent Sinclair yelled once more, and she ignored him. *Leave me alone.* Macy hugged her side, trying to lessen the pain, when she felt his fingers wrap around her upper arm. No. Holding her, he gently pulled her to a stop. It took him seconds to catch up to her, and his breathing hadn't changed, where she felt like she had run a marathon. Facing him, the sunlight blinded her for a second.

"Unless you're arresting me, you can't force me to stay." If she wasn't embarrassed enough, Macy's voice trembled, and she felt hot scarlet lines web her eyes.

Kayne loosened his hold when her muscles tensed against his palm and the tears welling in her eyes threatened to destroy his resolve. "You act like you're protecting someone involved with Officer Murphy's death, or you're protecting the spy. I have to know what kind of relationship you had with him."

He was making everything worse with his selfish need to know. The same single-minded drive he embraced when he left his pack to chase his demons. But he had to force her to make a move, to expose whoever she was working with because she wasn't working alone. A bead of sweat slid down the side of his face and he stopped himself from letting go of her to wipe it away. Accustomed to eighty degrees days of the mountains, the temperature of the desert had sweat beading on his forehead, and he could feel his shirt getting damp under his arms and around his shoulders. He hated the desert.

With his height, Macy had to tilt her head to see him better. In the warehouse his hair had been matted with blood, sweat, and dirt, hiding its true color. Agent Sinclair stood with the sun behind him, its cool shade of gold highlighting streaks of auburn that blended in dark brown while its ends touched his collar. The thin scar, a shade paler than his bronze skin, was a sliver from his left ear and curved under his jaw to end in a twisted cluster as if his skin pinched the blade. Macy recognized the intent. Someone had tried to cut his throat and failed. And if it hadn't healed, he had been human when it happened. He was used to surviving. While Macy analyzed his face, his grip eased but remained on her arm as he waited.

"I don't have to explain anything to you, Agent Sinclair. You're going to believe what you want." Macy thought she was going to be spared the 'I can help you' speech.

"I believe the evidence. You keep coming up in Officer Murphy's reports. You are said to be having a relationship with him outside of work. You could be charged with being the spy and an accomplice to whoever is behind the warehouses and White Cell," Kayne threatened. "I can help you if you tell me the truth."

There it was. She needed to protect herself. The voice inside her head told her to tell Agent Sinclair the truth. To tell him before it went too far, and it was too late to save herself. "I can't do anything about the reports. If the DRPD allowed their officer to falsify documents, it's not my problem. You can look at my time sheets, my open cases, and find out where I was and what I was doing. I can't falsify those when they're generated by a computer and signed off by command." Captain Dixon. Macy might be in more trouble than she thought. "You might want to go over the BPI's protocols and procedures."

"What was your relationship with the deceased?" *Tell me you didn't have one.*

Macy looked at the office, prayed Agent Pixley would retrieve her lycan, and back to Agent Sinclair. "I used to be part of the DRPD and we worked together. When I left for the Emergency Retraction Team, it was like I turned my back on them, like they weren't good enough. I chose a superior agency. I didn't keep many friends." Lying and digging a deeper hole. Would he tell her he knew or keep it to himself and add it to the case against her? "When the BPI recruiter offered me a position, I left the ERT. Officer Murphy didn't hold those decisions against me."

The BPI offered her a job. "You were treated differently when you transferred?" Kayne asked.

"You could say that. The ERT's purpose is to eliminate threats, no matter who or what they are. The BPI is the exact opposite. Its objective is to uphold the laws protecting paranormals. I'm sure you've noticed, it isn't at the top of everyone's to do list," Macy explained as she raised her left hand to shield her eyes from the sun.

"You protect paranormals? Your file states you have prejudice against shapeshifters and have expressed a dislike toward all paranormals." From the ERT, nothing but assassins with the government's blessing, to the BPI, and she was going to protect paranormals. Kayne doubted it.

Dislike. Negative, it's hate, pure hate. "My job is protecting them regardless of how I feel. If you're not going to believe me, don't ask the question." Macy closed her eyes, trying to control her anger, then met his glare with her own. "Agent Sinclair, I don't care if you doubt my integrity, my past with Officer Murphy, or how I deal with paranormals. It doesn't matter. Once you've torn apart the BPI and maybe the DRPD you'll walk away, and Desert Rock will be a fleeting thought. What's left of the BPI and the DRPD will be here for someone to pick up the pieces you're tossing to the ground. The citizens will be here and because of you they'll doubt their safety. I'll be here." Unemployed. Macy turned to leave, but his grip tightened, holding her, and she stopped.

True. "I don't doubt your ability ... it's clear the paranormals think you protect them, Doctor Locke said as much. You have his respect. Tell me you weren't seeing Officer Murphy on a personal level." It wasn't a question, it was a demand. He wanted confirmation. When she raised her hand to shield her eyes, Kayne automatically stepped to the side, blocking the sun. His height towered over her, and he half expected her to slink from him, the way Agent Pixley did, the way most did. Macy didn't. He was accusing her of being the spy, having an affair with a bad cop, and putting the BPI detectives in danger and she stood her ground.

"Negative. I wasn't having a relationship with him. I have a job to do, and having a personal life isn't part of the equation. I spend my nights on call, and my weekends training or working. Happy?" Judging my personal life? Macy doubted Agent Sinclair had a personal life.

"I'm not sure." Kayne looked at her Jeep, his truck, and back to her bloodshot eyes, bruises, and stiches. "Eliminate one person from the equation. Tell me about Sergeant Mayco and why he didn't tell you Mr. Barrette owned Pennsky warehouse?"

Macy was sick of his questions. "Sergeant Mayco didn't give me information because I didn't kill the Hunter Wolf form before it killed Officer Murphy, and I didn't gun down Mrs. Barrette. I work with Doctor Locke, a lycan, and you said I have his respect. I was being taught a lesson, Agent Sinclair. You doubt I protect paranormals ... well, as a human I'm not supposed to choose the shapeshifters over my own kind. Pretty fucking simple." God, did she betray Sergeant Mayco? Macy wasn't sure.

Something inside of him broke, making him doubt his intentions. It was her raw truth. Kayne thought there was something going on between Sergeant Mayco and Macy, but never would have guessed the sergeant held Officer Murphy and Dr. Locke against her. "Macy, I'm sorry. This case along with investigating the ersatz has taken its toll. I want whoever is doing this. They're killing shapeshifters and humans and using the Otherkin."

Macy bowed her head. Kidnappers. Serial killers. Guilt. "I don't have information for you."

Kayne wondered why she was lying, and why she continued lying when Captain Dixon wasn't there and no one from the BPI could hear them. "You know something and you're hiding it. I don't have to be a werewolf to know you're lying. If you're not with them, you're against them. It's not the BPI you have to fear, and it's not the DOJ. In the mortal world, you'll have a fair trial, maybe a prison sentence and maybe you'll live behind bars for the rest of your life. The shifters and mortals behind this won't hesitate, they don't care who you are. You witnessed the damage they're capable of doing. They'll kill you, like they killed Officer Murphy."

Agent Sinclair knew who killed David? Not possible. He was trying to get her to talk. Maybe being torn apart by a Hunter Wolf form was going to be her mercy. Macy shook the thought loose. Was she walking into a trap set by David? Absently, she watched Agent Sinclair's hand as if in slow motion, his fingers almost touching her when his movement dug in and she stepped back from his reach. "I'm not protecting anyone. I've told you the truth." Don't burn the bridge he's on, you might need him.

In an instant her strength drained from her, the bulk of it hiding under the lies, the investigations, and so much pain. She met Agent Sinclair's narrowed gaze and saw he was waiting for her to talk, to start babbling about her side, her explanation why, her lies or truths out for him to sense and judge. The silence stretched out as they stared at each other. He brought the interrogation to the parking lot under the guise of trying to help her and it left her playing in a minefield with him. *Macy.* She hated the way he said her name and the way it sounded familiar. She reminded herself Agent Sinclair wanted to talk, catch her in another lie, and wanted to twist her words, her actions, to fit inside of their damn reports. Without a word, she tugged her arm free from his hold, his fingers grazing her skin as she started toward her Jeep. Behind her, Agent Sinclair's footsteps followed, then his hand was on her shoulder, before he stopped her, she unlocked the door.

"Please, give me one second." Kayne took his hand back and waited for Macy to face him.

"I don't have any information," Macy repeated as she stared at her Jeep.

"You keep saying that. Did you recognize the symbol on the containers in the warehouse? Any information would help us." Kayne didn't think she did, if she had seen them before the Hunter Wolves attacked, but he had to get her talking.

Macy tried to remember the markings and if she had seen them at another scene. Harper's? She couldn't remember, but if she had, she would have made a note. "Negative," she answered as she faced him.

It was the first time she didn't lie. "All right. One more thing and you're free to go."

*Gee, thanks.* "What?"

"The tattoo you have on your back, what does it mean?" Kayne asked as casually as he could manage.

The feel of his heated hands on her bare shoulders as he held her came back in a rush and sent chills down her spine. He made a spectral out of her to see her tattoo. Macy narrowed her gaze and asked, "Why?"

"It caught my attention, and I apologize, again for my behavior. It's different," Kayne lied.

"It means nothing. Saw a picture and had to have it." Another lie. "Can I go?"

*Lying.* "That tattoo?" he asked, ignoring her.

"Affirmative, Agent Sinclair." Macy met his gaze and didn't like the doubt she saw. Turning from him, she opened the door, and when she was safely sitting behind the steering wheel, she closed the door and started the engine.

Kayne pulled a card from his shirt pocket and tapped the corner against the window. He held his breath, hoped she didn't ignore him, and waited. Slowly exhaling, Macy began manually rolling the window down. When it was halfway, warm vanilla carried on the breeze, and like ribbons, it feathered his face. He inhaled her scent, enjoying the pure fragrance lacking the harsh edge of dread and the office. It was Macy. In her Jeep, she was safe and believed she escaped the interrogation. Him. He hated baiting her. When the window was down, he wanted to ask if she took the doors and top off and drove through the desert. He could imagine her loving the freedom it gave her, then stopped himself from going further. Detective Gray. Suspect. Bait. Vampire property. Kayne was walking on fragile ground and wasn't going to risk getting any closer to her.

Macy stared at the fence and the empty lot beyond using the seconds to hide her pain. When she looked at him, she couldn't stop it from invading her eyes. "Agent Sinclair."

*Call me Kayne.* "Take the card. My personal cell number is on the back," Kayne started. "Call me anytime. If we don't stop them, if we don't find out who is doing this, the ersatz will be in every city, terrorizing people. And if White Cell does contain the contagion, it'll be on the streets and available to a public clambering to get their hands on it because they're scared. The relationship we have fought for between mortals and paranormals will be lost. The Requiem will be invalid. There will be another war between us, and if I know you, like I think I do, you don't want that."

*Damn, he's right.* Macy let his warning work through her thoughts, while his hand, flawless—after syn silver poisoning, and fights with Hunter Wolf forms—sat next to her hand marred with scratches, cuts, and bruises, and missing fingernails. She took the card, careful not to touch him, and after glancing at the number on the back, placed it in the cup holder next to her cell. The duffle bag sitting empty in the passenger seat reminded her the cost of escape was leaving her stuff behind. It didn't matter, she got what she needed. Macy took her eyes from the duffle bag and his card, and while holding his light amber gaze, rolled the window up.

Agent Sinclair stood with his wolf eyes narrowed on her and his wrecked truck behind him. It was evidence of the damage the Hunter Wolf forms were capable of doing and she forced herself to push it aside before she babbled a confession. Backing out, she refused to look at him, then turning the wheel she headed across the parking lot. It wasn't over. She could run, but there was no hiding. The DOJ and BPI put her in the center of their investigations. As she stopped and waited for the gate to rumble across the lane, she looked at his card. What would happen if the corrupted White Cell hit the streets? Total. Chaos.

Easing on the gas, the Jeep rolled over the track, and she left Agent Sinclair and his demand for the truth in her rear-view mirror.

"Come back, Macy," Kayne mumbled. *Come back and prove to me you're innocent.* He wanted to order her to turn around and explain whatever it was she was holding back. Hell, he would take her sharp tongue and belittling jabs over her silence.

At the warehouse, Kayne thought her feel resembled the ersatz, and their lack of a wolf spirit but not after today, the darkness strengthened the storm she used a barricade. Its viscidness sat thick around her as it built a barrier between her and the world. It was hard to judge an emotion as strong as her dread when it was alive, protective, and fed off her energy. Maybe it was fear's essential primal element she clung to and relied on when she felt backed into a corner. And Kayne backed her into a corner. If it was then he understood. Fear kept you alive because it evoked respect. You feared dying, you feared pain, and in turn, you respected those with the power to wield it and protected yourself from them. Dread, on the other hand, paralyzed you, made you a coward, created limits, slowed you down, and shaped second guesses. Kayne cursed as the silver glint of the spare tire disappeared behind the diamonds of the chain-link fence. Macy's dread was false, that much he knew for sure. Why he had felt it and why it was there, he didn't know. The damn investigation was confusing his thoughts and made frustration a constant feeling.

He kicked a rock with the toe of his dress shoe then started marching back to the office, dreading the hours in the breakroom, when his cell buzzed, and he groaned. "Sinclair." He stopped and faced the gate.

"I have confirmation Lord Daeland is in Desert Rock, and before you ask, no, I don't know his location," Michael reported, his gruff voice sounding like he was standing beside Kayne.

"Who told you?" *It keeps getting better.*

"His man Louie called, said Lord Daeland would contact you when you needed to know."

"Why didn't he call me?" Using his free hand, he wiped sweat from the back of his neck. With Daeland's authority and his place with the Council, he would be able to hide anywhere in the city and no one would tell Kayne. He was playing by the vampire's rules for the millionth time.

"Maybe he felt safer calling the Garrick pack, than the DOJ." Humor in Michael's voice traveled over the miles, giving away his smile.

Kayne doubted it, Daeland enjoyed toying with him. He mumbled, "Vampires." The only thing making it worth his time and patience was finding out Macy's connection to

Daeland and if he knew anything about Elijah's whereabouts. "What did he say?"

"You'll have to wait until nightfall before he contacts you, so says Louie."

The disdain in Michael's voice was hard to miss and made the corners of Kayne's mouth curve into a slight grin. Michael had a knack for pulling Kayne from the swamps of his thoughts and reminding him of reality and his place as the alpha of the Garrick pack. He made Kayne feel like he belonged in Feather River, and not chasing his demons. However, sometimes Michael lived in the past. He would prefer to have vampires as enemies rather than allies, and rather have Daeland and his Kindred cut ties with the Garrick pack. The reason Kayne's smile widened was Michael absolutely hated Louie.

Louie was an empath with psychic abilities and served as Daeland's theow. Having gone through the Ascension, Louie was half turned, and benefited from Daeland's power and authority, but that meant nothing to Michael. He viewed the theow and all theows as a vampire's personal slave, and as an old, stubborn werewolf he could not grasp the concept of wanting to serve a vampire. To him it was a sign of weakness to have a vampire own you and use you, then feed on the very essence of your life. What Michael failed to understand was that Daeland was one of the most powerful vampires in the world, who had helped establish the Council, and didn't go anywhere near his food supply. The crimson liquid went from vein to glass, a crystal glass with his initials engraved on the sides. Kayne considered Louie's place at Amaranth, Daeland's estate and home to his Kindred, and the theow's status as Daeland's second. Louie never left Amaranth, and he didn't wear the blood mark. In fact, there wasn't a vampire or shapeshifter at Amaranth who wore

Daeland's crest. It drove through Kayne. Daeland's presence plagued him, almost as bad as the blood mark.

A year ago, Daeland entered a stage of undead, known to vampires as the Affliction. Affecting them throughout their lives, the older ones wove in and out of its grip as time was the enemy and its attack over the decades made being alive, as much as they were, painful. In Daeland's case, a thousand years was a long time to live. If he wasn't at a council meeting, he was at Amaranth and spent his time alone in the darkness of his underground rooms. Except today, he was in Desert Rock, with his theow, and Macy.

"If Louie calls you, let me know," Kayne advised. "I need to know where Daeland is."

"Yes, sir. Anything else?"

"Negative," Kayne mumbled.

Tippi listened to Captain Dixon unload unfounded accusations against Detective Gray and stopped herself from rolling her eyes when he demanded she use her traits as an empath. She blamed Agent Sinclair for giving Captain Dixon the boldness to single out Detective Gray and was going to order the captain to stand down when Mercy Summit sent the results of the DNA tests to her tablet. Quickly fumbling with excuses, drowned by the captain's complaints, she left the breakroom and the office as fast as she dared without bringing attention to herself. Once outside, she marched toward Agent Sinclair, her blouse moving in the wind despite it being tucked into her slacks. Her DOJ badge sat at her hip beside her gun, and she carried her tablet. Echoing as she walked was the clicking of her black professional heels on the pavement.

"Congratulations, Agent Sinclair," Tippi mocked as she crossed the parking lot. Not the way she wanted to start the conversation, highly unprofessional, but seeing him, and having Captain Dixon's demands ringing in her ears, she couldn't stop herself.

"Sounds like Agent Sinclair is about to have his ass handed to him," Michael teased.

Without responding, Kayne ended the call. "Agent Pixley."

"You blindly followed Captain Dixon's lead, which had nothing to do with the investigation into the alleged spy. Instead, past cases, closed cases, were questioned, and he feels free to pursue Detective Gray. We haven't interviewed the other detectives, and yet, you made her the focus. If this farce of an investigation continues, and Detective Gray does go to her representative, you'll be fired for being incompetent as will Captain Dixon. And if by some chance Detective Gray is found innocent, you have destroyed her reputation in this city, and with the BPI." Tippi inhaled, trying to keep her temper under control.

Kayne told himself he played along with Captain Dixon to force Macy to reveal who she was protecting. *Not true.* He selfishly needed her connection to Daeland because he was taking the chance Daeland knew about Elijah. "Is that why you came out here?" Kayne asked as he met her glare.

Tension tightened Agent Sinclair's shoulders enough Tippi could see the ridges of his corded muscles under his shirt. She inhaled and second guessed her anger toward the alpha and focused on the real reason she searched for him instead of waiting for him to return. "Negative, Agent Sinclair. There are three things," she began. "First, Detective Ramirez is waiting in the breakroom. He was among the detectives at the warehouse. Second, the tracker on Detective Gray's car is active and working. She appeared on my tablet as soon as she left." Tippi couldn't hold her professional look under the conflict she felt about the tracking device.

Agent Pixley's reservations and accusations nearly had Kayne feeling guilty. "You said three things."

Tippi looked past Agent Sinclair to his wrecked truck and the empty parking space where Detective Gray's name was painted in white block letters. Detective Gray wasn't returning to the BPI, and she would never park there—her career was over. Especially since Agent Sinclair was involved. "What I said about Detective Gray is irrelevant, she'll never be found innocent, and only God knows what you have planned. There's nothing I can do to help her." *Alpha Grayson chose Lord Kayne to protect his Pureblood daughter. Lord Kayne found the wreckage, pulled the girl from the burning car, and she died on the side of the road in his arms.* "She's at your mercy and it pisses me off."

What the hell was she talking about? "Agent Pixley, are you going to tell me, or do I have to order you to?" Kayne threatened.

"Negative, sir. I received Detective Gray's DNA test," Tippi replied, as if she was making a confession.

"And?" Kayne's heart turned into a frozen lump of muscle that was lodged in his throat. Holding Agent Pixley's gaze, he knew he was right. He was right to have pushed Macy to leave and was right to have made her the main suspect. She would have to make a move, and when she did, Captain Dixon would follow. All Kayne had to do was keep the spider webs of his plan from collapsing.

"How did you know?" Tippi asked. She sat with Detective Gray for an hour and didn't sense her.

"It was a guess." *Daeland's blood mark.* "There has to be a reason for Captain Dixon's line of questioning."

"To use her as a scape goat, and when they find out what she is, they'll burn her at the stake. She'll have you to thank for it." Tippi checked the tablet, then reread the report, making sure she didn't make a mistake. No. Patient twenty-one, advised testing, lycanthrope virus, positive. Humanoid definition terminated. "Do you think she knows?"

"Negative." Macy's reactions were mortal. Like her fear. "How long has it been going on?" Kayne asked.

"There's no way of telling. But I've looked through her file and every test since she has been with the BPI is negative for the lycanthrope virus. I can check ERT's records," Tippi explained.

*Impossible.* "As much as I would like the attention of checking into her past, it's not necessary. The question is, what has CD4-T been doing to her?" Kayne saw her hooked up to lines carrying the antiserum to her veins. Damn, he needed to talk to Daeland.

"I don't know," Tippi answered. "It might explain why her wounds haven't healed. In the warehouse, under stress, and wounded, she didn't change, and I didn't sense her. Detective Gray was sitting three feet from me, and I would swear on a stack of bibles she's human. She doesn't feel paranormal." Tippi looked at the tablet, swiped the report, making it disappear, and took note of Detective Gray's direction. When she looked at Agent Sinclair, the information about the prior alpha and his family and their importance to him struck her. Yeah, it was a guess to test a BPI detective's DNA. "I know of only one kind of shapeshifter that can slip past a routine blood test." She waited for Agent Sinclair to admit he knew. Silence. He stared at her, almost daring her to say it. "A Pureblood."

Macy wasn't a Pureblood. Kayne grasped at his professional tone and said, "CD4-T has to be corrupting the test.

Pureblood or not, it's impossible to deny your wolf. The full moon would have forced her to shift. Detective Gray would have to have more control over her wolf than an alpha does, and if she took time off work every full moon, someone would have noticed. Plus, she isn't part of a pack, that makes her a rogue, and Doctor Locke would have had the Council intervene or would have forced her to concede and become one of the Gawain." Dr. Locke wouldn't have waited a hot second to have Macy in his pack. Kayne looked up at the sky, the crystal blue devoid of clouds stared back. "There's no way Detective Gray could have kept it a secret from the BPI and the other detectives. She would have made a mistake."

"One would think," Tippi mumbled. "You have an interest in her, Agent Sinclair. Detective Gray isn't who you think she is." Did she cross the line? Tippi didn't know as she waited for his response.

Kayne's eyes narrowed on Agent Pixley. Digging deep. "She isn't, Agent Pixley. My interest lies with finding Elijah and the spy, stopping the spread of White Cell, and putting an end to the ersatz. Detective Gray is a suspect, at the same time she has become an enigma in this case." A mystery he was going to solve. "She's on medical leave, so we're going to keep this between us for as long as we can. If the BPI, PD, and Captain Dixon or Commander Wilson find out *what* she is, they'll try to connect her to every shapeshifter crime in Desert Rock. They won't hesitate to blame her for Officer Murphy's death. Understand, this doesn't change my mind, but we need to protect her. I have to know her location."

"Affirmative, sir. With her name on Officer Murphy's reports, and Captain Dixon reviewing old cases, it appears someone knows." Tippi couldn't imagine who. Detective Gray was in more danger than being the spy.

"We're walking a fine line between the paranormal world and the mortal world, and I don't know which one is responsible for Detective Gray. Right now, we'll continue the interviews and try get as much information as we can. The spy remains our top priority, and I believe Captain Dixon is the person who knows about Detective Gray," Kayne advised. He found what he wanted. Did Elijah know about her?

"Why would he put on this charade of an investigation?" Tippi asked.

"What if it isn't him? What if he's nothing more than a puppet? We haven't seen Commander Arden." Kayne was guessing. "Have an agent do a background on the commander and find out where he lives and where he goes. We have to find him."

"Sir," Tippi mumbled as she checked the tablet. She didn't know the area, and didn't have to when Sanative appeared to look like a fortress/prison, and was the only building in that section of desert. "Do you want to know where Detective Gray is headed?"

"Affirmative." Kayne held his breath, noticed it, and released a slow exhale.

"Sanative. She's going to the one place she shouldn't go. Detective Gray's contact with Doctor Locke is going to make her case look worse. And after what Sergeant Mayco said about her to their command, I can't believe she would check on him." Tippi thought back to the warehouse. "Why did he challenge you?"

*Macy, are you running to your boyfriend?* He sounded delusional. "He has extended his protection to her and thought I was there to harm her. As for Detective Gray, she fought hard to protect you and Sergeant Mayco, and he nearly lost his life. In her eyes, when the Hunter Wolf infected him, she failed," Kayne replied. He knew the feeling. Macy was heading to Dr. Locke and he knew about her tattoo. At least he would protect her, as would his entire pack. "I know she's covering for someone." He growled his words, his frustration getting the better of him.

"Like herself. If she doesn't know she's a werewolf, instinct could be driving her, and she doesn't understand what's happening. It would explain her silence." Tippi glanced at the tablet, took note of Detective Gray's status, back to Agent Sinclair, and then the cars behind him. She didn't wait for Agent Sinclair to agree or disagree. "I'll tell Captain Dixon we're prepared to move forward. Detective Gray is going to lose her job regardless. When faced with being a werewolf, she'll need proof, someone to talk to, and counseling. Maybe Doctor Locke can help her. Her medical records specify the multiple times she's been hurt on duty, PTSD, and she routinely ignores her doctor's advice. This is going to, for a lack of a better term, do a number on her mentally and emotionally. Not to mention she will have to prove her innocence."

"I know." Daeland needed to contact Kayne and explain why Macy wore his blood mark, and they needed to protect her.

"Meanwhile, are you going to continue to follow Captain Dixon's lead?" Tippi asked.

"Affirmative. I don't have a choice. I think Captain Dixon is dirty. He may or may not be mixed up with the spy, but he's dirty." Kayne didn't look at Agent Pixley. Couldn't. Everything Macy knew—her life, career, and future—were about to be ripped away from her. Where would she go after her peers found out what she was? He wished he could have stopped her from going to Sanative and seeing Dr. Locke. The alpha gave her his pack's protection, there was no doubt, but he suspected something. When he learned she was a werewolf, maybe a Pureblood, he wouldn't hesitate to open his pack to her. The doctor's eyes gleamed sun yellow with possession. Strong. Independent. He saw Macy as a potential mate. Kayne's jealousy nearly choked him.

"Sir." Tippi waited a heartbeat, watched Agent Sinclair's conflict, and when he lost himself to his thoughts, she left for the office.

Kayne remained where he was, Agent Pixley's clicking heels fading, and stared at the gate. Pureblood. Cinnamon ringed with silver. They drew him in, gave him his past, and promised him redemption. Did he see her as a Macelaine's duplicate and held onto her with false hope? He didn't know. Macy was in his head and she was a werewolf. He drew a breath, could taste her vanilla, at the same time he hated to think Daeland was in Desert Rock to collect his Pureblood.

# CHAPTER SIXTEEN

Macy started out of the city with images of David, Sergeant Mayco, and Agent Sinclair whirling in her thoughts and the weight of them trying to cripple her. At each freeway exist she thought about turning around, and when the city sat behind her, she saw each turnout as a way of escape. She didn't stop and wouldn't let Agent Sinclair's warning, or his intimidation and fear tactics win. Driving the forty miles of two-lane road cutting through the desert her mind raced with the end of her career and what she was going to say to Sergeant Mayco. If she saw him.

Traffic began thinning, and after the first sign warning motorists Sanative was twenty miles ahead, it disappeared altogether, leaving her alone. The sound of the tires humming, the low mumbling of the radio, and the chaos of her head felt like someone had maxed the volume out. Along the sand-covered shoulder, the countdown continued with signs telling her not to pick up hitchhikers or animals, and Sanative was an active paranormal medical facility. The radio and signs didn't stop her memories from flowing and filling the spaces her fears left behind. Unlike human hospitals, Sanative's extensive ER was protected by electric fencing and gates topped with razor wire. Around the facility more than a dozen signs warned humans not to trespass, and the presence of paranormals. Beside the warnings were signs stating danger and do not proceed. Don't want lost humans getting confused and ending up with wounded paranormals.

When Dr. Locke transported her, he drove the black ambulance through the gates, and once at the hospital, hastily ushered her into one of the two emergency wards. Night had been turning the sky dark, making it hard for Macy to see where she was being taken. Like she cared when her nerves had been shot, the adrenaline drained from her, and she hadn't been able to think about anything except David's death. She hadn't been able to close her eyes without seeing the Hunter Wolf form tearing his body armor from him and hearing the sounds of David's body giving under its claws. Then there was the vague memory of the expression on Sergeant Mayco's face as Dr. Locke ordered his paramedics to take her to the ambulance. Later, when her head cleared, she realized there were going to be repercussions.

*"I shouldn't have to work with you."* No worries, sir, your career is over.

With the past, she shuddered. There had never been a need for her to go to Sanative, even if there was an ongoing case. After the prisoner had been treated, he or she was promptly transferred to a paranormal jail to ensure the safety of law enforcement personnel. Macy slowed, made a right, followed the curved drive, and entered the parking lot between two figures cut from stone. On the right side, standing fifteen feet tall, a female angel wearing a long gown that gathered at her feet, held a book, a medical symbol etched on the front, depicting Sanative. On the left a knight dressed in armor and holding a sword, his hands wrapped around the hilt, its point on the ground midst rocks, depicted the Gawain clan.

The name was taken from Arthurian legend and based on the character Sir Gawain. Dr. Locke and the men of the clan were referred to as Knights of Gawain, and were expected to be formidable, loyal, and defenders of all paranormals. The women, Ladies of Gawain, served as the backbone of the clan. They lived by strict rules and were examples of shapeshifters who had humanized their lives to better fit into society. Macy didn't know the inner workings of the clan but had skimmed through the Gawain clan's by-laws the BPI had on file. She always thought it was righteous, archaic, and bordered on ridiculous. Knowledge is power, and it had been important to understand Dr. Locke's views on humans, paranormals, and his responses to scenes, his clan, and Sanative.

*"It's like you have a connection with them."*

*Negative, I was doing my job.*

The hospital loomed in front of her, and she was going to have to face where she was heading and the potential for paranormals, lots of them, and they would recognize her. The bruises, stitches, and missing fingernails would give her away. Might as well be wearing a sign saying, *I got my ass kicked. Oh yeah, I kill your kind.* She didn't regret her past, her job, never would, but facing a crowd who believed she was nothing more than an assassin left her feeling like she should have brought a gun. She eased the Jeep over a speed bump as the parking lot opened and extended along the front of the stucco building. The immaculate landscaping of grass, trees, plants, and hummingbird yucca did their best to soften the hard lines. Like they were trying to make it appear more human, less paranormal, and less threatening. The lot was empty, not one car. While it unnerved her, it gave her a spot in front and close to the door.

As she limped along the sidewalk, she held her breath and approached a set of double doors. Preparing to reach for one of the worn brushed nickel the right side automatically opened, allowing a rush of cool, air-conditioned wind to sweep over her. The mix of stringent cleanser and ventilated air encompassed sat thick inside. She hated hospitals. Her anxiety grew as she anticipated facing shifters, the Otherkin, anyone, and straightening, she entered the waiting area. Empty. Macy's shoulders eased with relief, and she headed deeper into the large, airy space.

Small palm trees in black ceramic pots drank in the sunshine from several floor-to-ceiling windows and cast shadows on the rows of empty chairs sitting to the left and right. Like the parking lot, the reception area was void of people and sounds. In front of her sat another set of double doors, but acting as a sentry was a pale wood desk, and the upper half of a lean, dark-haired young man, whose badge told her he was the director. He watched, unamused as she approached, and Macy heard her heart pounding and her pulse in her ears. The fear he would listen to her, find out who she was, and immediately refuse her request teased her confidence. If he hadn't been watching her, Macy would have turned around, left, and pretended to have never been there.

"Can I help you?" His low voice carried an accent.

"BPI Detective Macy Gray, to see Sergeant Mayco," Macy answered. She presented her BPI identification, watched his chocolate eyes narrow and his brows crease.

Her insides rumbled with fear and felt like stones when they dropped to her legs, making her knees weak. Again, she was sure he was going to order her to leave. She was basically the enemy with an investigation hanging over her head. When he lifted his eyes from her ID and met her gaze, she waited to be told to go home. He didn't. He lifted a phone receiver, and in a language she didn't understand, began whispering, and several words later, he set the receiver on the cradle. He didn't order her to leave, didn't tell her to stay, didn't say a word, rather he let the silence—because she was the only person there—painfully draw out. Not knowing if he was going to let her see Sergeant Mayco or just let her stand there, Macy thought about leaving and going home. The pain killers were wearing off, letting the electric currents ride her muscles, and a throbbing to take hold of her face, and she didn't need the embarrassment of crying in public. Screw it, Macy wasn't waiting around.

"Macy, welcome," Dr. Locke greeted as he stood in the open door staring at her, his eyes glimmering with victory.

*Yes, I came running to you.* There goes her pride. If Agent Sinclair knew where she was, he would ask if they were in a relationship.

An hour later and she was watching Sergeant Mayco stare up at the ceiling, from the safety of an observation room. His bed, the term implied he was comfortable and there weren't silver shackles holding him down to a four-inch thick pad on top of a metal platform. At the sides and ends of the mat was enough room the medical staff could lean, stand, or sit on the platform itself and easily restrain him. That was saying something when the nurses, doctors, and staff were all shapeshifters, Otherkin, and paranormals. The shackles and chains looked welded to the platform and ended in steel plates bolted to the concrete floor. Going up and around each of his ankles, his wrists, and around his chest and waist, the bonds took away his points of strength. Her eyes traced the connections, the links, and she couldn't help but stare at the silver as it gleamed brightly under the caged fluorescent lights. Was it syn silver? Was it hurting him?

The bonds held his wrists to his sides, allowing two or three inches of freedom, while the ones around his ankles held his legs shoulder-width apart, giving no margin for movement. Macy could see Sergeant Mayco's right hand and watched his lean fingers create lazy circles against the mat beneath him. It was worse than the quarantine room. God, is this what she wanted to see? She didn't have an answer. She didn't know why she was there. She should have gone home. A chill skated down her spine and she raised her hand, touched the stitches, with the pad of her fingers, careful to not use her fingertips.

At some point, Macy left the chair, took six steps, and was standing close enough to the mirror she could touch it. He wore a loose, pale green cotton shirt and matching pants. There was no top sheet, blanket, pillow, only the mat, pajamas, and silver shackles and chains. His pasty skin, blond hair, and blue eyes stuck out from the black padding like a quick bite from a razor. There were no bruises, cuts, or scratches marring his skin, only three faded pink lines marked his cheek, while another went from his neck to disappear under his cotton shirt. She touched the stitches over her eye with her fingertip and winced from the pain. Sergeant Mayco had been attacked. Targeted like David? No, he would have died.

She stopped thinking about David, and looked at the wounds scarring her hands, and how she hadn't been cut by their nails. The slice above her eyes had been made from the pressure of the Hunter Wolf form hitting her with its fist, not its nails, she had stitches, and when it had held her by her throat, it hadn't cut her. Black and blue swallowed the area around her eye, purple and scarlet colored her neck, her sides, thighs, her ribs ached, and her entire body hurt with every tiny movement. She yawned, she hurt.

His wounds from the Hunter Wolf form were quickly healing and leaving unscarred skin behind. There was a part of her, blame it on sick curiosity, wanting to see his side and stomach and the wounds Agent Pixley fought to keep him from feeling. What did they look like? She bet it wasn't an open wound, and she bet he didn't have stitches. She couldn't see a bandage and there wasn't a rise in his shirt where it might have been. He was healing as fast as a lycan. As if hearing her thoughts, Sergeant Mayco turned his head toward the two-way mirror and stared.

His blue eyes sharpened and looked cold as ice as he whispered, "Macy."

Sergeant Mayco had never called her by her name. He didn't call anyone by their name, believing it would create a friendship. And friends made BPI detectives sloppy, weak, and targets.

Macy took two steps backward from the glass and whispered, "How can he?"

Dr. Locke rested his hand on her shoulder and steadied her. "Easy, he can't see through the glass. His wolf instincts are developing, and while they do, they are sensitive. They're telling him what he can't see, hear, or smell. He knows I'm here because I've shared my strength as an alpha with him. His wolf understands I might be his alpha, while Emmitt is trying to understand it on a human level. I'm also his doctor, which he does understand on a human level. You, on the other hand, I'm not sure. He might sense you're here because he knows you."

Regret like a wave of thorns washed over her. Macy should have followed Agent Logue out and never stayed behind. Leaving her team and searching for the wolf had been selfish. Single minded. Macy did find Agent Sinclair, a lot of good that did her. "He doesn't know me. He knows it's my fault."

"You saved his life. The wolf gaining strength inside of Emmitt senses you. Is there a reason he would recognize you?" he asked.

What? Had Agent Sinclair contacted Dr. Locke? Maybe it was when the doctor transported her. Or he was checking on whether or not she told him the truth about having never been there. *"You know shifters like you have a connection with them. It makes you too damn good for my liking. It makes you look like a shifter."* She could feel Sergeant Mayco staring at her.

"Macy, do you know why he would recognize you?"

"What? Negative," Macy snapped. After the interrogation and Agent Sinclair, she didn't have the patience or the energy to defend herself.

"Emmitt can't see you but knows you're here. Not a person, not a shapeshifter, and he didn't guess who you were. He knows you, Macy, are here. He called you by your name, not Detective Gray, your name. Despite not having full understanding or control of his instincts, he sensed *you*," Dr. Locke insisted and watched her.

Macy turned back to the two-way mirror, touched the stitches as if reminding herself they were there, and met his cold eyes holding his accusations and his wolf. Did he see her through his own reflection? Was he looking at the mirror picturing her, or was he watching his humanity being devoured by the animal inside of him? It was too much to watch and think about. It was wrong, seeing him was wrong, and giving into her weakness was wrong. Turning from him, she started out of the room.

"Macy, wait." Dr. Locke followed her out of the observation room and to the hallway where he caught up with her.

She didn't wait. She didn't stop. She had to get away from Sergeant Mayco, Dr. Locke, and get the hell out of Sanative. The BPI and Agent Sinclair believed she put the detective's lives at risk and being seen at Sanative would solidify their suspicions. Walking beside her, his hand lightly touched the small of her back, and together they made their way down the hall. With her emotions running wild and pain invading every part of her, she hadn't noticed the touching. His hand on her shoulder, his light touches to her neck and arms.

"What will happen to him?" she asked as she stepped out of his reach. If he noticed the space she created, he didn't say anything.

"In what way?" Dr. Locke asked and held her gaze.

Macy stumbled over words, not sure if they fit the questions, and worse, wasn't sure if she wanted to know the truth. His answer would explain what was happening to Sergeant Mayco, and what was happening to the others, the kidnap victims, if they lived. Agent Sinclair's warning came roaring back. If they didn't do something about it, if she didn't tell the truth, it would be her fault when White Cell and the contagion spread. It wasn't about her, the investigation into informants, or Commander Arden, it was about innocent humans ending up like Sergeant Mayco. She had to tell Agent Sinclair. Meeting his practiced gaze, she tried piecing everything together while dealing with the guilt eating her, all because she backed herself into a corner. Or walked into a trap set by Captain Dixon. Or David. What the hell had he done for them to kill him?

"I can feel the tension building in you," Dr. Locke noted, as he held her upper arms. "It's like a tornado of emotions."

Macy saw apprehension pass behind his calm doctor gaze and knew there was something else, something darker, like his secrets. A vague memory twisted its familiar feel around her, creating more guilt and she shouldn't be with him. It was wrong. She wasn't choosing shifters overs humans. Putting distance between them, paranoia ran through her.

"Calm down." He spoke softly, gently, his voice taking on its doctor tone. "You can't keep pushing yourself and bullying through the problems. Sometimes, you need to stop and figure them out."

"Negative," Macy quickly countered. She would bully through.

"If you let me through the walls you're living behind, I could help you," he offered softly.

*Help. Me.* "I don't need help." They killed David. She's positive Captain Dixon was one of them and Agent Sinclair was going to send her to prison. And she has no idea who they are. Macy needed more help than anyone could provide.

He held her, his fingers caressing her upper arms, and his body close to hers. When did their relationship change? He was touching her again, his right hand gliding up her arm to her neck, allowing the scent of his skin to drift around her. Riding over the understated smell of soap and hospital was the rich spice of his skin. A lycan. *Dr. Locke is a lycan,* she reminded herself. Macy toppled into her need to be reassured and she wanted ... needed someone to tell her it was going to be all right. She held his gaze, her helplessness drifting on the green and gold flecks of his eyes. The color wasn't the white yellow from the warehouse and any assurance coming from recognizing the difference remained out of reach when the warning screaming in her head grew louder. In response, his grip tightened, and the heat flowing from his hands and into her skin slowly soothed her nerves.

Macy took a step closer to him, seeking the comfort of his arms and the strength radiating from him.

"You're safe here, Macy," he promised as he drew her closer and wrapped his arms around her.

Safe at Sanative. Did she trust him? Did she need someone to protect her? Negative. His low rumble yanked her from the daze the spiraling chaos created. He couldn't do this to her. Macy wouldn't let anyone do this to her. If anyone found out a lycan was this close to her, that it was her choice, it would be the end of everything. She would be a traitor to her own kind. She wasn't living behind a wall. She was defending herself against lycans. They were the problem. Without another thought, she backed up to the wall and leaned against it.

"When will Sergeant Mayco shift?" Macy asked, her voice rough with her embarrassment.

Hesitating, Dr. Locke lowered his arms to his sides like he had given up. "The virus has already changed his DNA. He could shift today, tonight, tomorrow, I'm unsure."

"Is the virus from the altered Hunter Wolf form the reason the contagion has taken hold?" Sergeant Mayco hadn't had a chance.

"Yes. Not only are the altered Hunter Wolves bigger, faster, and stronger than their natural counterparts, their virus spreads, and begins morphing the mortal's DNA at twice the speed. The Hunter Wolf that attacked Emmitt had a concentrated amount of toxin in its claws. In a short time, the contagion attached itself to his cells and what should have taken a week, or at least his first full moon, happened in a matter of twenty-four hours," he explained, and walked to the other side of the hallway. "I think the forced acceleration is causing mutations and the jump in Death Bloom victims."

Macy knew he was referring to the Barrettes' case and it created another dozen questions which would remain unanswered since she wasn't part of the investigation. As her dread subsided and she felt more like herself, she shook off the need to have him reassure her.

"The Hunter Wolf forms are unable to change back to their humanoid forms after they die. If Sergeant Mayco shifts into his animal, his wolf, will he be able to shift back to his humanoid form?"

"I don't know. Henry hasn't shifted between forms. He's choosing to remain in his animal."

Henry, the lycan who followed her commands. "Can he shift between the three?" Macy asked.

"I believe he can. Agent Sinclair said he pulled Henry's wolf from him because he wasn't capable of shifting by himself. The power from an alpha gives the werewolf an anchor, and Agent Sinclair is a powerful alpha. However, under the best circumstances, it's traumatic and painful. He has chosen his wolf form as protection. A comfort." Dr. Locke hesitated.

"Tell me," Macy ordered.

"Grace died from a Death Bloom."

"How?"

"She wasn't healing the way a werewolf would. In order to give her time to heal, we tried keeping her in a medically-induced coma until she was strong enough to shapeshift. I couldn't stop the contagion," he explained.

Macy saw his regret and pain from failing her. The investigation was hurting everyone. "She had been attacked by her husband." Bites riddled her body. "Had Henry been attacked?"

"No. Agent Sinclair states he saw no wounds."

"White Cell. How fast would the combination push the contagion?" Macy asked. She didn't know how to react. She hadn't known the woman but knew Grace deserved better than a Death Bloom. The woman suffered at the hands of strangers and felt the betrayal of her husband. All Agent Sinclair did was save Henry from Mr. Barrette's fate. He hadn't saved Henry from the pain of loss.

"Since Henry had been infected with the contagion from taking White Cell, then attacked his wife, who then took White Cell, the combination acted as an accelerant and overloaded her system. There's no way to stop it."

"Even if given CD4-T?"

"The antiserum isn't strong enough to combat its effects."

Macy looked beyond Dr. Locke and the closed door of the observation room and wished there was something she could do. *There is something I can do.*

"I want you to know, we're watching Henry and we're watching Emmitt," he assured. "They'll be all right as long as there is someone to support them."

Alone. Macy had felt the emptiness over the last couple of weeks more than usual and battled it with her work. Sergeant Mayco wasn't going to be as lucky. She had no idea who was going to support him when, as a couple, he and his wife never hid the fact they detested paranormals, specifically shapeshifters. She hated her thoughts, but it was the truth. With his crossover, into the thing he hated most, they were going to have to deal with the repercussions. She had to stop it from happening to others, which meant taking a risk. Macy needed to go over the information on the memory sticks, analyze it, and find out who was behind the White Cell, the Hunter Wolves, and stop them from creating another level of lycan.

"I found vials of White Cell at the Barrettes' and had it tested. One of the techs said it looked the same as the vials found at Harper's warehouse. He said it didn't contain CD4-T, was different but wouldn't know for sure until he had it back at the lab. I haven't seen the report so I'm not sure of the outcome."

"Can you get me the report? A vial?" Dr. Locke asked.

"Negative." Macy pictured herself walking through the office—don't mind me, copying forensic reports—and trying to get into evidence. She wasn't going anywhere near Captain Dixon or Agent Sinclair when they were waiting to arrest her.

"You won't or you can't?" His voice changed, as if she was telling him, no, out of spite.

Anticipating Agent Sinclair pinning the scarlet S on her chest made her pause. She wasn't going to explain the extent of her problems, the investigation, and the end of her career to Dr. Locke, she didn't need his pity. Seconds stretched out and she watched understanding slowly register in his eyes and his contempt dissolved. "There's that."

"I'm sorry, Macy. You're not working anymore?"

"I'm on medical leave and have limited access to the office." Very limited. It wasn't a lie, but it wasn't the truth either. She leaned heavier on the wall and rubbed her shoulder. "You can call Rick Brindos and ask for the report. I'm not sure if they have allowed him to keep the vials for research or have booked them into evidence. He's interested in the bodies, and maybe between the two of you, you can find out what is changing the shapeshifters." Macy thought she was going to regret telling him, but it was too late. She was about to take the blame for crimes she wasn't responsible for. Which turned her thoughts to something she never thought was possible, Agent Sinclair. A damn lycan.

"And this Rick will work with me?" He clearly had his doubts.

"Affirmative. I've talked to him," Macy answered. She had to call Agent Sinclair.

"I'll call him. Macy, you look tired, and I can tell you're hurting. Is there anything I can do?"

She gave him a weak smile. "Negative, I'm fine. Who would have the facility to make and distribute tainted White Cell in those quantities, without anyone knowing?"

Dr. Locke groaned with her insistence. "No one on the street. It has to be someone big."

"There was a lab in the back of Pennsky warehouse," Macy explained. "I wasn't able to see the containers. Last I heard, no one recognized the company logo. Do you know where the equipment could have come from?"

"What I'm going to tell you, I have shared with the DOJ, no one else, and comes from a confidential source." His eyes wavered between human and his wolf.

"What I've told you is confidential and related to an on-going investigation." Macy wasn't going to be part of but was a suspect. "You told Agent Sinclair?"

"Yes. Why?"

The liar gets around. "The DOJ has taken over the BPI office, it figures it was him. The logos?" Agent Sinclair knew about the company logo when he was giving his 'I can help you' speech. He tried to bait her.

"The markings on the crates are from a small division of Renew Pharmaceuticals. They are the only company in the area with the resources. *If* they are responsible, and the equipment wasn't stolen, no one would question them. For a pharmaceutical company, the equipment was precisely designed for shapeshifters." Dr. Locke looked at her with pity in his eyes.

"You said *if* like you don't believe the equipment was stolen," Macy replied. Golden State Shipping. Renew Pharmaceuticals. Spies. Equipment for shapeshifters. Those were serious accusations, making the case bigger than someone off the streets transporting White Cell with the intent to sell. The BPI would have to investigate the corporations and those running the companies. With enough evidence the BPI and DOJ could get Homeland Security involved. The possibility she was too late scared her.

"The DOJ said they were going to talk to a representative from Renew. The equipment is worth millions. Renew wouldn't let it go, they would try to recover their money."

"If they wanted an investigation, they would need to file a stolen property report. Because Renew is human based, the DRPD is responsible for investigating the crime." Macy was beginning to doubt the DRPD's ability when David had been falsifying reports. If it had been stolen, and if not, how was the human public going to respond when they found out the pharmaceutical company, who had saved countless lives with CD4-T, was associated with kidnapping and murder? "What would motivate them to manufacture a corrupted version of White Cell?" Macy mumbled. Damn, she needed to go home.

"I wish I had an answer for you. This is putting all of us in danger. Is there anyone at the BPI who is willing to put the same time in you have and investigate this?"

"The DOJ is examining old cases." *Mainly mine.* "And asking questions. The BPI won't have a choice if there's evidence," Macy answered. She hoped what she said was true.

"I'll help them if I can. You need rest and I'm saying that as a doctor." He leaned forward, his right hand coming up and touching her forehead.

Macy waved his hand away. "I'll be fine. Mrs. Barrette had a Death Bloom, but it looked like Mr. Barrette attacked her the same way Henry attacked Grace. Did he?"

"I examined Mrs. Barrette's body." Dr. Locke inhaled, exhaled, and looked away from her, letting tension build. "Werewolf packs follow the structure of their animal counterparts living in the wild, as do therianthropes. It was only fifty years ago shapeshifters marked their mates. It was a way to keep the nature of the beast and the traditions of the animal close. It also played into the primal side celebrated among packs living completely separate from mortals and other shapeshifters. You could say it offered a mark of protection. Like a tattoo."

His hazel gaze narrowed on her, and she could feel him trying to judge what she was thinking. "Go on."

"A werewolf might mark its mate on the neck, back, or shoulder, repeatedly, because they heal. Some will bite, add an obsidian mixture to the wound, intending to make the marking ornate. The first time takes place after the relationship has been consummated. But a therian, a cat, is different. They will scratch and bite their mate across the shoulders or collarbone. It's not popular now, not when mortals see it as barbaric. Living in the open has changed the way shifters see the world and how the world sees them. Shapeshifters are no longer a secret group trying to protect their own, their traditions, and they aren't living in the shadows. They live in the gray area between being a mortal and a paranormal."

Macy understood his hesitation. The thought of being bitten and scarred was embarrassing and demeaning. She shook her head. Why anyone would want to be close to an animal was beyond her. Was it? She almost jumped into Dr. Locke's arms. "He marked her."

"Correct. She wouldn't have died from the wounds. We have no idea what the contagion, if he was infected by this new strain, does to their minds. His mate was dying and that alone affects the way one reacts. My guess, and this is just a guess, he feels her weakness, knows she's going to die, and goes into a rage. He can't control the situation, and he can't control the shift or his emotions. It doesn't help you were in his house, but I don't think it would have mattered."

"She was a mess," Macy mumbled. "Someone is kidnapping humans, infecting them with a corrupted contagion, and giving them an amped up version of White Cell. Instead of stopping the contagion from infecting the victim, it helps it along. They have the facility and the space to keep it all hidden. As if it couldn't get any worse, whoever is doing this isn't afraid of the law because they have spies in Renew, the BPI, and DRPD."

"You're innocent."

"Thanks for believing that. It won't matter if they have evidence." Macy squeezed the bridge of her nose. Her head throbbed, and her ribs felt like they were grinding against each other.

"I'm sorry, is there anything I can do?" Dr. Locke offered.

"Negative. I think you're part of the problem, no offense, and if they find out I came here it's going to make matters worse." Macy took a step, then stopped. Her mind told her to go home where she would be safe. Her instincts told her to save herself. "Doctor Locke."

"Please, it's Landon."

"All right, Landon." The name felt weird leaving her lips.

"You're thinking about trusting Agent Sinclair?" he asked, with no surprise showing on his face.

"I am. You don't like him, do you?" Macy sensed the same energy as when they had her trapped between them.

"Like has nothing to do with it. We're alphas. We remain in power because of our power, and we give orders, not take them. It's not easy to get along. I wouldn't trust him, but if you have information or think he can help you, you need to protect yourself."

Macy considered what he said, and it reminded her of the interrogation. "Can you really tell if I'm lying?" She knew they could. Everyone did. But maybe...

"Yes," he sternly answered.

*I'm in trouble.* "And an empath?" Macy asked, knowing the answer.

"Yes. They can pinpoint the lie. Empaths see emotions like threads. You're asked a simple question, much like a lie detector, you won't lie about your name, it's a truth, it creates an emotion, a thread. You answer a question, it's a lie, it creates an emotion, a thread. Each is different from the other letting the empath concentrate on the lies. With every answer you reveal more of yourself and your emotions."

A simple yes would have sufficed. "Right."

She held his gaze while she thought about the lies she had told Agent Sinclair and Agent Pixley. She was digging herself a hole, and if she didn't fix things, they would make it her grave. Macy needed to tell someone about the investigation into David's actions and her suspicions of Captain Dixon. She wasn't going to put Dr. Locke in danger by telling him when she had Agent Sinclair. Macy would put the target on him. Did she regret sharing information with him? Negative. Affirmative. Not because she didn't trust Dr. Locke, she did, she didn't want to make him an accomplice if they convicted her of being the spy.

With a deep inhale, Macy turned from him to stare at the end of the hall. If someone told her she would be having a conversation with Dr. Locke, she would have strongly disagreed. In fact, if someone told her, her innocence depended on a lycan, she would have threatened to shoot them. If only she had one human who believed her instead of two lycans. The lycans corrupted her world, and because of it, the humans thought she betrayed them.

"I see your struggle and feel your unease. If you have information, and you don't tell someone, you're putting your career and your life at risk. Whoever is doing this isn't going to stop, and if you don't have protection, you might get hurt." He closed the distance between them and touched her cheek with the back of his fingers. He slowly traced the bruise from her eye to her jawline. "If you want to talk, or need anything, let me know. I'm here for you."

Macy nodded. Hesitated, like she had another question. She couldn't involve him. Turning out of his touch she started down the hall, her mind telling her she was going to end up like David. Dead.

"Indulge me one question," Dr. Locke requested. "Please."

Macy stopped and faced him. He stood with his hand on his hip, his brown BDUs wrinkled from sitting with her, and his eyes gleaming. *Run.* Dr. Locke helped her, and she trusted he wouldn't go running to the DOJ, she owed him. Uncommitted about the question, she waited as her focus went to swallowing her pride, her fear, and talking to Agent Sinclair.

"I've talked about marks, their place in the lives of shapeshifters, and how they identify a mate. There are other marks. An alpha may have tattoos representing the pack, his territory, his origin, I have them. It makes me curious about the tattoo on your back. Agent Sinclair, a werewolf and alpha, risked being watched by a warehouse full of mortal law enforcement to see it," Dr. Locke stated. "Does it have a meaning?"

He had used a tattoo as an example of possession when he explained Mr. Barrette had marked his wife. Marked. Macy's eyes focused on Dr. Locke, not a lycan, but what he really was. Landon, a man, a doctor dressed in BDUs, his shoulder-length, sandy brown hair held back with a leather band, while his eyes were currents of emerald and gold expressing his power. She held his gaze and noticed his face remained blank, keeping all his thoughts hidden. As if it was happening all over again, she felt the heat of Agent Sinclair's hand holding her shoulder while his other hand grazed her skin, and moved her undershirt to reveal the image.

"Agent Sinclair asked about it this morning. I'll tell you the same thing I told him. I saw a picture and had to have it. The only darker meaning, I was a rebel without a clue," Macy answered. Before he could stop her and ask why she lied to him, she made her escape.

She didn't run from him; she remained calm as she left the hall, and walked through the reception area. The doors opened before she reached them, and leaving the hospital she started toward her Jeep. This was what her life had come to, her car meant safety. Escape. When she reached it without anyone intruding, she sat behind the steering wheel and relaxed. The damn tattoo bugged her. Macy didn't know life without it and couldn't remember ever getting it. Why would she get dragons? And swords? And it's meaning. She had no clue. She searched art books, had gone to tattoo parlors, traveled up and down the state of California asking questions and got nothing. She went as far as to do an online search and still nothing. David had asked about it, Agent Sinclair, and now Dr. Locke. What did they know that she didn't?

She wanted to hit something to relieve some of her frustration.

Macy started the engine and drove out of the empty parking lot. There were things about her life she didn't remember and didn't understand because of her injuries from the car crash. When she asked her grandparents, they explained the trauma of losing both parents at a young age created a type of amnesia and she should concentrate on the happy memories. Funny grandparents, she didn't have any happy memories because anything from before the crash was gone like someone had wiped her mind clean. Except for seeing her parents' faces when she dreamt about the car wreak, and when something reminded her of the smell of the fire. Those thoughts took her back to Agent Sinclair and the warehouse. Did she recognize him? Negative. She found out he was from Feather River and her imagination seized on it, then after being attacked by Hunter Wolves and the concussion, she was at her memory's mercy. She needed to let it go.

The past was the past, it was time for her to take care of her future by pleading her case and explaining she had evidence. Maybe she would tell Agent Sinclair her suspicions. Would he believe her after she spent the morning lying to him? She had to try. Cool air swirled out of the vents and through the Jeep as she drove past the guardians and onto the road, leaving Sanative behind her. Looking at her cell in the center console, along with Agent Sinclair's card, she convinced herself she didn't have to trust him, all she needed him to do was take the target off her back. Sure. No one was going to understand running to a lycan for help and then confiding in one about humans, but he was DOJ. It made him different.

*Keep telling yourself that.* They would make her the traitor, with or without Captain Dixon.

"Damn." Macy hated herself, her weakness, and the loss of control on her life. She hated depending on someone else for help. A damn lycan.

Left with no other choice, she made a quick turn, pulled to the shoulder, the tires kicking up rocks and a plume of dust that encased the Jeep before drifting with the wind. On the side of the road, alone and backed against a wall, she took the card from between the memory sticks and held it in one shaking hand. With her cell in the other and hating the feeling of being trapped, she stared at the glossy, white business card. It stated Department of Justice, Blood Rain team leader, Agent Kayne Sinclair, lycanthrope, a serial number, his office address, and the last line was a phone number. She didn't call the number on the front. Macy flipped the card over, almost dropped it, and entered the number from the back written in blue ink and neat handwriting.

One ring. Two rings. She thought about hanging up. Four rings. She looked at the screen and the red button that was begging her to end the call.

A low rumble answered, "Sinclair."

Sanative sat thirty miles off the freeway and forty miles off a two-lane road flanked by tumbleweeds, creosote brush, and trash that told the traveler whatever sat at its end wasn't good. Like there wasn't going to be anything good at the end of the phone call. Staring out the windshield, at the open desert, she wondered if she was doing the right thing.

"You've reached Agent Sinclair."

Macy closed her eyes, saw him staring down at her, felt his hands on her skin, and the strength of his wolf. She was losing her mind.

"Who is this? You've reached Agent Sinclair with the Department of Justice."

*Please help me.* "It's Macy."

Kayne's heart pounded when he heard her velvet voice and the unease breaking those two words 'It's. Macy'. She hadn't said Detective Gray, she said Macy. He believed she was going to trust him. Without requesting a break or alerting Agent Pixley he needed to step out, he stood and left the breakroom, the office, and went straight to the parking lot for privacy. Pacing back and forth, he did his best to sound impassive as he hit her with a million questions. Silence followed each one, then she hesitantly answered, her voice wavering, and then there was silence. When he stopped and asked if she was listening to him, he nearly lost control when she explained she had evidence and was working for someone.

*"I'm not the spy. I think I was looking for one."*

Explained her damned silence.

Someone, Captain Dixon, was making sure law enforcement focused on her. Was he trying to detract attention from himself? Maybe. Did he know she was a werewolf? Negative. Captain Dixon would have turned her over to the authorities. While she explained her side, guilt flooded Kayne's insides. She was exposing herself by trusting a werewolf, in an attempt to save her career when in the end she would lose it and the life she knew. Where did Daeland fit in this mess? He wouldn't know until the vampire called him. Would it be too late for her? Suspecting her secret was out, he had to assume Daeland planned to take his property back to Feather River and to Amaranth. Unless charges were filed against her, forcing her to stay in Desert Rock for a trial, if she made it to the jail unharmed, where she would have to prove her innocence. A mortal who had lied about being a werewolf, charged with murder, being a spy, kidnapping, and whatever else they added so she never saw the light of day. A death sentence would be a mercy.

With his thoughts racing, Kayne stressed he needed to see her, meet with her, and that's when she told him she would feel more comfortable if they met at her house. His heart nearly exploded. He admitted he got caught up in talking to her when he asked where she was and what she was doing. Silence followed, and several seconds later he realized she had hung up on him. He didn't care. Kayne stored her number in his cell, raced back to the breakroom, causally checked her location, and saw she was leaving Sanative and had been heading back to the city. What made her change her mind? Dr. Locke? Not possible. Sergeant Mayco? Maybe. He barely made it through another interview when he rechecked her position and saw she remained outside of the city and had stopped. Pinpointing her location, he learned she was at home, and he entered the address into the GPS. Macy didn't live within the city limits and he couldn't blame her. From Feather River, Moonlight was twenty miles off the main road, and another fifteen miles on a narrow two-lane road flanked by forest. Mortals didn't happen upon Moonlight. The distance from Desert Rock made it easier to visit her without anyone knowing where he had gone.

"Do you believe Detective Gray used the BPI and had ulterior motives?" Captain Dixon asked the female detective.

Pulled from his thoughts, Kayne watched Detective Gaines' blue eyes narrow and a flare of anger sweep through. She didn't like the focus on Macy. Captain Dixon asked everyone the same questions, repeated his demands, and it was getting them nowhere. He desperately wanted the interviews to end. Every detective believed the circumstances surrounding Officer Murphy's death were directly related to the warehouse and the possibility the suspects had been tipped off and planned for the BPI and PD. They also feared what had happened to Sergeant Mayco, but their real fear was the changed Hunter Wolves and the White Cell. With their fear came their silence.

"Negative, sir," Detective Gaines answered as her irritated gaze landed on the captain.

"Thank you, Detective. You can go," Captain Dixon dismissed her and watched her leave. "Was she telling the truth?" he asked as he faced Agent Pixley.

"Affirmative, sir. She doesn't think Detective Gray had ulterior motives. Detective Gaines has respect for Detective Gray," Tippi answered. The BPI detectives respected one another. "The conclusion is they fear the altered Hunter Wolves and the consequences of White Cell, and the threat it poses. Someone is targeting law enforcement, they have a target on their backs, and they feel helpless."

"In the condition Detective Gray is in, she isn't a threat and it'll give us time to finish the interviews tomorrow. I'm done here. As I'm in charge, and Commander Arden isn't present. I'm going to check on my detectives at the warehouse," Captain Dixon explained as he stood.

*His detectives?* "Where is Commander Arden?" Kayne questioned. "Is it normal for a commander to be absent this long while an investigation into his agency is in progress?" Was Macy working for Commander Arden?

Captain Dixon didn't have a ready answer and his hesitation told more than his lies were going to. "It's routine for him to visit other area offices."

"Standard protocol of the BPI." Kayne watched the rattled captain gather his folders and leave the room.

"He's lying," Tippi pointed out. She set her notebook and pen on the table beside a file, pinched the bridge of her nose, and yawned.

"Agreed." Kayne met Agent Pixley's emerald gaze. They accomplished nothing after hours of questions, hours of listening to droning voices, and hours made longer from the smell of their fear. He didn't know any more than he had that morning. "I'm going to check Detective Gray's desk and go over the information she gave us."

"I can't help feeling I've betrayed her trust," Tippi confessed as she looked at her notes.

"We've been lied to from the beginning. Why don't you check the sergeant's desk?" Kayne advised.

"Good idea." Tippi stood, and at the door faced Agent Sinclair. "Do you feel you've betrayed her?"

"Affirmative. I'm going to do as much as I can to help her," he replied and meant what he said, more than he realized.

Despite glares from the detectives, Kayne riffled through Macy's files, computer, and anything else he could get his hands on. Besides learning she had a thing for mints, notes, and pens, everything he learned about Harper's and the Pennsky warehouse, he gathered from the BPI's database. It was public record, just as she had said. The Barrettes had been mortal, Golden State Shipping owned the warehouses, and he found the connection to Renew Pharmaceuticals. Macy's question held his attention. Why were they taking the corrupted version of White Cell, when money wasn't an issue, and they could have gone to the hospital? No one would have questioned them. The local pride would have paid them to be inclusion into their fold. He had the feeling they had been infected against their wills and were secretly taking White Cell in hopes it cured them. Someone fed them lies.

Kayne had spent more time than necessary inspecting everything associated with Macy, and realizing he wasn't going to find the answers at the BPI office he had to move on. Heading out of the office for fresh air, he went to what had become his normal spot in the parking lot. There he rubbed the back of his neck and watched the golden sun sink in the scarlet cape of the western sky. A deep inhale gave him diesel, gas, and a hint of flavored smoke from a nearby restaurant and reminded him he was starving. He tried a selection from the snack machine in the breakroom, but the empty calorie foods wrapped in plastic did nothing to satisfy his wolf's metabolism. After the energy he burned through to overcome his injuries and syn sliver poisoning, he needed real food and a lot of it. But he wasn't willing to get caught at a restaurant. He would eat after his meeting with Macy.

Chayton and Russell checked in and reported they tracked down suspects connected to White Cell, questioned them, checked the leads they had been given, then returned to the office to go over the information and compare it to the reports. While they were another set of eyes on the same papers Kayne had scoured, he didn't think they were going to find anything. But it was worth a shot. Refusing to go back inside, he ordered Chayton to keep an eye on Macy's movements and if she left her house to alert him. The day left him frustrated and tired, and checking his watch, again, he gauged the time and decided he would wait thirty minutes then head in her direction. He didn't want to spook her.

One second. Two seconds. Three.

Kayne checked his watch, his frustration turning to irritation, and checked his cell. With no word from Michael, Daeland, or Louie, his patience was wearing thin.

---

# CHAPTER SEVENTEEN

**Darkness** cloaked the windows, its thickness pouring into the warehouse, adding weight to the dust-clouded air. In minutes, nightfall would render her blind, making it impossible to see the Hunter Wolf forms and their movements. As it was, she was squinting and struggling to see which direction Sergeant Mayco had gone. She lost him during the fight when several Hunter Wolves separated them, making them single targets. Macy ran down an aisle, the desert heat causing sweat to bead on her forehead and neck, and slipping under her body armor it touched her tattoo and burned. When an image of dragons and swords rose from the concrete like phantoms to hang in the air, she skidded to a stop and watched onyx explode from the tips of the swords while crimson welled under the dragon's scales and dripped to the blades. Her skin burned as if they had cut her, as if she was seeing what was happening to her, to her tattoo. When crimson caught ink, it traced a path from her shoulder blades to her heart where their ends created a full-size dragon.

*Not real.* Macy tugged at her armor, trying to free herself and to stop the burn from spreading, at the same time she cursed the damn tattoo and wished she had never gotten it. Her fingers grazed the stiff material, her skin burned, and her breathing came in panicked gulps. She was going to suffocate but not before she burned. A roar thundered in the warehouse, taking her attention from the dragon, and she knew the Hunter Wolf form found Sergeant Mayco. Macy took off, and following the echo raced down an aisle, focused on the light beaming at its end. Another roar pushed her to run faster. Almost there, she pulled her gun from its holster and prepared to fire. Crossing the mouth of the aisle, she stood in an empty hallway littered with pieces of sheet rock and bloody footprints.

"Take the shot," Sergeant Mayco ordered.

Through dim light, Macy twisted to face him, saw his cobalt eyes blaze bright artic, like a frozen ocean. His wolf. *I'm too late.*

"Take the damn shot," he ordered. "I don't want to die."

The target closed in, Macy's heart pounded, the heat surrounded her, and she could hear Mrs. Barrette's nails scraping debris and carpeting. *Have to take the shot.* She raised her hands, but had no gun. Did she drop it? She couldn't remember, and with a quick swipe of her hand, her fingers feathered the side of her thigh, and grabbing at nothing, panic erupted. She didn't have her gun and she was going to fail him.

Macy sat up, felt for her gun, and gulping for air, eyes wide open, the warehouse/hallway dissolved into her living room. The fireplace slowly came into focus, the oak mantel's dark grain and framed photos holding her attention. "Calm down." Deep breath, and she jumped with the hard rap, its echo rushing down the hall, and ricocheting off the walls, the thud, dulling by the time it reached the entrance to the living room. "It's not real."

She had been dreaming about the warehouse and the Barrettes. The image of Sergeant Mayco's wolf eyes and the dream brought guilt and bile to her throat. "Only a dream," she repeated. With several deep breathes the fog cleared and she registered the next round of knocking. She was at home, her Jeep was in the garage, and out of sight. No one knew she was there.

*Except Kayne*, Macy thought. *Don't go there. Don't call him Kayne. One conversation and a promise he was going to help doesn't mean he's going to believe you. He tried to bait you and jumped on board the blame Macy train.* With a shaking hand, she grabbed her cell, checked the time, and figured Agent Sinclair was on his way. The countdown to her confession had begun, and she would have to hand over the evidence of being a spy, just not the one he wanted. Would he believe her or arrest her? She didn't know but had to try to save herself and others.

The rapid thumping of her heart slowed to almost normal when another round of knocking bombarded the silence. Male voices clung to the tail end as they chatted on the other side of the door while she stared at the hall wishing they would leave her the hell alone. She didn't need this. She needed painkillers and sleep. With a chance of repeating the nightmare, maybe she didn't need sleep.

Another knock, louder, harder, and more demanding, had Macy giving up, if only to make them leave. She stood on weak legs, drew a slow breath in, and limped to the door. On the way, she straightened her tank top in preparation of greeting the waiting group, took a quick look at the skin over her heart expecting to see a dragon, felt stupid for checking, and pushed her hair back from her face. That was as good as it was going to get, because there was no doubt, with the stitches, bruises, and crinkled top, she was going to be a sight. With a sigh, she gripped the handle and eased the door open, then held it by its edge. Barely around the corner, she stared from a thin line between the doorframe and the door.

Two men. Two strangers. The one on the left in faded jeans, tan work boots, and a black T-shirt advertising a ski lodge, stared at her. His bald head gleamed in the puzzle pieces of sunlight filtering through the limbs and leaves of the Mulberry tree in her yard. His eyes weren't human, but weren't an animal's; they were a mangled combination of both, making it hard to guess what kind of shifter he was. For his eyes to remain tangled, he had spent some serious time in one of his animal forms. Eyes remained several feet behind the second man, who acting as the leader, narrowed his stare on her. The leader's eyes flicked between her, the side of the house, and the tree shading the yard. Macy's instincts blazed with a warning. She didn't need to be a detective or a trained observer for the men to put her on alert.

"Aren't you going to invite us in?" the leader asked, his thick voice sounding like he needed to clear his throat. In jeans, black work boots, and a collared shirt, she thought she recognized him from somewhere. His hair was longer, not shoulder-length, just past his ears, styled, and the only word to describe the color was calico. His straight body, tight muscles, and stance choreographed his anticipation for a fight.

Her instincts rode over her. Lycans. They were at her house, and they wanted inside.

"Negative."

*"They won't care who you are, they will kill you. Just like Officer Murphy."* Kayne. Agent Sinclair's warning echoed in her head.

"Please," he asked with a smile. His canines lengthened, their sharp tips touching his bottom lip. "I asked nicely."

Not only no, but hell no. "No." Macy slammed the door.

Calico advanced, fast, his large hand wrapping around the inside edge, stopping it, and the wood cried out from his grip. She shoved back, her ribs burning, her shoulders aching, and a fire tracing a path down her spine. *Hurts. Everywhere.* Using her shoulder and all her strength, she shoved harder to have fire erupt in her chest. When a booted foot abruptly stopped the door, it bounced back at Macy. She leaned to avoid the worst of the force, regained her footing, and heaving harder, her body protested the strength and muscles she was trying to use. The door inched toward her, proving she wasn't budging it and he was playing with her. Outside there were more voices—some mumbled, some clear—the worst of them being the rough laugh turned growl growing closer.

"Wrong answer, Detective Gray," Calico mocked as he poured himself into her house. "Is this the way you treat all your visitors?" He didn't walk into her house ... his size, power, and strength filled it, taking it over and sucking the oxygen from the space.

Detective Gray. They don't care who you are.

Chills raced over her skin. Calico knew her and was standing in her house staring down on her, his mass taking the expanse of the hallway. There was nowhere to go. Macy took a cautious step backward to see if he would follow. He didn't. He thought he had her trapped. Good for him. She needed to get to her kitchen where she kept a spare gun. The Ruger 380 wasn't her H&K .45 service gun, but it was loaded with six rounds of synthetic silver. Did she need to kill them all? Negative. She needed a distraction and enough time to grab her cell and get the hell out of the house. Surely, they wouldn't chase a human down the street. Right? Macy backed up slowly, out of his reach, while trying not to instigate a reaction. When she thought she created enough distance, she turned and made for the kitchen, hoping the adrenaline numbed her pain and kept her going.

The lack of footsteps behind her gave her a sliver of hope he didn't take chase, and the excitement fueled her. Maybe the lycan decided invading a BPI detective's house was a bad idea and left. And if he didn't? If he threatened her, she was going to kill him.

She raced barefooted into the kitchen and made for the counter, when two Hunter Wolf forms entered through the sliding glass door, their large bodies absorbing the space between the counter, the door, her gun, and her freedom. Skidding to a stop, she backed up, each step feeling like she was retreating and was back at the warehouse. The Hunter Wolves stalked forward, she backed up, two steps for them, zero for her. As fear tangled with desperation, she knew they were the hard to kill kind. Not altered, but like Agent Sinclair had called them, ersatz. The sick yellow around their huge, black pupils was their insanity and weakness.

*Should have called Agent Sinclair sooner,* Macy thought with regret. Every word he said was coming back to haunt her. Because she tried to keep her actions a secret, the bastards had her trapped in her own damn house. If she fought the lycans in human form, she might have a chance. It wasn't a good choice, but without other options, it was the only choice. She edged the counter, her fingertips feathering the concrete, its cool feel threading into her fingers up to her palms that were damp with sweat. The Hunter Wolf forms matched her movement, one taking a step to her left while the other went to her right. It was slow progress, but she was getting closer to her gun, and from there she might make it to the door. Almost crazy from the mixture of hope and failure, she took another step and readied to grab the gun from the drawer.

Long fingers wrapped around her upper arms, causing shock to spike inside of her. She hadn't heard their approach and hadn't felt them behind her. Twisting, she used her heels to kick her captor, then using her bare feet on the wood flooring for better grip, twisted harder. He lifted her, leaving her striking air as he growled, tightened his grip, and squeezing her arms, wrenched soft whimpers of pain from her.

"This didn't have to happen. You should have cooperated," Calico said as if giving her a lecture. His broad shoulders and wide chest blocked her view of one of the Hunter Wolf forms behind him. "But the easy way isn't something your kind understands."

*No, BPI detectives don't do things the easy way, that's why we win.*

The wave of rage coming from him had her considering it might be wise to do things the easy way, at least until she found a way of escape. The thought he had to be powerful enough to keep the others in check combined with his rage and lycan strength was starting to scare her. As if sensing her intent, yellow eyes tracked her, then narrowed on Calico's every move, their chests rising and falling with their heavy inhales. She wasn't going to make it out unharmed. They hunted her down to hurt her. Knowledge and fear burned in her middle. He leaned closer to her face, loose strands of white, black, and brown hair falling forward to feather his red cheeks. With his face next to hers, she wondered how long he spent in his animal form and what part of his human mind had died.

"If you know me, then you know I'm being watched," Macy warned, thankful her voice held. *Lying.* Not a smart move. Like it mattered, she had been lying all day. Maybe she should tell him about Agent Sinclair and his pending arrival. Her instincts warned her it was a bad idea, and she should keep it to herself. Her comment didn't play well, it won her more pain, making her head drop, her chin rested on her chest, and she tried to convince herself he wouldn't squeeze her arms from their sockets.

"Chin up, Detective Gray." Calico curled his finger, placed it under her chin, and raised her face to his. "After I expressed my desire to talk to you, Captain Dixon assured me there would be no interruptions."

*Bastard.* The pain eased, and she released the breath she had been holding. "Is this his way of trying to scare me?"

Calico laughed and replied, "He isn't that smart. This is my way of making sure you're the spy."

His fetid breath misted her cheek, bringing bile to her throat, and she resisted the urge to gag. Turning her head, a scant sliver, she attempted to put distance between them. "Why do you care?"

"I need to make sure my spies are safe, and they remain in place. This will give Captain Dixon time to gather the evidence for your conviction. Because you've decided to leave with me, you'll miss getting arrested, the trial, and will become one of the most wanted criminals in the state." He stopped, thought slipping into his multicolored eyes. "You won't be able to leave me."

Spies. More than one. "I don't believe you," Macy shot back. Where the hell was Agent Sinclair? She hated herself. Unless Calico was telling the truth, and one of his spies was keeping Agent Sinclair from leaving the office. Why would he leave the BPI, the interviews, and detectives when she wasn't going anywhere? *Please. Please, Kayne.* She didn't want him to find her empty house or her body. She had to stall Calico. "You can't do the job yourself, so you're forcing Captain Dixon to your bidding."

"Forcing? Everyone has a price and his was immortality. All it took was one promise," Calico bragged. "He said he was tired of being a weak mortal."

"You're going to infect him," Macy mumbled. Captain Dixon was a crappy human and letting him crossover would make him shitty lycan.

"No, I'm not. Wouldn't waste my time." Calcio's eyes wavered between wolf and human as if he also thought Captain Dixon was worthless. "I would give him White Cell and let my crossbreeds play with him."

He knew about the warehouse.

"And me?" she asked cautiously. She stopped the thought of being held prisoner, infected by one of his monsters, and turning into one of them. She would become like the beasts in her kitchen. Or die from a Death Bloom. The Death Bloom would be mercy. Unless she went into Blood Rage and became a monster bent on killing.

"I have plans for you," Calico answered. He raised his hand, and with the back of his fingertips, feathered the stiches.

Was that a yes or no? Macy struggled to get away from his touch when he started laughing and took several steps backward. "Terrorizing you, while it's a thrill, makes my boys a bit crazy. And I don't want them attacking you, Macelaine."

"Who?" Macy raised her head, met Calico's inhuman gaze. "You have the wrong person."

"No, I don't." His glare held her when he began explaining, "All these years. Do you know the work, time, and patience I've had to have in order to get my plan where it is? David was supposed to hand you over at Harper's warehouse where my crossbreeds would have taken possession of you. His greed forced me to sacrifice Pennsky, the perfect training place. Should have known better than to trust a fucking mortal."

"David was a spy?" Macy mumbled to herself. He was going to turn her over. He was working with shapeshifters.

"No, and yes."

"What about the Barrettes?" she asked, figuring she didn't have anything to lose.

"Always the detective. They didn't work out." Calico took a cell from of his pocket. "I have her. Blow the building."

*What does that mean?* "What?" Panic. Macy squirmed, fixed her eyes on the man holding her, and tried twisting to see Calico. "What building?"

"Pennsky," Calcio replied easily. With satisfaction on his face, he returned the cell to his pocket.

A thousand thoughts flew through her head, all of them a variety of pleading that clotted in her throat before she could say them. The warehouse was thirty minutes outside the city limits and sat off the highway. If someone was able to call, it would take the fire department at least forty-five minutes to respond, and by then, the worst burn victims would be dead. Dread returned with the memory of the warehouse, and she risked looking to the windows and saw the sun was coloring the sky with smeared hues of red, gold, and plum as it began its descent. Nighttime would make finding victims difficult, if not impossible. And time didn't play fair when fire was involved. Black smoke would choke everyone, including the shapeshifters, and soot would cover them from head to toe.

Calico reached out, took her chin in his fingers, and twisted her face only stopping when their eyes met. "I know they're your friends," he said with a laugh. "The very people who betrayed you. There should be some small part of you that's pleased with me."

"Murdering innocent people isn't payback." Macy held his eyes, saw nothing. No regret, remorse, or if he gave a damn. Nothing. Cold. She wondered what else the man was capable of doing.

Calico released her like he was trying to control his anger at the same time his eyes wavered between azure and burnt red. "Righteous, just like your father. With your past, you would kill every paranormal if you had the chance. Your own kind. I hope your father is turning over in his grave." He glanced at the backyard, then back to her when he grabbed her hair, and leaned close. "What is that? What is that smell?"

My father. Hell no, Calico didn't know about her family, he's insane. Macy couldn't smell anything except her house, the vanilla candles sitting on the counter, and the sweat, a musky, wet dog scent, from the man restraining her. Keeping her confusion to herself she remained silent. He was losing his focus in his thoughts, and she wasn't going to provoke him. She watched him, tracking him, and wasn't sure if he was asking her or his Hunter Wolves.

"Don't test my patience. I don't have to wait to put my plans into action," Calico growled as his eyes turned wild and distant. "Your attitude will change soon enough. The precious BPI, your bureau will believe you're responsible for the explosion, leaving you no choice." With a step backwards he gauged her weakness, the smirk curving his lips, letting her know he didn't fear her or the BPI. "Let her stand."

The man obeyed and lowered her to the ground. When her feet met the floor, she refused to look defeated or rub her arms. "No choice for what?"

"You're a born killer, Macelaine. Do you think it's an accident you chose the ERT and the BPI?" Calcio saw surprise cross her face. "Yes, I know your past. And I know those agencies gave you the freedom to kill without guilt. Having worked for both, you know their protocol and the way they operate. But you're loyal. Really, saving Sergeant Mayco? He was going to burn you, and you still protected him. I had to take drastic measures to ensure you wouldn't be able to save yourself. The BPI and the DOJ following Agent Sinclair's lead will blame you for the warehouse, guaranteeing you can never return to the mortal life you once knew. You will never be able to show your face because of your crimes. Do you know what the punishment is for a werewolf who has committed the crimes you have?" He grabbed her, pulled her closer, and leaned in until his lips were a sliver from hers. "Death. The hands of justice move quick where shifters are concerned. Back in the day, the mortals would have publicly executed you. And that's what you would deserve, after blowing up the warehouse, the evidence, and killing all those law enforcement officers who trusted you."

"You. Are. Delusional," Macy swore.

Holding his gaze, she feared challenging him and pushing him would cause her more pain. Macy didn't know what his plan was but knew she didn't want any part of it. She jerked her head, and his fingers gripped her chin, and closing in, he smelled her hair, his nose making a trail down to her ear, and neck, like a dog. After feathering her collarbone, he rose and met her gaze. With a growl and flash of wolf eyes, he put space between them as if she were poison.

"Elijah, they blew up the warehouse. We need to get out of here." Eyes, the man who had been holding her stared at her, then Calico. Elijah.

He turned, his hair following the curves of his shoulders, and started toward the front door. Macy watched him and hoped he was leaving. When he rounded on her to meet her gaze, she took a step back. "Derek has a shot for you to make sure you come quietly, then we're going for a ride."

When Elijah had finished talking, Derek pulled a syringe from his back pocket, and taking the lid off exposed a needle. Not today. She wasn't going to be unconscious with the Hunter Wolf forms looming. Before Derek grabbed her, Macy cocked her fist back and delivered a solid punch to his throat. A guttural cough sounded as his left hand went to his neck, then she kneed him in the thigh, sending him backward and into the counter. Without waiting, she ran out of the kitchen, away from the Hunter Wolf forms, and straight at Elijah.

He waited like a wolf for its prey, a sick smile curving his lips, and his canines lengthening. His height worked against him, her height working for her. Macy ducked under his arms, slid across the wood floor, and into the hallway. Angry yells echoed behind her, dying out under the sound of pounding footsteps. She needed more speed. One step. Two steps. Like a dream the door sat open. *I'm out of here.* Thoughts of the BPI hunting for Elijah and then shooting him filled her head at the same time sparks fired at the base of her neck, and spreading over her scalp, shot down her spine. As quickly as she understood what was happening, her head snapped backward, and her feet left the floor. The air held her for a second before she landed with a thick thud on her back and her head smacked the ground. Pain seared, enveloping her in a world of fog.

Macy lay stunned, blinking to stay conscious, then forcing her eyes open she stared up at the blurred ceiling. Each labored breath tightened a metal band around her aching rib cage. One of the bastards had pulled her by her hair and to the ground. Into the floor. Closing her eyes, she prayed Kayne would drive up and save her from whatever they were going to do. She would tell him anything he wanted to know and things he didn't. Warmth slid down the side of her face, the liquid seeping from the stiches above her eye and lip. Blood. If they got off on fear, what were they going to do with fresh blood? She didn't want to know and didn't want to be unconscious around them. Pushing herself to focus on the light fixture above her, she prayed for her eyes to adjust. The bronze fixture, the room, and the dark figure remained a blur wrapped in a slow spin while muffled words drifted through the haze.

His orders about the blood, the car, and getting out of there thundered in her skull. By the time he finished, her eyes focused enough to see him. Elijah was an inch from her face, waving his hand back and forth, light touches swept over her nose and cheeks from the strands of hair hanging from between his fingers. She tried rolling to her side but couldn't without pain streaking across her forehead and erupting in her rib cage. All Macy could do was watch him as he let the hair, her hair, fall to the floor.

"If you were one of the bums off the street, I would kill you. Dime a dozen. But trying to escape four werewolves and my crossbreeds ... well, that's the kind of audacity I was hoping for." Elijah smiled at her, his face held a shade of Hunter Wolf form and his canines grazed his lips. "Still, you need to learn a lesson, and you'll stand for that."

Derek knelt by her head, put his hands under her arms, and lifted her as if she weighed nothing. The pain cascaded through her like lava, making Macy shake from its intensity. She tried talking, but mumbled sobs escaped her, causing blood to mist her mouth. Her head rolled with the movement and nausea spilled to her stomach, threatening her throat. The haze hadn't cleared when the sting of a needle punctured her skin and cool metal slid deep into her flesh.

"You're not your own. You're one of mine. You'll kneel before me," Elijah ordered.

Darkness slithered to the edges of her vision, distorting his body, while confusion made it impossible to form a thought. As the cloud of unconsciousness forced itself on her, she kicked again, silently begging Derek to squeeze her arms until she screamed. Pain might keep the darkness at bay. *It's all for nothing,* her mind mocked. Macy wasn't going to escape them when the tranquilizer was pulling her under. With the admission she wasn't going anywhere, her knees folded under her, Derek's grip tightened, and she started to sink to the floor.

"Watch as werewolf royalty kneels before a convicted rogue with a death sentence," Elijah mocked. The others joined him, and the rough growls of the Hunter Wolf forms sounded. "Pureblood, the ways I'm going to use you ..."

As if Elijah's words cut the strings holding her, she slid down Derek's thighs. Her body crumpled to the floor, his laugh echoed in her house, and inside her mind. "I'm not who you think I am."

"Yes, princess, you are."

*I'm not your princess. I'm not the spy.* With a weak moan, she closed her eyes and the world crashed.

## CHAPTER EIGHTEEN

"Agent Sinclair," Chayton started as he skidded to a stop.

The heat had gotten worse throughout the day, and it showed in Chayton's blue T-shirt. Sweat darkened the cotton under his arms, down his back, and at his waist as did Kayne's button-up. The shock creasing his face and the worry darkening his eyes made Kayne hesitate. *Don't be Macy.*

"What?"

"There was an explosion at the warehouse," Chayton explained in a rush.

"No." Disbelief swallowed him in an instant. The people. The evidence.

"Affirmative. The entire back half including the lab." Chayton looked toward the east. "Captain Dixon was hurt in the blast and ordered the BPI and the PD arrest Detective Gray. He believes she is responsible."

"Captain Dixon," Kayne growled. The man was hell bent on convicting her, an innocent woman. Chayton's demeanor held DOJ formality and not the familiar relationship they had as first and fourth, alpha and pack. "Was Commander Arden there?"

"Negative. No one has seen him." Waiting for orders, Chayton's body tensed, and his almond-shaped, mocha eyes met Kayne's calculating gaze.

He wasn't going to worry about the missing commander … yet. "What about emergency responders, have they been called?" he asked. "Fire Rescue, Haz-Mat, Rapid Response, ambulances, Sanative?"

"Affirmative. The detectives and agents on site have taken care of the priorities, and what they were unable to achieve the detectives here have secured. It is a matter of time before the PD and the BPI are at Detective Gray's house. I do not believe she is behind the blast."

"Neither do I." After Officer Murphy's death and the way the BPI treated the PD, they'd take pride in taking Macy into custody. Getting there before the BPI and the PD meant he needed to leave immediately. "I have to beat them." Kayne could see the questions forming in Chayton's stare as his fourth questioned the leader of Blood Rain, but more importantly, he was questioning him as the alpha of his pack. He would, if and when he found out what was going on, explain everything to him. At the moment, Macy was the only person connected to the explosion, and he needed her.

"Damn, they'll find her guilty of every crime in the High Desert." Until they find out she's a werewolf. Possibly a Pureblood with connections to the paranormal world, the Council, and Daeland. "All her work will be for nothing. They won't think twice about linking her to the ersatz. If she makes it to the jail alive. Macy must have figured something wasn't right and that's why she called. No one else but the two of us knew we were going to meet. I have a bad feeling about this," Kayne mumbled more to himself than Chayton.

"Macy. You were going to meet with Detective Gray? You know, you cannot get in the middle of this," Chayton warned. "With the explosion, they are sure she is the spy, and they will close the case. The DOJ's part in the investigation is over."

"As long as Elijah is out there with his ersatz, it's my business. Whoever Detective Gray is protecting is using her. She's prior ERT and a decorated BPI detective, it makes her a risk. When they take her into custody, they'll use extreme force, and because they think she betrayed them, she'll be killed and her evidence conveniently lost," Kayne explained. He stopped himself from pouring out details about Daeland, then reconsidered. If anything happened to him, Chayton would be responsible for explaining the situation to Michael. Kayne stopped and faced his fourth. "Swear this will remain between us."

Sweat crawled over his skin and slid down his temples. "You have my oath."

"Macy wears Daeland's blood mark, and he's here, in Desert Rock, has been for two days. That makes it pack business. It makes it all of our business. If Elijah pushes a confrontation between mortals, shifters, and the Veiled, the Council will descend on this city and they'll bring hell with them."

"Lord Daeland's blood mark," Chayton whispered. Absently, he stepped back and watched Kayne transfer gear from his truck to his newly rented car sitting in Detective Gray's parking space. "Nice car."

Kayne glared at him. "Make sure to tell Agent Pixley what's going on. I don't need Commander Wilson breathing down my neck because I'm not here." He climbed behind the wheel of his bright red SUV and surveyed the arsenal sitting in the passenger seat. His thoughts racing, he stopped and considered what he had said. Kayne faced Chayton. "Where is Commander Wilson?"

"He is safe at the warehouse and has shapeshifters getting the mortals to safety."

"Good. When I know something, I'll call you. You need to have Blood Rain ready," Kayne ordered as he started the engine. "If White Rain is available, I want them."

"Affirmative, sir." Stepping back, he put space between him and the vehicle as Kayne backed the boxy SUV out of the parking spot.

Kayne left Chayton watching him and prayed he wouldn't run into problems. He stopped at the gate, the image of Macy with her bruises and stitches filling his vision. Staring at the street, he watched sharp lights of several fire trucks and ambulances flash as their sirens screamed in the evening air. He didn't want to think Pennsky warehouse was going to be the beginning of Elijah cleansing Desert Rock of his presence. Would he burn everything? If he did, every law enforcement agency and the fire department was going to have their hands full.

Out of the city and free from traffic, he increased his speed down the two-lane road flanked by open desert and stretching out into miles going deeper into nothing. The only distraction came from the railroad tracks cutting a swath alongside the narrow stretch of asphalt. Time sped up, corrupting his thoughts, and with nothing to take his attention from them, the miles multiplied, and worry intensified. On his left side, the sun sank below the mountains, making the headlights that automatically came on cut through twilight while the wind grew stronger, and the dust in the air hid the peaks of the tallest mountains.

As the miles disappeared behind him, night cloaked the desert, giving the vastness a primeval edge as if it held onto its ancient beginnings while the road reached out in front of him. Kayne was convinced he was lost. The GPS, silent for miles, seemed to have abandoned him, as if it knew he wasn't from the area and was tricking him into driving deeper toward the desert's wilds. Every second turned into wasted time, and pushing his anxiety he took his cell and started to call Chayton to confirm Macy's address. *No way she lives in the middle of nowhere.* Before he finished, the female voice of the GPS ordered him to turn left in one thousand feet. He kept the screen open, just in case, placed the cell in the center console, searched for the upcoming turn, and doubted there was going to be anything of significance.

To prove him wrong, a sign for a housing development, bright with lights, told him to turn right, he was entering a vacation spot he could call home, and please enjoy your stay. Leaving the main road, he slowly drove around a corner to see green lawn bordering each side of the entrance. On the right side, a waterfall backlit with spotlights welcomed him to Tawny Ridge. Macy lived outside of the city in a quiet neighborhood and was a werewolf who was responsible for an explosion that might have killed her coworkers. It didn't make sense. If she wasn't the spy, and Captain Dixon wasn't, then who the hell was? The missing Commander Arden? Kayne wished he had answers.

He wove down streets crowded by trucks and family cars, following the female's orders, and taking in the neighborhood. One street led to another, and another, and continuing through the honeycomb of homes apprehension rode his thoughts and his second guessing began clouding his decision. Was he expecting to catch Detective M. Gray plotting her next move? Was she waiting for him in wolf form? He didn't know what to think and it drove him crazy. Macy called him. Kayne growled. Macy blew up the warehouse, was waiting for him with evidence, and would answer all his questions. That's funny. Someone was setting her up. If she answered the door, with her split lip bleeding and her stiches staring at him, was he going to tell her about the warehouse? Negative.

Kayne knew he would start mumbling about why he was there. *Good evening, wanted to let you know I've been hunting Elijah, he's responsible for my wife's betrayal and death, the murder of an alpha and his family, and if I can pin the ersatz on him, he'll face a death sentence. Again. No one will care you're the spy when they find out you're a werewolf. And you are. Your life as you know it is ending and your career is over. Hey, while I'm here, one question, how do you know Daeland? He's a vampire lord and you have his crest inked on your back. Can I check it for fang scars?* If Macy shot him, he deserved it.

Kayne checked the address, canceled the GPS, and turned the headlights off as he pulled up to the curb, parked, and killed the engine. Thankful for his rental, his fear one of Elijah's spies would see him at her house eased. Hopefully, they wouldn't recognize him. He didn't want to think he was putting her at greater risk for the same treatment Henry and Grace received. If there was a chance his actions brought Elijah out of hiding, Kayne was going to be there.

Deep inhale. Exaggerated exhale. She trusted him, a DOJ agent and werewolf, enough to call him. Kayne eased his grip on the steering wheel, tried to calm his nerves, and accept the hunt for Elijah was getting to him. An alpha for twenty-three years, a werewolf for two hundred and thirty-eight, a soldier for the Coterie, a short term as a lord with the Council, and this was bothering him. If he admitted to himself, he had been on edge for months, that the anticipation of something happening was making him crazy, it might make the case easier to handle. Maybe. The looming mystery didn't have a reason ... no, it added to his anxiety.

The details had his instincts on high alert as his senses were giving him information faster than he could process it. And Daeland was in the middle. Kayne needed to get to Macy before the BPI and the PD showed up with guns drawn and prepared to take her in dead or alive. After doing a quick sweep for people, he got out of the SUV, and once confident no one was outside turned to the interior.

He took off his shoulder holster, placed it on the driver's seat, fumbled with his shirt and tie, and free of them, tossed them to the backseat. Beside his discarded clothing, Kayne reached for the DOJ T-shirt and pulled it over his head. A warning screamed with the sound of a car and he scanned the area. Leaning farther into the SUV he pretended to look for something, because he didn't need a family seeing him arm himself and then call the police. When the car turned, he quickly replaced the single carry holster with a dual carry, and after adjusting it to sit snug around his back and arms, he placed a Smith and Wesson 1911 in each pocket. Kayne worked to loosen his belt, and with the leather in his hand shoved a magazine pouch onto the length, forced it to stay at his hip, and slipped it through his belt loops. He quickly repeated the process on his right side. As added protection, he grabbed a knife, sheathed it at his ankle, and then reached for his cell. The warehouse had been a painful lesson. It didn't stop him from thinking he looked out of place and ready for a war. At least until you noticed he was wearing slacks and dress shoes.

Frustration took bites out of him as he wondered what game he was playing, and by whose rules he played them. If he was playing at all, rather he was a pawn to be used. Like Macy. Damn, there was a better way to fight. He was a powerful werewolf, one who preferred to be in his Hunter Wolf or on all fours, without worrying about clothing and weapons. The game, tangled with mortals and shapeshifters, was all wrong and had the worst consequences.

Kayne checked his gear, his mind wild with what facet of Macy he was going to see. The arsonist. The spy. The Pureblood werewolf. Macy the injured BPI detective. There was the chance Elijah was watching and waiting for him to make the first move, which would allow Elijah to trap them at the same time. Kayne should have considered backup. Without law enforcement's presence, he would have to deal with Elijah himself. And he knew exactly how he was going to end the man.

He internally shrugged, locked the SUV, and started down the sidewalk leading to her house. There was nothing in the air, no clues indicating she was home or had run. At the edge of the sidewalk the air changed, and the first threads of her fear reached out. Kayne released a string of curses. He wanted to be in wolf form with heightened sight, hearing, strength, agility, and protection. He did not want to be lurking around at night like a mortal. Closer to the dark house, weak silver light of the crescent moon turned the little, yellow flowers along the walk to a dull, buttery beige. Farther down the sidewalk and deeper onto the property, he took in the landscaped yard, the flowers, and the walkway. This was Macy's home, the house of a mastermind spy and arsonist. It jarred the accusations against her.

Everything since he arrived in Desert Rock had been wrong. He wasn't any different. He survived months of living with a storm raging inside of him and he wanted to apprehend Elijah, put the ghosts in their graves, and end the desperate need for forgiveness. Then Macy happened. Who was he? Alpha? DOJ agent? When had the two merged? The agent part of his life leaked into his personal life and both wanted her.

"Talk to her, get the evidence, and get out. Simple," Kayne mumbled.

The rustling leaves sent their scratchy whisper floating across the night sky while the breeze brought him stronger tastes of who had been there. It twisted through him and the all too familiar scent of werewolf, ersatz, and Macy met his nose. They had been at her house, and it was the feel of her pain riding the air and growing thicker the closer he got to her front door. Someone knew she was home, alone and un-protected, making it easy for the ersatz to take her from her own house. They took what they wanted while he was wast-ing time at the BPI office interviewing detectives. A growl rumbled from his chest, rising to his throat as he stood with his hand on the handle of her front door. Kayne inhaled, searching for her scent, and met the familiar tang of evil. *Eli-jah.*

He tried the brushed nickel handle, and easily turning the door swung open to a black hole, the inside of the house sat in front of him. Stepping across the threshold, he met cold anger mixed with currents of emotions. The toxic concoction washed out from the dark, bringing her pain forward as if carried by a tidal wave. Another step and Macy's soft vanilla scent sat all around him, her essence thick and washing him in her passion. Had he felt it before? Negative. The ware-house? Maybe. Silver ringed with cinnamon. Every detail—the moonlight, her scent, the feel of the storm, and the hot desert night—added to his imagination. He didn't need the chaos. Kayne struggled to shake it free, and with the moon-light behind him he followed the hall to the first room and entered what he assumed to be her living room. He let his eyes adjust to the darkness, and waited for a noise, anything telling him she was there, and he hadn't missed her. A whisper, like leaves on the breeze sounded behind him, in the hallway, and not from the trees in the yard. Maybe she hid from them. He turned and stood under the arched entrance between the hall and the living room and waited for the sound to repeat.

*Come on, Macy.* Nothing.

He was making himself crazy. Not taking a chance by yelling out her name, Kayne reached for the light switch, at the same time a shadow broke the sliver gleam on the wood floor. Instinctively reaching for his gun, he started to take it from the holster, froze, and left the barrel covered by leather. Long fingers wrapped around his neck, squeezed, and the shadow moved in front of him to block the light. He let go of the grip and the gun silently slid back into the holster. Kayne clutched the wrist, made of stone, and struggling for air he fought to loosen the hold as the soles of his dress shoes squealed on the flooring. His airflow slowed, his mind fogged, and instinctively his body started its transition into his Hunter Wolf form.

"Shift and I'll kill you where you stand, Alpha."

The threat, sounding distorted, was enough Kayne let go of the wrist and the hand holding him. With his arms hanging limp at his sides, his fear eased and his wolf sank, and humanoid features slipped into place. "Let go."

"I should kill you. I should rip you to pieces and have your pack eat what is left." An angry, restrained roar rode the low voice. It wanted loose. Rage begging for freedom.

Kayne could feel it switch from cold to hot as if a frozen wind carried a fire. A growl sounded, the grip eased, and thinking he was free, he took a step back. Daeland jerked him farther into the hall, and with the walls passing in a blur, shoved him to the floor. His chest hit, hard, the air rushing from his lungs, and his protest lost.

"Tell me what you smell," Daeland demanded. On one knee, he held Kayne to the ground.

In a pained breath, confusion bucked his previous thoughts and tangled with what he thought he knew. "Blood. I smell her blood." Elijah hurt her. Why did it call his wolf?

"That's right. When they came for her, she feared for her life and fought them, and they drugged her and took her." Daeland's whisper barely restrained the heated anger sitting in every word. With his hand on the back of Kayne's neck, he shoved his face to the floor one more time, like a show of power, before letting go and backing across the hall. "Do you know what he has, Wolf?"

"A Pureblood," Kayne answered. He got to his feet, brushed his pants off out of habit, straightened his holster, and rubbed his neck. "Who wears your mark."

He pushed Daeland's insult to the side. All the vampire had to do was call and explain everything from the beginning, like a normal fucking person. But it wasn't the way of the vampire. Games, secrets, hints of nothing and more hints of pieces equaling life and death was their twisted way. Damn night crawlers drove him crazy.

"Yes, Lord Kayne, they have a Pureblood," Daeland confirmed with scorn in his voice. "They have Garrick's daughter, Macelaine." The vampire pushed each word through his thin lips as if using them as a threat. Daeland cast him an onyx stare, one second, two seconds, and he gave Kayne his back and walked down the hall. He hated it, and following Daeland, Kayne walked to the living room.

"Drop the *lord* bit, I'm not calling you Lord Daeland." He ignored the part about Garrick's daughter. Wasn't real. He had held Macy in his arms and felt nothing. Agent Pixley sat next to her and admitted Macy felt mortal. Even if there was a sliver of a chance it was true, Kayne accepted redemption for the past was a dream. Elijah's capture was the only way he was going to be able to silence his demons and bury his ghosts.

"How did you get in the house when you need an invitation?" Kayne asked.

An ancient curse, created by powerful religious leaders, known as the Godsend, kept vampires from crossing a threshold of an innocent mortal's residence. The innate enchantment was passed on during the bleeding and took root inside of the vampire when their mortal souls died. The vampires saw it as a disease they didn't have the cure for. Everyone else saw it for what it was, a Godsend. Would Macy knowingly give Daeland access to her house? Kayne wanted to say no, except the vampire was standing in her living room.

"You would be better off dead," Daeland grated and walked to the fireplace.

"What are you doing here?" Kayne remained where he was.

Daeland moved with an air of elegance werewolves didn't possess, would never possess. Young vampires took up space, as if they didn't understand what it meant to be dead, and their mortal side was fighting to hold onto their life. The old dead, like Daeland, had a way of not being, a way of existing when they chose, as if at any moment they would fade into the air like a vapor. Standing before Kayne silent, motionless, like a demon carved from the shadows Daeland embodied those traits.

"What are you doing here?" Daeland countered. "Besides putting her life at risk."

"Spare me. My presence isn't the problem. Yours is. I don't believe Macy is Garrick's daughter. She's a werewolf, I'll give you that, and I'll admit your mark on her has me questioning your sanity," Kayne shot back. "You can't seriously expect me to believe a BPI detective is Garrick's dead daughter." Macy's age would match.

"Why not?" Daeland countered.

Kayne paused. Despite Daeland's attack, and his ridiculous notion Macy was Garrick's daughter, he couldn't stop the relief from having the vampire in front of him. Their friendship spanned a hundred years, it gave Kayne freedom to express his feelings about the Council, Elijah, the politics of the pack, and he didn't have to hide his true self. Like he did when he was working with the DOJ. Staring at Daeland, he couldn't stop from remembering the last time they met. Behind the gates of Amaranth, inside of Daeland's inner sanctuary, Kayne watched the once powerful death-wielding vampire shuffle across the stone floor wearing a plain white T-shirt, draped on his thinning frame and a pair of loose cotton pants, hanging on thinner hips. In addition to his decomposing body, he wore his dark hair pulled tight from his face, making his equally dark eyes look sunken and gaunt. His usual olive skin was tight, translucent and stretched over the bones of his face, hands, and toes, revealing withering veins.

Daeland had stopped feeding and had been dying.

It was only a matter of time before one of the elders saw how far the Affliction progressed, and fearing Daeland wouldn't be able to care for his coven, would try to put him to ground. That was a week ago. He wasn't the same, he was the vampire Kayne remembered. He was the threat nightmares exemplified. At six foot, six inches tall, the same height as Kayne, Daeland's presence carried weight. In order for him get back to his full health, he had to have fed from dozens of people. Or a dozen strong paranormals. Obviously he had his fill, for the black, button-up dress shirt sat taut around his muscled chest, and his deep blue denim jeans, fitting snug, hinted at muscles. His dying skin was no longer pallid; instead, the olive with hints of soft bronze of summer and his Italian descent hid the veins beneath, and his dark eyes held a level of life. His black hair hung loose at his shoulders its waves tucked behind his ears. He wasn't in the throes of the Affliction. If mortals saw him on the street, they would believe he was a thirty-something man. Whatever had grabbed him from the brink of a dark sleep had to be important. It wasn't Macy, it couldn't be.

"Did you hear me?" Daeland demanded.

"I heard you."

"What?" His eyes bled from vampire black to coffee brown.

"It's good to see the Affliction didn't send you to ground," Kayne answered.

He didn't want to face the Council on his own and feared the evidence proving Elijah was alive and actively damaging the relationship between mortals and paranormals would fall on deaf ears. The Council didn't care about the wellbeing of paranormals, let alone mortals, their concern focused on protecting the Veiled, and their privacy. He planned on using Daeland's influence with the Council. Kayne needed the vampire.

"Don't change the subject," Daeland ordered, halfheartedly. He turned around, placed his hands on the fireplace mantle, and bowed his head. A mortal gesture. "My priority is Elijah. He has Macelaine. When he realizes who she is, he will use her. I want to blame you. Damn everything, I want to blame you, but my current state ... I should have been here months ago."

"I'm not going to turn away your help, but I think the Affliction has you believing she's Macelaine. I know her, I've talked to her, and she lives as a mortal. She doesn't shift. A Pureblood cannot deny their wolf."

Daeland spun around to face Kayne, and seethed, "Don't insult me, Alpha. I know the truth. We have to leave."

Kayne took a step, stopping the vampire, and they faced each other, leaving a sliver of space separating their chests. "Don't throw your authority at me. I don't care. I'm not leaving. We're not leaving. I want answers."

"You created a mess by coming here, and now Macelaine is in the hands of the very person you've been hunting like a rabid dog," Daeland growled.

"I'm an agent with the Department of Justice and I'm investigating a case, which gives me the right to be here," Kayne argued, letting his anger loose on the vampire. "Why don't you explain why you are here?"

"I have."

"She isn't Macelaine. The child died. I know, she died in my arms. I heard her heart stop," Kayne admitted softly. Part of him knew she was Macelaine. Her eyes proved her identity. Silver, as if it was molten liquid held back by raw power. Was he going to believe what the vampire said? Not yet. He needed answers and proof. He couldn't risk believing in redemption. The warning in his head was telling him to be quiet, Daeland's power and position with the Council exceeded his own, as did Daeland's years, meaning the vampire could hang him up by his skin.

"Working with the mortals has weakened you, Kayne. Do you trust everything you see?"

Kayne took a step away, ending the stand-off between them. He needed space. He wanted time to think. Both were never going to happen. "Macy Gray is a BPI detective, and a suspect in a case. The BPI and the PD are on their way here right now. There was an explosion, and her superiors believe she's responsible. They're going to arrest her. All I want are answers."

"Why are you here?" Daeland asked.

"She called me. Said she had information."

"You knew she was different. You said you knew she was a Pureblood. How did you find out?" Daeland visibly relaxed, his shoulders following their natural curves, and he took his familiar stance, his left hand resting at the waist of his jeans.

"She was injured, and I saw the tattoo. Afterwards, I had her DNA tested," Kayne explained. "I know Purebloods can fool blood tests." He stopped talking as the image of her cinnamon eyes ringed in silver stared at him. "I want answers."

"Macy Gray is Macelaine Grayson, daughter of Garrick and Sabine Grayson. What other reason is there for her to wear the blood mark of my kith?" Daeland asked through a breath as if he had said it a thousand times.

"Your kith?" Kayne turned to burn energy, paced, and stopped. *Not Kindred.*

"My signature from my land and a time when blood bound carried power and the world hadn't moved on. There's an extra sword and the extra dragon head holds that sword in its mouth. Our names are intertwined in its center. Macelaine is mine." Daeland gave Kayne his back to stare at the empty house.

"If you extended your protection to her because you believe she's Macelaine, then why mark her for the world to see? You put her life in danger," Kayne accused Daeland's back.

"She has worn my signature her entire life. I could not predict the future and what threats would come for her."

The pending arrival of the PD and BPI was forgotten as Kayne's mind played the scenes at the warehouse, and excitement flowed freely in his veins with the chance redemption was in his grasp. The empath hadn't given him memories of his past. It gave him the answer. Macy was in the images plaguing him while he chased the ersatz. He saw her die in his arms, smelled the fuel from the wrecked car, and choked on the smoke. There were too many questions.

"You feed from her." The words tumbled from his mouth, tasting weak and foul, and part of him wished it was true. It would make her less enticing. Less needed.

Daeland became a blur as he grabbed Kayne by the throat lifted him off the floor. "Never. Never utter those words. Do not belittle her. She is part of me."

Kayne's eyes blazed amber as he pulled a gun from its holster and shoved it into Daeland's neck. The shot wouldn't kill him; syn silver wasn't a threat to vampires, but it would hurt like hell and take time to heal. "Put me down. I'm done with your attacks."

Daeland slowly lowered him, and letting go, put distance between them. "She is mine."

"I got it. If you want me to believe you, you need to do some explaining," Kayne stated. "It's that simple."

"If law enforcement is headed this way, we don't have the time. I have a car ready. We'll discuss it as we drive." Daeland checked the house, gazing at the photos on the walls, the books on the coffee table, and the glass of water. Walking over to the glass, he lifted it to his face.

"Where are we going?" Kayne asked, getting his attention.

"Elijah's lab. That is what you want, isn't it?" he replied absently.

*Damn him.* "You knew Elijah was alive this entire time? Hell, on earth is in the desert, and you use Macy as bait while Elijah kills people?" Kayne took a step forward. "Why didn't you tell me?"

"The Council's spies were investigating. They didn't want to destroy the network they created," Daeland explained. "And you could not be trusted."

"That's wrong."

"I'll not stand here arguing with you while time slips from us." Daeland walked to the open door and stopped.

"You are going to explain whatever it is you know," Kayne demanded. He continued down the sidewalk, leaving the house and Daeland behind him.

"I know her life," Daeland whispered. He inhaled her scent, and drawing it in savored the threads matching his own. "They took what is mine."

# CHAPTER NINETEEN

**He wasn't** going to report Macy's kidnapping; the BPI and PD could report her missing when they didn't find her in the house. And Kayne didn't want to waste time telling them why he left Desert Rock. When it was settled, he hoped Commander Wilson would listen long enough to understand before arresting him as Macy's accomplice. If Kayne found Elijah, he wouldn't have to defend himself or Macy. *If* he found him.

Daeland drove from the house and out of the neighborhood as if he had been there a thousand times. Meanwhile, Kayne absently watched the houses pass and explained to Chayton he needed to go to Macy's and look for the evidence. Then told him he was with Daeland and they were going to find her and Elijah, while conveniently leaving out the part about her being Garrick's daughter. Until there was proof, Kayne refused to spread a destructive rumor. Like he refused to hope redemption was real. If Macy was Macelaine and there was a chance she accepted her life, would she forgive him for failing her? He stopped the shudder crawling down his spine and focused on the present. He wouldn't say anything about her. Her identity would remain a secret and her life safe from a situation he couldn't control.

Through the development, Daeland turned onto a dark highway, and headed away from Tawny Ridge, Macy's empty house, and the BPI. Kayne prepared to make the last call of the night, its weight hanging over him like a knife about to drop. He dreaded calling Commander Wilson and, in the end, opted for Agent Pixley, who reported the BPI and PD hadn't been able to take Macy into custody because she had run. She asked if Kayne knew anything about it and he said no. He explained after Macy confessed to having information, he planned a meeting with her and had clearly missed her. Pushing his luck even further, he told Agent Pixley his suspicions surrounding Captain Dixon. She didn't act surprised, and without missing a beat, asked where he was headed. Kayne answered the best he could without telling the truth. He didn't need another agent thrown into the mess if things went bad. The situation had changed from mortal to paranormal. Agent Pixley wasn't part of the Garrick pack, bordered on mortal, and was a DOJ agent. By the time Kayne had taken care of his whereabouts, an hour had slipped by.

"If we find Elijah and his lab, how are we supposed to stop him?" Kayne asked, sitting back in the cream-colored leather seat.

"Stop him?" Daeland questioned with astonishment in his voice. "It depends on the state I find Macelaine in. When I have her and she's safe, I will decide how long he lives."

"How long will it take us to reach him?" Kayne saw chaos in the future.

"Another hour. I let her slip through my fingers." Daeland took his eyes off the road long enough to look at Kayne, his features highlighted by the green light of the dash.

*So did I. I held her in my arms.* "Explain how you know she's Macelaine." Kayne turned slightly to see Daeland better.

"When Sabine was pregnant with her, the moon threatened to kill the child by demanding she shift. As you said, werewolves cannot deny their wolf, and Purebloods are vulnerable to their wolves when emotions run high. Garrick and I made the decision Sabine would stay at my house, surrounded by my coven during the full moon. This would allow the combined power of the coven to hold her in trance through its strongest phase. It worked for a while, but sadly, with each full moon and each denial of the shift, her wolf demanded more. After months of refusing the moon and her wolf, the struggle took place every day. Sabine knew the risks involved and wanted to have the baby at home. That lasted a couple of days. In her seventh month the need to shift became overwhelming, and her wolf overpowered her. The sun had begun its rise when Garrick woke to her screams for help. There were six men who helped him bring her half-shifted body to my house, and we did what we could to save Sabine and the baby."

"You helped them?" Kayne asked cautiously. *Why don't I remember this?* Kayne struggled to think back to the young Moonlight pack, as it had been known, and couldn't place ever hearing about the Pureblood's birth. He would have known since he had served as security for Daeland.

"I've helped a great many people. You can't forge allies with lies and threats. We are people, Kayne. Before we became something else, we were people. Humanity is a thing, not a kind of person. And while we hid in the shadows together, we helped one another." An air of superiority laced Daeland's words.

"The elders as individuals didn't see it the same way, and neither did the Council. They wouldn't want you helping an alpha save his unborn child, especially a Pureblood," Kayne pointed out. The Council didn't want anything or anyone to upset their power base or authority over all paranormals and allowing Garrick to keep a Pureblood would make them look weak.

"The Council saw Macelaine's birth as a way to separate themselves from superstitions and the past," Daeland replied. "They had aspirations of living in the open and among mortals. It wouldn't serve them to kill those deemed unfit by a darker age."

Unfit. They were considered abominations.

Kayne witnessed Garrick's leadership and strength when he was sent to observe the alpha during the pack's probation period. It had been his responsibility to reject or accept the petition for the Council to recognize the Moonlight pack as omnipotent and its history have its own chronicle. Alpha Garrick kept the traditions of the pack, the wolf, and their lives, and was the reason he chose the Moonlight territory. He didn't have to worry about the alpha playing into the politics of useless hatred and rumors between paranormals and factions. Kayne couldn't stop from thinking those ideals killed him and his family.

"Make no mistake, there is a price to pay for everything," Daeland replied softly. "Early in the beginning, we knew the birth wasn't going to be easy, then when her wolf forced the change it grew deadly. Without the convenience of a hospital, Garrick used his wolf and his strength as alpha to stop his wife's shift long enough we could safely deliver the baby. Where Sabine was healthy and strong, Macelaine was weak and dying. Purebloods are rarely healthy. Threatened with mutations, birth deformities, and being delivered half shifted, most of them die. There are those who say death is the price for believing you can have a normal life. Death and the loss of a child."

"Not everything in legend is true. We are walking, talking examples of it," Kayne mumbled with irritation. "Why didn't Garrick give her his strength? As an alpha, he could have used the essence of the pack. He was the strongest among them."

"Despite the Council's order giving Purebloods the right to live, the myths warning us they're uncontrollable, power hungry, and bloodthirsty created a lifetime of fear. Garrick favored the old ways, the traditions of the past, and had he given Macelaine a taste of the pack and the power it held, his wolves would have seen it as putting the pack at risk. They would have challenged him for alpha and then challenged Sabine to take the second from the pack, and the child would have been killed. While I believe Garrick didn't fear losing his life in a challenge, he was a powerful alpha, he did fear they would go to the Council and petition to have him destroy his daughter. If anything happened to her it would have destroyed Sabine. And Garrick."

The sight of Kayne delivering her battered body to Amaranth played as if Daeland was driving straight into it. "The Council listens to you. Had you explained the situation, Garrick could have given her his strength and the power of the pack. With a statement from a lord, the Council wouldn't believe the rumblings of the pack." Kayne stopped and stared as the headlights cast a bright beam on the asphalt.

*Macy had been dying.*

Garrick hadn't used his power to save her. The blood mark of his kith. Daeland saved her. His blood. "You. You don't feed from her. She feeds from you. You saved her at birth with your blood. She didn't die after the car wreck. Macy responded like a vampire. She went into a coma to heal her wounds. Once you had her, you saved her again. She's part of you, and you keep her from shapeshifting."

Kayne sat straighter, his anger burning through his understanding. "Without your blood, she didn't stay under your influence, and your weakness allowed her wolf to grow stronger. She's changing. Macy didn't shoot the therian-lion because she knew it was dying." Kayne's excitement sat in his words.

His questions were getting answers. "In the warehouse, I couldn't feel her because of you. Even the new wolf from the warehouse sensed *what* she was. Macy was facing losing control, being found out by the mortals, and they would have sent her to prison, damn they would have killed her, all because of your self-induced Affliction." He ended with fury running through his words and the need to protect her rising from his middle.

His wolf saw what she was, recognized who she was. Kayne thought the empath was punishing him with memories of Elijah and Eryin, making them worse with the memories surrounding Garrick's death and his failure. His mind created the illusion. It was showing him what Elijah wanted all along. Macy. *"He found what he was looking for."* The Hunter Wolf told him exactly what had happened.

"By the time I knew the Affliction was upon me, I was unable to stop its progress. I was surviving on her strength, and it was her strength keeping me from going to ground. I could only hope she didn't lose control over her wolf and shapeshift. I needed time to find a way out of the abyss," Daeland confessed.

Daeland losing himself? Not likely. "How have you kept her a secret all this time?" Kayne asked. "Who raised her, knowing she was a Pureblood?" It was curiosity. He wanted to know who would risk their lives by defying the Garrick pack and knowing there was a group of werewolves prepared to kill the Pureblood.

"She never left Feather River. Macelaine had a bond with Garrick's territory, much like you do as alpha, and it gave her the strength she needed. Plus, I couldn't take the chance she would shapeshift. As you pointed out, she needed my blood to stay under my control. Macelaine grew up, and after moving beyond puberty the risk became less and the bond with the territory faded. Completely under my power, she went to school, college, and after her grandparents died, she moved to Desert Rock."

"She was living in her father's territory the entire time," he mumbled. She was living in his territory. Macelaine Grayson never left Moonlight. He had been near her the entire time. "Her grandparents died?"

"Jeremiah and Sarah Browning. They died from old age, and no, they were not mortal. They were empaths who could have helped her if she shifted. They had the protection and benefits of being part of my coven."

"No one in the Council is going to be happy with the lies you have wove around her. Add in the years you've deceived them, and they'll find a reason to dismiss you. And after you're stripped of your authority, they'll take Macy," Kayne pointed out. "What you did was selfish even for you."

"I have status in the Council, and they cannot dismiss me," he corrected with arrogance. "They knew there was something wrong when I didn't go to ground. I was forced to quell their questions and rising doubt before they started investigating. Luckily, I had you, your lack of being there for your pack, and your obsession with finding Elijah to use as a distraction."

"I'm going to let that slide. If Elijah has Macy, then what will he do with her?" Elijah was unstable and dangerous in the past; what he could be doing to Macy made Kayne fear for her life.

"The ersatz are mutations and because they aren't pure, they're dying. Macelaine isn't the only Pureblood he has kidnapped. I'm assuming Elijah needs their perfect DNA. As for the mortals, he hopes they will serve his cause. I understand, in the beginning, he didn't know Macelaine's real identity. She was a detective among many he wanted to use for his own purposes. You saw her house, she lives alone, has a willingness to kill, and the capacity to do it well. I'm afraid that is the Pureblood in her, even the need to be alone. Purebloods set themselves apart because their senses drive them so hard." Daeland paused. "While Elijah has been recruiting followers, kidnapping people, and creating his vulgarities, there is another working in the shadows. We've been waiting for her. She's a vampire from Estonia, from days of old, and is most likely responsible for the empaths at the warehouse. If Havana learns Macy is Macelaine and a Pureblood, she will use her against me and the Council."

"You know what they're doing to the empaths?" Kayne asked.

"The Council has been investigating the reported kidnapping of Purebloods. Then, when the BPI recognized a pattern, Doctor Locke reported what was happening. That's where I've been."

"Why would he do that?" Kayne hadn't liked the doctor, and now he disliked him even more.

"I'm with the Council and he reports to me about his territory. More so, since the ersatz have been evading law enforcement and the threat of White Cell has increased. He mentioned a BPI detective, who he had a relationship with, had been injured. Funny thing, he never said it was

Macelaine and didn't tell me he saw her tattoo. Any questions he had about its meaning were answered when you made a point to see it. He called and reported you and the challenge you provoked in front of mortal witnesses." Daeland gave him a sideways glance.

*He gave her his protection and the protection of his pack.* Kayne shifted in his seat, the leather whispering against his dress pants. He planned to defend himself, like a kid in trouble, when Daeland raised a hand to quiet him.

"I dislike the doctor." There were more colorful words he had for the man.

"I believe the feeling is mutual. After his report, I knew I needed to do something."

Dr. Locke knew about Macy. If he knew, who else did? Kayne shook his head, shoving the thoughts away. "What about the vampire, do you know her?" he asked. He knew the answer was going to have a history. One he wasn't sure he wanted to hear.

"Too well. Her full name is Havana Saint. One hundred years ago, the Council sentenced her to fifty years in ground for forcing her theows to mate with one another then she tried to infect them with the lycanthrope and therianthrope viruses. She hoped to have a supply of Purebloods to feed from. The experiment failed and her theows died. If she knows about Macelaine ..." Daeland gripped the steering wheel making the polished wood inlay groan.

"Why would she want Purebloods?" He reached for the pieces of the puzzle and tried connecting them to the new information. In return, his mind threw everything at him at once, including how he felt about Macy. The feel was primal and his need to get her back consumed his thoughts. Under it, his need for revenge, and the need to right his wrong sat in his grasp. Forgiveness. Redemption. Revenge. Kayne wanted to have her with him at Moonlight, with the pack, and at home, where she belonged.

"Havana is not strong, and never will be. Hating her weakness, she convinced herself, if she drank from a Pureblood, she would absorb their power, and therefore gain their strength. Macelaine is a Pureblood from one of the strongest alphas of our time and Havana knows my history with her. I don't want to think about what will happen when Havana finds out."

"Macy has your blood, Garrick's blood, and you're in her head. If Havana is working with Elijah, she already knows. She will drain Macy and kill her, revenge sated," Kayne responded. He took a breath, realizing the importance of what he was about to say. If there was a chance Havana didn't know, there had to be a way to get Macy from them. "Can you decrease your hold on Macy, so she can shift?"

Daeland looked at Kayne, his eyes flickering between onyx and chocolate while his emotions turned them wild. "Never. Macelaine doesn't know what she is. If she started shifting into her wolf form, it might destroy her." Turning his attention back to the road, as if it might tell him something, he drove on. When he spoke again, his voice was low, his concern evident. "I fear she would lose her mind."

"I know how Macy feels about lycans, she's been witnessing their violence for years. If she shapeshifts, she might hate herself, but she would be alive, and would have time to accept who and what she is. Daeland, I've seen her fight, she's strong. Her father's spirit lives inside of her, and she has an unyielding will. If she had the ability to shift, she could save herself."

It was a gamble, and he didn't like it any better than Daeland. He didn't fear a Death Bloom, there wasn't a contagion corrupting her DNA. Unlike an infected werewolf, Purebloods didn't fight themselves, the mortal and wolf were one with the wolf spirit and shifted between their wolf form and Hunter Wolf forms with ease. Kayne, an alpha, couldn't match the strength and speed of a Pureblood.

"Can you?" Kayne asked, pushing for an answer.

"I can try to ease the influence. The shift isn't the only problem we're facing. If Macelaine does survive, her memories will flood her mind. She would relive the accident, her parents' deaths, and feel the void of their absence anew. She would remember you and the pack. All of it combined with shapeshifting might plummet her into insanity."

*Keeps getting better.* "At the warehouse, she recognized me, as I recognized her." *She looked at me with cinnamon eyes ringed in silver the same way she had before she died.* "She doesn't understand what's happening and is going crazy trying to figure it out." It was Kayne's turn to look at the road. "Macy has been hurt several times over the last few months and has been hospitalized. Her body is saturated with CD4-T, what happens if they try to infect her?"

"That is something I cannot answer," Daeland replied. "Depending on how they try, it might force the change. Or do nothing. You said her control was slipping with my condition. How much?"

"She's using her senses and her wolf's instincts," Kayne started, and slightly turned to face Daeland. "A half-shifted therian-lion was running down a hallway, toward Macy and three of her team, and she didn't shoot. She disobeyed a direct order. She claimed it was dying from a Death Bloom."

"Was it?" Daeland asked.

"Affirmative. But she didn't shoot it. It was charging her team. If Macy were mortal, she wouldn't know it was dying, she would have protected her team, followed orders, and shot it full of synthetic silver. She didn't need to shoot it because she *sensed* it was dying," Kayne clarified.

"If her wolf is coming forward it may have weakened the bond. I might not have to do anything. Combine her current state with high stress, high emotion, and she feels threatened. She will defend herself. She will shift."

More silence, weighted by worry and riddled with tension, moved between them, the truth they had to face adding more stress to the problem. Kayne let the silence stretch out, using the time to wrap his mind around what was happening.

"Have you ever wondered why the Council gave you the Moonlight Territory without the traditional challenge?" Daeland's smooth voice broke through the silence.

The question jerked him from his thoughts of what he was going to do when they arrived at Elijah's lab. And if he was going to act like an alpha or play the role of DOJ agent. If Macy's innocence remained in question, Kayne would have to arrest Elijah, not kill him. Why him? Had haunted him for twenty-three years. He failed to protect Garrick and his family and as punishment, they kicked him out of the Coterie, dismantled the group, and made him alpha of the pack. Forever reminded. Did Kayne need confirmation? Negative.

*Why the Council marked me a coward?* "I failed Garrick, denounced my lordship, and the Council needed an easy target," Kayne answered.

"A little dramatic, and no." Daeland gave Kayne a shielded gaze. "Macelaine lived. I had to have an alpha who would accept her when she returned. That someone needed to rule the pack and make the necessary sacrifices. I planned for the day Macelaine would return to Moonlight."

Kayne stared out the windshield, watching the scenery blur in the sudden realization Macy was alive and out of the past as Macelaine next in line to the alpha. It sent a spike driving through his heart, making his chest ache with sadness with the idea he would lose the Garrick pack. Macy wouldn't force him out. Daeland might. The Council might. Kayne wanted to keep his pack. He served them, faced challenges, and successfully protected his wolves through The Requiem. The pack was his.

"Macy is replacing me?" Kayne asked. His voice was low and a poor attempt at smothering his sudden anger while adding misery to the last forty-eight hours.

"No. She needs an alpha when she returns to Moonlight. Of course, it depends on your future with the DOJ." Daeland glanced at him, then back to the road.

Struck a nerve. "I'm here because of Elijah. He murdered Garrick, his family, and part of me blames him for my wife. When he's dead, and the ersatz are eradicated, I'm leaving the DOJ," Kayne answered. He told himself as much when he was at the warehouse with Macy. "That doesn't explain all of this."

"First of all, Elijah has what is mine. Second, Havana and Elijah don't know she's the first of her kind," Daeland answered.

"Purebloods come from every species," Kayne argued. "You said they've kidnapped others. How is she any different?"

"Vampires aren't capable of bringing shapeshifters through the Ascension because the vampire's blood acts as a contagion and tries to destroy the animal spirit. The animal fights back and the mortal loses their life. I shared my blood with her when she was seconds old ... it was a risk, but there was no other choice. When the accident nearly killed her, I gave her my blood. She has been blood bound to me. Never before has it happened."

Daeland didn't make her a theow, he made her his daughter. "She doesn't heal from her wounds and has the weaknesses of a mortal. If she has been drinking from you and is a Pureblood, shouldn't she be healing?" Kayne asked.

"In theory. Her wolf lies dormant, she doesn't have its strength, its power, and I haven't seen her in months. Plus, you said she has been given CD4-T. Maybe it's weakening her," Daeland replied as he touched the screen. It changed to a map and gave them a time of arrival.

*You left her in Desert Rock alone.* "You planned for her return. Why did you wait until Elijah found her?" Kayne asked. "This could have been avoided."

"As the years slipped by and she remained a secret, I saw no reason to change things. Then she started working in law enforcement, people knew her, it made taking her out of her life more problematic. I didn't want to explain to her what she was and exposing who she was when Macelaine Grayson was dead. The time had to be right for all concerned."

The vampire's demeanor changed, his shoulders tensed, his tone went from relaxed to cold, and he stared forward. Kayne couldn't use his werewolf senses on him. A vampire didn't have enough of a heartbeat to give a reaction to the truth or lies. It was as if they were just words and their meaning, the truth and the deception behind them stopped existing. But something wasn't right, Daeland, without a heartbeat, looked like he was in pain.

"What's wrong?" Kayne asked. "What's going on?"

"She is not well," he mumbled. "The bond remains. You will drive. I have to keep my strength."

Daeland halfheartedly checked the review mirror before pulling to the shoulder, his hand slipping from the steering wheel and slamming on the brakes it sent the SUV skidding on loose gravel. When they stopped, Kayne jumped out, went to the driver's side, and helped the vampire around the front of the vehicle and then inside. After racing back to the driver's side, he got in and sat behind the wheel.

"What are they doing to her?" he asked. Back on the road, he pushed the SUV to eighty then ninety, and pushing it further, he hit ninety-five. Wouldn't do him any good to crash. He might live through it, he knew Daeland would, but he would lose Macy.

"Macelaine is scared ... the bitterness travels the line between us as a current. I cannot stop it and I cannot help her," Daeland growled. His hands gripped his thighs, his fingers digging into his jeans.

"How strong is the bond?"

The headlights cut through the night, giving them the nothing surrounding him. The empty desert held the night and the black snake of roadway. The farther they drove the more he worried he wouldn't reach her in time. There was no way, if they found Elijah, backup would reach them in time. He checked the map to see they had thirty minutes.

"Faint. My bond with her is weak, I cannot influence her, and it leaves me with the strongest emotions," Daeland whispered. His head rolled to the left to see Kayne.

"She might be waking up. Knowing Macy, she will think about what has happened. The explosion, her job, and the betrayal of Captain Dixon. She knows she's alone and has lost everything she worked for." Kayne hoped he was right.

His thoughts went to Officer Murphy and making Macy look guilty, to guilty. Her name was on the paper trail to both warehouses, she was present at both warehouses, and the

Barrettes'. Between Officer Murphy and Captain Dixon, they set her up. They had been pushing her and waiting for her to fall apart.

"She didn't because she's a werewolf, a Pureblood, and somewhere deep down she knows," Kayne mumbled. Lost in his thoughts, he was talking out loud and trying to add everything up.

"I can hear you and read your thoughts, Kayne. They are as bright as a light shouting in the dark. How long has this been going on?" Daeland asked as he sat straighter.

"According to Macy, six to eight months." *When was the damn road going to end?* Kayne cursed the distance and pushed the SUV faster.

"If Elijah and his spies have been planning this and they have successfully made her look guilty, mortal law enforcement will hunt her down."

"They are. Only they're doing it in Desert Rock. Per protocol, the BPI, PD, and the DOJ will label her a fugitive, and her picture will be everywhere. Macy knows the severity of what they are doing to her and what they have taken from her."

"How many spies does Elijah have?"

"Unsure. They could be in every law enforcement agency. I'm positive Captain Dixon is one of them. I understand he was hurt in the blast, but if he thinks Elijah tried to kill him, he might turn on him. If he's smart and doesn't want Elijah to finish the job, he'll confess and demand protection." Kayne checked the map, his speed, and calculated how many miles a minute they were traveling.

"Macy didn't know what they were doing?" Daeland asked. As he struggled to keep his strength his English crumbled, letting his Italian accent weave through.

"I think she was trying to piece it together. When I questioned her, she was guarded, like she was protecting someone. Today, Macy visited her sergeant, he was wounded by a Hunter Wolf. Afterwards, she called me, saying she had evidence. I don't know who ordered her, or why, but she was investigating another detective." Kayne stopped, the interview going through his thoughts. She lied about her relationship with Officer Murphy. Damn. Did she get close to him to investigate him? "Affirmative," he answered himself. "I think she was investigating Officer Murphy. Because he was on a drug task force? Was the spy? Did he have connections to the warehouses?"

"You are rattling on. Do you know why Elijah chose Desert Rock?" Daeland asked, interrupting him.

"Negative. Both warehouses were in desolate locations, making it easy for him to store White Cell, hold his prisoners, and infect mortals. There was a maze of containers in Pennsky as well as empaths and victims. One of the victims was the owner of Golden State Shipping, which would have given Elijah access to any shipping method of his choice. They could have shipped White Cell, ersatz, or anything they wanted all over the world." Kayne looked at Daeland. "Anywhere in the world."

# CHAPTER TWENTY

Voices floated over her, their tones coming and going, then riding on the painful pulse reverberating against her skull slithered into her head. She was alive. Licking her dry lips, she tasted blood, from which wound she was unsure, then drool slipped from the corner of her mouth to slide down her chin to her neck. Macy swallowed thick saliva, like bitter oil, at the same time fumes clung to the inside of her mouth. What the hell did they give her? Where the hell was she? As quietly as possible, she tested her arms and legs. From the pain and stiffness in her muscles, and the warmth of metal on her skin, she understood they had been driving for a long time, and they handcuffed her.

With the voices gaining strength, consciousness traipsed through her mind, giving her fragments of the day. Each one attacking her like a bombardment of ammo in the guise of the spies, wounded detectives, agents, and techs that were working at the warehouse. Had they died? Had anyone survived? What was Kayne doing? Adding to Captain Dixon's list of charges against her. Had the BPI gone to her house and found she was missing? They made her a fugitive. She swallowed the tears begging to fall as desperation flooded her, and damn, she wished Elijah would tranq her again so she could ignore the pain, the situation, and the thoughts racing to the dark side. She was helpless to stop the torrent and knew, if she couldn't escape, she needed to make a decision. The pressure from her tears grew heavier as the end of her life teased her like a descending cloud to sit thick in her throat and on her mind. She wasn't going to let them infect her with the contagion, become a lycan, and spend eternity living like a monster. An ersatz. She would take her own life, or push them, forcing them to kill her.

*Death by shapeshifter.*

*A coward's choice.*

Macy sank into the seat, refusing to open her eyes to see her guards, the shapeshifters, and didn't have to when she sensed them. Their strength and essence marked them as lycans and were needles on her skin. The feeling darkened her thoughts. The vehicle jumped, her body slid to the rounded edge of the seat, the chains jingled, and her muscles contracted. She tried raising her hand to steady herself, but it stopped short, and she felt a tug at her waist, and groaned. They didn't handcuff her. She wore waist shackles. The cuffs at her wrists were connected to an eight-inch length of chain linking the chain around her waist. Macy moved her feet to feel metal digging into her ankles. Another length of chain ran from the one at her waist to her ankles where it split to the right and left cuffs. The restraints would leave her with just enough slack for her to walk, slowly, not run. Mocking her efforts to stay quiet, the rattling continued and alerted the car full of lycans she wasn't asleep anymore.

"She wakes. I probably shouldn't have given you the full cocktail, since you're recovering and all, but you did try to escape," Elijah said from the front passenger seat. "Couldn't take the risk."

Macy ignored him as her body dealt with wounds pulsing with her heartbeat, and the residual haze from the drugs fogging her thoughts. After swallowing hard and stopping the urge to empty her stomach, she could do nothing but rest against the lycan beside her. Through half closed eyes, she saw Elijah as a dark blur, while in front of him, darkness hung like a blanket, suffocating the sky. She couldn't see oncoming traffic, street signs, streetlights, billboards, or anything indicating their location. They could be anywhere. She had no idea how long they had been driving or in which direction. It confirmed her fear that no one was going to find her.

"Here we are." Elijah shifted in his seat to see her. "Home sweet home."

*Home?* Macy didn't have a response.

"I'm surprised you've been able to keep your secret from the mortals," Elijah began.

*I don't have a secret. Not anymore.* He droned on with his human voice tortured by his wolf, something about lying, and her eyes fluttered closed, her mind chugging along in its pitiful state beside her uneasy stomach. *I should have told Kayne everything. Is that my secret?* Guilt quickly replaced worry, and she sank deeper into the fathoms.

The engine and their conversation faded, the car slowed down, and easing over ruts in the road the vehicle lurched on. Drifting on the haze, Macy saw Kayne, expertly dressed and commanding authority. His appearance changed and he wasn't Agent Sinclair the lie detector for the DOJ, he was another man from another time. With dust shading the beads of sweat on his forehead, and his rich chocolate eyes wild as if he was on the verge of losing control, pieces of his ripped T-shirt clung to him. She didn't know where he had been or how he found her. With shaking, bleeding hands, as if he had been in a fight, he reached for her. Kneeling in the dirt, his jeans tore to expose skin, and loose strands of brown hair fell forward and caught in his eyelashes. *He found me once, he will again.*

"Macelaine," Kayne whispered. Like aged whiskey, his amber eyes blazed while he repeated her name, pleading for her to stay awake, his grief making his voice unrecognizable. Searching her face, he stopped when he saw the cut above her eye.

Was she seeing the past or the present? Maybe the future?

Kayne lifted her to cradle her in his arms, and Macy felt his uncontrolled rage wrap around her while a chill, like sorrow, rolled from him with its hardened edges. He was affecting her, making something inside of her change but it wasn't enough. What she needed was out of her reach, he was out of her reach. He couldn't save her from herself. He couldn't save her parents. The sorrow from their deaths drowned her, and she gave up the will to go on and felt her arms and legs go numb. It was over. Her weakened body molded to his hold. She met his amber gaze and watched layered knowledge replace the calculated DOJ agent. There was something else churning inside of him and making him crazy with emotions.

He loved her.

He was scared.

Kayne thought she was dying.

With her weak exhale, her chest caved in and pain stole her breath. When he said her name, she struggled to open her eyes to see him and met an onyx shroud that crept closer and threatened to take her from him. She couldn't breathe. She wanted to stay with him. Her heartbeat slowed, ending the drumming in her ears, and stopped.

*God, I am dying.*

*"Losing you."*

Macy jerked, sat straight up, and scooted as far as she could, chains singing, from the lycan beside her. She was losing her mind. Sitting back, her head felt like it split open, her shoulders burned, and her stomach rolled, but she was up and awake. She was not leaning on a lycan and sure as hell wasn't dreaming about Kayne. Agent Sinclair. Lowering her head to her hands, Macy rubbed her left eye and then gingerly touched the stitches over her right eye and felt dried blood. *I'm human.* Was she trying to convince herself?

Elijah laughed, a deep, rough rumble. "I should have warned you about the tranquilizer. Doc puts her mixes together with shifters in mind, not mortals, so it packs quite a punch. Wasn't sure how it was going to work on you." He talked like they were having a casual conversation between two friends. He gave her an arrogant grin. "Live and learn."

Macy held his stare through heavy lids as the SUV slowed and drove into a dark garage, cutting the stars from her view, and stopped. She wasn't escaping. It made her decision necessary. *Fuck you.* She wasn't going to live as an ersatz.

"I thought your wounds would have healed by now. You're weak like a mortal and I don't know what's causing it. I'll have to ask the doctor. It might be CD4-T," Elijah added absently. "They've given you enough."

Her wounds were healing. It had to be the drugs playing with her mind. Macy didn't understand him and the things he said confused her while his underlying tone sent ice shards across her skin.

"You don't have to say anything. Remember, I can sense, and taste, what you're feeling. Like your fear, and the little bite of anger you have coursing through your veins. Coming from you it tastes sweet, a bit like dessert." Elijah glared at her, then turned his attention to the lycan beside her. "Jake, take her to the lab. I want her in a tank. Do not let Havana touch her. Do you understand?" Elijah demanded. He opened his door—the interior light blinded Macy—got out of the SUV, and without waiting for an answer, slammed the door closed.

Obeying like an obedient dog, Jake opened his door, allowing light and heat to rush in and warm the cool air. The dry scent of creosote brush drifted to her, making her thankful she was still in the desert. Where else would she be? Feather River. Why? Because Elijah was from there. *Losing my mind.*

Opening her door, Elijah ordered, "Get out." His chest heaved with his inhale, as if there was a physical fight between rational and insanity.

*I'm in the clutches of a madman.* Macy waited for the heat to roll over her skin and her stomach to settle before attempting to move. When it didn't, she gave up and slowly scooted across the leather seat with the dull sounds of clinking chains following. With no one to stop him, his violence would continue. They believed she blew up the warehouse with everyone in it, and when they go to her house to bring her in for questioning, she won't be there. If they hadn't already searched her house. Macy looked guilty. Evading law enforcement and fleeing the scene of a crime, they'll say.

Agent Sinclair would be helping collect evidence against her, if he hadn't been in the explosion. Captain Dixon would put out an all-points bulletin, an APB, giving her description to every law enforcement agency in Southern California, maybe in the US, and the California Highway Patrol would add her to their AMBER alert system. Every citizen in the state would be looking for the rogue BPI detective guilty of aiding shapeshifters and killing law enforcement personal, and innocent humans. Her record would be tagged as a threat, DRPD, ERT, BPI, proceed with extreme caution. They'd prepare to take her down with extreme force.

The memory sticks she left on a side table in her living room, figuring she would plead her innocence and hand them over to Agent Sinclair were worthless. If they found her, *if,* and it was a big if, and if Macy lived through whatever Elijah had planned, they would execute her for the lives lost at the warehouse. And they would add David's to the list.

Elijah would go free.

The ersatz would continue.

She had to admit as sad as it was, execution sounded better than staying with Elijah. Macy sat at the edge of the seat, turned, and placed her bare feet on the railing, her jeans covering the cuffs. She gauged the distance to the ground and decided her height, brain haze, and sickness from the tranquilizer, plus the shackles, made hopping out impossible. She wasn't confident she would be able to stand, she was pretty sure she would crash into the concrete face first and break bones. No one had to tell her there was going to be pain coming her way. She'd be damned if she was going to start it herself.

*Not yet.*

"Do not let Havana touch her, do you understand?" Elijah repeated. His wolf's eyes gleamed despite being out of the interior light's reach.

"Affirmative, sir. If she insists?" Jake asked cautiously. He glanced at Macy, who remained seated, her feet on the edge, the light on her back, and back to Elijah.

Jake's muscled shoulders pulled the brown BDU top tight, the style reminding her of Dr. Locke's. His boots differed from the tactical type police officers wore, looking like military combat boots. His bald head gleamed with sweat from the heat, and under his right dark brown eye was a tattoo. It was Asian—a symbol or a letter, maybe, she wasn't sure—and the ink was a shade darker than his skin. You had to stare at him to notice it, and she bet few people stared at him. If they risked it, they didn't question him. It had her wondering why Jake, a lycan with his massive body of muscles, didn't like whoever Havana was. She faced Hunter Wolf forms, therians, and the Otherkin, knew their capabilities, and the threats, and had fought back and she was human. What did Havana do to scare a lycan?

"Put her in a tank. Lock the door. Turn the lights on," Elijah answered with sarcasm in his voice. "Think you can handle that? Now stop wasting time and take her inside."

*Lights.*

Jake faced her, his dark eyes narrowing. "Let's go," he demanded.

Macy swayed. "I can't."

To make her point, she raised her cuffed hands as far as they would go and shook them. Jake's narrowed gaze locked on her, his irritation evident when he grunted, and approached her. He walked with caution while checking the cuffs around her wrists, and when he reached her, he pushed her jeans up her legs and checked the cuffs at her ankles. What was Macy going to do, beat him up and make a run for it, in shackles? She couldn't stand, let alone run. She wasn't wearing shoes and didn't know where she was, other than in the middle of nowhere, with the desert surrounding her. His hesitation toward her had her thinking back to Elijah and what he said about her. There's no way Jake believed him.

Satisfied the locks were going to hold and she wasn't going to escape, he grudgingly grabbed her upper arms, and lifted her from the SUV. His fingers tightened on her, making a fire spread from her arms and ribs, and her body shuddered. After taking several steps from the SUV, he gently lowered her until she was on her feet. When he released his hold, her knees buckled, hit the concrete, and a cry escaped her lips. Suddenly Jake was there, stopping her from falling forward and held her off the ground. A wave of nausea rolled to her throat, its current sloshing in her stomach, and lightning blasted behind her eyes. Macy was helpless, defenseless, and dependent on the enemy for help.

"I don't understand," Jake griped. "Elijah is losing his mind."

*Makes two of us.* "I'm not who you think I am," Macy mumbled as sandpaper scratched her throat with the words.

"We'll see." His big hands wrapped around her arms, and he lifted her to her feet, and holding her, the warmth from his touch spread across her chilled skin. When she was half certain she could stand by herself, because she didn't want him touching her, Macy straightened and put space between them. He stared at her, seeming to study her, grunted, and stormed back to the SUV. With her feet shoulder width apart, for better balance, she took a step to watch Jake.

"Don't move," he ordered, his voice harsher with her than Elijah.

Macy closed her eyes, wished for escape, then opened them.

Jake pushed the door closed, leaving the sallow glare from the crescent moon the only light, its halo barely reaching into the hanger. When Macy's eyes adjusted to the dimness, she saw old plane parts sitting abandoned and covered in dust and spiderwebs. There were crates cluttered in the dark corners, giving the feeling the place hadn't been used in years. Abandoned. Same as Harper's and Pennsky warehouses.

"Hurry up," Jake ordered as he headed deeper into the hangar.

Macy trailed behind him her chains clinking with each small step and echoing in the emptiness as they skated across the concrete. She chose her steps carefully; she was barefoot, and didn't want to risk falling. After a dozen steps, she heard his boots before she saw him marching back for her and stopping, she waited. *Sorry I'm not walking fast enough toward my death.* Getting ready to be picked up and thrown over his shoulder like a bag of bones, she tensed. When he gently lifted her and cradled her to his body, intimately, his touch crawled over her and she wanted to be back on the ground. How low was she going to go? Macy didn't look at him, as she drew her arms in, attempting to create space between their bodies. He dismissed her efforts, walked to the only door, its old wood, peeling paint, and rusted hinges adding to the abandoned look. Jake set her on the ground, and when she held her balance, he stared down at her, considering her.

"I sense it," Jake admitted as he gave her his back. "Like everyone else, I doubted it. It's there. You're not natural."

"Does my humanity offend you?" Macy mumbled. *Like being on the right side of law enforcement.*

Jake ignored her, placed his palm on a square, and activating a white light it glided to the bottom then back to the top, and the cover slid open, revealing a keypad backlit by highlighter green. They had palm vein authentication and number code. High tech. His body blocked the illumination from glaring on her and she stood in the dark as she waited for him to enter the code. A secret code. He made no move to hide what he was doing, and for a second, she strained to see the keypad and numbers, and gave up. *Why? Won't matter when I'm on the inside.* Losing herself to the dread, she stared at the rickety door when it slid open with a whisper, revealing a dark hallway. The rundown appearance contrasted with the modern technology, giving the place a surreal feel.

He faced her, his thoughts in his dark eyes, then bent down and unceremoniously picked her up and carried her to another door, where he put her down, repeated the process, and resumed carrying her. Caged lights lined the hallway, their scant glow enough Jake could see clearly, while she struggled. When they reached another panel, he entered a code, and the door opened with a swish. The next keypad lit up dark violet, and reaching out, he entered a string of numbers, and the door slid open. Time was quickly dwindling. The final door would condemn her to no escape, and a *tank,* guarded by a light.

One Havana couldn't pass. What kind of paranormal was affected by light? Macy didn't want to know.

Jake set her on the floor, faced the keypad, and hesitated, his finger hovering over the numbers. With his height towering over her, he turned enough to meet her gaze and she saw pity. "Knowing who you are, you're right to fear this."

*What the hell?* Macy took a step backwards. "You don't know who I am."

"I do, Princess."

She watched the door open with the familiar swish, and a bank of stringent cleanser poured out. Macy's lungs burned as her thoughts raced with the knowledge they cleaned the tank. It was opposite of the warehouse where dirt, blood, bones, and remains littered the area. Elijah said it had been the Hunter Wolf forms' play area. Was Jake about to leave her in Elijah's playroom? It was a horrible thought, and one she tried to bury. The longer they stood there the stronger the scent of blood became. Old blood with a metallic edge, and no amount of chemicals were going to get rid of the stained air. Macy's mind tossed her back to the Barrettes', the heat, the stench of their imminent deaths, and took another step backward, the chains clinking on the concrete. The Barrettes' fate waited for her. She wished they would kill her like they had David.

"Ersatz," Macy whispered. *The madman is going to infect me, and I'll die half shifted and scarred by a Death Bloom.*

Fear and desperation sank with the violet light cast by the keyboard. Macy watched his long arm reach for her and backed up, tripping over the chains, and nearly falling. He gripped her arm, jerked her close to him, twisted around, and shoved her into the tank. Slipping on the smooth surface, she caught her balance despite the chains tangling around her ankles, and landed on her knees. The tank, like the corridor, was air-conditioned, almost cold, and as dark as the hallways had been. She shivered and fought the urge to rub the chill from her arms. If she could have. Denim brushed against the floor and the clinking of her restraints disappeared, evaporating into nothing as if the room absorbed the sounds. She searched aimlessly in the dark for Jake and saw nothing, heard nothing. Then she felt him brush her, and with her heart pounding in her chest, she turned her head back and forth, trying to guess where he had gone. A slight touch to her left shoulder had her twisting and her hair drifting with the breeze as he circled her.

"You can't see me?"

"No. Happy?"

"I can see you clearly," Jake growled, the deep rumble dying in the silent room.

*Stop playing with me.* "Is this what you do to your victims?" With her strength and patience spent, Macy lowered to sit on the back of her thighs. She didn't sway and nausea didn't push itself to her throat. She felt the difference and it sent a rush of nervous energy through her. The drugs were finally wearing off. Shitty timing. Around her, Jake moved soundlessly in the protection of the dark. She couldn't see him, didn't try, because she wasn't going to play the game. Macy sucked in a surprised yelp when his rough fingers gripped her upper arms, and kneeling in front of her, pulled her close. Tightening his grip, her ribs hurt, her heart raced from the pain, and the feel of his clothing against her chest made her cringe.

"Not my victims. I wanted to test you," Jake whispered, his lips at her ear. "He's obsessed with you and now they're saying Elijah is insane."

"He is insane," Macy whispered back. There were too many things happening—the tank, Jake's closeness, and Elijah was somewhere waiting. They kept saying things she didn't understand, making it difficult to guess.

Macy bowed her head when her side erupted in pain and her forehead rested on his chest. His hands slid down her arms to her hips, and for a breath they stayed like that. Her head on his chest, his hands on her hips, and she knew she was losing her mind.

"He thinks you hold secrets," he whispered. "Old secrets."

The air moved when he shoved her backward, the chains tugging on her wrists, waist, and ankles, forcing her to the floor. Helpless to stop him, she stared up at the ceiling.

"Don't move."

"I can't," Macy scoffed. He pinned her to the floor, making any chance of disobeying him impossible.

"I'm going to remove the restraints."

Relief was short lived. The cuffs were coming off and he was going to leave her there. Macy wouldn't escape. She would pay the price for crimes she hadn't committed, and if she made it out of the tank, she would have to know the codes to the doors and if that was possible, she would have to pass the palm vein scanner. Guaranteed failure. Macy felt him tighten the slack in the chains as he grazed his hand across her hips. The feel making her stomach roll, and her insides seize from the violation. There was the clinking of chains, the feel of his knuckles, as if he had the back of his hand digging into her stomach, and in one quick motion, his weight and hands were gone. The sickening swishing sound of the door closing followed the muted thud of the locking mechanisms and she was alone. It was still dark, she was still lying on the floor, and escape had eluded her.

After years of protecting herself against the contagion, fighting paranormals, and defying death, she wasn't going to live through this one. *I'm going to die in the tank, and I won't know why.* Macy's weak grasp on her panic splintered, and she opened her mouth to scream until her throat bled. A whimper left her lips, and she closed her mouth. Like the noises, the tank would steal it from her, and she would be admitting defeat. Elijah would have won. She inhaled and exhaled, trying to let go of her fear, and stared up into the dark.

A flash of dark purple blasted in the room, and squeezing her eyes closed, she turned her head from the brightness. As the bright bursts behind her eyes began to recede, she slowly opened them, to a dark violet light. The same as the keypad. No. Macy recognized what it was, lifted the hem of her tank top to see the material glowing, then back up at the ceiling where from several places the dark purple gleamed.

A black light lit up the tank. It wasn't a good thing. A black light never was.

Like denying her panic freedom, she couldn't stay lying down, looking defeated so she forced herself up. Once sitting, she gingerly dabbed the blood from the cut with her top, saw it had stopped bleeding, and checked the stitches. It hadn't been torn open. Now it was time to see what the tank was. The left and right sides were solid walls, made from the same soft material as the floor. It was continuous with no seams or corners, and everything including the floor, the walls, and the door was white, and glowed like her tank top. A shiver traced over her skin, and she wished she was back in the dark.

Under a black light, body fluids glowed. The crime scene techs used it when a paranormal thought they could cover up a crime. It was a convenient little gadget when they used it, not so much now. There were a few chemicals known to clean blood off a surface, clean it to where it didn't show up under a black light. They didn't seem to think the tank needed such cleaning. The smell of cleanser assured her she wasn't sitting in fresh fluids or infected blood, but the sight of the glowing marks told a different story. The door wore scratches, dents, and stains, while along its edge there were human handprints mixed with animal prints. Silent and deadly, the glow promised there was going to be pain, because that's what happened in the tank. Macy made a circle, and when she faced the front, she froze. A window in the shape of a square going from the top to the bottom took up the front of the tank. On the other side, sitting in the shadow of the dark violet glow, sat equipment and medical instruments.

A lab.

The lab where they created the Hunter Wolf forms. The ersatz. She wanted to ask why. Why had David started the betrayal and why had Captain Dixon finished it by putting her there? She didn't understand why he handed her over to the shapeshifters. The enemy. Macy approached the front, and leaving inches between her and the glass, sat against the right side wall. Drawing her knees to her chest, she leaned back and tried blocking out the distorted blue/white glow from fluid stains sitting on either side of her head. She wouldn't let fear take over. She rested her forehead on her knees, careful not to touch the cut, and closed her eyes. The weight of Captain Dixon's lies and betrayal slithered over her skin like a snake, poisoning her thoughts and feeding her fury. Elijah was going to make her an experiment.

Bastard.

If he infected her and she lived, she was going to return Captain Dixon's favor and kill him. She would listen to him beg for his life, and when he was crying, she would tear him to pieces. If he hadn't been in the warehouse. "I hope he burned," Macy mumbled, and the room ate the sound.

# CHAPTER TWENTY-ONE

The night sky sparkled with stars that stared down at them as a desert wind carrying sand peppered the SUV. Kayne eased the vehicle over deep ruts and chunks of broken asphalt and slowed when the tires sank in soft dirt. Every time the vehicle bounced, he knew Daeland had lost his mind, and they were heading to nowhere. The lack of confidence made him quiet, like Daeland's silence made him crazy.

"Do you feel her?" Kayne asked. He turned, missing a ditch, and gave Daeland a sideways glance.

"Her emotions are erratic. I can't pinpoint if she's scared, hurt, or if they have drugged her again," he answered. Drawing his fingers through his hair, he rubbed the back of his neck, and looked out the window.

"I learned Macy had worked for the ERT." Kayne quickly glanced over, making sure he was paying attention, and back to the road. "ERT is the Emergency Retraction Team. Their job is to eliminate the threat by any means necessary. The BPI recruited her and made her the sharpshooter for her team. I'm saying, she's trained, and if she's capable of defending herself, she will." *Please be all right.* Kayne's body was practically vibrating with the need to put an end to Elijah, the past haunting him, and to fulfill his role as guardian. *Redemption.*

"Her training will help. The struggle inside of her will be a weakness. Macelaine is fractured." Daeland sat straighter. "We're here."

*Fractured.* As a Pureblood, Macy didn't need to accept her wolf, but it had been dormant and the divide could cripple her. As her guardian and alpha, he could help her. Save her. Kayne slowed the SUV when a chain link fence glittered in the headlights. "What is this place?"

"A military base. It's been mothballed. Here there is plenty of space for labs, trucks, and they can come and go as they please, and it's in the middle of nowhere. I understand it resembles the warehouses," Daeland replied. Craning his neck, he looked up at the top of the fencing.

Razor wire topped the tall fence, a sign warned of electricity, and on the other side under the crescent moon was an endless desert. "We're going to have to cover a lot of ground. The area is too large for the two of us. We must make it over an electric fence, find where they're hiding her, then we have to get in, and get her out without being seen or heard. We won't make it."

"We won't be alone. This involves the Council, and they have sent a team from the Coterie. They'll be here in minutes. Meanwhile, send for your DOJ team. That gives us a couple of hours to take care of Elijah, Havana, and get Macelaine out of there." Daeland looked at his watch, checked his cell, and gazed out the windshield.

"The Coterie?" Kayne asked. The banned force of shapeshifters and paranormals was back and active.

"Elijah proved dismantling the Coterie was a poor decision, and, with this blatant act against us, we can't have him and these creations exposing the Veiled. More so, we can't have his actions creating resentment between those living in the open and the mortals. Someone must enforce Council law. Mortal law enforcement hasn't been enough," Daeland replied.

"The Coterie. Defying the Council. This risk isn't like you. It's been twenty years." *Years that felt like an eternity.* "You don't leave your house, you were heading to ground to disappear into obscurity for years, maybe decades. Why now?"

"It's forty-five days away from being twenty-four years. When Elijah murdered Garrick, he ended a powerful alpha, a loyal adherent to the Council, and destroyed a family. He took Macelaine's parents from her and would have sought her out if he knew she lived. I had to protect the last of the Grayson lineage," Daeland replied. "And to keep her safe the Coterie is a must."

Kayne wanted to believe Daeland cared about Garrick's lineage and Macy's life. He couldn't. The Coterie was reinstated, the Council was enforcing their powerbase, and Daeland no doubt had his secrets and plans. As Garrick's daughter, the last Grayson, and a Pureblood, what was Macy worth?

Daeland looked at Kayne, his eyes darkening. "When I have Macelaine, I am taking her to Amaranth."

"You can't. The BPI, DOJ, and the local PD want her for blowing up a warehouse. Remember, she's Detective Gray. She must go back to Desert Rock and prove her innocence. I need her testimony. I have to prove Captain Dixon and Officer Murphy were both working with Elijah," Kayne explained. "Then she can return to Feather River." *To the Moonlight pack.*

"Her identity will be in the open, leaving you helpless when the media begins destroying her. They will say she pretended to be mortal. They will think she betrayed the citizens of the city, and no one will believe the captain and the officer were criminals. Further, the Council will insist Doctor Locke protect her, and he will follow their order. Are you willing to put Macelaine in his charge?" Anticipating Kayne's flare of anger at the mention of the doctor, Daeland smothered his pleasure with arrogance.

"You ask a question you know the answer to, as a threat. I'm not taking the bait. This is bigger, dammit, she's a witness," Kayne argued as images of Dr. Locke and Macy teased his jealousy. Staring down at the cream leather with wood inlay steering wheel he squeezed, making it moan in his grasp. He wasn't jealous. There was no reason to be jealous.

Placing his scotch on the rail of the deck, he inhaled, trying to suppress his anxiety and the increasing tension in his shoulders. There was a storm coming. He had known it for months.

"The traitors built the case around her and dropped her in the middle of their plan. They were doing it to every detective and officer they wanted. They blackmailed them ... at least the ones they couldn't buy. You can easily prove she's innocent without her being forced to endure their questions." Daeland stopped and looked at Kayne. He sat in the passenger seat silent, as if his essence of life ceased to exist. "She can come home under the Council's recommendation. She's a Pureblood who carries my blood in her veins. Macelaine never belonged with the mortals."

Daeland's voice broke his concentration, and Kayne shook himself. "You left her with the mortals. This is because of you. You can't give her to the Council. She needs to clear her name, otherwise she won't have a chance for any kind of life. Macy is a detective and takes her job seriously, she'll turn herself in before she adds another lie. You know that. She won't lie to appease you. Or anyone."

"I am not discussing this with you, Lord Kayne, I am telling you," Daeland growled. As quickly as his anger struck out, it was gone. "Backup has arrived."

Kayne grabbed Daeland's sleeve before he opened the door. "We're dealing with Macy Gray, a detective in the Bureau of Paranormal Investigations. I told you she had been with the Emergency Retraction Team," he repeated, looking at Daeland's clear eyes. "When I said they take care of threats by any means necessary, I meant their job is to hunt and kill shapeshifters, paranormals, and she's the sharpshooter for her BPI team. She kills, and she has started using her werewolf senses and has no idea what it means. Macy isn't the child Macelaine. She's an adult, she doesn't know you, doesn't know you're a vampire, and she thinks I am part of the reason this is happening to her." *Tried to use her as bait.* "If Elijah and Havana harm her, she'll be on the defensive. You need to be careful."

"You talk about Macelaine as if she will kill anything in sight," Daeland accused.

"She caught Elijah's attention because she does." Whatever delusions Daeland had about her, Macy was a killer. There were second guesses, the memory of her protecting the new wolf, Agent Pixley, her sergeant. In the end, he wasn't going to give in, it was better to be safe than sorry. Macy knew how to kill.

The soldier stood by the door. He didn't interrupt them, didn't stare into the window with impatience, he remained silent as he waited. Kayne saw his face, knew he would wear a mask to hide his skin, and black on black fatigues. There were no insignias, patches, or animals depicting a shifter background, and there were no fangs identifying him as a vampire. He was a ghost. The Coterie didn't play by the mortals' rules.

"We're going in, and I'm taking back what is mine. I suggest you remember what he took from you and from the Garrick pack. Elijah escaped a death sentence. He serves that punishment tonight." With the last of his words, Daeland opened the door and left the SUV in a wind of warm air.

Kayne felt played. Daeland brought up Eryin's betrayal and the pack to manipulate him. The memories surfaced one after another, in a wave of old pain tasting sour from age. Elijah seduced Eryin to get close to Kayne, and in turn, learned about the security provided for Garrick and his family. He knew Eryin's betrayal wasn't his failure. His failure was not protecting Garrick and his family from Elijah and the rogues following him. Eryin played Kayne then, and Daeland was playing him now. Sadly, he wanted what Elijah had, and it gave Daeland power. Taking a deep breath, he shed the remains of the memories, opened the door, and got out. With or without Daeland's cooperation he was going to take Macy back to Desert Rock to testify and clear her name. When she was safely in Feather River, he was going to finish the job he started. Kayne was going to find the people responsible for the poisoned White Cell, all the spies within the BPI, and the PD, and he would make sure he destroyed every lab.

The night's wind gusted around him, blowing his hair into his face and making the chain-link fence rattle, while sand rode the air, grating across the hard-packed ground. Grains skated over his dress shoes, reminding Kayne he wasn't dressed for a mission. If he was going to take part in the Coterie's rescue-turned-revenge, he was going to need a change of clothing. Or not. The fear of shifting and the repercussions following were the furthest thing from his mind.

Daeland was in charge of the Coterie team, giving Kayne the freedom to fight any way he chose.

Kayne jerked the cell from the clip at his hip and hit the number for Chayton.

"Agent Logue," he growled.

"I need Blood Rain and White Rain at my location. Brief the teams there will be ersatz, number unconfirmed. Advise medical there will be victims, number unconfirmed. The place is an abandoned military base," Kayne ordered.

"Copy. Be advised the teams and BPI agents found files on six others, all part of the BPI and the DRPD. Captain Dixon targeted them for Elijah."

"Are they in custody?" Kayne asked.

"Affirmative."

"Where is Captain Dixon?"

"Hospitalized and under guard. He was injured in the explosion, and feeling betrayed, confessed to his part in Elijah's plot. Agent Sinclair, we found cases of White Cell being transported out of Desert Rock. This is bigger than Elijah, there is someone else involved," Chayton explained.

Kayne wished the captain would have burned with the evidence. If they didn't stop the ersatz, they were on the threshold of having the trust between shifters and mortals damaged beyond repair. The Requiem and twenty years of work gone because of greed. With the relationship between mortals and paranormals decaying, the mortals would turn to White Cell and there would be unstable ersatz on the loose and countless deaths. If the ersatz lived. The Death Bloom had become their savior.

"I understand. I need you here ASAP," Kayne stressed.

"Copy. There is something you should know about Detective Gray," Chayton said hesitantly, the anger in his voice fading.

"What?" He stared at Daeland, the group of vampires and shapeshifters, and watched them prepare.

"Wait a minute." Chayton's voice faded out as he spoke to someone else, authority holding his orders. "Captain Dixon explained Elijah believed Detective Gray is Macelaine Grayson, Alpha Garrick's daughter, and focused his attention on her. Because of his fixation on her, some of the mortals and paranormals he enlisted started cutting ties with him. Except Captain Dixon. He did not believe Elijah, but knowing how desperate Elijah was for Detective Gray, tried to blackmail him. Captain Dixon put a price on her head and was in possession of a file with newspaper clippings of anything relating to the car crash. It cannot be possible."

"Does the captain believe Detective Gray is Macelaine?"

"Negative."

Kayne took a deep breath, tasted dust and the warm night air, while the silver cast of the moon mocked him as he stood on the wrong side of the fence. "Who else knows about the file on Detective Gray?"

"Blood Rain," Chayton responded.

"Excellent. Make sure it stays that way. Elijah tried to kill him, his part in the crimes has been exposed, and now Captain Dixon is desperate and wants revenge. Has anyone heard from Commander Arden?" Kayne might have a chance if he could keep Macy's identity a secret.

"Negative."

"With everything going on and he's still missing. I don't like it. Have someone question Captain Dixon," Kayne ordered.

"Affirmative, sir. Kayne?"

"What?" Cinnamon eyes ringed with silver. She was real.

"You did not correct me when I said it was not possible. Detective Gray wears Lord Daeland's blood mark. Is she Macelaine Grayson?" Chayton's voice was nearly a whisper.

"Affirmative. Get the team here as fast as you can, and make sure you keep whatever files on Macy out of the hands of the BPI. She must appear mortal in the eyes of the law. I'm going in with the Coterie."

"Detective Gray is the Pureblood daughter of Garrick." The line went silent, save for the whispered words in Chayton's native tongue. "The Coterie. I wish you had taken me with you. I want to be there when Elijah dies. The crimes he has committed against the mortals and paranormals, and what he tried to do Detective Gray ... Macelaine," Chayton growled.

"I know. Understand, I couldn't risk you or Blood Rain if this didn't work out. There are vampires here, you need to use caution. Only brief the team when there are no mortals around."

"Affirmative, sir."

Kayne ended the call, his mind racing with what he learned. With Captain Dixon's confession/accusations against Elijah, he would be able to prove Macy's innocence. She was closer to going home. Only if he found her. They were wasting time. Frustration fed on his impatience, and turning, he needed to find Daeland. Instead, he faced the yellow glare of a werewolf holding a stack of gear.


"Your fear is like an open wound, freely bleeding, and draining you. I can taste it's sweetness despite the glass."

Macy jerked awake, the back of her head hitting the wall behind her. "Damn." She was beginning to hate her dreams. At least it wasn't Agent Sinclair. Rubbing her eyes, she kneaded her shoulders, sat back, and stared at her prison. *I'm not going to make it out of here. I'm losing my mind.* Looking at the cell, she lazily checked the door, the grisly handprints, and stains, and turning, leaned forward, straining to see through the lights and into the lab. Her anticipation was twisting with her fear and creating outcomes she didn't want to face.

"Look at me."

Macy's instincts raged as she scooted backwards, realizing the voice hadn't been a dream. The intense feeling of impertinence in the woman's words sent chills skating down her spine. Was this Havana?

"Elijah covets you if he put you under the protection of the UV lights."

"UV lights," Macy repeated. She shook her head, trying to loosen the hold the voice had on her. She didn't hear it as much as she felt it like a breeze against her thoughts. As if it was one of her own.

"They protect you, from me. You have my curiosity. Let me see Elijah's prize." Her accent threaded through her words, drawing them out.

"No," Macy mumbled. No way. From where she sat, the unlit lab was empty of people, except for the voice sliding on the air through the darkness and into the tank.

"A trade then. I'll let you see me if I can see you." Out of the shadows, a woman appeared at the edge of the black/violet halo while the soft shadows belonging to the equipment turned to distorted edges fraying around her thin frame.

Things, details, made people solid. Their shoes, hair, skin, and weight made them part of the world. The woman could have been wearing a skirt, pants, or a dress and Macy wouldn't have seen the outline. Fearing what she couldn't see, Macy scooted farther from the window, trying to get out from under the feel of the woman's gaze. She didn't move with tension riddling her muscles like a shapeshifter, she drifted closer. Empath. She must be an empath. Macy doubted her conclusion when the air carrying her acted like it feared her. *It's shock,* she told herself. *Drugs and injuries. Shock.* She was losing her mind.

"Girl, we made a deal. Now come closer, so I can see you. I promise, I can't pass the layers of glass between us. Elijah has made sure the windows are strong enough to withstand the strength of his creations." Each word clung to a curve as she spoke.

Creations. She had to get out of there. Macy watched a void of emotion hold the woman's face in its grip, and knew whatever the woman was, human or not, she was lying.

"Come."

Another whisper, and Macy's mind slipped, the image in front of her not matching the influence infecting her. No. Helpless to stop herself, she inched toward the window. The soft echo of warning beating through her muscles didn't stop her. The cuffs of her jeans scraped the floor with muted pulls of denim while the woman's urging continued to fog her thoughts. Macy stopped, knelt on her knees, and sat on her heels. She needed to remember the woman was there to harm her, kill her, infect her.

Emerald eyes blazed from the dark, stealing Macy's attempts to clear her mind. With a sliver of space separating her trembling fingertips from the glass, a deep voice broke through, breaking the trance. Her mind snapped. Seeking the familiar feel, she clung to it as it repeated the warnings, and its warmth invaded the chill. Without waiting, Macy quickly crawled, tripping over her arms and feet, backwards across the tank, only stopping when she crashed into the door.

"Vampire," the woman squealed. She tilted her head. "You have a master. Tell me his name." The tempting velvet voice shattered and sounded like breaking glass. "Tell me."

Macy scurried from the door to a corner where she smashed her body against the wall. Its coolness sank into her skin the same way the word vampire sank into her thoughts. It isn't true. *This is Elijah's way of torturing me.*

"Tell me your master's name," she ordered.

Macy battled the heavy demand as its claws dug into her mind. At the edge of light, she watched the woman pace, back and forth, the gleam in her eyes sliding in and out of the shadows. She couldn't answer. Didn't have an answer. A hiss slithered through her determination to stay sane, at the same time the air distorted and the woman was standing in front of the window. Her skin shining in the hue, her eyes narrowed and bled black, like coal from a pale face. Macy screamed a short blast of surprise when the woman's skin blackened and curled around the bones in her hand, and she vanished into the darkness.

UV lights. Fear. Vampires. Panic. Fucking panic. "Vampires aren't real," Macy tried convincing herself. "Are. Not. Real." *Like lycans and therians hadn't been real. The Otherkin. Shut up.*

Her hands went to her eyes when bright lights lit the lab, drowning out the dark purple inside of the tank. When the shock faded, Macy opened them to see the expanse. On her left, a set of metal double doors opened, letting guards and

Hunter Wolf forms enter the large room, while to the right, cabinets, chairs, refrigerators, freezers, and equipment she had never seen before lined the wall. Taking up the center were two L-shaped, stainless-steel islands, complete with their own sinks, shackles, and chains. Tables with knives, needles, and other devices sat under clear plastic. It made everything at Sanative look archaic in comparison.

People stood around and between the equipment, but the woman was gone. Maybe she had never been there. Like it was a comfort, Macy spotted the guard who locked her up standing beside another woman wearing a white lab coat. Was she the doc? She watched them talking, their lips moving, their arms animating their conversation when Doc pointed to the tank, at her. She couldn't hear what they were saying or the commotion in the lab. The tank was soundproof. Closing her eyes in disgust, she had to accept the woman had never been there, or the woman had been inside her head, raping her thoughts and deafening her ears with her demands. A new dread entered her world. No, vampires aren't real. The woman wasn't real.

"Vampires," Macy mumbled while watching the pantomime on the other side of the glass.

Movement from across the lab took her attention, and following the other's focus, she saw three dark tanks. How many are there? She couldn't see inside them and couldn't tell if there were more on her side. While the lab continued to come alive with people and their commotion, she tried keeping track of who was there, but her mind was busy trying to stay together and not crumble under the strain. She was having a difficult time sorting through the jumbled mess, then one by one the tanks lit up bright with glaring light, revealing its prisoners. Macy sucked in a breath.

Human aquariums.

Their torture was being watched.

Across from Macy a female huddled in the corner, her long, auburn hair, used as a shield, hid her face, tucked in knees, and her body. Mumbled curses left Macy's lips in a whisper and stalled when a male stood in tank two, hands at his sides, and staring over the lab met her gaze. A feather of familiarity drifted through her and she shut it down. She didn't know him, them. Her eyes left tank two, and moving on tank one held a naked male, from his open throat a veil of crimson stained his chest, his limp body rested against the wall, legs stretched out before him, arms loose at his sides, hands sagging on the floor. The crisp room buckled under red and white, turning it into a grotesque melting candy cane. Scarlet lines slid down the wall, her eyes followed the slow descent to his tanned side and the thickening pool beside his thigh. Macy stood and limped to the window as her instincts started taking over. Elijah was mocking her knowing she was a detective whose job it was to prevent exactly what was happening. She tracked the viscous scarlet creeping forward, and when it didn't stop, because it was warm and pumping from the wounds riddling his body, she tried convincing herself they hadn't murdered him. That he didn't die with her sitting across the room from him.

Tank two's heavy gaze continued to narrow on her, his eyes taking in her cuts, bruises, and the blood staining her tank top. It was clear to her, since she was standing and could see the tanks, he wanted to know what had happened to the others. Outcome for one may be the outcome for them all, and she, better than anyone, understood. Macy held his gaze while a thousand thoughts flooded her mind. She had to tell him about the dead man, warn him about the vampire, and wanted to know if there were others. With frustration building, she closed her eyes and saw the pictures lying on the table and Agent Sinclair's flawless fingers pointing at them and demanding she tell him what had happened to the missing.

*Hard to keep track of transients. The BPI doesn't investigate humans.*

Agent Sinclair needed to ask the DRPD about the missing persons, not her, not the BPI. He won't. He thinks she blew up the warehouse and skipped town. Because she was an arsonists, kidnapper, and murderer. Damn Captain Dixon and David, they could go to hell. She glanced back at the door, reminded there was no way out, back at tank two, when recognition struck her, and she was sure he had been one of the missing persons. With her attention on him, he turned his head in the direction of the female's tank. She answered by nodding and giving a small shrug. She had no idea if the woman was alive. He looked at the other tank and she shook her head, no. A simple gesture confirming the man's death. Tank one died alone in the dark while his cries for help were stolen by his fabricated prison.

*I wonder if he saw me while he was being torn apart.* Macy shut down the thoughts. If no one was going to find her, she had to do what she has done her entire life, she would save herself.

Locked behind Elijah's impenetrable glass, the tension in the lab was becoming palpable, and it was infecting the tanks. She couldn't help but stare at tank two across from her, deciding it was better than looking at the broken body in the middle of tank one's abusive crimson and offensive white. Tank two wore blue sweatpants, the waist clinging to the protruding bones of his pelvis. Without a shirt, his thin shoulders stuck out from his body, as if they were too big for him. He gave her one last look, and with slumped shoulders, turned away and hobbled to the back of the tank. Green, purple, and yellow marked his back between the dark brown of new scabs and bright red skin from fresh cuts. His blondish-brown hair stuck in clusters on the top and sides of his head.

It was their responsibility to protect them, the humans and paranormals, and the DRPD and the BPI let them down. Macy let him down. Elijah was responsible for the missing persons all along. They hadn't left town, moved on, or found a new place to live. She believed most of them were here, had been here, somewhere. They had been in the tanks. Then there was Henry and Grace. The Barrettes. Their fates sealed by a madman. The dead were the lucky ones. Except Henry. Macy's gaze blurred as she stared at the crimson stains of the tank. Sometimes death was an escape. *Stop. Think.*

Mr. Barrette's shipping company was an asset, whether Elijah wanted expedited paperwork with no questions, or clearance to ship the corrupted White Cell across the nation. Staring at the tanks, her mind seized on Elijah trying to use Golden State Shipping to transport his Hunter Wolf forms anywhere. Maybe Mr. Barrette had told the madman no. And Renewed Pharmaceuticals? Did they create the corrupted White Cell on purpose? In league with Elijah to infect his victims with the contagion.

"They don't find you. You find them. You kidnap them and infect them. You have a never-ending supply of disposable victims," Macy accused. She didn't care if he heard her or not.

Elijah casually approached the window, stopping when several feet separated them. "Maybe."

*He can hear me.* "You're insane. Your spies aren't good enough to cover the crimes. The BPI will find you. You will go to prison for the crimes you've committed." *Agent Sinclair will find you. Maybe. Hopefully.*

Elijah took a step. "You aren't a detective anymore, Macelaine. I don't fear the BPI. I'll prove to you I do what I want, when I want, and the extent of my control, and how this works. I'm going to give you demonstration. What do you say, one last hoorah for Detective Macy Gray?" Elijah waved his hand toward the tanks. "You'll choose one." He pulled a coin from his pocket and met her gaze. "Heads or tails?"

"Wh-What?" she stammered. What was he going to do?

"Easy. Heads. Tails. Choose one." He flipped the coin, once, twice, a third time. "Heads, she dies. Tails, he dies. Simple." Elijah's eyes flickered between russet and gold, and the corner of his mouth pulled in a half smile.

Macy met tank two's eyes and saw fear in their sunken depths. Tank three remained huddled in the corner, oblivious to what was going on. *Good for her.* "I'm not playing." She scrambled for something to distract him. "Why am I here?"

Elijah ignored her question. "They can hear you. When you choose, they'll know you're responsible for killing them. Like you failed to save the other from my crossbreed."

"I'm not playing your game," she repeated. *Please stop this.*

Elijah tossed the coin into the air, caught it, and turned it to the underside of his wrist, and covered it with his left hand. "Ready?"

"Stop this," Macy demanded. She looked at tank three to see the woman staring back. Damn. They were waiting to hear which one of them was going to die.

"Does this disturb you?" he taunted.

He knew the answer. Like all shapeshifters and their damn games, he wanted her submission. "You know it does. Are you happy?" Macy replied.

"No. Does it disturb you?" Elijah flipped the coin.

"Yes. God, yes. Stop this." She watched the coin as it flipped in the air, he caught it, and flipped it again.

"Good girl." Taking the coin, he held it in his large palm, then acted like he was going to shove it back in his pocket.

A wave of relief swept over Macy and her shoulders sank a sliver, but she wouldn't be caught off guard. She was look-ing at the tanks when he slammed something against the glass, and she stumbled backwards. Elijah pressed the coin to the window, showing the chosen side. "No."

"Heads it is," he growled.

"No!"

"Yes. The girl."

Helpless to do anything, she watched the woman scram-ble to one side of the tank then to the other, like a mouse on a wheel, only stopping when the door opened. She faced the Hunter Wolf form, her back smashed against the glass, and her cotton top shoved up, exposing her spine. From the entrance the Hunter Wolf form stalked toward its prey, stopped, stood in front of her, and roared.

"Stop this," Macy demanded.

"I can't. Won't. At this point her fear has taken his control and he's acting on instinct," Elijah explained. His eyes locked on the woman, his muscles corded under his shirt, like he was losing himself in the moment.

The lab watched. Elijah watched. She watched. Tank two watched Macy.

The Hunter Wolf form grabbed the woman by the throat, lifted her, and her pants slid down thin legs to pool on the floor. From her knees, yellow, black, and green snaked up her thighs to create a tight bud. Death Bloom. The Hunter Wolf form snarled, drew its clawed hand back, like he was going to punch her, then speared her chest. The entire lab heard breaking bones and tearing flesh as cotton sank in, more bones snapped, blood poured, and her high-pitched scream died. It jerked its hand back with the woman's dead heart in its palm and shoved the organ into its mouth. When it swallowed the lump, it held her by her arms, and chewing on her neck, her head dropped to the floor with a heavy thump. Blood splashed the window, the wall, the Hunter Wolf form, peppering the white with scarlet.

Bile soared to her throat at the same time Macy's knees buckled and she hit the floor. *Nothing I can do.* She swallowed, hard, not wanting Elijah to see her weakness but couldn't stop disgust from crawling over her. It chilled her skin as if it was a physical thing and she knew what she had watched. What she allowed to happen. She looked at the people in the lab and saw they had gone back to whatever they had been doing before the show. Macy sat on her butt, her mind replaying the scene and the sounds.

"Did you see the Death Bloom? Of course you did. I did her a favor." While the Hunter Wolf form continued devouring the woman, he faced her. "You asked why you're here."

Macy forced her eyes from the tank to Elijah's where they focused. "They'll find you." Her voice was a drained version of itself. "They'll find you."

"Not likely. This has taken years. I had to turn mortals into werewolves and therians. As you witnessed, not all of them survive, then I had to secure those with the assets I required. It's busy work. But I digress ... when the Doc has your Pureblood DNA, she'll add it to the accelerant, I've named Resurgence, and the newly infected will shift on their own. No moon. No alpha. They will be free. You, Macelaine, will have helped my cause and your father's soul will cry out in anguish."

Macy didn't know the details of a crossover, most clans keeping their traditions a secret, but understood what he was trying to do was wrong. Not wrong but an atrocity. "You can't manipulate me," she replied and stood. The tank sat higher than the floor of the lab, making her taller than Elijah. With the combination of purple and white lights, she noticed the thin silver lines sparkling in the glass. *Strong enough to keep Elijah's creations inside.* Syn sliver threaded throughout the window. "I'm not one of your mindless followers. I'm not one of those." Macy looked at lab and the people who were mindlessly obeying a madman. She gained strength in sounding like herself and not the helpless victim she envisioned.

A part of her, one of the fractured pieces bobbing inside of her, thought she should take the risk and ask why he kept calling her Macelaine, a Pureblood, and talking about her father. She would be damned if he thought he had gotten inside her head, so she stopped herself. And it was impossible to concentrate on one thing when there were threats coming from everywhere and she wasn't sure if she wanted out of the tank or if it was the safest place. Her thoughts raced and her eyes focused on the blood, the dead, the Hunter Wolf form, and it made her problems feel weak. She was a detective. Her entire life spent in law enforcement.

Sitting by and watching wasn't in her human DNA. If there was a chance to get the others out, then that's what she had to do.

Elijah watched her, lost in thought, as if he was seeing her for the first time, then masked his reaction and turning in a circle, gazed at his prisoners, his eyes lingering on the dead bodies. "You would be surprised at the number of people who want to be a shapeshifter. One day, you're a myth, a thing of lore, creating nightmares, and being the monster people threaten their children with. In an instant it changes and you're a hero with the power of immortality. I'm giving them what they want, for a price." His cheekbones lifted under his skin, tightening the flesh around his dark gold eyes and across his forehead.

Macy would make a deal with Satan for her gun. "Is that what you tell yourself?" she asked dryly as if she was bored. "You take their life from them. You experiment on them, turning them into some corrupted version of a Hunter Wolf form. Animals, things, murderers, and then cut them lose on innocents. You make them do your dirty work. Just like Captain Dixon and Officer Murphy."

"Captain Dixon didn't believe me. He doesn't believe in you. He saw you like one might see a vault full of money and did anything I asked, until he used you against me," Elijah responded. Losing his composure, his hands flexed, forming fists, loose, fist, loose. His body looked trapped inside of his clothes as he walked closer to the window. His humanoid features continued to slip while his lycan features sharpened. His hands grew while his shoulders pulled his shirt tight across his expanding chest.

With his advance, tension tightened her muscles as doubt cast a shadow over her actions. "He wasn't good enough, Captain Dixon, but you know that, don't you? I killed your Hunter Wolf forms, I mean a lot of them, by filling their bodies with syn silver and Captain Dixon didn't stop me." It was her turn to close in on the window. "You have a problem with your new and improved creations. The infected are dying from Death Blooms and the survivors are going insane, and when we find them, they die from syn silver. We can't confirm their identities because they don't shift back to their human forms. It's difficult to test DNA once it's been polluted by syn silver. And damn does it course through their veins. Their bodies turn to mush and we don't know who they are, and we can't tell their families they're dead. Part of me doesn't care, because if they trusted you, they deserve to die," Macy taunted, her voice rising.

The frustration over the kidnapped victims, the dead, and being held prisoner turned into fury, and engulfing her insides it sent heat up her neck and into her arms and legs. Was it possible Captain Dixon and David wanted to betray the entire Southern California BPI division and the DRPD? Not possible. They couldn't do it by themselves, they needed help. *Mostly because only one of them is alive*, she thought coldly. She stopped her line of thinking before they strayed to Agent Sinclair and his accusations took root. A flurry of unstoppable puzzle pieces flew at her. There had to be others in the police department, someone watching the jails, someone making sure no one entered information in the NCA, and maybe there was someone in Sanative.

She risked taking her eyes off Elijah to search the lab for her guard. He had been wearing the same kind of fatigues as Dr. Locke's employees. When she didn't find him, she looked back at Elijah and a breath caught in her lungs. The bones of his face swam under his skin, fluid, large and rounded, and turned his skin sallow. She watched, mesmerized, as more of his wolf pushed through the surface. He wasn't a natural lycan. No lycan had ever shifted that slowly, that purposely, it was impossible. Unless he was experimenting on himself. A warning went off telling her, she should stop pushing him. Anger was a weapon and if she used it carelessly, she would force him to infect her or feed her to a Hunter Wolf form. Being dog food would take the decision of death by shapeshifter out of her hands and whatever sick plan he had would be over.

"You're here because you're going to help them become like me." Elijah raised his hands, flexing them in front of her as curved brown and beige nails grew out of his humanoid fingertips. Holding her gaze, his calico hair sank into his skin, revealing thick veins pulsing against his skull.

Macy couldn't stop her heart from trying to escape her chest and her heartbeat from keeping time with his. With his change, her hair felt heavy on her head, the air in her lungs felt hot, and burned when she tried to exhale and gulp fresh air. It was panic, nothing more, and he was doing it to her. Like Kayne and Dr. Locke at the warehouse. Fighting for calm, she took a deep breath and saw for the first time his actions were going to work for her. Elijah presented her with a sick reality, and one she couldn't believe had taken her so long to understand. She didn't have to worry about her job, protocol, the BPI team doubting her, or the DRPD questioning her loyalty. There was no protocol. No Sergeant Mayco. No one. Macy was free of them. It gave her control over her actions and her hate.

With more rage than she could control, she went to her hands and knees, making their faces even, and crawled across the remaining distance. There was power building inside her and it felt good, its sweetness and promise of violence saturating every cell as she crept to the window. Elijah met her, a sliver separating his changing form from the glass. On her knees, she placed her palms flat against the window, felt the first quiver of energy sink into her palms and a numbness hit her fingers, reaching all the way to their tips where she was missing fingernails. Pushing the slight pain away, she was aware it was syn silver, and drowned it under the freedom to say and do whatever she wanted.

"You and your monsters sit at the bottom of the food chain." She laughed, and the tangle of anger and fear scared her. "You'll never be as good as mortals. You surround yourself with worthless beings to make yourself feel better. You're nothing but a bully who attacks the weak. You are a coward. You are a monster. Hell, your kind invented the word. The question is why? Why create more trash?"

Elijah's eyes blazed with his wolf and his canines lengthened, a growl running through each exhale, his chest heaved. "You righteous bitch. Mortals forced us into hiding, then forced us to live in the open. Dealing with them made us weak and turned us against our own. Our traditions are lost, and our packs have become meaningless. You and mortals have tossed our ways out, drowning them under weak terms so we don't give you nightmares and while you have tried to change us, you have destroyed our existence. Who is the monster?"

"You will always be the monster." Macy met his gaze. "Do you know what I do to monsters? Do you, Elijah? I kill them." It was harder than she expected to control her breathing. It was harder to concentrate when the stinging from the glass was racing to her elbows, traveling up to her shoulders, and inching toward her neck. "You kill innocent people."

"Innocent? In the name of the law, how many paranormal kills do you have, Detective Macy Gray?" Elijah snarled the question, making it hard to understand him. "Are you judge and jury for the paranormals?"

"Don't use me to justify yourself. It would be easy to ask you how many human kills you have throughout your pathetic life, but I don't care. You'll pay for them all," Macy countered. There was ice in each of her words, and when she heard her voice, she didn't recognize herself. Hate, freedom, whatever it was, was changing her. "Paranormal or human, it doesn't matter, you kidnap and murder *people*. That makes you the monster, it always will. You don't have the power to deny the beast living inside of you."

"How many of us have you killed?" Elijah snarled at her.

"Not. Enough." The words left her mouth with all the hate she could feed into them while images of David, the Barrettes, the dead man, and the woman sat in front of her.

"I find it hard to believe you don't care about the mortals I've killed or the mortals I've infected. Like the one behind me. I have gone through great lengths to corrupt your precious BPI so there will be many more. Do you care about that?"

Her hands clenched into fists. "I'm going to kill, and when I do, it's going to be you. That's what I care about." She felt a calm sweep over her. Her skin went from warm to hot. Sweat beaded on her forehead, neck, and arms, at her waist, under her hair, and her legs felt wet inside her jeans. Her clothes molded to her skin, feeling tight and restrictive. The aches, cuts, and bruises were forgotten under her desire to get out of the tank to kill him. For a second, she thought about her job. She did care about the innocent, right and wrong, and what it would mean to kill because of hate and anger. It was a natural reaction, a natural question coming from her conscience. If she did what she wanted and ended his life, Elijah would win, and she would be no better than him. Macy would become a monster, without his contagion.

"Can't control her? I thought you were stronger than a mortal. You have lost your touch, mighty wolf," the woman mocked. She checked the UV light, and took a step backwards. "Let me have her first."

"Havana, you'll not touch her," Elijah replied.

Macy recognized the voice and the lithe way the woman seemed to drift, as the person she heard earlier. It meant their interaction had been real. It meant vampires were real. Her eyes darted between the two and she told herself she needed to deal with one thing at a time. When Elijah's eyes gleamed with true hate, not the tired, surface hate provoked by moods, but cold and pulsing with threats, she knew which button to push.

"Mighty wolf?" Macy taunted. "I think not. If she can push you around, I know I can." When the vampire made eye contact with her, the thought she sealed her death flashed before her.

"Do you, Pureblood?" Elijah seethed. His deep growl thundered inside the tank and in her ears.

Havana's surprise creased her face for a split second then was gone, quickly replaced with squeals of laughter. Macy's own quick breaths joined the rapid beating of her heart and together they pulsed in her ears. Elijah gave Havana a death stare then stormed from the lab, his hair trailing behind him.

"He's going to get his prize." Havana's eyes lit up with humor as her laugh echoed.

Macy darted to the right side of the tank and put her back against the wall when a flash of tank three scampering like a mouse made her feel defenseless. *I'm as good as dead.* The foreign material mocked her retreat, her bare feet slipping on the seamless wall/floor, and with each passing second, her thoughts and fears betrayed her. Death by Hunter Wolf form. Maybe Elijah would kill her himself. Checking the lab, she hoped Havana had been playing with her, and her eyes went to the other tanks. Tank two was watching with anticipation, knowledge of what awaited, and regret. The people in the lab stopped what they were doing, their attention focused on her. They all stared at her like she was a foreign entity. An oddity at a sideshow. The walking dead. With the familiar swish, the door opened and Elijah's transforming body poured inside. His corded muscles stretched down his arms and she wondered what punishment she provoked.

"I know the damage your body can take. Unlike the mind, it heals, leaving no trace of torture behind. Something you should consider. When I'm done, how long do think it'll take for you to lose yourself?" Elijah growled.

"I am lost," Macy replied. "Always have been." *No loss there.*

Elijah ignored her and stalking closer, his power fed his wolf, allowing it to lick at her fear. Macy felt it as if he was touching her and recoiled. Like a phantom, his animal rose above the human side, pressing Elijah down somewhere in his dark depths. The instinct to run forced her to move and she skirted to the left, to the window, and watched as he matched her steps. The eyes of their audience pinpricked her back, and she knew she resembled tank three. He blocked her from crossing the tank, and Macy cut to the right, wanting to go around him, her fingertips grazing the soft material as her inhales burned her lungs. Air touched the nape of her neck before he hauled her backwards, taking her balance. With her hair fisted in his hand, she tripped over her feet, and struggled to stay upright. Elijah's laugh turned bark mocked her as he dragged her, her feet slipping on the floor, to the window. When he changed his grip, she finally gained her footing and felt his large hand holding the back of her head, his fingers around the side, the tips of his claws touching her face. One scratch and the contagion would be in her blood stream.

Elijah's laugh ended abruptly when gripping her tighter, he shoved her face against the glass. "Your lie is over. I'm not playing your game, Macelaine. Tell me it burns," he growled, pushing the length of his body against her and smashing hers against the window. "It's syn silver." His lips moved against her left ear. "How many times have you used it on a werewolf, like me?"

Macy whimpered, the burn traveling through her skin and into her bones where it attacked her nerves as if they were out in the open. Then it was gone, she was in the air, mere seconds ticked by when she landed on her back at Elijah's feet. The first stings from him ripping hair from her head crawled over her scalp, her back and ribs crunched, and his hideous laugh invaded her ears. Panic's energy spread through her, and reaching up, she frantically grabbed his thick wrist, her fingers barely circling the corded muscles. Black spots danced in front of her as she held onto him and tried stopping him from choking her. Elijah squeezed and her mind screamed in terror as the tendons in her neck contracted and she dug her nails into his skin. When his muscles bulged and thickened, she tore dried ribbons of flesh from his wrist. He was shapeshifting. Macy's grip weakened then slipped on his fluid muscles, flaking skin, and soft hair. She couldn't stop herself from gagging when bile shot to her mouth, forcing her to swallow before she choked.

Elijah's howl of laughter mocked her struggle and disgust. "It's a juxtaposition. The dying flesh of the mortal and the new growth of the animal." Lifting her from the floor by her neck, her arms and legs hung. Was he going to eat her heart? He drew her closer and growled, "Macelaine, it's time to free the wolf within."

He held her in front of him, shifted his weight to his front leg, and eased his hold. Macy quickly gasped for oxygen, sucking in the searing air and worked to get her footing. When she stood, she turned her hips, and using all her strength, kicked the muscle above his knee. Elijah didn't flinch. His hold constricted. Her grip on his wrist tightened. The pressure continued until she stopped breathing, and gray crept in from the edges. He was going to strangle her to death. Fighting to stay awake, she watched his inhales coming in impatient huffs as he raised his free hand. With her legs flagging and her vision blurring, she watched out of the corner of her eye as his closed fist cut through the air. Macy tried to raise her hand to block the hit as dark spots clouded her sight. The hit struck her in the side of the head, nausea poured in, her balance vanished, and she stumbled to the side. The tank faded in and out. On her hands and knees, her head hung, blood dripped from her, and she pushed off the floor as more blood slid down the side of her face, cheeks, to soak into her tank top and color the white in scarlet. She was a victim in a tank. Macy crawled to one side, and sitting with her back against the wall, rested her chin on her chest. Her vision blurred then was taken by shadows and she couldn't stay straight or upright.

*"I know how much punishment your body can take."*

Macy whimpered as warm blood cooled on her skin.

That's what he did in the tank. He isolated them, beat them, and broke their bodies. He broke their minds. Their wills. His deep laughter echoed in the soundless cell as if it was another weapon.

*This is the chamber of horrors and Elijah is its master.* It was Macy's last thought, too slow and too late. She lifted her hands in a feeble attempt to protect herself when he swept in for another strike. When his kick landed, she cried out, her head exploded with pain, and she flew across the tank, her breath escaping her. Landing in a limp pile on the floor, Macy blinked and the bright white world of the tank shutoff like a light.

# CHAPTER TWENTY-TWO

**After** bypassing the electric fence, Daeland ordered the soldiers into teams of three to search the grounds and the structures. With the combined speed of shapeshifters and vampires, they covered the area in a matter of minutes instead of the hours it would have taken mortals.

The advantage didn't calm Kayne's nerves when every building held an abundance of trash, old vehicle parts, and remnants of the military base. There wasn't any evidence of Macy or Elijah. The deception behind the condition of the base reminded him of Pennsky warehouse. If it was anything like the warehouse, he wasn't going to see ersatz, Elijah, or the lab until he was in the middle of an attack. Which added to his worry, like the four teams canvasing the base might trip an alarm alerting an army of ersatz of their presence and their location. What would Elijah do if he knew the Coterie was there? What would he do to Macy? The same wariness clawed at him every time he entered a hangar.

Kayne assumed Elijah's arrogance kept him in denial, and no doubt, he thought the explosion at the warehouse guaranteed no one would look for him. Why not? He had been manipulating mortal law enforcement for months. Did his arrogance have him believing the Council was ignorant of his actions? Maybe. If he had a spy in the Council, it would explain the lack of fear. He thought of Jaxyn. He would have to ask Daeland about the vampire, and the lead that had him investigating Pennsky. Elijah had easily manipulated Kayne and nearly killed him.

The spies could be anyone and be everywhere. Kayne looked at the werewolf, Steve, and couldn't stop the accusations from flaring. Not under Daeland's rule. Daeland wouldn't hesitate to kill a spy. A hangar came into view, and he let a growl of frustration rumble in his chest at the sight. The crescent moon's dull glow couldn't penetrate the inside, but it was enough he saw debris littering the ground. Without entering and wasting his time, because his patience were shot, he wasn't surprised to smell the same gritty sand, old dust, and rotting parts like the others. He started to leave when the wind changed and the faint odors of sweat, gas, and shapeshifters wafted out. Keeping his back to the wind, Kayne inhaled, exhaled, faced the hangar, and deepened his breathing to search for the heavier scents layering the air. Excitement coursed through him, and he dulled it before he got his hopes up. No one reported seeing anything resembling security cameras, alarms, or sensors, but the possibility remained at the back of his mind. He needed to be cautious and not take a chance by barging in and alerting Elijah to their presence.

The hangar's width accommodated anything from a helicopter, a small plane like a Cessna, or semi-trucks, and was as tall as it was long. The attached depot matched the hangar—large, weather beaten, and abandoned. Like Pennsky. Kayne stopped at the entrance, the toes of his boots over the concrete separating the outside from the inside, and saw tire tread impressions in the beige powder covering the floor. Following the tracks, he saw the outlines from boots, several men by the size, and another set from bare feet. His heart stopped in his chest. Scuff marks showed where Macy must have fallen; they chained her, the hem of her jeans dragging behind her restricted steps continued until they stopped. Boots came back, replaced her prints—he was carrying her—and with the next step the boot's impressions became sharper. Macy couldn't walk. Whether it was from being drugged, the chains, or they hurt her he didn't know. Fury caught him, his wolf howled, and he tasted the familiar silky iron of her blood on his tongue.

They hurt Macy.

Kayne held a growl in his chest, sidestepped to the building, and flattened against the outside wall. Steve and two vampires, both clad in black, and wearing hoods to cover their faces, watched him. He motioned the team to the hangar, then looked at Steve, who mirrored his actions and took his gun from its holster. He didn't know the vampires, or what they looked like, but didn't have to give a verbal order for them to wrap themselves in the shadows and do a search. Without worrying about discovery, they swept through night's embrace, creating a tinge of jealously in him. Werewolves didn't possess the ability to hide in the shadows and they didn't have the lithe agility of their movements. Werewolves were animals, brute strength, strong presence, and guided by primal instincts. Brutal and primeval.

While Kayne waited for the vampires to finish their search, he shifted his focus from Macy, his imagination making him insane, to the lack of security. Was it an invitation? Negative. Was Elijah delusional? Affirmative. With his back against the metal siding, he counted the passing seconds, and his attention went straight to Macy. Tired of waiting, he left the wall and stopped when the shadow rippled, and a vampire stepped out from the darkness. Lifting his mask, he revealed a slender face and narrowed green eyes.

"It's clear. One door. It's protected by a code and palm vein access control."

*Damn.* "Noted." Kayne stared out into the night, feeling time's weight as it let Macy slip through his fingers. "Is there another entrance anywhere?"

"Negative."

"I guess we're going to have to knock."

Kayne followed the tracks, Macy's soft impressions, the chain snaking with her, when the scent of her blood stopped him. Kneeling, he counted the drops and imagined the cut above her eye bleeding. "I'm coming for you," he promised as he stood.

In mid-step, Daeland gripped the back of Kayne's shoulders. "Pain. Suffering." The rest of his words were intangible, falling to the thickness of his Italian accent and growls.

"We found her. My team will breach the door. Take your team and position them along the perimeter. No one leaves here." Kayne's voice deepened with the need to get through to Daeland and break the throes of Macy's emotions. His hand slipped from Kayne's shoulder, and his fear that Elijah was pushing her was becoming a reality. What he was doing to force her to shift, Kayne didn't want to imagine. Elijah proved he would hurt her.

"Follow Lord Kayne's order," Daeland demanded, his voice raw.

*Total.*

In silence, Daeland's vampires vanished.

*Chaos.*

Kayne reminded himself, when backup arrived, he was there as an agent with the DOJ, searching for a BPI detective, suspected of blowing up a warehouse with law enforcement inside. Not an alpha of a pack, rescuing the Pureblood were-wolf child of a dead alpha, and following the demands of a vampire lord who was clearly losing control. And that said nothing of Elijah and the vampire assisting him in creating the ersatz.

*Total chaos.*

"You need to join your team," Kayne ordered.

"Macelaine is losing the battle." Daeland shook his head. "She'll relive the pain and emptiness of losing her parents. The void will push her too far. I will lose her," he whispered. Not waiting for Kayne to respond, he turned and slinked out of the hangar.

*Stay with me, Macy,* he thought as he faced the soldiers. "Let's do this."

Kayne fought at Macy's side, knew she was calculating, and after watching her with her team, he thought he knew who she was at her core. She wouldn't lose herself to Elijah, Havana, the threat of their torture, or the betrayal at the hands of the people she was sworn to protect. Macy was fighting Macelaine. The half living as a mortal and her wolf demanding she give into her true self. It wasn't a question of if she was going to turn, but when. When Macy did, she would have her wolf's strength to help her kill more efficiently. It would help her kill as a Pureblood.

Steve approached the door, making sure to leave space, and raised his gun. They weren't going to waste time decoding the pad and disabling the palm vein sensor, when shooting it would get the attention from inside and draw a guard or two outside. Getting ready, the vampires wrapped the shadows around them and disappeared into the dark. They were waiting for the go sign from him when deep, mumbled voices drifted into the hangar. Pointing to the stacks of crates, Kayne and Steve hid behind them. The door opened with a muted hush, letting a group of men march out, the static of charged air trailing behind them. Within seconds, its claws took hold of the hangar, telling Kayne someone was intensifying their power, infusing their wolf, and the pressure forced the weaker men to leave. Using his senses, Kayne analyzed the energy and recognized the corrupted signature as Elijah.

There was only one reason he was building his power and permeating the air with his wolf's essence ... he was trying to force Macy to shift. Kayne's wolf howled as he tracked the men while they walked farther into the hangar, their struggle to control their wolves failing. The backlash washed the area, its wave slamming into Kayne and Steve. As they held onto their control, the voices grew closer, the guard's mumblings nothing more than deep rumbles, their wolves close to taking over. Kayne stepped out from behind the crate, Steve following, and stopped in front of the group. You had to strain to see them, to notice the thick shadows as they left their perches to emerge from the dark and they took their positions behind the four unsuspecting werewolves.

"I need one for questioning," Kayne ordered.

A man wearing brown BDUs and combat boots stepped out from the group, a rough growl dressed up as a laugh echoed in the hangar. "You're trespassing."

Kayne didn't respond. He watched the others search the hangar, looking for his backup, maybe, or looking for their own backup. The leader was the one he needed to question, the others and their fate was in the hands of the vampires.

Pointing to the leader, he said, "I need him."

"Stay where you are. Travis, pull the alarm, get the lights on in here, and get backup," the leader ordered.

"Copy, sir."

Travis turned, two others nodded, and mirroring him faced the door. Kayne didn't have to wait long before Travis grunted, his head snapped to the right in an ugly pop, and blood splashed to the cement floor. The second man's growl turned scream ended with a mix of ripping flesh and breaking bones, while the third scrambled backward to stand beside the leader. After the vampires separated the men's heads from their bodies, they tossed them. The wanted effect, nearly making Kayne grin.

The standoff ended in a tangle of bodies when the man on the left darted in, rushed Steve, and bending low tackled him to the ground. The vampires left their victims, their shadowed bodies, like ghosts, racing to the fight. Kayne took his gun from its holster, pointed it at the leader, stopping him, and they watched the vampires fight to separate the two men. With roars and growls, the man continued his assault on Steve. The vampires grabbed his arms, jerked him backwards, at the same time they lifted him, as if he weighed nothing, and forced him to stand. Steve stood, by himself, brushed the sand and dirt from his black BDU pants, and returned to Kayne's side.

"Where's Elijah?" Kayne demanded.

"Who?" the leader asked. He wore a smirk, like there weren't two dead men behind him.

Kayne gave the vampires a slight nod, and whimpers bubbled from the man's parted lips, drool slid down his chin, dripped to his shoulder, and his head fell forward. "He isn't dead. But he will be if you don't answer my question."

The vampires stilled, and the weak whimpering ended. When Steve stepped to the side, Kayne froze as the tension-filled air warned them of Daeland's presence. No one saw him. No one saw the shadow until the leader's legs swung in the air and Daeland turned him and slammed him to the ground. Into the concrete floor.

"Where is Macelaine?" he demanded.

The leader made choking sounds as his response while Daeland held him for several seconds. "Tell me."

Kayne lightly grabbed Daeland's wrist. "We're done asking him."

In silence, Daeland let go and in a blur of motion left the leader. The man grabbed his throat, started coughing, and sucking air. "I'll kill him," Daeland threatened.

Kayne had no doubt. "Since you can't talk, you're going to unlock the door for us ... yes?"

He didn't try to respond, confirming Kayne's assumption—Daeland crushed his trachea. It would heal, in time, if he was given the time. He glared at Kayne as he got to his feet, and still holding his throat, he nodded to his partner.

"One move and he will join the others," Daeland warned, the words forced from thin lips while his entire being shook with his anger.

"Let's go," Kayne ordered. "How many guards? How many people are inside?"

The leader raised his right hand, showing all five fingers. *Five? More like five dozen.*

When they reached the door, he punched a series of numbers into a keypad, the palm vein sensor remained blank, and when Kayne thought he wasn't going to open the door, lights flooded the hangar. The keypad turned red for a split second, changed to blue/violet, and went blank.

Damn fool.

Daeland roared.

A shocked scream broke the silence, and they watched Daeland lift the second man off the ground, his face turning purple, and fighting for his life, his humanoid features caved under his wolf. Kayne knew Daeland's strength and wasn't surprised when the man's head separated from his body in a wet, flesh-tearing squeeze. Behind him the rustling of ripping fabric alerted Kayne to the leader's shapeshifting. Holstering his gun, Kayne grabbed the leader's throat, sinking his partially shifted claws into the soft flesh. The leader growled, failed to finish shifting, and when Kayne felt tendons tightening, he tugged. Pulling his half-shifted hand back, he opened a gaping wound with a gale of scarlet, and the leader dropped to the pool of his own blood. Kayne meet Daeland's onyx stare, and with the leader's throat in his hand, his fingers wrapped round its warmth and his heartbeat pounding let it drop to the ground. The Coterie executed their mission with ruthlessness, the evidence had been in his hand. Like the ERT and the BPI. Kayne thought about Macy as he wiped his hand on his pants.

"The keypad has been disabled. It was protected by UV light. If they have it here, it'll be everywhere," Kayne warned.

"Noted," Daeland replied.

"We need to get inside." Kayne nodded to Steve as he continued to wipe the sticky remnants from his hand.

The werewolf unholstered his gun and approached the door when it burst open, and an alarm blared inside the hangar. Kayne pulled his gun free of the holster at the same time Steve backed up, and ersatz, more than he could count, flooded the hanger.

"Engage," Daeland ordered. With rage alive in his eyes, he met Kayne's gaze. "Find Macelaine."

Adrenaline shot through Kayne, and his team of four skirted the rush and slipped inside, leaving a tangle of growls and roars behind them. They raced down the narrow hallway, prepared to battle ersatz and shapeshifters. Leading the way, Kayne felt like he had been running forever when the hall turned to the right, and he skidded to a stop, the men behind him crowding him. He stared at a split. Three doors lined the wall to the right, each with a keypad. To the left, three doors matching the right side, each with keypads. Kayne checked the right side, and before he reached the first door, there was another short hallway with a set of double doors at its end. Time was wasting. Kayne growled, looked at the doors, and wanted someone to tell him where to go.

"Where are you, Macy?" he whispered.

A scream came from the short hallway and double doors. His wolf howled with fury. It wasn't the answer he wanted.

"How can you call her wolf when you haven't infected her?" Havana asked. "Stop, you are driving the crossbreeds insane."

"I do as I please. I found her. She's mine." Elijah continued working the bindings while around him, the crossbreeds began pacing, their hulking bodies making shadows.

"You claim this mortal?" Havana asked as she watched the stalking crossbreeds. "Why?"

"None of your business," Elijah barked. He buckled the last binding to Macy's ankle and stepped back.

"We will see," Havana challenged.

The vampire edged the table, making sure not to draw attention to herself, and slinking to Macy's side, leaned in, only stopping when she was a breath from her cheek. Elijah had opened the gash above her eye, the stitches tearing from her skin, and it bled freely, down the side of her face and cheek. Her split lip oozed, staining her teeth and lips, while each weak inhale and exhale made her ribs grind against each other.

*Don't touch me,* Macy wanted to scream at the woman as she struggled to open her eye.

"No," Elijah growled. "I am warning you, Havana, do not touch her."

Macy's body felt heavy with pain, and wasn't responding, and her mind, struggling through the murkiness, didn't want to know what was happening. Elijah yelled, she flinched, his voice thundering over her. She wasn't in the tank anymore. Through the slit of her left eye, she saw the blurred ceiling, rafters, and lights, and turning her head saw the woman. Havana. The vampire. She tried scooting away from her, the restraints, at her wrists and ankles stopping her. They strapped her to one of the tables in the lab. She didn't have the strength to struggle, and her weak tugs confirmed her arms and legs were useless. Oh God. Fully conscious, Macy's insides shuddered when a cold breeze feathered her cheek; its chilled breath, carrying rot, touched her skin and floated to her broken nose. With a ragged pull of air, she held her breath, and turned her head to see Elijah.

"You've proved to be entertaining," Elijah taunted. "You have a captive audience." He grinned, like malice, and grabbed her face.

Macy squeezed her eye closed as Elijah held her hair, lifted her head off the steel table, and turned her to face another set of tanks. A man sat at the glass, staring, a line of blood running from his nose, ears, and his left eye. His crimson lips parted as if he might say something, then they closed.

*Dying is easier*, she wanted to tell him.

"Look at her. Does she look familiar?" Elijah asked.

With one eye, Macy looked from the man and strained to see the next tank.

"I'm going to make her look like you, then I'm going to kill her. Detective Gray's body will be found, and the investigation will end," Elijah explained. "You'll die a spy, a traitor, and a murderer. Your name will be a curse on their lips."

Macy's vision blurred. She closed her eye, and swallowed bile. Her life was over, and as if it couldn't get any worse, he was going to kill an innocent woman.

"What have you done?" Havana demanded, fury sharpening her voice.

Macy thought she sensed fear in Havana's words, but she was losing her mind, and trusting herself was impossible. She wished Elijah would let go of her. Her skin crawled when cold fingertips trailed up her arm to her shoulder, their light touch hooking her tank top and pulling it to the side. Her heart sank to her stomach, and Macy knew what Havana was going to see. Her mark. The tattoo branding her and leashing her to a forgotten past.

"Get away from her," Elijah repeated. He took a step and reached for Havana.

"What have you done?" Havana demanded as she backed away. "You'll pay for hurting her."

Elijah shoved Macy up, and her shoulders screamed with pain, the restraints cutting into her wrists. Doing her best to move with him she tried to ease the tension in her legs.

"It's nothing," Elijah assured. "You're scared of a tattoo?"

Elijah released his grip, she dropped to the table, and hitting the back of her head saw bursts of white light. The dreams. The tattoo. She was going to learn the truth. From a vampire.

"Nothing?" Havana questioned hotly. "It's an ancient crest, a signature of blood, of a powerful vampire and his brutality. There are only two people who wear that mark. Lord Daeland and his daughter. It ties them together."

*No. No.* Macy didn't want to believe Havana. *Vampires? No. No.*

"It means Daeland has fed her from his vein," she whispered.

"That forgotten relic doesn't know who she is. Nothing about him is powerful," Elijah argued.

They were talking about things that had nothing to do with her. She isn't Macelaine. Macy pulled on the restraints and failed when exhaustion and her weakened muscles stopped her. Giving up, she gave into being lost in thought, and her mind spun around the tattoo and its meaning. She screamed when pain ripped into her arm, and jerking, craned to see with her good eye. Blonde hair covered Havana's face as her mouth latched to the crook of Macy's right elbow. Cold lips rested on her warm flesh like bands of unforgiving metal as the vampire's needle teeth sank into her skin. As she fought harder to get her arm out from Havana's grip, she screamed and screamed. With a wet slurping sound flooding her ears, Macy lost control and let every ounce of worry, anger, frustration, and hate pour from her through her scream. When she couldn't breathe, she sucked air, and screamed again, her voice rough, tired, and raw. Macy turned her head, looked at the tank, and saw the man was standing and watching her, his eyes wide with fear and his pale face inches from the window.

*Help me.*

"Havana," Elijah thundered. The muscles in his shoulders bulged, his chest heaved, and red colored his cheeks.

The varying growls sounded distant, faint, as the threads of unconsciousness began weaving around her. Macy's breathing slowed, the lack of air crushing her chest. Her head lolled to the right, toward Havana, and she watched in horror as the vampire's head bobbed with each drag, her thin shoulders caving in as if her entire body drank from her vein. Elijah's shifting body stood over her, over them, his hands a mix of Hunter Wolf form claws and humanoid hands. He took a fistful of blonde hair, and jerking Havana backward, yanked her teeth from Macy's arm. Tears welled in her eyes, relief and fear battling for their place, and she sucked in another strained breath as the salty drops stung open cuts. Raw oxygen attacked the gaping wound at her elbow, and she knew she was in for another round of shock.

"I warned you, Havana," Elijah started. "You'll be punished."

Macy worked to see her arm, had to see the damage, and saw bright scarlet tangled in pink flesh. The bend of her elbow was missing. Gone. White bone blazed on either side of the joint. Tears streamed down her cheeks, her breaths coming in hard, short pulls. All of this and she was going to die on the table as a traitor. She jerked the restraints, her legs and arm protesting. The pain spread but she didn't stop, she jerked harder, desperate. Her mind raced as she stared at the mess of her ravaged arm, then at Elijah and Havana. He was holding the vampire off the ground while scarlet covered Havana's lips, teeth, mouth, cheeks, and crazy as it was, she looked fragile, small, and grotesque. Elijah let her go, their eyes met, and Havana spit a chunk of flesh to the ground.

"You are unhinged, untrustworthy, and a risk," Havana fumed, her accent twisting her insults. Her arms hung at her sides, her hands fisted, her defiance feeding Elijah's anger. "You lied to me. You lied to all of us."

"Shut up, Havana."

"You stupid mut. He blood marked her. You have Macelaine Grayson, Daeland's daughter."

"Daeland's daughter," he mimicked Havana's accent. "Macelaine Grayson is the late, great Alpha Garrick's daughter. I have his Pureblood. She has kept her secret from the mortals for years. The moon doesn't rule her, and she doesn't live with a pack because they don't know what she is. Do you know what that means? No rules, more power, and freedom. Her DNA will transform the crossbreeds." He laughed. "Kayne, her loyal guardian, the ignorant ass, couldn't tell who she was."

*Kayne.* Elijah knew Kayne. Macy closed her eyes and prayed for unconsciousness while unhindered tears streamed from the corners of her eyes. She begged for mercy, was quickly denied, and the darkness never reached her. The words Elijah said, Dr. Locke's questions. Macy's own instincts gave her information while around her the answers were a million times more painful than the damage riddling her body.

No. Her head lolled to one side as denial escaped her.

Her wounds would have killed a human.

She healed quicker than other people.

Sergeant Mayco's accusations drifted. Her mind raced with the scene at the Barrettes' house, the sound of her heartbeat in Macy's ears, and she had sensed Mrs. Barrette's death. The warehouse. The feeling of familiarity as she looked at Kayne; she knew him, knew his face. The image of him leaning over her, his soft voice trembling with worry, and his amber eyes holding his fear. The dream where she saw him. Macy shook her head with the memories of the warehouse.

"Not the warehouse," Macy mumbled through tears. The car crash. *He found me once, he will find me again.*

"You don't know the truth, you fool." Havana's strangled voice jerked Macy from her thoughts.

"And you do," Elijah shot back. It wasn't a question, and he wasn't waiting for an answer.

Havana took several steps back, putting distance between them. She narrowed her eyes on Macy, smoothed the front of her dress, with bloody hands leaving scarlet smear marks trailing down the front of white fabric. She hit Macy with an onyx glare, then shifted her gaze to Elijah. "You think Macelaine, Detective Gray, has kept being a werewolf a secret? Purebloods can't deny their wolves, she would have gone insane."

"If you're going to repeat old tales, shut up." Elijah monitored the lab, his crossbreeds, and turned his insane gaze back to Havana.

"She hasn't had to keep her secret because she doesn't know. Look at her. She isn't healing, she's bleeding to death," Havana pointed out, as if the obvious eluded Elijah. "I tasted Lord Daeland."

Warm rain on rusted tin wrapped around Macy like a haze, and she tasted a sweet liquid thick like honey and spiced like wine. She fought the memory, lost herself in the silky iron on her tongue, and licking her lips, felt the cut. *What am I?*

Elijah looked at her. Her swollen eye. Broken nose. Missing elbow and the blood dripping to the floor. "Go on."

"She doesn't heal. The moon doesn't rule her. She doesn't live with a pack. Her veins carry the blood of her vampire master. You didn't know about the intimate relationship between the Moonlight pack and Amaranth? Instead of plotting Garrick's death, you should have paid attention to his wife," Havana teased as she closed in on Macy. She cleared her throat and spit a thick chunk of meaty tissue to the floor where it landed with a slap. "From the moment she was born, she has been drinking from Daeland. His influence over her has stolen her ability to shift and drove her wolf into a dormant state. He stripped a Pureblood of her wolf. She's mortal. An unforgivable sin. And he calls me a menace."

"I can make her a crossbreed," Elijah countered. He stared at Macy, his confidence faltering.

"Hyenas are smarter than you. I said there was another inside of her head. Had I known it was Lord Daeland, I would have left you to your insanity," Havana seethed.

Elijah met Macy's gaze, his gold glare drilling into her. "A vampire can't steal a shapeshifter's animal. If it was possible, your kind would have crippled us."

"A vampire has never successfully turned a shapeshifter into a theow, I know because I tried, because the shapeshifter's animal spirit naturally rebels. The battle between the animal and the influence of the vampire causes the mortal's mind to suffer. But this isn't your typical vampire/werewolf relationship. Daeland saved her life with his blood, and when he did, he shared his essence, his death. Macelaine's wolf spirit accepted his death into itself where it has been blooming and growing stronger for decades. She is his blood slave. The greedy bastard took it further and made her his daughter. He lives inside of her head."

Havana touched Macy's lips. "They have touched, caressed the flesh of Lord Daeland, and drank his essence freely," she whispered absently, trailing her fingertips along Macy's swollen lip. "I will tell you how to break the bond, if you promise me another taste of her." Havana's eyes drifted over Macy's body as if she was deciding which part of her, she would sink her teeth into.

Elijah leaned closer, his mouth grazing the blood-smeared cheek of the vampire, and grabbed her by the hair. "Havana, you'll tell me, or I'll flood this room with UV light and turn you to ash."

"As Lord Daeland's blood slave she has never shifted. He has kept her wolf in trance, it's the key to breaking the nexus.

Unlike the infected, Purebloods don't accept their wolves, they are their wolves, and when she shifts into her wolf form, Daeland's control will be nothing more than a memory. She'll be the Pureblood you want. I want what's owed before Lord Daeland storms in here with the Coterie, Kayne, or god forbid the entire damn Council."

"You live in the past. The Coterie doesn't exist, and I have someone in your precious Council. Daeland doesn't know where I am, he's in the deep of the Affliction. As for Kayne, because of his guilt over Garrick, he has driven the Council crazy with his single-minded determination to find me. He left his pack for the DOJ and is currently in Desert Rock playing agent. He has important matters to take care of ... like dealing with an explosion, trying to save as many mortals as possible, and convincing the BPI and DOJ Macy is behind it all," Elijah boasted.

*It's true.* She wanted to sink into the table with defeat. There was no one to save her, and why would they? She killed people and was a spy. She was a vampire's blood slave.

"You might be able to manipulate the alpha, but you know nothing of vampires. If you have her, you have Lord Daeland. He sees her, feels her, and knows the punishment you have dealt her. He knows where she is," Havana warned, and turned her attention back to Macy. "She doesn't show any signs of being a Pureblood, it means their nexus is strong. I don't know why he worked so hard for her when Purebloods by nature are hard to control, and more trouble than they're worth. Really, I think I was doing them a favor when I drained them, all those years ago. The Council doesn't appreciate anything," Havana said flippantly. "Did you hear me? Elijah, what are you doing?"

"All she has to do is shift," he growled. Climbing on top of the table, Elijah positioned his body over Macy to straddle her. His weight crushing her and increasing the pain.

"You're not strong enough to call her wolf, and if you managed it, you cannot control her. She's a Pureblood. She has Alpha Garrick's strength and Lord Daeland's evil."

"I'm not a lycan," Macy protested. "Or a vampire's slave."

"You are both, child," Havana mused.

"Hear me, Macelaine, daughter of Garrick," Elijah growled as he loomed over her, his eyes blazing with insanity.

He smiled, exposing lengthening canines, his hands turning into claws, and reaching for her he held her by the neck. Macy wanted to scream. She longed to escape ... not the lab, but the tragedy her life was becoming. Hot, sour bile sat in her mouth, and she tasted its weakness wrapped in sweet iron of blood. When the BPI team, the people she swore to serve and protect, found out what she was, they would kill her. A wet, guttural moan left her lips, its sound a gross imitation of a laugh. She was becoming the exact thing she hated. Her entire life had been a lie. Everything she knew, everything she trusted was burning to ashes.

"Your wolf rises from your mortal depths to obey. Give me your wolf," Elijah demanded through a growl.

Macy's muscles constricted, the tendons threatening to detach from her bones, and her skin heated in a rush. The wounds and hard pain damaging her body faded, and turning warm, spread out to her arms, down her legs, as her heartbeat pulsed in her ears. "No," Macy begged through clenched teeth. "No."

"Yes, Macelaine, free your wolf." Elijah squeezed her body between his knees and thighs, his corded muscles bulging through his jeans.

Macy stared up at him, watching his theatrics with sweat beading on her forehead and her lungs squeezing around her quick inhales. With each second, parts of her thoughts splintered, she fought her body, her past, and struggled to hold onto herself. Macy Gray. Her mind weakened under the strain when shadowed figures stalked from the edges of her vision, pushing through her memories to sit in front of her. Kayne, the ends of his hair sitting on his shoulders, stood beside her father and looked down at her. Her dad gave her a gentle smile, and holding her gaze, his eyes bled to liquid silver. When she met Kayne's amber stare, he gauged her. He knew who she was, why he needed to guard her, and the danger surrounding her. *Pureblood.*

The memory swept her up in its current of emotion and abandoned her in the car. No. She didn't want to relive the nightmare.

"Macelaine, look at me," Sabine urged as she leaned over the seat, and reaching for her, began talking.

Her voice carried her fear and panic, and Macy felt its intensity like she was there. Needing sound to infuse her mom's words, Macy wanted it to destroy the haunting silence that had plagued her all these years. "Tell me. Tell me." As if she could see Macy, her eyes darkened and new pain started in Macy's stomach, spread out and burned in her veins. She knew if she didn't hear her mom's message right then it would be lost. Macy struggled as her body continued to shift, making her skin feel alien. Her jeans tightened on her thighs, and her bra dug into her sides. Elijah was going to turn her against her will. "Help me," she pleaded and closed her eyes.

The world transformed and went silent.

The scene came to life when her mom grabbed her hands, the hands of a child, and squeezed. Gunshots rang out, a window shattered, the car jerked to the left, swerved to the right, and another gunshot blasted. After gaining control, her dad faced her mom.

"Hurry. It needs to be done," he ordered.

Someone was trying to kill them. Meeting her dad's heavy gaze in the rearview mirror, she begged, "Dad. Mom. Don't leave. Don't leave me."

In the rearview mirror her dad stared at her, his daughter, and with grief in his eyes he held her. Then, as if loss overwhelmed him and he might change his mind, he tore his gaze from her and to the mountain closing in on them.

"Do it."

Sabine nodded and turned her attention to Macy. "You are Macelaine Grayson, Pureblood daughter of Garrick Grayson, alpha to the Moonlight pack. You belong to the Moonlight Valley and the wolves who thrive in the mountains. Keep our love alive by keeping your wolf in your heart." Her mom touched her dad as her hand clamped around Macy's wrist.

"Don't leave me," she begged through the fiery pain burning between them. Her mom slipped into a daze and began reciting a spell with words she didn't understand, and when her mom was finished, she broke the trance and sank in her seat.

"Daeland keeps your essence alive. Daughter, you need Kayne. He is your shield," she whispered.

Power coursed through her, its heat saturating her body as it traveled into her hands, up her arms, and into her chest. Another gunshot sent the car ricocheting off the mountain side. Her mom's eyes widened as it slid sideways, tossing her against the passenger door, and her head crashed into the window, breaking the glass. Macy stared at the scarlet sliding down the remaining shards of window as time seemed to slow down.

Meeting his gaze, she cried, "Dad, don't leave me. Stay with me."

"I love you, my daughter," his rough voice thundered in the car. Knowing it was the last time they would look at each other, her dad's eyes rolled liquid silver. "I love you."

"Dad."

He roared, and Macy's heart broke.

In the past she felt loss, but it had been distant, cold, as if it had detached itself from her. With new energy grief and pain slammed into her, flayed her heart, and she held her breath as her heart ached from the emptiness carving a hollow cavern inside of her. Macy couldn't let it consume her. If she lost control, she would lose herself. Fragments of her past toyed with her as they revealed themselves and she couldn't deny the truth any longer. *I'm losing you.* Kayne failed to protect her and her family, and he watched her die and thought she was buried and gone. Until the tattoo. Kayne recognized her by Daeland's blood mark.

"I'm a lycan. Pureblood." Macy squeezed her eyes shut, making them hurt and forcing hot tears down the sides of her face. Doubt and denial crumbled under the pressure of her wolf.

"You are an arrogant bastard. You can't force her wolf. She's the daughter of an alpha. An alpha you couldn't kill," Havana protested. Standing beside Macy, she glared at Elijah.

"I killed him," Elijah grated through clenched teeth.

"Not in a challenge. Not in his territory. You murdered him in cold blood. Your greed will cost you. You lost everything before and will lose it again," Havana warned as she took several steps backwards and whispered curses.

Macy rolled her head, saw Elijah, the person responsible for her parents' deaths, and wanted to kill him. Restrained and wounded, she could do nothing but wish she was free. Behind him, Havana hovered, her attention flicking to the door, the tanks, and over Macy. Her eyes bled black, her lips pulled back, revealing fangs, and the feel of their points in Macy's arm made her skin crawl.

"*Surma edasimuuja*," Havana whispered. She tugged on Elijah's shirt sleeve, and hissed, "You brought the death dealer here. I warned you, and now you will pay."

"I'm convinced you have dirt in your skull from being in ground. Garrick is dead, his spirit is gone, and there's nothing he can do. The Moonlight pack is weak and falling apart because Kayne is drowning in guilt. That gives me the advantage," Elijah growled and jerked his arm from Havana's grasp.

Rage swept over Havana, sharpening her cheekbones, and a thick nail extended from her finger when she pointed at Macy, her eyes wide, and yelled, "How do you think she survived a crash that killed her parents? Lord Daeland." Havana's head jerked. "She has the ultimate savior, and he's here for his daughter."

With her warning, an alarm blared, overwhelming the lab with its sharp ringing and covered the chatter of the others. The sound caused Havana and Elijah to pause. Relief flooded Macy knowing someone was going to find her and she wasn't going to die a traitor. Delusion told her she would be able to clear her name. Her heart sank when she remembered the truth. They would find out she was a lycan and hang her anyway. *I need Kayne.* Macy coughed, a mist of blood stained her lips, her chest tightened, and ached. Kidnapped. Beat. Feed on. Macy learned her life was a lie. How do you come back from that? You don't. You fall into the deep end of your mind and that's where you stay.

Broken.

Havana yelled over the alarm, "I've been in ground before and will not go again. You face him alone."

One minute she was there, seething at Elijah, staring at Macy, and the next Havana was gone. The alarm turned off, silence flooded the lab and sat thick, as red lights started flashing. People took their positions while Hunter Wolf forms raced around equipment, and the doors burst open.

Elijah squeezed her throat, his nails digging into her skin, and he leaned down. "I'll be back, Pureblood. We aren't finished." He let go of her, hoped off the table, and barked, "Guard the damn doors. Don't let anyone in."

Macy remained restrained and defenseless, as roars echoed with the fight, equipment fell and crashed to the tiled floor, pieces littering the lab. Above her, the combination of red and white lights flicked off and on, adding to the chaos. Was she going to die on the table while they fought around her? No. He found her once, he would find her again.

False hope. Macy needed to save herself. Determined to fight, she sat up as far she could, her right arm dead on the stainless-steel top, and she searched for Elijah. Catching sight of him, he disappeared into the thick of Hunter Wolves. He was gone. Without him watching her, Macy pulled the restraints at her ankles, and her left wrist. They didn't budge. She was too weak to get the bindings to move. Pain flowed inside her, and like knives driving into her wounds, it searched for her nerves and cut them to shreds. Macy collapsed in defeat. She didn't know how much longer Elijah would leave her there before coming back to continue his torture.

With tears falling, her helplessness ate whatever determination she mustered, causing Macy to doubt if she was going to live. She couldn't take any more pain and faced the edge of giving up and letting go of her strength. A quiet suffocated the noises of the lab, her thoughts, and she waited for her body to give into the injuries, blood loss, and shock. The noiseless calm lasted seconds when a feather of awareness crept up her neck, the soft vibration humming in her mind. The familiar feel of his wolf reached out, its threads searching for her, and wanting to find her it flooded her with hope. Kayne was there. Like he had been after the car crash. And at the warehouse when he stared down on her. The intensity of his touch, the heat in his amber eyes, and the feel of his presence proved his need to protect her.

Her guardian, her shield hadn't given up on her. Kayne was coming for her.

# CHAPTER TWENTY-THREE

An alarm wailed, alerting Elijah of their presence while above Kayne LED lights glared against metal walls. He raced down the hall toward the set of double doors and prayed he was heading in the right direction and Elijah hadn't run with Macy. His senses targeted a splinter of an essence, and pushing his power, a hum inched into his mind, into his wolf, telling him she was there. Macy. An excited rush swept through him, and stopping at the doors he gripped the handle and pulled. Denied. It was locked.

"Stand back," Kayne ordered.

Steve and the team of vampires took their positions behind him, guns ready for whatever was on the other side. Kayne's hand thickened, his fingers elongating, and holding the handle in his clawed hand, he used his wolf's strength to heave the door. It easily flung open, and letting go, it flew into the wall where it stayed. A wall of ersatz met them, their heaving bodies stalking forward. Without waiting, Kayne rushed into the brightly lit room, dodging swinging arms, as his backup spread out. After the warehouse and knowing they were dealing with ersatz, he wasn't going to fight them. It was an absolute waste of time. Kayne raised his gun and fired two rounds of syn silver into the head of a charging ersatz

"Don't fight them, their contagion is poisonous. Shoot them in the head," Kayne ordered. He met zero resistance; the power of working with others like himself gave him strength. No questions. No mercy.

Steve didn't hesitate, and mirroring Kayne, fired two shots, and the second ersatz, missing part of its skull, fell to the ground. The vampires concentrated on people in their humanoid forms, plowing through them as the lab erupted in gunfire, and more ersatz fell.

"Get Elijah, we'll take care of the Hunter Wolves," Steve shouted over the noise. He fired and another body fell in a crumpled mess.

With the soldiers efficiently dispatching the attacking ersatz, Kayne didn't need to reply. He rushed through a group of paranormals—some in humanoid form and others in animal form—toward the center of the lab where he skirted fallen equipment, and the thickest part of the commotion. When the way cleared, he saw his target. Elijah. He was kneeling on a table with someone pinned beneath his legs, under him, and in his grasp was a bloody bag of bones. Steel bands wrapped around Kayne's chest, squeezing and mocking his attempt to save her, as the sound her heart stopping echoed in his ears. No. He failed the first time and would not fail the second.

"Get away from her," Kayne demanded. Power emanated from Elijah, causing him to conceal his fury as he slowly approached the table.

Looking up as if dazed, Elijah straightened, raised his hands, and slowly turned to face Kayne. His wild eyes stared, blood covered his lips, cheeks, and his smile revealed crimson-stained canines. Macy's body went limp as the truth of Daeland's worry sat in her bleeding cuts, bruised face, and swollen eye. Crimson smears colored the skin around her mouth down to her neck, and to her arm where a ravaged vampire bite bled freely. Her white tank top was a medley of scarlet, pink, and crimson, and there were dark stains on her jeans. If she didn't get help, she was going to bleed out as he watched. He wanted to tell her to shift and save herself.

"The guard dog has taken up the quest to save the Pureblood, a second time. You fool, your attempt at redemption is weak and pathetic." Elijah slurred his words, his voice low and carried a growl. "It's no wonder the Garrick pack is crumbling."

"I don't need redemption," Kayne lied. Looking at Macy's unmoving body fed his fury at the same time it revived the emotions of his past. He didn't need redemption. He ached for it. While he needed deliverance from his past sins, there was something more ... it went deeper, and calling him, made him crazy. It teased a coming storm that haunted him and amped his anxiety.

"You never were a good liar," Elijah remarked halfheartedly. With one long nail he pierced Macy's cheek—she didn't react—and using it like a hook turned her head to the side. Elijah gave Kayne full view of her face, and he watched blood seep from between her swollen lips. "She isn't going anywhere," he assured as he jumped from the table to stand in front of Kayne. "I have her. I've uttered the magic words, shared her blood, and broken the bond she has with Daeland. She's mine. There's nothing you or that relic can do to stop me." Behind Elijah, two ersatz approached Macy, and half turning to keep his eyes on Kayne, ordered, "Take her to the compound."

Kayne took a step forward, panic pushing him, as one of them lifted her unconscious form from the table. The only indication she was alive was the soft cry she made as it shifted her in its arms. "Stay where you are."

"You're the one who needs to stay where you are. They'll kill her, and you know they will. They live for it," Elijah warned.

"Macy," Kayne mumbled, letting her name caress his lips. He stopped walking, his stare focusing on her arm and hand as fresh blood surfaced, the crimson drops landing in the pool on the floor. His heartbeat spiked when she moaned, tried to turn her head to see him, failed, and went limp. "I will kill you."

"There's the challenge I was expecting from you," Elijah growled. He checked on the retreating ersatz, and when they were safely out of Kayne's reach, Elijah met his gaze.

"I'm not the one you have to worry about. The Coterie is here, Daeland is here, and there is no one to save you from your punishment." Kayne readied to fight Elijah and get to Macy before he lost her.

"Daeland is just as weak as you are. Only he doesn't hold onto the past the way you have. Which makes me think you can't let the thing with Eryin die, can you? See what I did there. Eryin is dead. That's right, by your hand," Elijah taunted.

"What do you care?" Kayne countered.

"You killed her in order to protect a Pureblood." Elijah's rage swallowed his eyes, and there was marked tension in his shoulders. "Your wife. One of your own. You turned your back on the pack."

"She died a traitor," Kayne replied calmly.

"Strong words. You're too late, again, just as you were when I killed Garrick." Elijah looked behind him. "I have labs and crossbreeds everywhere. With her DNA, a Pureblood's

DNA, I will create a new breed. No rules, no moon, and no one will stop me. You can't win."

"You're insane," Kayne shot back.

Behind Elijah, the ersatz headed to an open panel. Their banter was wasting time.

"Am I? Look at what your precious mortals are doing. They're exploiting you for your strength, your senses, and your ability to heal. How long do you think it will take before they figure out they don't need you, they need your DNA? They'll dissect you to create a superior hybrid. You'll be their trash. I've proven, by lacing White Cell with Resurgence, a crossbreed is possible. And now I have uncontaminated DNA."

"All you've proven is you can infect mortals, kill them, and if the crossbreeds live, they go insane and die," Kayne started. "You can't change nature and destroy the animal spirit."

"Such a purest. I can and I will. Then when I'm done with her, she'll be a shell of the Pureblood she once was. And I'll sell what's left to the highest bidder. Maybe Daeland. What do you think the going rate is for a damaged Pureblood?" Elijah asked.

*Damaged.* He was so close to having her. What would this do to her?

"Outside of her territory and our traditions and beliefs, she's nothing, just another werewolf. But it doesn't matter, because you won't have the chance to use her." Kayne gauged Elijah, the ersatz, and raced to think of something to stall for time. "If you've broken the bond between Daeland and Macy, why isn't she healing?" *She's dying.*

Elijah paused, doubt creasing his face, then it was gone. "I'll force her wolf from her, and she'll heal."

Kayne's heart felt like it dropped to his knees when the panel door started to close, leaving him to watch the ersatz disappear with her. He was going to lose her. The breath he had been holding was pushed from his lungs when Elijah's shoulder caught him in the chest. Off balance from the driving force, Kayne stumbled backward and slammed into an examination table. His back arched over the metal edge, his boots leaving the floor, and he struggled to stay upright. Raising his arm, Elijah drove it down, stabbing Kayne in the left shoulder. Thick nails gashed Kayne's skin, and rearing back flesh clung to Elijah's claw.

Blood welled from the holes, soaking Kayne's black T-shirt, and while he struggled to get to his feet, his boots slipped in the pool of Macy's blood. His combat boot came up, and kicking Elijah, Kayne forced him back, giving him room to scoot across the table. As he landed on the floor his hands extended and shifted into Hunter Wolf claws. His wolf howled in his ears, a growl filled his chest, and desperation to get to the panel door worked his nerves like electricity. Kayne checked his surroundings, and reminded himself he wasn't there with the mortals' DOJ, he was there with the Coterie.

Freedom.

Elijah's face elongated, his hands turning into claws, his shoulders expanding, and his teeth changing to his Hunter Wolf's. At the same time Kayne's T-shirt tore at its seams as the muscles in his shoulders thickened and morphed into his Hunter Wolf. They remained across from one another, walking from between the tables and into the open. Anger, hot and starving, fueled Kayne as he caught sight of the people behind giant windows. Cells. The lab was able to watch the prisoners. Experiments. There were three on each side of the lab, each bright with light, and white walls, except for the dead. Ravaged bodies broke the gleaming scarlet and stark white patterns. Had Macy been in one of them?

"Every minute you're here, she moves farther away from you," Elijah taunted. Grabbing a handful of surgical instruments, he threw them at Kayne.

He stepped to the left and out of the way of the syringes, scissors, and most of the flying objects missed him, save for the two scalpels sticking out from his flesh. Kayne roared as sharp pain tracked down his arm, and pulling them free, he tossed them. "She's mine." *Always has been. Always will be.* The admission struck Kayne with more force than any hit Elijah could muster.

"Macy doesn't know you. Kayne Sinclair will stay true to following the rules like a lap dog. You won't break mortals' law because we live in their world, and you work and take orders from them. Mortal law states, I have to stand trial for my crimes." Elijah sidestepped, and circling Kayne, led him away from the door.

"No mortals. You were sentenced to death by pack law. As alpha, I enforce those laws," Kayne assured.

"If you kill me, you will kill Detective Gray's innocence. The mortals will find her guilty of being a spy and a werewolf, and your little Macelaine will be added to death row," Elijah threatened. He smiled, his lips drawn back from his canines, as if he had won the fight.

"You shouldn't have tried to blow up your accomplice," Kayne pointed out as if he was talking to someone sane. "Your pet, Dixon, turned on you."

Elijah shrugged like he didn't care, giving Kayne a second to charge into his chest with his shoulder, and hearing Elijah's gasp, and ribs cracking under pressure, Kayne shoved harder. They were wrestling for control when Elijah wrapped his arms around Kayne, and holding him tight, sank his nails into Kayne's shoulders. His roar rumbled with pain as he fought to free himself from Elijah's grip. When it weakened, Kayne leaned as far as he could, and bringing his arm back, he targeted the vulnerable area between Elijah's shoulder and socket. With a direct hit, he held Elijah's gaze. The wet sound of tearing skin, muscles, and popping tendons wasn't good enough ... Kayne jerked his claw backwards. Elijah snarled, let go of Kayne, and his arm fell limp at his side.

"My crossbreeds will kill her." Elijah limped back, his arm swaying from his socket.

*Not if the soldiers find her first.* Kayne didn't respond when he was confident, he was going to finish Elijah. "You weren't strong enough to kill Garrick. You aren't strong enough to kill me."

"I won't have to. My crossbreeds will do it for me," Elijah replied easily.

"I doubt that," Kayne growled. Around them the fight was shifting in the Coterie's favor. At the main door, there were therians and werewolves in humanoid form, werewolves in their Hunter Wolf forms, therians in their beast forms, and vampires rushing the lab area. "There's no way out."

"I haven't survived this long to have you stop me," Elijah countered and backed up. "This isn't over. What I have started others will continue."

"Not if I stop them," Kayne promised.

"Macelaine waits for me."

Kayne's chest burned with his breaths, his instincts pushing him to attack, and his worries and fear taking his attention to Macy. With a roar, he rushed Elijah, just as a new group of crossbreeds charged into the lab. They surrounded Elijah, becoming cannon fodder under the shapeshifters, beasts, Hunter Wolves, and the vampire's attacks. As they swarmed him, he drifted behind the chaos, and getting lost in the tangle of bodies, Elijah disappeared. Kayne searched the crowd, jerking his head back and forth over the others, and frantically searching the doors. Elijah was gone. How? Wanting to roar and growl in frustration, Kayne pushed through the mass, going for the only door that mattered. He headed toward Macy.

Was Kayne there? Had she heard him? She didn't know. Her mind was a tangle of a forgotten past, a lost future, and pain. There was so much pain. In the arms of the Hunter Wolf form, a coldness settled in her wounds, creating a false numbness she eagerly embraced and wanted to drown in. The denial didn't last long when it let go and her breath gusted from her as she hit the concrete with a hard thump. Landing on her side, she cried out and cringed as her ravaged arm was pinned beneath her. Black rolled in, she felt consciousness waver, and with the strength she could muster she forced herself to stay awake. One slow breath, a second, and when she was breathing easier, she tugged her arm out from under her, and rested against a wall.

The pain was inching back, like a low wave waiting to become a tsunami. Macy had to accept if Kayne was there, the chances of him fighting through the horde of ersatz in the lab and then finding her was a sliver of hope she wasn't prepared to bet her life on. She needed to save herself. There was no way she was going to let them take her, not again. Not to Elijah. Macy wouldn't survive his torture. She was already guilty of being a lycan spy, lying to the BPI, to humans, and she wasn't going let Elijah use her DNA to create more of his monsters. The second Hunter Wolf form joined the first, and standing in front of her, their opaque yellow eyes told her they were dying. Elijah couldn't fight and keep control of his monsters.

Without Elijah to keep them under control, she had become their target and she wouldn't last long. The image of the woman being attacked in the tank filled her eyes as Macy mumbled curses and scooted down the wall. It was, and she knew, a pathetic attempt of escaping them. Two steps, they moved together, and the desperation to run and get away consumed her thoughts. She wasn't going to give up. One step. Two steps. Three and she bumped into a crate. Checking for a way around it, she noticed it resembled the ones from Pennsky warehouse. They all did. They were stacked in the corners and along the walls. The BPI needed to find the lab and the evidence. Would it be enough to keep her from going to prison? She could have laughed. She was a lycan. A werewolf. Nothing was going to stop her from going to prison.

Her thoughts ceased when more Hunter Wolf forms stuffed the hallway. Macy struggled to stay standing upright while she searched for a way out. Her eye blurred when she tried to see the end, but cleared when a woman's headless body came into view. It looked as if it had been deliberately placed against the dingy, green wall, a pool of blood spread out from around it, the hole from the Hunter Wolf form taking her heart, seeped. There were others; dead, broken bodies of men and women strewn everywhere. It reminded her of the warehouse, of the lycan and his wife, and quickly, the images from every crime scene sat in front of her. They were never going to stop killing.

With her emotions sitting inside her like weights, and despite her efforts of ignoring her instincts, they pushed forward, through the tangle of human worries. The strange feeling enveloped her, and drawing it in, she gave herself over to the wolf's embrace. Strength exploded inside her, its intense blast too much to control. She slid down the wall, her right arm limp on her thigh, and dropped her head to stare at the floor as heat started in her middle like a fire and spread over her, leaving pain in its wake.

*Help me*, Macy begged.

The thick woods surrounded them, and kneeling in front of her, his board shoulders promised protection, and with his silver eyes bright with his wolf, he smiled. She felt his love and pride as he placed his hands on her small shoulders.

"Macelaine, embrace your wolf." His rumbled voice held his power, and he squeezed her shoulders.

Macy shook her head no, she couldn't do it, she would fail like she had when the car crashed. She wanted to reach out and touch him, to feel his strength, and comfort, to tell him she loved him.

"I'm your alpha and I gave you an order."

With the sun blazing in the cloudless, cerulean sky, heating the day and making the grass under her bare feet warm, Macy shook her head no.

"Daughter."

She shook her head no.

"You're strong. You're a Pureblood. Go and run."

As if she was a child, she obeyed. No more lies. Like a catalyst, her resolution made her skin stretch, her muscles tighten, and she let go of her control. Drowning inside of herself, she heard someone growling, roaring, and trying to yell. Her pulse beat in her ears and pain sank deeper into muscles as the wolf within demanded its freedom. Macy watched her tank top fall to the floor, followed by her bra, and when she gained strength, she struggled to stand.

Halfway up the wall, the seams of her jeans split open and cool air caressed her heated skin and sent her back to the floor.

Macy failed.

She didn't know what she was doing. She didn't want to die from a Death Bloom. As if in a dream, her parents' voices strengthened, submerging her, surrounding her as if they were beside her. Their presence replaced the emptiness of their deaths, and as if they were there to guide her, her life came alive around her. She reached out, trying to touch the images all the while letting the heat and the pain of the wolf within flow over her as if it were heated water. Memories, images, and emotions fed her cries as hot tears fell to the floor. She groaned as her bones shrank, then reshaped, her skin grew tighter around her shifting body, and her muscles reformed. Helpless to defend herself, she watched Hunter Wolf forms approach. She retreated, feebly crawling, trying for more time, and backed into another wall.

Her cramped muscles forced her to use it to inch up its side, and stood half shifted and in pain. They roared, advanced, their gazes locked on her. Damn, she was going to die by shapeshifter. Macy focused her thoughts, gained strength, and in a blistering minute stood fully shapeshifted in her Hunter Wolf form. Her heart pounded, at the same time her body embraced wild rage. The pain of losing her parents, her past, and the life she created played before her, feeding her fury.

Macy saw her targets and attacked.

With his wolf driving his instincts and adrenaline coursing through his veins, the toxic mixture fueled his imagination to invent every possible horror. Kayne punctured the door with his clawed hands, and pain erupted as he left blood, broken nails, and torn skin sliding down its serrated edges. Peeling the metal back, he tore it free, tossed it behind him, and prepared to fight a horde of ersatz as he jumped over the remains of the panel. When he entered the darkened room, a growl rumbled in his heaving chest, and his lips pulled from his canines. The space was littered with crates, boxes, and equipment. His failure, defeat, and anger swallowed him like the silence in the empty room. Covered in blood, and no one to fight, Kayne gave up his Hunter Wolf and melted into his humanoid form.

There would be no redemption. Only loss.

He was going to add another failure to the list, and it would become a memory that haunted him. Like the vision of Macy strapped to the table, unconscious, injured, her wounds bleeding, and Elijah straddling her like he owned her. Kayne should have let the soldiers fight Elijah and followed the ersatz. Sweat beaded on his forehead and chest to slide through dust, leaving tracks on his bare skin. A part of him knew he needed clothing—mortals were on their way, and he didn't need to be found naked—but the other part of him didn't give a damn. With his thoughts carving a path to the dark side, Kayne stared at the hallway stretching out to the left and right, like thin, ravaged veins. Left? Right? He chose right, then told himself, *One foot in front of the other.* Every one of them felt heavy and slow.

When there were a dozen steps behind him, he found himself in another hallway, and through the open door he met white lights casting rectangles on the opposite wall. He was behind the cells, their doors hung open, like Elijah's crossbreeds tore them from their hinges. It didn't surprise him, with the amount of power riding the air, the fight, and Elijah fleeing, his crossbreeds lost control and attacked the prisoners.

*And Macy?* Kayne didn't have an answer. Instead, he tracked the trail of carnage they left behind. Searching deeper, he caught the scent of blood, denying it could be hers, its tangy call riding the air, heavy and fresh, while its essence mingled with death.

Intertwined through it all was another scent bringing his wolf up inside of him and begging for a taste. Kayne opened his mouth, inhaled deeply, and tasted the air with his tongue. Macy. His wolf howled in his ears as the threads of her blood sank into his pores, burned his control to ash, and roaring, he went into a frenzy and began tearing through the hall. One after another, he tossed crates out of his way, making them crash into the wall, and sending shards of plastic and wood flying. Farther down, he threw lab equipment, anything in his path, anything keeping him from finding her. The scent of her blood drove him, making him blind while turning his search into charged desperation. He didn't know how far he had stalked when the hall opened to a small storage room littered with more crates and equipment.

*Where are you?* As if in answer, Kayne stopped, his heart in his throat as dried dots gave way to blood spray, giving way to splatter where they stopped in thick, crimson pools. He tried walking, but his legs, stiff like rebar and tight from fear, wouldn't obey him. They didn't kill her. They wouldn't kill her. She fought back. Not in her condition. She had been unconscious when the crossbreed carried her out of the lab.

Kayne went over her background, BPI, ERT, he had watched her fight, and saw her survive a hit from a crossbreed, and was aware enough to pull a knife and defend herself. The sight of her strapped to the table unconscious and bleeding had him doubting she was strong enough to defend herself, much less fight. She would have had to shapeshift, alone and without guidance, the entire time her past corrupted her reality. Echoing was Daeland's warning, Macy would lose her mind during the transition. If it happened. He refused to believe it was possible when Macy was a Pureblood. She and her wolf were one. And if the shift and her past overwhelmed her, and she lived, it would be the end. He rejected the idea and continued searching, refusing to believe the blood belonged to her.

He didn't believe she went insane, or the crossbreeds killed her while he was fighting Elijah. Especially after everything she survived, like the twenty-three years under Daeland's influence, denying her wolf, her true self, and facing the worst of the paranormals. Rounding another corner, he stopped, unable to take a step when the gore and violence brought his fears to life and spread panic through him. Through a red haze he saw Macy's clothing torn to shreds, covered in blood, scattered on the concrete. He roared, the sound dying under the varied voices coming from the other end of the hall. His wolf flowed over his skin as he relished the thought of killing crossbreeds. Heavy steps and the thought of revenge goaded him. Kayne made for the voices, his fists clenching and unclenching.

As he marched, new fur protruded from his sweat-slicked skin, his face elongated to steal his humanoid features, and his wolf emerged. He was going to kill them all. Shouts, yells, and orders echoed off the concrete walls and brought Kayne to a standstill. Those were not the voices of crossbreeds. He shook his head, trying to dislodge the grip revenge, pain, and Macy had on him, and listened. Did he recognize them? Affirmative. The red haze drained from his mind, his wolf sank, and knowing he had backup, went back to searching. Back to trying to find her. He roared her name and felt senseless. A gleaming trail led to another, and another, and he lost his hope.

"I found a body," someone yelled.

Kayne's head jerked up, hope sparked, and he hurried around tossed boxes, his bare skin glistening with blood and sweat. Dust drifted around him while the edges of the crates scraped his bare legs and hips. Wading into the sea of agents and detectives, he pushed through those who stood and stared. He didn't care, nothing was going to stop him ... then he met Agent Pixley and her emerald glare.

Commander Wilson stepped out from behind a locker, and putting his hand up he stopped Kayne from going any farther. "You aren't wearing any clothes."

"Move," Kayne growled. On instinct, his wolf rose, his eyes changed colors, and his senses opened. His wolf was close to the surface, and it wanted out. It longed to hunt, stalk, and kill.

"Negative. The fight is over. You can growl all you like, but it won't help you. The DOJ is here, *Agent Sinclair,* and you are naked," Commander Wilson warned. "Get yourself together and put these on." He took a pair of sweatpants from an agent and shoved them at his chest.

Kayne glared at him, inhaled, calmed, controlled his breathing, and jerked the pants from Commander Wilson. With little care he tugged them up his legs. "Now move," he demanded.

"Negative. You aren't going anywhere in the state of mind you're in. It's over. The fight is over. You need to calm down," Commander Wilson ordered. "Or I'll have you removed."

When they arrived at the base, they checked the hangar, and found the remains of several lycans in humanoid form, their throats ripped out and their heads missing. Tippi didn't think it could get worse, but she was wrong. The lab was a thing of nightmares with the dismembered bodies of Hunter Wolves nearly covering the entire floor. She knew, through Agent Logue, Agent Sinclair had been in the middle of the fight in his attempt to save Detective Gray. The evidence he had been there were his abandoned guns and holster. He shifted to defend himself. He shifted to fight. Tippi watched the confrontation, noticed the marked tension in Agent Sinclair's shoulders, his harsh breathing, and gently gripped his right arm. With his aggression and anxiety amped up from the fight, he wasn't blocking her, so it gave her an opportunity to ease some of his stress. Opening herself to him, his emotions slammed into her like a truck.

Tippi inhaled and hoped her voice held. "Calm down. Control your wolf, there are mortals here."

Her cool grip shocked Kayne's heated skin, sending shivers across his body, and jerked him from the haze. He looked at the worried gazes around him and knew he had gone too far. "You're right," he replied. He raised his hands to show he was in control. "I'm leaving."

Agent Pixley gave him a tight smile, released her hold, and stood by Commander Wilson. Kayne took a couple hesitant steps, and feigning leaving, sidestepped them, and immediately found what they didn't want him to see. Fragments, bits, things he should have recognized as mortal but his brain, fighting the sight, made them unrecognizable. Closing his eyes, he blocked out the talking, and opened them to see remnants at his feet. Sections of a mortal's body lay in a thick layer of blood. An arm, bloody and broken, a leg, a hand, pieces, and the blood, it was everywhere. The crossbreed tore her apart where he was standing.

"No. No," Kayne whispered. "Not like this."

"Agent Sinclair," Commander Wilson warned. "Dammit, let him search."

Kayne walked around the bigger pools of drying crimson, searching for a sign it wasn't Macy, and praying it was someone else. Really, he prayed the crossbreeds killed each other. He stopped, frozen in mid-step as a wash of icy awareness tightened around his spine. Hidden under a piece of cloth was dark hair. The color wasn't right. Was it his mind playing tricks on him? He couldn't be sure because of the amount of blood soaking the mane. He pushed himself to get closer, needing confirmation he had failed, and she was really gone. With hesitation gripping him, he shoved the box aside and mentally prepared to see Macy. Scraps of frayed skin glared white against the thick mass of hair, making his stomach roll into a ball of ice, and it almost sent him to his knees.

All he wanted was a chance. One chance to prove he could protect her. He failed her, and letting Elijah escape, failed the DOJ. Kayne gave up. With his head hung, he turned, left the corner, his eyes glancing over objects and people, and walked. When someone brushed his arm, Kayne turned, met their stare, growled, and continued. People crowded around him, sucking the air from the room, and suffocating him with their presence. They talked about evidence, the bodies, and getting the forensics team inside. It reminded him the DOJ and the BPI were there. His freedom with the Coterie had come to a fruitless, violent end.

"Agent Sinclair, you did your best. It's time for you to get out of here," Tippi advised. A team of agents had prepared tranquilizers, anticipating Hunter Wolves ... it didn't mean they wouldn't use one on Agent Sinclair.

*My best?* Kayne felt her inside of his mind, trying to understand his emotions and take away his pain. The memories haunting him brought him the same pain he felt when Macy had died in his arms. "Stop. The pain is mine," Kayne whispered. *Mine alone.*

He met Agent Pixley's gaze, held it for a heartbeat, then it drifted to a claw. Kayne stared at it. Hope swept in as he left the agent, and maneuvering around crates, he shoved a shredded box, finding another claw, ripped from an ersatz. No, crossbreed. Tossing boxes, broken crates, and crushed plastic containers, he found a body—its torso badly torn, its bowels a tangle of glistening pile on the floor, and blood soaking its fur and body. Elijah's creations weren't stable. Again, Kayne prayed they fought and killed each other. Was it possible? He raced back to the clumps of hair where forensic technicians wearing biohazard suits had converged on the mortal's parts and were placing them in black bags. Around them agents with cameras lit the space with flashes.

Kayne saw bright dots and blinked. "Enough. Stop."

Not far from the hair and blood, a woman's shoulders, and part of her torso sat next to the wall. He bent down, his shaking hands grabbing and lifting the fleshy chunk off the concrete, and saw a hole in her chest but no tattoo.

Dropping it, Kayne closed his eyes; there wasn't enough skin to see her tattoo.

"Come with me. You need to let them gather the evidence," Tippi urged. "You're getting in their way."

"Elijah is gone," Kayne mumbled as he stood. He wiped his hands on his sweatpants, then looked at them. Crimson stained the lines in his palms, and he clenched his hands into fists.

"I know." Tippi watched him lower his hands, and with her heart pounding in her chest, held his arm, and guided him around agents, detectives, and forensic technicians. "We have taken others into custody."

"I couldn't stop him," Kayne confessed. He raised his hand to scrub the back of his neck as if doing so would ease his throbbing head, then stopped. Instead, he stared at the crimson staining his palms. "I couldn't save her. Macy."

Before leaving for the base, Tippi helped Agent Logue and Agent Kriss conceal information regarding Detective Gray and her real identity. The records would prove she was mortal, had been kidnapped, and it would keep Macelaine Grayson dead and buried. And the past in the past.

"He made you choose between saving her and stopping him. Anyway, we didn't get him either. If he built this place, he would have had an escape route. The desert is a big area," Tippi said, trying to assure him.

Kayne allowed Agent Pixley to lead him farther down the hall and was mildly surprised she hadn't said anything about Macy's death, when he treated her as if she was the spy. His insides felt hollow with the thought. Not wanting to wait for forensics to confirm the body was Macy, he used his senses. He dissected the scents, but there were too many of them for him to know for sure it wasn't her blood, and it wasn't her body. His instincts told him the body lying hidden in trash was Macy, except he didn't want to believe she was gone. Really gone. There was nothing Daeland could do to save her. Kayne saw her eyes bleeding silver, like molten silk, and his heart sank into grief. Maybe it was easier to believe she was dead than believing Elijah took her and she was out there somewhere, alone and suffering from Elijah's torture and delusions.

Kayne's borrowed sweatpants hung on his hips, while his chest, back, and arms were riddled with wounds, and he knew sorrow radiated from him. He walked barefoot toward Chayton who had watched him lose himself in the past, blatantly ignore the future, and distance himself from the pack. His fourth followed him when he left for the DOJ and continued to help him fight the ghosts haunting him. The ghost had been brought to life long enough to tease him with redemption, then her life was taken.

"Agent Sinclair," Chayton greeted with his approach. Dirt covered the knees of his BDUs, while a faint handprint over his pocket shifted with his gait. "I need to talk to you. Alone."

Kayne looked at him, meeting almond eyes framing the bright copper of his wolf. The aggression and concentrated power weaving through the air kept the shapeshifters on edge and their instincts on alert. Chayton was displaying absolute control over his wolf, and it made Kayne feel weak. Without asking for an explanation, he nodded. Something in Chayton's stare demanded attention, and he was in no condition to protest. More so, he needed the distraction. Agent Pixley was right, the fight was over, and he had a job to do, losing control would get him removed from the scene ... hell, the DOJ. If that mattered anymore. With Elijah's escape, Kayne needed at least one witness to prove Havana had been there, then he needed to make sure the Coterie and Daeland were clear of the mortals.

"Agent Sinclair, this way, and I suggest we hurry," Chayton insisted. He started down the tunnel, giving Kayne and Agent Pixley his back.

Kayne waited, faced Agent Pixley, and saw her eyes narrow as she watched Chayton. "What is he going to show me?"

"You have to see for yourself," Tippi answered.

There was nothing in the green depths giving away if Agent Pixley knew anything or where Chayton was taking him. He was sure they wanted him out of the way. None of it mattered when the cold fact remained the same—they were too late. He reminded himself of his job, forced his self-defense to kick in, and bringing numbness it patched the fractures Macy's death created. It didn't stop him from thinking about the last couple of days, the way she felt against him, her fight with the crossbreeds, the questioning turned interrogation, and how he had planned to use her as bait. The situation could have been different. Regrets created anger, and infecting his thoughts, Kayne considered turning his back on the mortals, the DOJ, and leaving Desert Rock. He would go back to Feather River, to his life and his pack. This was the mortals' mess. Elijah. Tremors of fury tumbled through him, renewing the need to kill him.

"Agent Logue is waiting for you," Tippi urged. She felt his rage and heartache twist him and battle for attention every time he looked back. Agent Sinclair needed to get out of the depot.

"Where the hell is he taking me?" Kayne repeated. Did it matter? *I'm being an ass.*

"Follow him." Tippi stood her ground, held his gaze, and saw the hurt in its depths. "Go."

Kayne obeyed, and with rushed steps caught up with Chayton. "I'm not in the mood for this. If you haven't noticed, Elijah is gone, I don't know where Daeland went, there are vampires here, and I have to explain everything to Commander Wilson. If you're trying to get me out of harm's way, I appreciate your help, but I have a job to do," Kayne rambled. He stopped and watched Chayton. "Chayton." Kayne growled his name, expecting his fourth to stop. "I'm ordering you to stop this."

Chayton ignored him and continued down the dimly lit tunnel, leaving Kayne behind.

"Macy is dead."

"Time is of the essence," Chayton replied over his shoulder.

Damn him. Green paint gave way to gray walls of cinderblocks and dim, yellow lights protected by wire cages. Another a couple of yards the tunnel widened, and Kayne saw tire tracks. Had Elijah used it to escape, after his crossbreeds killed Macy? Or did he take her with him? He didn't know. Wouldn't know until forensics completed testing the remains. His mind raced and he barely noticed when the tunnel opened, and they walked into the night. Behind them, the chorus of muffled voices carried down the concrete walls as they worked the scene without Kayne.

Chayton turned, his boots grating on the gravel, and faced Kayne. His eyes flashed copper with a challenge, his body tensing, and a growl left his lips. "Alpha Kayne."

*Alpha Kayne?* "Remember who you are threatening," he warned.

"I know who I am threatening. It is you who needs to remember who *you* are. You are an alpha, a pack leader, and lord with the Council. You have the strength and authority to protect her." Chayton's wolf eyes softened, deliberately fading to dark brown.

"Don't start with me," Kayne ordered. *I failed to protect her.* No one is given a third chance. "I've had it. I have responsibilities and need to get back."

"Negative. Agents found a command center, complete with computers, and the video feed from the cameras stationed all over the facility. They have evidence proving what had been happening in the hangar, depot, lab, and in the cells. They have proof of everyone who entered the depot. Agent Kriss kept everything from the moment you entered the lab ... equipment malfunction, from the humans. It looks like there are days' worth of video."

It would prove what he had been saying for months. And would be the last time anyone saw Macy alive. "I want a copy of it tonight."

"To do what?" Chayton asked.

"To see her," Kayne whispered. "To see what happened."

"After all the years you have spent chasing the ghosts of your guilt, stop." Chayton inhaled, his chest rising. "I have stood by you and will continue to stand by your side, but you have to remember what you are, and the world you live in. Remember your pack is your true family. If you do not, she will be lost."

"Macy is dead. Or gone and better off dead. I couldn't protect her when she was a child, and I have failed a second time. For fuck's sake, I thought she was working with Elijah, and planned to use her as bait. She called me for help, and what did I do?" Kayne yelled at him, letting his frustration and his pathetic guilt have the freedom it wanted. "I wasted time, and he took her."

"Much has been revealed. Captain Dixon kidnapped Commander Arden, the same way he had the Taylors taken from their home. It is why we could not find him. In his confession, he told us where to find Arden, and the commander explained Detective Gray put herself in the center of the case when he asked her to investigate Officer Murphy and specific detectives. That is right. Had you met with her, she would have handed over the information she collected. Only Commander Arden knew, and when he disappeared, she did not know who to trust. She was trying to protect him."

Kayne tried interrupting, but Chayton cut him off and continued. "Mr. Barrette, owner of Golden State Shipping, collected over three million dollars in fines, and had pending charges for transporting White Cell, along with mortal and paranormal trafficking. He was losing his business. The DEA and FBI kept it quiet until they could charge him without a threat of his associates fleeing and losing the case. When Elijah infected him, it broke the operation open, which included Stephen Gomes, CEO of Renew Pharmaceuticals.

"Before Elijah got to Mr. Gomes, he hung himself. He did leave a suicide note explaining how Elijah was blackmailing him. The techs found the evidence on his computer's hard drive. Elijah planned this, Kayne, and when he leaned about Detective Gray's real identity, he concentrated his attention on her. Because of his obsession with her and the fact she was a BPI detective, several of his coconspirators left with their assets. We are tracking Elijah's use of the assets to find them. Captain Dixon found out about Detective Gray from Officer Murphy, and together they tried blackmailing Elijah. They demanded money for her life." Chayton looked from Kayne to Sanative's black ambulance. "We have evidence, witnesses, and Captain Dixon's confession. The case is progressing, and Blood Rain is taking over the investigation."

"Elijah is free. It's my job to find him," Kayne replied.

"Negative. The DRPD has issued an all-points bulletin, the BPI has launched a statewide manhunt, and the DOJ is sending the case nationwide. The Council recognizes the threat Elijah poses and will have the Coterie investigate. He will be found, and he will be punished. Your priority is your pack. You are their alpha," Chayton explained.

Kayne stared at the inky sky and the stars gazing down at them as if absorbing the actions of the night. He lost his position in the Coterie and the DOJ in one night. "My replacement?"

"Commander Wilson requested me," Chayton answered.

Chayton was the perfect person for the job. It didn't make leaving any easier. "Fine."

"It is about time I got through to you," Chayton replied with relief.

Kayne glared at him—DOJ agent, and fourth in line to the Moonlight pack—and watched a smile tug the corners of his mouth. When he stepped back, he turned his head toward a black ambulance sitting silently in the dark.

"Doctor Locke is here," Kayne growled. He didn't want to face him and answer questions when he was responsible for Macy's death. No doubt the doctor would blame him.

"I found her. She was hiding." Chayton touched the dusty palm print on his chest. "The gods know after living without a pack, and surviving Elijah, she deserves a true alpha who will protect her. Kayne, you are just beginning to understand the meaning."

"Macy is alive?" Kayne asked, his voice weakening. Hope lit up in all of its cruel glory as the images of the hall flashed through his mind.

"Affirmative. Go to her." Chayton looked at the ambulance.

A Pureblood. The pack gained Garrick's descendant. He had been given another chance at redemption. Kayne met Chayton's gaze, and warned, "Regardless of how we feel, Macy is a Pureblood. With her first shift, she escaped Daeland's influence, and free from him, she killed and tasted blood. That makes her dangerous."

"She will need the strength of her alpha and her pack," Chayton answered.

"Chayton." Kayne couldn't talk. He wasn't going to fumble over words, so he gave his fourth his forearm.

Chayton gripped his in return and they stood there for a heartbeat. Then, Kayne let go and started over to the waiting men and Macy. *I'm a fool.* Kayne wanted to ask someone, anyone, when did he lose control over his emotions? He battled his past, the nightmares haunting him, and Macy changed them. Her presence changed him. Stranded in the eye of the storm, he knew she would see him in the calm.

With his approach, he saw Daeland and Dr. Locke standing beside the van. "I thought you said you were taking her to Feather River, to Amaranth," Kayne said, repeating Daeland's words. "She didn't need to be with the mortals." He didn't acknowledge the doctor and wouldn't.

"Doctor Locke has given me an idea. Evidence proves Elijah kidnapped her and infected her. It only makes sense, as a victim of a shapeshifter attack, he would transport her to Sanative for treatment. Her identity as Macelaine Grayson, Pureblood, will be kept a secret. In Desert Rock, she will do what *you* want. Detective Gray will clear her name," Daeland explained. His black shirt showed signs of fighting, everything else about him looked as if they weren't in the desert with carnage behind them. "She will be able to return to Feather River as Macy Gray."

"Not if Elijah has told anyone." Kayne was getting what he wanted. Macy was going back to Desert Rock, she would clear her name, and hand over evidence, but he didn't trust him. "I don't—"

Dr. Locke cut him off. "Macy shapeshifted to defend herself and killed two Hunter Wolves. As a detective, she knows she has committed a crime. Macelaine, however, regained her memory and is having a hard time understanding the difference between the past and the present. I need you to be careful." Shaking his head, his yellow eyes dimmed. "She's been asking for you. We only have a couple of minutes. She's a BPI detective who has been attacked and I have to transport her to Sanative before mortal law enforcement asks why I'm waiting."

Dr. Locke took offence to Macy asking for him. Good. He no longer had a connection to her. Kayne nodded, unsure he would have been able to reply with his emotions overriding his rational thoughts. Part of him fought for control—he was an agent—and the other fought for Macy. He was an alpha. He looked at Daeland, cast him a dark glare, and in silence walked to the back of the ambulance where he took three quick breaths.

*Macy asked for me. She wanted me.* With those thoughts, he opened the door and met cool air. The sterile scent of cleanser and the artificial smells of medicine drifted out, a dim light clicked on, and he stepped inside the ambulance. Two more steps and he was in the cabin, sitting beside the gurney. Macy's arms rested at her sides on a cotton blanket that covered her waist and legs, while her face, free from worry, appeared calm. Macy hadn't backed down, she defended herself, and continued to fight for her life.

Kayne didn't know when he scooped her into his arms and held her close to him until he felt her heartbeat against his chest. Macy's long, chestnut-colored hair feathered his arm, the large, blue T-shirt with Sanative's emblem on the front hung on her shoulders, the ends of the blanket draping over his bare feet. Her breath came in easy inhales, her chest rising and falling in the silence, while her heartbeat sounded in his ears as a soft rhythm only he should know. He moved from the bench seat to the gurney, and cradling her, Kayne squeezed her, looked out the back and into the night, and felt time closing in on him.

"Macelaine," Kayne whispered, letting her name move his lips.

He lowered his head and nuzzled her neck, smelling the skin behind her ear, and gently ran his tongue up the side of her face. Her taste sat in his mouth, telling him everything he needed to know. The salt was from her tears, blood from her wounds, and the darkness he sensed was the vampire coursing through her veins. Relief settled in him when there was no evidence of the blood sharing Elijah boasted about. He hadn't been strong enough to force her wolf from her, and he hadn't been strong enough to bind them together.

They were words ... empty, like Elijah.

# CHAPTER TWENTY-FIVE

Macy remembered Agent Logue finding her, taking her from her hiding place and into his arms, then handing her over to Daeland who called her daughter and placed her in the ambulance where Dr. Locke had given her clothes. She had done her best to sit through his questions and quick examination before sleep took over and he left her alone. Sinking into exhaustion, she kept the memories playing, using it to stop herself from seeing the images of her parents, the hall, the Hunter Wolf forms, and shifting. Agent Logue. Daeland. Dr. Locke. Ambulance. Repeat. My life was a lie. Agent Logue. Daeland. Dr. Locke. Ambulance. Repeat.

Her senses flared when someone approached, rousing her from her light sleep, and she died inside knowing it was because she was a lycan. Had been all along. Then there was Kayne. Had they found him? She wasn't going to open her eyes fearing it was her imagination, a new nightmare, or a delusion created from shards of the present and her past. When warmth wrapped around her—through her T-shirt, and into her skin—she wanted it to fill the void of reliving her parents' death. Macy turned in the arms embracing her and the protection they promised, and letting her defenses down, she relaxed, and allowed herself to let go of the pain. Safety lasted a second when her mind, turning on her, brought images of the Hunter Wolf forms to her eyes, the taste of their blood to her mouth, and the feel of their skin tearing to her hands. She saw the tank, Elijah, and the vampire. No. Macy sat up, strong arms held her tight, and it spurred panic through her, making it difficult to differentiate between the lab and the hall. Fearing being trapped, she fought harder.

"No more pain." Macy twisted in the arms holding her.

"Macy. Stop. I'm here," Kayne pleaded softly, trying not to add to her fear. With her sitting on his thighs, he pinned her arms down, held her upper body, while she kicked at the gurney and fought to get her grip with her feet. Keeping her in his arms had gotten harder with her improved strength. He reminded Chayton she was a Pureblood, and he hated to think what he would do if she shifted.

Macy wrestled against the hard hold, the pain, and hurt invading her life, and the past tricking her mind. Images flashed, she twisted, fabric wrapping around her legs and tangling between them to keep her from standing. Against her will, her hands shifted to her Hunter Wolf form claws, and she felt her wolf swimming inside of her, waiting to get free. It was a reminder she was one of them. An animal. She wouldn't shapeshift. Never again. Using her strength to deny her wolf, she stopped the shift.

"Macelaine, hear your alpha," Kayne whispered.

*Kayne is your shield.*

His warmth feathered her ear as his soothing song caressed her fear, eased her fight, and relaxing in his embrace she drew in his scent, the feel of his skin, and his crux. The whisper deepened, the verses drifting through her memory and into her wolf. Understanding the words and their meaning, she clung to his promises, and accepted strength from him while his arms gave her a home. Her home. Her past. The truth.

When she stopped fighting, Kayne eased his hold, and breathed, "Open your eyes." Brushing hair from her cheek, he searched her face and was amazed the cut over her eye had healed, her arm had healed, and there were no signs of her injuries. One shift. The strength of a Pureblood.

Macy obeyed and saw Kayne staring down on her with amber wolf eyes. Past or present? The heated look confirmed it was real, and she responded with her own. Silver. Like her father's. "Kayne."

"I'm here," he replied. "I thought you were dead."

"I was." Macy watched amber flare then bleed to coffee brown, and she shook herself. "At the warehouse, my tattoo. You knew."

"Affirmative," Kayne answered. He ran a finger over the unmarked skin where the cut had been. "You're healed."

Within the safety of the ambulance, she had searched her body, her face, arms, sides, and tested her ribs to find herself healed. Perfect skin. No pain. She healed when she shifted. The intense look in his eyes felt like it went straight through her to another person. A person she didn't know.

"You didn't tell me," Macy accused, suddenly angry.

"I wouldn't let myself believe you could be alive. If you were, I could lose you all over again." Kayne gazed at her as a waterfall of emotions flowed through her. "If I told you, would you have believed me?"

Over the last couple of months, she questioned herself. Her recurring nightmare. The Barrettes. The lycan at the warehouse. *You know shifters like you have a connection with them.*

"I'm not sure," Macy answered honestly. Even with her memories, she wasn't prepared to accept what had happened to her. "I don't believe it."

"Acceptance will take time," Kayne assured, hoping she believed him.

Acceptance. She almost laughed. "I remember Feather River, my home, and Daeland. I remember you and why you were there," Macy whispered. "Then it's pieces." Elijah wanted the Pureblood dead and ended up killing her parents. She was the reason her parents had been targeted and murdered.

"It's just the beginning," he whispered back. Kayne's attention splintered when he sensed Daeland and Dr. Locke closing in, their presence like a ticking nightmare threatening to separate them. "Macy, there is video feed of the lab and what happened. Those responsible will be caught and charged. You'll be able to clear your name."

They'll prove her innocence. The happiness lasted a second, and Macy swallowed her reaction. They'll watch what happened when she was in the tank with Elijah. The beating.

Kayne watched her shutdown. Kidnapped, beaten, and attacked. "I'm sorry. I wish I would have found you sooner."

His darkened gaze gave away the sadness and told her he was thinking about what Elijah did to her. She needed to change the subject. "Daeland. My memories of him are scattered." She grabbed her elbow, imagined the missing flesh, and shuddered. "I know he's the reason for the tattoo. I don't know why I have it?"

Kayne heard her voice break and wanted to ease her pain. "Daeland is powerful and has authority among the paranormals. He gave you the tattoo to keep you safe." Not a complete lie.

"Did I drink Daeland's blood? Is it possible?" Macy asked with disgust in her voice. She knew it was the truth, couldn't deny the feeling, just like her instincts told her she knew Kayne. Still ...

Kayne held the back of her head with his right hand, her hair in his fingers, and caressed her back with his left. His fingers moved up, down, up, down. "Yes. He saved your life when you were born, and again after the car crash by giving you his blood. Vampires can enthrall mortals, and paranormals ... that's what he did to you. With his influence over your wolf, it remained in a dormant state," Kayne explained. "Do you understand?"

He took her wolf. Could he do it again? "I think so." Macy didn't understand. "What will happen to me?"

"The charge of arson has been dropped, and your disappearance has been reported as a kidnapping. Elijah targeted a BPI detective, abducted you, and took you to the lab where he infected you. It means Doctor Locke is going to take you to Sanative. Being there will give you time to recover and deal with the case," Kayne explained.

With the mention of the case, Macy reminded herself she was still, for a limited time, a BPI detective. Medical retirement, lycanthropy contagion, humanoid status eliminated. When she straightened, he lowered his arm, and she felt the muscles in his legs tense. Before leaving him, she took in his bare chest, his half-healed wounds, and the way his skin felt against her body. As much as she wanted to be near him—he felt safe—she needed to act like a detective. Macy wouldn't drag him into the chaos of her life or the pending investigation and trial. Her mistake with David served as proof she shouldn't get close to anyone. In the scant space between the gurney and the bench, Macy stood, swayed, the blanket dropped, and putting distance between them, gingerly sat down on the edge of padding.

"What about Macelaine Grayson?" she asked as she tugged the blanket to her legs. She might be wearing a T-shirt and cotton pants, but she wasn't wearing underwear or a bra, and had been naked in front of too many people. "What is going to happen to her?"

When she stood, Kayne's hands slipped from her waist, and he kept from steadying her when she looked like she might collapse. He hated the way he missed her. After holding her for minutes, he felt whole with her near him. Watching her struggle with the blanket, he was moved to help her again, but knew she needed to get through the night by herself.

He cleared his throat, making sure his voice held. "Everyone knows the child along with her parent was murdered twenty-three years ago in Feather River. Detective Macy Gray is alive and living in Desert Rock. The two are not connected in the mortal word."

She heard her father's roar and the tires squeal, and barely stopped herself from covering her ears. Twenty-three years. Macy had been living a lie for twenty-three years. Too much to handle. She was going to lose it. She wasn't a distraught human overwhelmed by tragedy. She was a lycan, and when lycans lost control they got shot. Macy knew because she shot them.

"I'll be medically discharged from the BPI for the lycanthrope contagion. I've lost my job and the life I created." She sounded weak and she hated it. "What am I supposed to do?"

Kayne saw her eyes well with tears and wanted to hold her. How did he tell her, after what she survived, her life wasn't her own? That Daeland and the Council were in charge of her fate. "After the trial, you can return home."

"To Feather River? I have no one there." She wasn't going to stay in Desert Rock. The trial was going to put her in the spotlight, and then the public would know what happened.

She would be the BPI detective who was kidnapped and infected. In Feather River her choices were between lycans and vampires. Not good options. Nowhere to go and no job. Macy winced as her doubts took over her future.

Guilt darkened his mood. He lived in her home. "You have Daeland and I. We're here for you." Selfishly, Kayne wanted Macy at Moonlight with him, not at Amaranth with Daeland and his coven. Moonlight was plenty big for the both of them, and he would do what he promised all those years ago—he would serve as her protector. *Redemption.*

With her emotions bouncing between rage and sorrow, Macy didn't say anything in return. She didn't know what to say. Her thoughts focused on what she lost, what she was, what she did, and her body cried for sleep. She had nothing, and reality became a heavy weight she didn't think she was going to be able to crawl out from under. Inhaling and exhaling, she folded her hands in her lap, and stared at the blanket. How to ask a million questions in seconds?

Kayne watched her withdraw at the same time her desperation spiked. "I'll be there, in Desert Rock, to finish up my part of the investigation. When it's finished, Agent Logue is taking my place. If you want, I can visit you at Sanative, but only if you want me to. I can help you with the past. I can answer your questions." His voice was rough with need. He feared she heard it and would block him out. "I want to apologize for the way I treated you. I wanted Elijah. He murdered your parents, and you."

She gave him a sideways glance. All these years he sought revenge for her parent's deaths. "Had I known what was at risk, I would have helped you. The information I told you about is on memory sticks, at my house. Anything I can do to help put Elijah and Captain Dixon behind bars I'll do," Macy stated, avoiding his question

Did she want Kayne seeing her at Sanative? God no. She wouldn't drag him into her life when the taste of the Hunter Wolf form's blood caused her heartbeat to speed up. He didn't need her. He was an alpha and didn't need what Havana described as an uncontrollable, murdering Pureblood. The sole person responsible for her parent's death. Who would want that? No one.

"After disobeying Sergeant Mayco's direct order to take Mrs. Barrette down, Commander Arden drew up my separation papers. He was going to fire me unless I investigated Officer Murphy, the officers close to the case, and BPI detectives he thought might know something. It's why I couldn't tell you the truth. I haven't spoken to him in days, and I didn't know where he was. I thought he might have cut ties with me." A growl ran through her words, and she wanted to cry but feared if she started, she wouldn't stop. "I wasn't seeing anyone, romantically, because I wasn't going to put their life at risk."

They trapped her. "The DOJ found him, and he explained your involvement." He couldn't ignore her lack of an answer and it burned through him. She continued withdrawing from him. Fine, if she wanted to push him away, he wasn't going to beg to be near her. Kayne stood, anger and hurt building in him. "The DOJ and Commander Arden have the evidence to clear your name. You're a victim and witness to the crimes, nothing more."

Macy regretted hurting him and regretted seeing the shift from Kayne to Agent Sinclair, but it couldn't be helped. As selfish as it felt, she wasn't going to worry about his feelings when her life was being turned upside down. Damn, she was sitting in a Sanative ambulance in borrowed clothing, waiting to be transferred.

"Agent Sinclair, we need to leave," Dr. Locke insisted.

"Understood." The doctor's voice and edge of possession it carried grated on Kayne's nerves and ate at his patience. He thought he was taking her away from Kayne, but he wasn't.

Macy watched him give her his back and gazed at the black ink tracing down his spine the same way she had the first time she saw him. She wondered if one of them marked him the way Daeland had marked her. Ownership. Master. He stepped down, his muscles flexing with his steps, his bare feet crunching the sand, and then he was out of her sight. This wasn't real. They weren't real. It wasn't possible for him to jump from the past to the future and into her life. Not now, not ever. She didn't know him. There were twenty-three years sitting between them.

"Kayne," Macy called after him. She sat straighter, clutching the blanket to her chest, and realized they were watching her.

"Macelaine," Kayne whispered. He turned around and rushed back to the ambulance. "Macy."

"You found me once. Saved me. I knew you would again," she confessed. "Thank you." Macy's eyes gleamed silver in the light of the ambulance, drawing attention from Dr. Locke, Daeland, and Kayne.

For a heart-wrenching second, Macy looked at Kayne with the same wounded eyes as the child from his past. Was that the redemption he had been seeking? He didn't know. He would do anything to have her say his name and look at him. "You're welcome."

Daeland stepped around Kayne and placed his hand on his shoulder. "Time slips from us, and you have a job to do."

Macy tore her gaze from Kayne when Daeland took the steps, his height making the cabin look small, and broad shoulders and body filling the narrow space. When he sat down beside her, she scooted away from him while Havana's squealing and the sucking sound of her tearing into her arm flooded her ears.

"Macelaine, I won't hurt you," Daeland promised, placing his hand on her leg. Her cinnamon eyes darted to Kayne and back to him. "I'm here to protect you."

"It's just ..." Macy didn't know how to say she didn't want to believe in vampires, and Havana scarred her for life.

"A vampire bit her—"

"Havana," Macy blurted out.

Damn the vampire had been there. "Havana tore her elbow from her arm and left her bleeding. You have to remember, until tonight, Macy didn't know vampires existed," Kayne explained, defending her fear. "Might explain why she's cautious of you." He met Daeland's onyx gaze with an amber warning.

"I understand." Daeland faced Macelaine. "Havana was here, and she hurt you?"

"Affirmative," Macy replied as she stared at Daeland's hand on her thigh.

"Did she say anything to you?" Daeland asked, his onyx eyes drilling into her, and the pressure of his hand increased as if giving her a silent warning.

She felt the pressure, looked at his hand, and then met his gaze. Was she going to lie to a vampire? Affirmative. "Negative." With nervous movements, she clenched and unclenched the blanket. *When my wolf accepted Daeland's death into itself, I became a blood slave, and his daughter.*

Kayne couldn't stop the curved grin when she lied to Daeland.

"The Council will hear of this," Daeland promised. "I won't hurt you. No one will."

Macy nodded, keeping her gaze on Daeland, who wrapped his arms around her and blocked Kayne from seeing her. *Fine.* Kayne turned and started walking. No matter what she said, he wasn't going back to the ambulance when he was confused. Was she denying their relationship or was she accepting the past they shared? He didn't know. He did know he didn't need the pain from rejection. Kayne marched barefoot on sand, gravel, and thorns, and ignoring them all, made his way back to the tunnel, and back to his job. He wasn't going to think about Macy being at Sanative with Dr. Locke, who clearly wanted her there.

"Kayne," Daeland called.

He kept marching toward the tunnel as if he hadn't heard him and toward mortals.

It took a second for Daeland to catch him, grab his arm, and stop him. "Do you have anything to confess?"

He glared at Daeland, then looked at the ambulance when the engine started, and its headlights came on. Macy was leaving. "Negative."

"I know what you did. I can smell the pack on her. I can smell you on her. You have started the binding. Your actions were selfish, and they put her at risk," Daeland accused.

"She is the Garrick pack. The Moonlight pack. Macy should be bound to it," Kayne argued. "I'm not interested in your opinion."

"Indeed," he replied. "Before you think she's part of Moonlight, remember she's my daughter. I'm ordering you to protect her from the mortals' law. I trust you can handle lying to them."

"Order me? I'll protect her because I'm her guardian. Her shield. And coming from you, that's priceless," Kayne mocked. "I can't help thinking you planned this entire mess. The Affliction, Macy's changing, her finding me at the warehouse, Elijah, and his crossbreeds. You have what you want ... power over the Coterie, I'm leaving the DOJ, and you have Macelaine, Garrick's Pureblood daughter. What power play have you concocted? Is this a way for you to take my territory?"

"The territory you left?" Daeland let the question hang between them. "I can take it whenever the desire strikes." Kayne started to argue, but Daeland raised his hand, silencing him. "I don't want anything from you, territory included. This has been coming. The mortals and their laws aren't enough. Like I said, Elijah proved their incompetence. You will never know how deep this goes, or for what reasons," Daeland explained. "The Council has its secrets. I thought you understood."

Daeland had his secrets. Kayne's eyes blazed amber, his lips pulled back, revealing lengthening canines, and a growl rumbled from his chest. Letting his fury and hurt take hold of him, he prepared to unleash a tirade on Daeland.

"Agent Sinclair."

Daeland smiled, his fangs touching his bottom lip. "Agent Sinclair, you're being summoned."

Kayne shut his anger off like a light switch, and backing down, the instinct to protect the Veiled was stronger than his need to yell at Daeland. Besides, losing his temper in front of the mortals would be another strike against him. He needed to be in Commander Wilson's good graces if he wanted to stay close to the case. Without a word to Daeland, he faced the agent, and signaled he would be there in a minute. The agent waved him off, and Kayne turned to finish his threat. Daeland was gone. The noises, shadows, they were all gone. Macy was gone. It didn't seem real.

"Agent Sinclair," Chayton called.

Kayne didn't answer. Feeling defeated and tricked, he ambled through the night toward the tunnel. A desert breeze blew around him, washing him in its threads of desolation and causing him to pause. He relished the emptiness and drew a clean breath, free of blood, fear, Elijah, and vampires. But mainly Macy.

"What were you talking to Lord Daeland about?" Chayton asked, as he fell in step.

Lord Daeland. You mean manipulating liar. "Nothing we can discuss here," Kayne responded. "The agent, he had a question?"

"A report," Chayton answered. "Agents and detectives are closing in on finding Elijah's other warehouses in Southern California, and agents are also checking every building owned by Renew Pharmaceuticals and Golden State Shipping. When news of the BPI and DOJ's raid on this facility, Elijah's near arrest, and then disappearance, hit Desert Rock, some of Elijah's accomplices left town, while others came forward."

"I'm sure they'll want to make a deal," he responded like he was listening.

"Affirmative. Their confessions and the information they are giving will help us find—"

Kayne barely noticed when they stopped walking. He was nodding when he needed to, commenting when appropriate, all while staring into the tunnel. His thoughts were not on the case, Elijah, and the upcoming raids on the various properties. They were stuck on Macy. She lied to Daeland knowing he was going to sense the deception. To hide what Havana said to her? How much did the vampire know?

"Why did it take Doctor Locke nearly half an hour to transport Detective Gray? She had been attacked and infected. I don't want to hear it was because of you." Commander Wilson stood beside them, his questioning stare darting from Kayne to Chayton and back again as if he didn't trust either of them.

Kayne dragged himself out of his thoughts and looked at Commander Wilson. "Mr. Northrip tortured Detective Gray, giving her substantial injuries. He was working to stabilize her," he answered. He saw her strapped to the table, bloody and dying, and then saw her flawless skin and silver eyes.

"I see. I want you to go back to Desert Rock and be the liaison to the BPI. When Detective Gray is able, I need you to question her," Commander Wilson instructed. His hand rested on the butt of his gun, while sand from the hall and tunnel dusted his BDUs.

Kayne rested his left hand on the edge of his borrowed pants, then moved his finger over the gathered waist. "Agent Logue is capable of questing Detective Gray," he insisted, his voice returning to normal "I would rather stay here." Far from Dr. Locke.

"I want Logue here. And while you're there, get some sleep. It's an order," Commander Wilson countered. "We'll talk about how you found this place later."

"Agent Sinclair, your truck is over here," Chayton directed.

"Copy, sir," Kayne replied to Commander Wilson, and turning, followed Chayton.

They walked in silence, over the desert terrain, and through the maze of vehicles. Waiting for him wasn't the rental; thankfully, it was his truck. Kayne rounded the front, noticing the bodywork, the windshield, passenger window, and the driver side window. "I didn't have time to call a mechanic or anyone to have body work done." Kayne knelt and checked the axel, stood and checked the paint job. "Who did this?"

"Doctor Locke had a werewolf from his pack fix it. Said it needed to get done so you would get the hell out of his territory." Chayton was walking down the side of the truck.

"He said what?" Kayne demanded. Anger flared where the doctor was concerned, and making it worse was Macy. She was with him.

"Relax, it is done. Now get in, go to Desert Rock, and wait for us, you are of no use here." Chayton opened the driver's side door. When an agent approached, he backed up, talked to him, and returned to Kayne. "Here, a detective found your guns in the lab where you *dropped* them."

Kayne noticed the emphasis on the word *dropped*. Next to his destroyed holster and both guns were the shredded remains of his clothing and boots. Shapeshifted without fear of breaking the law and it felt freeing, natural, like his true self. Once behind the steering wheel, he took the ruined holster and guns, leaned over the center console, and set them on the passenger seat. He eased back in the seat, relishing sitting down. "Thanks."

Chayton closed the door. "Agent Pixley and Agent Kriss helped me destroy the DNA test and exchange it with another, then made sure her medical records stated she was mortal. You need to thank Agent Pixley, she risked being caught. We have done all we can on our end."

"Good." Macy was going to stay Macy.

"We protect our own. The mortal world does not deserve to know about her. They do not care that Purebloods exist," Chayton added.

"Affirmative," Kayne agreed.

"She will be given the chance to create a new life."

"Affirmative."

"If you are going to continue with one-word answers, I am heading back to the depot." Chayton landed his glittering eyes on Kayne. "All right, I am leaving."

Kayne thought he should say something, when from behind Chayton, someone was yelling for him. "Now you can go."

"Affirmative, sir." He turned, then turned back. "When the pack finds out she is alive, and it does not need to be soon, some will believe and embrace her. But others, I fear, will see her as a threat or a lie. A power play on your part."

"Agreed," Kayne replied. More threats and lies than happy homecoming. How long could he hide her identity when Elijah knew and he was loose?

Chayton shook his head at another one-word answer. "You have to protect her, help her, and bring her home."

"That's my plan." Kayne started his truck, bringing the diesel engine to life.

"Kayne, do not worry about Doctor Locke, Daeland, or anyone else. Macelaine has lived her entire life alone, she knows what she wants, and does not question her instincts. She fought for shapeshifters at the same time mortals focused on destroying her. Do not fear their influence."

"I know." Kayne stared at the night, the crescent moon, stars, and open desert. The wilds of it had embraced her.

Macy had been strong as a child. He knew better than anyone that she was her own person and that's what scared him. She will placate Dr. Locke, Daeland ... damn, she lied to him, and even himself, by telling them what they wanted to hear, and once their attention found something new, she would do whatever she pleased.

"Go help her," Chayton advised. He gave Kayne a half smile before heading in the direction of the tunnel.

Kayne backed up, turned the wheel, and stopped. He stared at Chayton's silhouette, the lights, the hangar, and the mass of SUVs, trucks, and diesel pushers they used as mobile forensic labs. Then he watched the crime scene investigators and forensic technicians, all wearing biohazard suits, haul more equipment into the hanger and tunnel. Roaming around the assembly were videographers live streaming to the DOJ and BPI. He wanted to be in the middle of it all, and at the same time was thankful he was going to Desert Rock. The gods knew he didn't need to see the cells and have his tired mind throw images of Macy at him. Kidnapped. Beat. Macy learned her life had been a lie. And she faced him with strength. Or had a death grip on her control. Finished turning around, Kayne headed down the rough dirt road, trying to miss holes, channels created from rain, and the same rocks he dodged hours earlier.

"Macelaine Grayson," he whispered, letting the name roll from his lips and not from grief but with emotion. She was alive. He didn't know if he was comfortable with the name, when he knew Macy Gray was his storm. The storm that knew him without knowing her past.

He turned the wheel, drove the last bit of dirt road, and stopped before crossing the fog line, his headlights cutting across the deserted highway to fade into the depths of the dark desert. Her scent—vanilla, wolf, and vampire—lingered on his skin as if it belonged there, but her distance hurt him, and he wanted her touch gone. After rolling down the windows, the rush of night's clean air swept through the cab as he drove onto the highway and gained speed. The air may have cleansed his skin, but it didn't take away the sting from her refusal. She had ignored his assurance he would be with her and would visit her.

Kayne thought about her hesitation and her fear on the air as she crawled out of his embrace. Separating them. Did he expect her to accept her new life? He wanted her to. With regret, he needed the doctor's help. Kayne tightened his grip on the steering wheel. What was he thinking? Macy didn't belong with him, to him, she was the daughter of Alpha Garrick, blood daughter to Daeland, and protected by the Council. He had served as her guardian when she was a child and failed. What did he have to offer her? Despite his doubts, Kayne couldn't stop his scattered thoughts from concentrating on her words. Macy remembered him.

*"You found me once. I knew you would find me again."*

*"I'll always be there, Macelaine."*

The desert's warmth washed his bare skin in the mellow aromas of sage and sundried leaves, taking Macy from him. He growled, and losing the battle with his resolve, rolled up the windows. Kayne inhaled, caught her faint scent, and shuddered from its power over him.

"She needs time," he told the inside of the truck. Then reminded himself he needed to take solace in having Macelaine Grayson alive and within his reach. She was going to return to her territory of Moonlight, with him, her shield.

# CHAPTER TWENTY-SIX

**Headlights** sliced through the hanging night, exposing patches of new and old asphalt while giving glimpses of creosote bushes hugging the road. On the sides of the ambulance, stars broke the black sky, and like arrows, pointed to the crescent moon Macy was staring at.

"Do you want to talk about what happened?" he asked and gave her a quick look.

Macy sat in the passenger seat, the T-shirt and cotton pants swallowing her, and had rolled the window down to stare at the night and passing scenery. Dr. Locke had given her his medical advice, which she promptly ignored, and stayed where she was. She didn't move, her legs were folded under her, nearly formless in the pants, and was leaning against the frame, putting her face next to the open window and in the rush of wind.

"I won't judge you. Anything you say will be protected by doctor patient confidentiality. You can't keep it bottled up," he warned.

*Yes, I can.* "There's nothing to talk about." There was everything to talk about. The pressure from keeping the unfairness, the lies, and the end of the life she had created was currently building and she knew if she didn't cut some of the pressure loose, she was going to explode. Already her head throbbed, her muscles ached, and her stomach felt like it was full of lead. The explosion was going to leave a mess.

"You need to talk. The tension coming from you is tangible. I can feel it rolling from you in waves. It feels like fire on my skin. I also feel your power, its aged, not the usual electric spark of new crossovers."

Daeland. Her father. Her mother. They made her who and what she was. A Pureblood.

"There are emotional stages you go through after being infected, much like grieving. It allows you to process what has happened."

Macy could smell the Hunter Wolf form's blood, despite Dr. Locke using two containers of disinfectant wipes to clean her up. "I wasn't infected. My parents were Pureblood lycans, murdered lycans, and a vampire lord saved my life with his blood, and now is claiming to be my father. He took my memories." Sitting straighter, her eyes thick with silver, she faced him. "I was born this way. I've been *this* my entire life. It's not a full moon, there wasn't an alpha present, I was alone and shapeshifted. No Death Bloom. It means I have shifted more than once. And you knew," Macy accused. *Like Kayne.*

"Lord Daeland saved the newborn daughter of Alpha Garrick. You're a Pureblood from a strong line of alphas, and that makes you werewolf royalty, and you have the protection of one of the most powerful vampires with the Council. And because he blocked your memories you are responding like a newly infected." Dr. Locke gave her a sideways glance. "I didn't know. Yes, I suspected you had ties to the paranormal world after I saw the tattoo ... but I never would have endangered your life. Anyway, if I wanted to confirm you were a werewolf, I would have tested your DNA. I didn't. I watched you and gave you my pack's protection."

Macy eyed him, and staying silent felt there was something else he was going to say.

"Please call me Landon."

Macy stared at the side of his face waiting for him to continue.

"All right. I'm an alpha, and I saw your determination, felt your strength, and was drawn to you. I want you, Macy, not a myth. The mortal Detective Gray caught my attention." Landon's quick gaze blazed bright yellow edging on white as if certifying his truth. He inhaled, his chest filling with oxygen, his eyes bled to green with gold flakes, and he looked at the road. "There aren't many mortals, let alone mortal women, willing to confront paranormals, take abuse, and keep going. You wore bruises, scraps, and lacerations like they were part of you. In your fight to survive, your fingernails were torn out. And you just lied to Lord Daeland, of the Council, knowing full well he was going to know."

Macy looked at her hands and the new fingernails, having forgotten about them as memories of Daeland trickled in, giving her a comfortable feeling for him, as if she knew him.

"I'm not telling him anything. I blame him. He let me live a lie then came back, had me knocked to my knees, and ripped it from me." Macy didn't know what to say to his admission. "No, you're right, I wasn't knocked to my knees. I was investigated, presented as bait, kidnapped, beat up, and fed on. Elijah's Hunter Wolf forms tried killing me, and in turn I killed them, tore them apart." Pureblood.

"I understand this is a shock. You don't have to trust Lord Daeland, not yet. You seem to trust Agent Sinclair."

Landon's voice carried a thread of jealousy that turned his eyes to white sunlight. What was she going to say? "I knew him. It feels like I know him." Not a lie.

He seemed to consider her answer, the silence thickening between them. "You're correct when you guessed you had shifted before. It's said you shifted as a young child. You ran beside your father, and with the pack, proving your power. At the time shapeshifters were starting to cast off the old ways and wanted to live free among the mortals. Your existence was part of the new future and that's what started the protests among the pack's numbers. Fearing for your life Alpha Garrick requested Agent Sinclair, then a soldier with the Coterie, to become your guardian. He was with you every day and the two of you were never without the other, until you died. It broke him. It's not a secret he's spent the past twenty-three years hunting Elijah in attempt for redemption. You're alive and he thinks you need a guardian. He thinks you're his redemption."

*Kayne, broken.* He's anything but broken. *Redemption.* "How do you know this information?" Macy asked. What other information did he have? Kayne hadn't believed she was Macelaine, but recognized the blood mark, and knew who her master was. Why hadn't Landon recognized it? He lied to her. Like everyone else.

"Every faction has a chronicle. Your history is in Moonlight's, what is now known as the Garrick pack, records. It states Agent Sinclair was with you for seven years, and during that time you were enthralled with him like a twisted version of Stockholm syndrome. No one can blame you when you were a child depending on your guardian. How do you feel about him?" he insisted.

Embarrassment seared Macy's cheeks and chest as if she had been lit on fire. Stockholm syndrome. *Damn him.* She wanted to answer just to put an end to the conversation. Wind blew through the open window, rustling her hair, caressing the nape of her neck, and brought his smell to her.

Kayne's intimate whispers were in her thoughts and his heated touch was on her skin. Was she reliving her infatuation with her guardian the same way she relived her parents' death? Macy had no fucking clue. No. When she didn't acknowledge his offer to visit her, he took offense, was hurt, and she felt its raw edge. She could see herself sitting in an observation room, in the same oversized clothes she was wearing, Kayne safely behind the two-way mirror, as Dr. Locke explained to him she suffered from a twisted version of Stockholm syndrome. Poor child. Macy was better off alone. Denial was a bitch. Instinct told her she needed Kayne, and she wanted to be with him, but she wasn't going to tell Landon anything. Information like that would be used against her.

"I said it's like I know him, he's from my past which is a twenty-three-year-old lie. Present time, he's the agent who planned to use me as bait. Sided with Captain Dixon, questioned me like I was the spy and devil incarnate, doubted my loyalty to the BPI, and would have put a scarlet S for spy on my chest. How it must burn through him, I'm innocent." Macy hoped her rebuttal was going to be enough he left her alone. Fatigue gnawed at her, making her thoughts dark and everything worse somehow, if that was possible.

"He's an agent with Blood Rain, it's his responsibility to investigate leads, and make arrests. That said, after causing a scene in order to see your tattoo, I'm surprised he didn't contact Lord Daeland requesting authorization to retain his property. Agent Sinclair ignored DOJ protocol, the Council's law, and put your life at risk with paranormals and mortals. He acted recklessly. The Council will punish him for his actions." Landon did a breathing thing, reminding her of

Sergeant Mayco. "He left his pack to chase a ghost and turned his back on the Council."

*I'm not property.* Landon had serious issues with Kayne, and she couldn't blame him. Why hadn't he called Daeland? Because her death, his failure, broke him. Why would he open an old wound? But the tattoo ... He had spent hours in the warehouse wounded, suffering from syn silver poisoning, and under the influence of an empath and didn't trust himself. She saw him gazing down at her with old pain in his eyes. *Stay with me.* Confusion warped her thoughts, creating doubt, and she didn't know what to think.

"He was investigating the Hunter Wolf forms and was right." What if he had stayed in Feather River? She would be dead.

"This is who you are, BPI Detective Macy Gray. You fought shapeshifters and paranormals, and killed them, when required. By their hands, you have endured loss, betrayal, pain, and after losing your mortal life, they thrust you deeper into the darker side of the paranormal world. I don't see you wanting to take the first step and engage the stages necessary to overcome your hate. No one accepts the things you have gone through without tears, anger, and hating the unfairness of what happened. I've been helping people for a long time, and you have me worried," he explained.

"Before I can go through the stages of acceptance and accept being a lycan, I have to face my past. My parents were murdered and the man responsible kidnapped me in order to use my DNA, then tried to kill me. Let's talk about my current situation, the investigation into my conduct and a trial." She tugged the collar of the T-shirt, and the sides wrapped around her. "I don't have a job." Sanative loomed over her like a hangman's noose.

"I'm sorry. You need time and I'm not giving you any. You'll have the time and the resources to understand the stages at your disposal when you get to Sanative." He hesitated, glanced at Macy, back to the road, and back to her. "I would be honored if you considered the Gawain pack. I told you how I feel about you, and with us, you would never be alone."

She turned to stare up at the crescent moon and felt its pull. An offer to join the pack, be with Landon, and see Sergeant Mayco every day ... no way, wasn't going to happen. Never. Ever. She gave the moon, the stars, and the infinite darkness one last look and met his hopeful gaze. "Thank you, I'll think about it. I'll certainly have the time. You need to realize, right now I see myself as a monster. I am what I hate. I am what I've killed."

"Step one. I want to repeat everything I said, but I realize how useless it will be at this point. We all learn, and you will too, there isn't a kind of monster, or a level of monster. There are people, we are people, and monsters live inside of us all. Captain Dixon and Officer Murphy serve as proof," he said in his calm voice.

He was right, damn him, and his words were useless. At least some of them. Macy stared at his hazel eyes of green and gold and thought about David and Captain Dixon's betrayal. Her life had been in their hands, and they easily gave her up to the monsters.

"Gods forgive me, I'm sorry," he whispered. "Macy, I don't want you to hate me."

"What?" Did she miss something? A breeze of regret drifted around her, suffocating the innocence in the fresh air. When he met her gaze, she saw pity in their gold and emerald depths. Pity for the weak.

"I have cared for you for a long time, and I've proved it by giving you my protection. I've also admired your strength and your loyalty. This hurts me and I couldn't live with myself if you hated me." He slanted his head, gave her a shielded gaze, and looked back at the road.

She listened to his confession and didn't know what to say. Landon clearly didn't like Kayne, not because he was an alpha, DOJ, or had left his pack. Landon didn't like him because he was close to her. When she was a child, he had been her guardian. Her shield. She wasn't a child. The heat in Kayne's amber stare had made her heart race while she craved the feel of his skin. Landon's accusation about being infatuated with Kayne might be true. He was a piece of her past she recognized and wanted. She needed answers and a solid foundation.

"I don't understand. I'm not going to hate you, couldn't hate you."

"While I want to believe you, I truly do, you don't know why this concerns me."

"Then tell me," Macy demanded. She didn't like the fear coming from him.

He gripped the steering wheel, his knuckles turning white, then inhaled and exhaled. "I can fabricate the effects of the contagion, like you have been infected, but I can't hide your lack of injuries. The report stated you had been attacked, chained, taken to the facility where you were beaten. When we get back to Sanative you will have to appear hurt and wounded, as a mortal." His voice reached out to her, as if he was continuing to apologize.

"What are you going to do to me?" Macy didn't want to know. She knew. The icy feel of the tank surrounded her, making her body quake with pain.

His soft, glowing eyes gave away the truth of his future actions. "I'm going to hurt you. Because you heal quick, it'll have to be extensive."

Pain and fear made up her world. Macy held his gaze, letting his words sink into the scars scoring her insides while the resonances from Elijah's beating burned her skin. *"I know how much damage your body can take."* This wasn't the same. She needed to protect Kayne, Daeland, and Macelaine. "You. Only you and in private. I won't be humiliated."

"You have my word. We'll stop, no one will see us." His shoulders tensed. "Please forgive me."

Macy gave him her back, wrapped her arms around herself, and sank in the seat and stared at the moon. As if understanding her emotions and reminding her she wasn't alone, the wolf within raged. She saw it standing on its hind legs, its front raised to the sky, its black nails cutting through air as if trying to reach her. *I'm right here.* Sharp barks turned to a low howl, and echoing in her ears, it stood on all fours and stared at her. After enduring the coming pain, embarrassment, and proving to the world she wasn't crazy, she would wear her scars, and get revenge.

The wolf within howled a song of praise and promise, its eyes glittering silver in the moonlight. Her wolf within understood. Then like the wind captured its spirit, it disappeared.

THE END

Silver Tears
Moonlight Territory (Book Two)

Macy Gray lost it all; her career with the Bureau of Paranormal Investigations, the life she created in Desert Rock,
and worst of all... her mortality. Thrown into the world of
the paranormal, her real identity as Macelaine Grayson,
daughter to a murdered lycan, continues to be a secret
and her life shrouded in lies. Living in Feather River, home
to a vampire lord, his coven, and Kayne Sinclair, alpha of
his clan, she knows she can't hide forever. If she wants the
truth, she has to face Kayne, who holds the keys to a past
she can't remember.

After decades of chasing his enemy for revenge and seeking redemption, Kayne assumes the role as alpha of the
Moonlight pack. While he works to heal the wounds left
behind from his absence, his attention is on one woman,
Macy, the only person who can grant him forgiveness.
Kayne failed to protect her in the past, can he redeem
himself and protect her from the enemy bent on destroying her? Or will Macy remain out of his reach and out of
his life?


Coming soon

M.A. Kastle resides in sunny California with her family and two German Shepherds. She is the author of the urban fantasy series Cascade Saga, Cascade Wolves, and Moonlight Territory. For news about upcoming books, news, or book signings visit her at Facebook, Instagram, and Twitter.

Facebook @Makastle
Instagram @Makastleauthor
Twitter @Makastle